CW00665590

# Kiss and Tell

## Leo McNeir

# Kiss and Tell

## Leo McNeir

enigma
publishing

Also by Leo McNeir

*Getaway with Murder*

*Death in Little Venice*

and published by enigma publishing

enigma publishing
PO Box 1901, Milton Keynes, MK19 6DN

First published 2003
© Leo McNeir 2003

The moral rights of the author have been asserted.

The events and characters described in *Kiss and Tell* are entirely fictitious, and any apparent resemblance to real people, companies or occurrences is entirely coincidental.

All our Rights Reserved. No part of this publication may be reproduced, stored in a retrieval system, or transmitted, in any form or by any means, electronic, mechanical, photocopying, recording or otherwise, without the prior permission of the publisher.

A CIP record for this book is available from the British Library.

ISBN 0 9531742 1 2

Typesetting and cover design by *specialist* publising services ltd, Milton Keynes

Printed in Great Britain by The Baskerville Press, Salisbury, Wiltshire

Leo McNeir is a linguist and lexicographer and has edited eight dictionaries in fifteen languages in the past decade, the standard works in their field.

*Kiss and Tell* is his third novel, following the successful publication of *Getaway with Murder* (2000) and *Death in Little Venice* (2001).

He lives with cookery writer Cassandra McNeir and their cat, Mog, in a three hundred year old cottage in a Northamptonshire village.

They have four children between them and a narrowboat on the Grand Union Canal.

# Dedication

For Maureen and Nick

# Part 1

It was a misty morning, the best time of the day at the best time of the year, with the sun rising above the horizon through veils of pale cloud. The jogger pounded the towpath of the Grand Union Canal between Yore and Hanford where the waterway followed the contour line in a series of gentle curves, flanked by woods and meadows, fields and paddocks. It was early May, and the countryside was alive with lambs and blossom.

He gulped in great mouthfuls of the clean air, rejoicing in muscles that he had carefully honed over the past few years in the fitness centre and on the local pathways. The walkman beat out the rhythm in time with his fists, thrusting like the pistons on a steam locomotive. This was his favourite route. Today it was a deserted landscape, not a boat, not a cyclist, not an angler in sight. Not even the lugubrious heron that took flight as soon as he raced into view. On a straight section over firm ground, he glanced down at his watch. Nine minutes forty-five seconds so far, according to the stop-watch dial. That was nearly ten seconds inside his best time. This was a memorable morning.

For the next fifty metres he had a clear run before the path became rougher, and branches from overhanging trees were liable to lash his face if he was not especially vigilant. Then it was over the canal bridge and on to the final killer section up the steep meadow to the main road where he had a flat run for all the last mile home. He squared up to face the challenge and accelerated the pace. Today he would beat his record.

On a day like this, even the meadow seemed less of a mountain to climb, though he knew he had to treat it with respect. A pity to get a stitch from over-enthusiasm at this stage in the run. It was when he was almost in sight of the road, in a patch of scrub and bushes, that he saw it up ahead. The colour first caught his attention, bright red in amongst the green and yellow leaves and grasses. Reluctant to slow down, he told himself it was just a hold-all that someone had left behind, and he moved over to skirt it in a wide arc.

But a further glance told him it was obviously not a hold-all. He could see a trainer, a Reebok like his own, and curiosity was beginning to draw him nearer. The red fabric was the lower half of a jogging suit. Startled, he realised that someone was lying on the ground, half-hidden by a bush. Perhaps they had collapsed through running too hard; it was easy enough on this hilly terrain. There was nothing for it but to investigate, and he swung reluctantly back towards his original course.

Kneeling beside the prostrate shape, he began to pull back the bushes to take a closer look. Suddenly, in horror, he tasted bile as he realised that the form had no head. He was staggering back starting to retch when the blow came. He was completely unprepared for it. One moment he was straining backwards in the undergrowth, the next there came a sickening explosion on the back of his head, a blinding light and a rapid descent into darkness. He never saw his attacker, never felt the walkman being lifted from his belt or the watch snatched from his wrist. As he was released by his assailant, he hit the ground and began tumbling down the slope. His momentum carried him a long way, almost as far as the canal itself.

The whole episode had been witnessed by no one and, as the unconscious jogger rolled to a halt at the bottom of the meadow, he was seen only by a solitary heron on the bank. It flapped inelegantly into the air, settled its head back like a pterodactyl and flew out over the fields through which ran the silver strip of water.

# Part 2

The car cruised slowly down the high street, past rows of cottages where spring flowers made a bright spectacle against honey-coloured stone. It was a conspicuous machine, a Mercedes-Benz in metallic silver, that would have looked just right parked on the drive of a country manor house. The bright, late morning sunshine glinted off the coachwork, and the car rolled to an elegant halt outside the village shop. Dark tinted windows made it difficult to see the driver, and it was only when he emerged that the few passers-by in the street, the shop-keeper putting up a notice in her window and two neighbours from behind net curtains, could get a sight of him.

The man stood for a few seconds taking in the view. The street was generously wide, flanked by stone houses, a few of them thatched, a few with wisps of smoke curling from chimneys. On the opposite side of the road was a pub, *The Two Roses*, with window boxes filled with primulas in blue and yellow, ivy covering part of the stonework and tubs of multi-coloured wallflowers. Beyond the shop and two more cottages stood the church, slightly raised and set back from the road, behind neatly trimmed hedging. It had a strong, tall, crenellated tower contrasting with the delicate stone mullions of its windows in the Early English style.

Those who were watching, saw a tallish man of medium build with dark short hair. By any yardstick he was good-looking, and his appearance was aided by the cut of the jacket and the expensively casual line of the trousers. The clothes were under-stated, as if he was taking care not to compete with the opulence of the car.

In the shop he was greeted by Molly Appleton, whose husband Richard was seated in the booth that comprised the post office. One or two customers were browsing at shelves, only thinly disguising their interest in the stranger.

"Good morning," Molly said brightly. She suspected that the man had not come in for a pint of milk and a loaf of bread. "Lovely day. Can I help you?"

"Yes, I hope so. Good morning. I'm looking for Marnie Walker's place. Do you know it?"

"That would be Glebe Farm."

"Glebe Farm," the man repeated dubiously. "The person I'm looking for is an interior designer."

"And a very good one." The comment came from a stocky man in his late fifties, bull-necked, in tweed jacket and country check shirt, emerging silently from behind a stack of shelving.

"That doesn't surprise me," said the stranger. "It was the farm address that made me wonder."

"Marnie's converting it," Molly said. "She lives down there ... with her friend. They've been there since last summer."

"Right."

"Mind you, they've fitted so well into the village, you'd think they'd been here for years. Very nice people."

"And she lives there with a friend," said the stranger.

"Yes," chimed in one of the other customers, a woman with white hair.

"Just the two of them. I heard she was a widow."

Molly stared at her blankly. "Well, you won't have any trouble finding her," she said to the visitor. "Take the road round past the church and go through the first field gate on your left. Just follow the track down. Keep bearing to the right and you can't miss it."

"She'll do you a jolly good job," said the bull-necked man. "She did a first rate ... *makeover*, I think she called it, for my cousin Dorothy Vane-Henderson at Hanford Hall. Excellent."

"I see. Actually, I'm not looking for a designer. This is more of a social call."

"Oh that's nice," said Molly. "I didn't realise you were a friend of Marnie's."

The stranger turned towards the door. "I'm not. I'm her husband."

# Part 3

This had to be the perfect spring Saturday. The narrowboat boat glided past two anglers on the canal bank, its engine running quietly a little over half speed, barely any wash at all spreading behind it. Only one of the men looked up. He could make out the name *Sally Ann* on the bow and was pleasantly surprised that the steerer of the boat raised a hand and smiled in his direction. It was a lovely smile. He had an impression of a slim figure in navy sweatshirt and blue jeans, and short brown hair.

"Any luck?" she called out across the water. Her voice was attractive, deeper than he expected. The angler shook his head. The steerer smiled again. "Never mind. Next time." She turned her attention to the bend ahead, swinging the boat clear of the shallow bottom on the inside of the curve. On the hatch cover, a sturdy black cat sat up and stretched.

Straightening up, Marnie Walker increased engine speed, drew in a deep breath and enjoyed the view. In a sunlit landscape she could make out the tower of the church in her adopted home village of Knightly St John. She estimated arriving back at her mooring in under ten minutes. On all sides, fields extended away into the distance, some of them still showing the undulations of mediaeval ridge and furrow, now home to sheep and lambs. On the other side of the canal, crops were sprouting, with reflections from the sun visible in puddles left by the rains of the past few days. Even with the thump and clatter of the diesel engine under her feet, this was a peaceful and refreshing sight.

She was lining up to approach a bridge on an awkward bend when a face appeared in the hatchway, and she was joined on the stern deck by a girl.

"Right, Marnie. That's the washing-up done." The girl looked around and recognised the position. "Good. Just in time. Nearly home." She was almost as tall as the steerer, who was five foot seven, and had ultra-short blonde hair, pale skin and thin sharp features. She was just seventeen but looked younger with a slender boyish figure.

"Anne, can you pop up to the front and check nobody's coming through the bridge hole."

"Sure." She skipped nimbly along the gunwale on the outside of the boat and held up a thumb as an all-clear signal before walking back to the stern.

After the bridge they stood together for a few seconds, taking in the scenery. The trees in every direction were shading pale green with new foliage, the bushes were filling out and no longer transparent, and the countryside was splashed with yellow where fields of oil-seed rape were flowering. Cows and sheep were grazing in warm sunshine.

"No rough winds shaking the darling buds of May here," Anne said.

"Nope."

"I love that poem." Anne laughed brightly. "I don't suppose anyone'll ever write anything like that for me."

"I don't think people do that sort of thing any more," said Marnie.

"Never mind."

Ahead they could see the start of the long, sweeping right-hand curve in the canal that ended at their mooring. Visibility on that side was hindered by the spinney that extended some fifty metres inland, but through the treetops they could just make out the uppermost chimneys of Glebe Farm, their home since the previous summer and still undergoing restoration.

*Sally Ann* rounded the curve and Marnie eased her over to the outside edge of the canal in preparation for docking.

"Do you see what I see?" Marnie said, pointing ahead. "We've got company."

"Someone you know?"

Marnie shook her head. "Don't recognise it. Not one of the Little Venice crowd. We'd better pull in alongside *Thyrsis* so as not to block our visitor in."

"They can't have realised it was a private dock," said Anne.

Marnie had thought of putting up a sign along the lines of: 'Private – mooring of N/B Sally Ann', but she had decided that would look possessive and unwelcoming. She was beginning to have second thoughts as she eased back the accelerator and lined the boat up to slip gently beside *Thyrsis,* the boat moored just beyond the entrance to her docking area.

In *Sally Ann*'s place now stood a boat of about fifty feet in length painted all over in grey, either primer or undercoat, a not uncommon sight on the waterways. No name was visible.

She slowed *Sally Ann* to nudge the side of *Thyrsis*, which belonged to her lover Ralph Lombard, and dropped the rope she was holding round a mooring stud on his boat, when she saw movement from the corner of her eye. A window was sliding open on the boat in the dock. The face behind the window was indistinct, as if the person on board did not want to be seen.

"Can I help you?" A man's voice. His tone gave the impression that helping was the last thing on his mind.

Marnie was uncertain how to answer a question that she felt she should be asking him.

As she stepped down onto the bank, the man called out again. "I say ... don't you realise this is private property?"

Marnie stopped. "Actually, I did know that. I'm the owner."

In reply, she heard only a muffled grunt, and the window slid shut, leaving her alone on the canalside. She felt like Alice in Wonderland, where everything was the opposite of what it should be and where she, the owner, was the trespasser. Anne had finished tying up the bow rope of *Sally Ann* and now came to stand beside her.

"What was that about? He sounded stroppy. Doesn't he realise it's a private mooring?"

"Apparently not. Must be some misunderstanding. Perhaps he thinks he's somewhere else."

"I wish he was," Anne muttered.

The hatch at the stern of the grey boat slid back, and the door opened to reveal a man of about forty, thin, balding and in shirtsleeves. He hesitated in the hatchway before coming out onto the deck, eyeing Marnie and Anne with suspicion.

Marnie decided to make a fresh start. "Good afternoon."

"Hallo. Did you say you were the owner of this property?"

Marnie and Anne walked forward. "Well, yes. It's not how I usually introduce myself, but it seemed appropriate in the circumstances. I'm Marnie Walker." They stopped beside the grey boat, and the man looked down at them appraisingly.

"And that's your boat."

"*Sally Ann* is my boat, that's right." Technically, *Sally Ann* still belonged to Marnie's sister Beth and her husband Paul, but that did not concern him.

"And the other one?"

"*Thyrsis* belongs to a friend of mine. Is that relevant?" Marnie was becoming impatient at being interviewed by a complete stranger, and a trespasser at that, about her legal position while standing on her own property. She thought it was time the man explained himself. "I don't think I caught your name."

"No."

"Look …" Marnie began, "You're welcome to stay around here, of course, but at some point it would be nice if I could put my boat back in her dock."

"Yes." He looked at Marnie thoughtfully. "I think there's been a misunderstanding."

"I rather think so, too."

"I thought this was Ralph's place."

"You know Ralph?" Marnie was taken aback. "He didn't mention that anyone was coming."

"He didn't know. I sort of … guessed. It was a typical Ralph kind of joke."

"What was?"

"The name of the boat … *Thyrsis* …the Scholar Gypsy … the Oxford connection. I saw it there, knew he had a place in the country, had a boat and put two and two together."

"And made five and a half," Marnie heard Anne whisper at her side.

"It's certainly his boat," said Marnie, suppressing a smile. "Good guess. But his *place in the country* is miles from here in the next county."

"I see. Well, I'd … er … better pull out and let you have your mooring back." He retreated into the cabin.

"Not over-endowed with charm," Marnie said quietly.

They heard the engine of the boat start up, a smooth-running modern diesel, unlike the old Lister two-cylinder on Sally Ann. They returned to their boat, and Marnie switched on the ignition. The engine began thumping rhythmically away under the deck, faint puffs of light grey smoke blowing from the exhaust at the stern. The anonymous boat eased out from the dock across the whole width of the canal, and the stranger manoeuvred backwards and forwards a few times to bring her round in the channel to draw alongside Sally Ann.

"Would you mind if I tied up alongside Ralph's boat?" he called over to Marnie.

"You can tie up anywhere along this section while you're in transit." She hoped the hint was subtle.

"Good. This'll do fine."

Too subtle. They eased Sally Ann into her slot and made her secure.

"That man doesn't seem to know the words sorry, please or thank you," said Anne.

Marnie smiled. "Amnesia."

"You reckon?"

"Didn't you notice? He seemed unable to remember his own name."

"I wonder who he is." Anne lifted the cat from the roof. "Come on, Dolly." She put the cat down on the deck, and it leapt silently onto the bank. All three of them made their way through the spinney in stripes of sunlight, stepping round puddles. The air smelt fresh and clean. For Marnie and Anne this was heaven, and they walked companionably, enjoying the early warmth, absolutely where they wanted to be. For Marnie it was the culmination of her desire to run her own show. For Anne it was the starting point of a career that she hoped would give her a life like Marnie's.

They emerged from the spinney into the farmyard where the cluster of buildings was starting to look more finished. Glebe Farm was still in the throes of reconstruction, but it was coming together and looking more like a home with each month that passed. On the far side of the yard in front of them stood the main farmhouse, like all the buildings constructed in stone the colour of set honey. The windows were still boarded, but its stone mullions were visible and its proportions were balanced and pleasing to the eye. At rightangles to the house it was joined on the left to a row of three cottages, one occupied since the previous autumn by Jill and Alex Burton, newly married, the others still in progress.

Marnie and Anne turned to the right, walking across the cobbled yard towards the outbuildings set apart from the houses. Here, there was a group of small barns, all built of the local stone. One of them, known as the *office barn*, was their workbase, with a bed-sitting room under the roof for Anne. The few other barns were used for storage. One of them housed Marnie's classic MG sports car, a 1936 model TA, fully restored, in British racing green. It was her only car since her Rover GTi had been destroyed by a bomb in London in January, and she was still wrangling with the insurance company about its replacement.

Anne slid back the barn door revealing full-length windows, while Marnie opened the wooden door into the office and picked up the morning post. Anne followed Dolly in and took a fax message from the machine. She put it on Marnie's desk, beside the cat who had taken up station under the lamp. It was a routine fax from their main client, Willards Brewery, confirming dates for the completion of projects. Marnie sat and read through the message, absent-mindedly slitting open the mail with a paperknife.

"Those dates are okay, aren't they?" said Anne. "No surprises."

"No surprises," Marnie echoed. As she picked up the first of the letters, a small piece of paper fell onto the desk. It was a note written in a bold hand that had a familiar look. As Marnie read it, she frowned.

*Hallo Marnie*
*It's been a long time. I read about what happened to you in the papers. I missed it first time round - abroad on business. Nearly murdered, car bombed! I was worried about you, thought I'd look in. I'm in the area – I'll call back in the next few days. Hope you don't mind. A lot to catch up on.*
*Love,*
*Simon*

"And he spoke as if he knew me?" Ralph looked bewildered. "I don't really have any boating friends as such on the cut."

It was Sunday, and they were having breakfast on *Sally Ann*. Ralph had driven back early after attending a seminar for a few days at All Saints College Oxford, where he was professor of economics. During the night the sky had clouded over and a breeze had sprung up around dawn, bringing a brief shower that had left everything washed clean and fresh.

Marnie got up to make a second pot of coffee, stepping over Dolly who was busy taking care of a saucer of milk. "Well enough to think he'd found your boat just by seeing its name and making the Oxford connection. He said it was a typical Ralph joke."

Ralph stood and looked out of the saloon window. "His own boat doesn't give any clues to identity ... or to anything else. What did you say he looked like?"

"Not very tall, about my height, say five-seven or eight ... slight build ... very short hair, dark, receding. About your age, at a guess."

Ralph continued staring out towards the stranger's boat. At six feet tall, he could just stand in the cabin without having to stoop. In his mid-forties, with brown hair and brown eyes, he had kept himself in trim. Having known him for two years, Marnie still thought Ralph an unlikely figure to find on a canalboat. He was one of the best-known economists in his field in Europe with a worldwide reputation. All Saints had offered him a personal chair, a professorship, the previous year, but now he was arranging to leave his full-time post for freedom as a 'visiting professor' with a number of college engagements each year, spending the rest of his time on writing and research.

Marnie had first met Ralph when she had pulled him out of the canal one dark night in Oxford. A dark night in all ways. Ralph had been trying to commit suicide. Since then, his depression had lifted with her help, and their relationship had developed. Now they were planning to marry at some unspecified future date.

"Oh well," he said, taking his place at the table, "we'll find out soon enough, I expect."

"I thought he was creepy," said Anne. "Oh sorry ... I shouldn't have said that if he's your friend, Ralph."

"*If* is the word."

Marnie brought the coffee-pot to the table and sat down. "I must say, I agree with Anne. I don't want to be disloyal, but I couldn't imagine him knowing you, somehow."

"Academics can be a strange breed. And knowing me doesn't make him a friend." Ralph laughed. "Could be quite the opposite!"

"But presumably, if he wasn't a friend of some sort, he wouldn't come to visit you."

Marnie poured Ralph some more coffee. Suddenly, Anne craned her neck to see through the window. "There he goes!" All three faces peered out in time to see their visitor setting off through the spinney in jogging gear. He was running with his back to them, and Ralph strained trying to recognise him.

"Any wiser?" Marnie said.

"Good heavens ... I don't believe it ... it *can't* be ..."

"Who can't it be?" Anne asked.

"It's not easy to be sure at this angle, but I think it's ... no, surely not ..."

"Obviously not the closest of friends," Marnie muttered.

"It's just so improbable. What's *he* doing on a canalboat?"

"*He* being?"

"If it's who I think it is, it's Anthony Leyton-Brown."

"I've heard of him," Marnie said. "I think."

"No need to sound surprised," said Ralph. "He's hot news at the moment."

"Isn't he that MP caught up in sleaze?" Anne joined in.

"That's the one."

"And he's a friend?" Marnie asked doubtfully.

"Sort of." It was a very un-Ralph reply.

"Meaning?"

"If it is him, I've known him most of my life. We were at school together. Because of our work we've often bumped into each other, but I wouldn't exactly call him a friend, more a kind of ... lifelong acquaintance."

"So why do you think he's come looking for you?"

"Is that what he said?"

"I got the impression he'd just spotted your boat and thought he'd tie up nearby," Anne said.

"Any port in a storm," Ralph muttered. He looked serious.

"Storm?" said Marnie

"You know ... all this business with the under-age call-girl. The stuff in the papers. Yet more sleaze for the government."

"Which one is he?"

"Marnie, don't you ever keep up with the news?" Ralph, who devoured every newspaper and listened to every news bulletin, found it hard to grasp that some people, including Marnie, did not live the same way.

Marnie reminded him of this. "And I know it's part of your work to keep on top of it all, but I've also got a full-time job and a life to lead. And there are just so many people in this government who seem to be involved in some scandal or other, it's quite hard to keep up with it all."

"The tabloids were full of it about two weeks ago," Ralph said. "They spoke of almost nothing else."

"I read the *Guardian*," Marnie replied slowly, trying to look superior. "Well, when I get round to it I do. I have a busy life."

Anne laughed. Ralph smiled at them, raising his hands in surrender. "I give in. Okay, let's forget sleaze for the moment. What are your plans for today?"

"I've got preparations for meetings on Monday and Wednesday, plus two letters to write. After that, if it's fine, I'd quite like another trip on *Sally*. Any takers?"

"Lunch on the boat?" Anne suggested." Marnie nodded.

"Room for a stowaway?" said Ralph.

"Even a tabloid-reading stowaway," Marnie agreed generously.

• • • • •

By noon the cloud cover had broken up and they had set off on *Sally Ann*. Preparing to stop for lunch out in the country, Ralph had produced a bottle of Spanish sparkling wine, *Cava*, from the fridge, and with olives and cashew nuts to keep it company, they drank a toast to a perfect spring day.

There were now only a few clouds spread out over the sky like scattered sheep on a hillside. The real sheep were grazing among the trees that came down to the water, and a warm smell of fresh growth hung in the air. Marnie breathed in deeply and wondered if that was the smell of wild garlic or something filtering up from the galley.

Anne went below to check that the table was laid and returned announcing that they could eat in five minutes. Marnie pointed ahead. "We can tie up after the next bend ... there's a nice view up that steep field to Hanford Hall."

Ralph kept *Sally Ann* out in mid-channel. "Isn't that where you did the redecoration for that strange woman?"

"That's it. Anne calls her *Mrs Frightfully-Frightfully*. Mind you, I'm not complaining. It was a complete makeover on the whole place ... literally money no object. I wish there were more people like her around."

Lunch was garlic bread followed by baked trout with almonds, roast peppers and a mixed salad. As they began the first course, Marnie noticed it was almost one o'clock and put on the radio for the weather forecast. She left it on for Ralph to hear the news headlines. It was the usual mixture of hospital waiting lists, cuts in the defence budget and a report on negative equity for home-owners. They were about to switch off when the news reader began the next item:

*Concern has been expressed in government circles about the disappearance of Anthony Leyton-Brown, MP for the Docklands West constituency in London. Mr Leyton-Brown has not been seen since reports appeared in the press about his alleged association with a teenage girl who had been working as a temporary researcher in his Westminster office. We have an interview with the wife of the missing MP, plus comment from his agent and a statement from the Globe newspaper in which the original report appeared.*

"Do you want to hear about that MP?" Anne asked.

"Might as well," said Marnie. "So he's in hiding ... in our back yard."

Ralph agreed. "He decided to lie low after the photos appeared in the press. That was two weeks ago."

"And the government's getting worried about what might have happened to him," Anne said.

"I doubt it. They probably told him to keep out of the way. The last thing this government wants is any more scandal. They've been plagued by it."

The newscaster began an interview with the MP's wife, Melissa Leyton-Brown, and Anne turned up the volume.

*... the whereabouts of your husband, Mrs Leyton-Brown?*

*I wish I knew. He left home on the morning those photos were in the paper, and I haven't seen him since.*

*You really have no idea where he is? I think many of our listeners will find that hard to believe.*

*It's the truth. I have no reason to lie to you.*

*Has he made any attempt to contact you in the past two weeks?*

*None at all.*

*You must be concerned, Mrs Leyton-Brown.*

*That would be understatement. I'm seriously worried about my husband. He's been hounded by the press, and I just hope they realise what they've done.*

*I must put it to you, Mrs Leyton-Brown, with great respect, that some might say your husband brought this on himself.*

*As far as I'm concerned, this has been a case of entrapment. It shows the depths to which the media in this country have sunk.*

*Did you know the , er, researcher who appeared in the photographs?*

*No. I don't think so. My husband has several people working for him at any given time. They come and go.*

*The newspaper alleged that she was fifteen. You didn't think it strange that he should have someone so young working in his private office in the Commons?*

*Not at all. In the past he's had school leavers on short spells of work experience. A lot of MPs do that. It's good experience for them, usually the children of constituents.*

*How did he come to have this particular girl working for him?*

*I don't know. She must have applied, I suppose. I think that's how it usually works.*

*Knowing your husband as you do, where do you think he might have gone?*

*If I knew that, I'd contact him myself ... and I certainly wouldn't be telling anyone in the news media.*

*You sound very upset, Mrs Leyton-Brown.*

*How do you think I should sound? My husband has been harassed by the gutter press. It's disgraceful. I just don't know how they can get away with this. We seem powerless to do anything to stop them. The media are out of control in this country.*

*You don't think they have a duty to report on the lives of the people who run the country and set standards for everybody else?*

*Not when they deliberately set out to trap people and make up lies to suit their own ends.*

*That is a serious allegation, Mrs Leyton-Brown.*

*I'm sorry ... I can't ... It's so unfair ... I just ...*

"That poor woman," said Marnie. "Do you really think he hasn't spoken to her?"

"I certainly think she's telling the truth," said Ralph.

"But that's terrible, just clearing off and leaving her to face the music all by herself."

"Perhaps he thinks they're bugging her phone. Perhaps he's trying to protect her."

Marnie was incredulous. "*Protect* her ... by running away?"

"Perhaps he just can't cope with it," said Anne.

Another interview came on.

*... who has been the agent for Docklands West for many years. Mr Haslam, do you have any knowledge of the whereabouts of Anthony Leyton-Brown?*

*None. My last contact with Anthony was the day before the newspaper articles came out. We had a regular business meeting in my office, made a few appointments, had a drink in the Conservative Club. That was it.*

*So ... business as usual.*
*Absolutely.*
*And you don't know his whereabouts?*
*I've already told you that.*
*How did he seem when you saw him last? Was he in any way different?*
*Not at all.*
*Did he seem to have any particular worries ... anxieties?*
*Nothing out of the ordinary ... the problems of constituents, routine office matters ...*
*Did he mention his research staff in the Commons?*
*No. He handles all that side of things from Westminster. I just deal with local issues in the constituency.*
*Who appoints temporary research staff?*
*Sometimes people write in offering to do voluntary work in the office for a while. Sometimes Central Office might offer someone who wants a short-term assignment. It depends. But I leave all that to Anthony.*
*Does anyone vet the applicants as to their suitability? After all, an MP's office is full of confidential papers.*
*It's a matter of personal judgment on the whole. It depends on the circumstances.*
*Did you meet the so-called 'researcher' who was in the photos that were printed?*
*No.*
*Do you normally meet them?*
*Sometimes ... if they come with Anthony to a meeting.*
*But not this one?*
*No.*
*How do you and the other constituency workers feel about his disappearance?*
*(Pause) I shall have to be careful what I say here.*
*Are you worried about possible action from the press?*
*Huh! No. I'm concerned that I might lose my temper and use bad language on your programme.*
*You don't think Mr Leyton-Brown has brought the problem on himself, having a relationship with a schoolgirl?*
*That's ridiculous! A respected and respectable Member of Parliament has been dragged through the mud by the gutter press. They've used foul tactics to entrap Anthony. It's time something was done to stop this kind of thing from happening.*
*You wouldn't want the media to be gagged to prevent them from exposing sleaze and corruption?*
*I didn't say that. But if they don't act in a responsible way ... they'll find themselves in trouble.*

"Do you think it was a frame-up, Ralph?" Marnie asked.

"Well ... some journalists are unscrupulous ... no doubt about that. But he was photographed in a compromising position. That can't be denied."

"You saw the photos yourself?"

"In the *Globe*, yes."

"I didn't think you read that sort of paper. No, I mean it, really. I'm not joking."

"I read most of the nationals every day. They rarely tell you what's going on, but even the tabloids have some sharp journalists. I like to see the range of opinions. It's a way of picking up clues about what's really happening. Ah, this sounds like them now."

" ... *but we stand by our story and our right to print the truth. The photographs published in the Globe two weeks ago were taken by a staff photographer, not a freelance, and we can vouch for their authenticity. They were taken with a long lens in the garden of the MP in question. We did not invade his privacy unnecessarily, but took the view that this story was definitely in the public interest. We have not infringed the voluntary code of conduct to which Globe International Newspapers are signatories. We regret any distress that publication may have caused the family of Mr Leyton-Brown, but our concern to report news of national interest led us to the editorial decision to publish."*

*That was the end of the statement from Globe Newspapers. No one from the company was available for interview this lunchtime. The MP himself is still in hiding, but one thing is clear ... this story is not going to go away.*

Anne turned off the radio. A thoughtful silence descended on the cabin. Marnie spoke first. "I still think he should at least reassure his wife that he's okay. You can't just run away like that. Do you think he'll have heard that broadcast?"

"Probably."

"You know him, Ralph. What do you think he'll do now?"

"Contact her, I expect."

"But what's he going to do in general?" Anne said. "He can't just go back in a few weeks time as if nothing's happened, can he?"

"There'll be strong pressure on him to resign, won't there?" said Marnie.

"It's not that easy," said Ralph. "Major's only propped up by the Ulster Unionists. They can't afford a by-election they could well lose."

"Is his seat a marginal?" Marnie asked.

"It's a Conservative seat. That's marginal by definition these days. I'm not joking. They haven't won a by-election since William Hague got in back in '83."

"But what choice does he have? Either he denies the photos, which he can't, or he admits it happened and tries to make an excuse."

Ralph agreed. "Short of a miracle, his situation looks hopeless."

# Part 5

Monday morning was bright and warm when Marnie set off for her meeting in Ralph's car, leaving Anne in charge. She tried not to care about the impact the elderly Volvo might have on her image.

It was a normal start to the week in Knightly St John. Ralph was working on board *Thyrsis*, connected to the rest of the world by his new Internet link. Anne was studying Marnie's scheme for a Willards pub near Foxton Locks before sorting out that week's invoices. Dolly had not been seen since breakfast and was probably curled up in a sheltered spot practising her beauty sleep.

It was a normal start, apart from the presence of the most wanted man in the country living on the edge of their community on a canal boat. At least that was the assumption. Of Anthony Leyton-Brown there had been no sighting since early on Sunday.

By the end of the morning, Anne was beginning to worry. What if he had done something desperate under the strain of it all? But he was a politician, and Ralph had often said they were hard-bitten, tough as old boots. But even so ...

She put aside her pen and made for the door. Down by the docking area everything was quiet. The three boats lay at rest at their moorings, only the open side doors on *Thyrsis* revealing that someone was on board.

Anne shook her head and decided she was being foolish. At that moment a stubby green boat came into view in mid-channel, skirting the anonymous grey boat and *Thyrsis*. It was painted in the workaday livery of British Waterways, shaped like a steel punt with an open hold and a small cabin at the stern. It was piled with branches, plastic bags and the regulation supermarket trolley. Anne gave a customary wave to the steerer who hailed her and began pulling in towards the bank. She had seen him before, one of the regular men for this sector, but they had never spoken.

"Hi. Can I ask if you've you seen any strange characters along here?"

Anne's eyes flickered involuntarily towards the grey boat. "Strange ... in what way?"

"Hanging around," he said, "cruising up and down, maybe looking at moored boats."

"Everybody does that on the cut," said Anne. "That's what it's all about."

The man looked exasperated. "I know. That's what I told them in the office. But they said I had to ask everyone I saw and warn them."

"*Warn* them? What about?"

"People have been breaking into boats, stealing stuff. And there's been the odd mugging." He looked at the grey boat. "I haven't seen that one before. D'you know whose it is?"

"It belongs to someone our friend knows. He's just passing through."

"Okay. Well, make sure you keep your boat locked whenever you leave it unattended, right?"

"Right."

"And be careful when you're walking alone ... be vigilant."

"I can't think anyone'd want to mug me."

"You'd be surprised. Someone mugged a jogger on the towpath near Yore last week ... gave him a nasty knock on the head."

"Must be pretty fit to catch a jogger," said Anne.

The man pushed the boat away from the bank, pressing the accelerator to move off. "The police are treating it seriously. You be careful now."

Back at the office barn, Anne picked up the message pad to write a note to Marnie about the boatman's warning. To her surprise, the top page already had writing on it.

*Missed you again! This is becoming a habit. Back later in the week.*
*Love,*
*S*

• • • • •

An hour later Anne was comparing the merits of different Internet servers when Marnie breezed in, dumped her briefcase on the desk and went straight to the kitchen area at the back of the office.

"Hi! I'm back. *What a morning!* How're things?"

"Okay. How d'you get on?"

Marnie switched on the kettle. "Not bad. Jeffries was there. You know what he's like ... wants to discuss *every* tiny detail. Still, I think he trusts me now ... even though I'm not a man. Anything happen while I was out?"

"I've put a few messages on your desk ... and a fax from the plumbing suppliers."

Marnie paused in the act of spooning coffee into the pot. "Don't tell me ..."

"No, it's all right. The hot-water tanks are in stock ... they'll deliver Thursday. We're back on schedule."

"Hurray!"

Marnie walked over to her desk as the kettle began rattling and picked up the pile of messages. Anne saw her reach the hand-written note from S. She saw the frown cross Marnie's face, saw her read the note again, crumple it and drop it into the waste-paper bin. There was a pause before she moved on to the next message.

"Shall I make the coffee?" Anne called across in a casual tone.

"No, it's okay. I'm on my feet."

Marnie went back to the kitchen area, where Dolly was loitering with intent by the fridge door. She bent and stroked the cat absent-mindedly, not noticing that the kettle had switched itself off.

"Any luck at the garages?"

"Garages ... oh yes. I managed to call in on one. They don't make the GTi any more. I'll have to have a rethink." She brought the mugs over, while Dolly purred at her milk.

"Marnie, did you see that message? We've got another stranger round here."

"It's okay, Anne."

"My message about the mugger, I mean."

"Mugger?"

Anne explained about the warning from the British Waterways man. "He said the police are making enquiries."

"Great," said Marnie. "I expect that means we'll be in for a visit from an old acquaintance."

"DCI Bartlett?"

Marnie nodded. "What's the betting? It'll be him or Marriner, at a guess."

"Sergeant Marriner's not that bad. At least he doesn't look so stern as Mr Bartlett."

"Wait till they're carting you off in chains under suspicion."

Anne laughed. "I'll take my chances. But seriously, Marnie, the police are warning everyone on the cut to be extra careful. I'll make sure I lock the office every time I go out, so no one can come in while I'm away."

Marnie looked down at her desk. "Good idea."

•  •  •  •  •

Anne enjoyed her routine. It anchored her life and work. Each day at around four she would gather up the post and head off up the field track to the village shop to post letters and collect a few groceries. But on that afternoon she had begun her expedition earlier than usual, telling Marnie she had an idea, wanting to avoid the children coming out of school, to reach the shop before the rush. She was on a mission and wanted Molly Appleton's attention to herself.

"Hallo, my dear. You're early today. Rush hour hasn't started. Richard always says we can set the clock by you."

"I'm deliberately early today, Mrs Appleton. There's something I want to ask you."

"How can I help?"

"It's about tabloid newspapers ... "

"Oh, yes."

"In particular the *Globe* ... "

•  •  •  •  •

There was a knock on the door of the office barn, and it swung open to reveal Ralph standing on the threshold.

"Hallo. Did I give you a shock?"

Marnie's face relaxed into a smile. "No, of course not."

"You looked rather ... startled."

"The effort of concentration. Come in."

"Am I interrupting you?"

"To be strictly accurate, yes, but it's a welcome interruption."

Ralph kissed her warmly and Marnie responded. "Do that again," he said. She did.

"Well, well," said Marnie. "Romantic interludes in the afternoon. Do you fancy ... a drink of anything?"

Ralph sighed. "I knew it could only go downhill from that point. I'll join you if you're having one. But don't you want to wait for Anne to get back from her post run?"

"She won't be back for a while. She's gone off on what she described as a mission. I'll put the kettle on. Any sign of our new neighbour?"

"He looked in on me about an hour ago." Ralph paused while the water gushed into the kettle. "He's obviously been badly shaken by what's happened."

"He was quite rude to me yesterday. Do you think that was out of character?"

"I'd think it was a sign of his troubled state of mind. He's quite paranoid ... convinced he's being hounded."

"That figures," said Marnie. "What about his wife ... has he been in touch with her?"

"I asked him about that ... persuaded him to ring her. I've lent him my mobile."

"He hasn't got a phone?" Marnie was incredulous.

"No. That's been one of the problems. His mobile's battery has run down and he's got no means of recharging it on the boat."

"No generator?"

"No petrol."

"So now you're incommunicado until he gives it back."

"I'll survive. Anyway, I've got a new one coming any time now. That one was fairly basic, and I saw a special offer, so I thought I'd upgrade."

"And you'll manage to work it?"

"Mock not." He looked sheepish. "Actually, I've arranged for an expert to set it up for me. You know what I'm like with technology."

"You must still make sure you get the old one back."

"I will. Anthony promised to drop it in when he'd finished with it. And I don't like to disturb him. He seems to spend much of the time sleeping ... said he didn't know what day it was. I don't think he was pretending."

"Sounds like he's close to having a breakdown. How was he when you spoke to him?"

"On the brink of tears, I'd say ... not totally coherent. He's a sick man, Marnie."

A rapid movement past the window caught Marnie's eye, and in seconds Anne pushed open the door, coming in backwards, her arms filled with a bundle of newspapers tied round with string.

"Any more of this and we'll have to buy a yak!" She staggered theatrically across the office and dropped the huge package on her desk with a weary sigh. "It's a miracle there are any trees left in the world at all."

"Are you going into the recycling business?" Ralph asked.

"I'm going into the research business."

"I'm getting nervous already."

Anne opened her desk drawer and took out a pair of scissors to cut the string holding the bundle together. "I never imagined there'd be so many of them in a fortnight."

Marnie said, "I thought you were just going to find out from Molly who took the *Globe* and go and get the ones with the Leyton-Brown articles in."

"I did ... and this is the result. She told me there were three people who had the *Globe* delivered. The first one said he just put them in the bin each day and didn't recommend rummaging in it."

"Good advice," said Ralph.

"Yes. The next one said he kept his for the Scouts' waste paper collection. They were coming on Saturday, but I was welcome to have them if I wanted. They were bundled up in his shed. Here they are. I accepted the offer before I saw how much stuff there was."

Marnie could not believe it. "All that is just two weeks' editions of *The Globe*?"

"Plus the *Mail on Sunday* and the *News of the World*. I hope the articles are in here somewhere, after all this effort." She settled down to the task of sorting out the *Globe* from the rest while Marnie and Ralph went back to the other side of the office.

"Why the research?" Ralph asked in a quiet voice.

"You know Anne … she has to get to the bottom of things."

"I expect the *News of the World* will help her do that … " Ralph noticed Marnie's expression. "Sorry. But why read up on Anthony?"

"We ought to know the background if he's on our own doorstep."

"*Blimey!*" It was Anne. She glanced up. "Er, sorry … *News of the World* … "Feeling that no other explanation was necessary, she resumed her task. Ralph smiled at Marnie.

"Know-all," Marnie muttered. "Anyway, how do you know what … "

Before she could finish the sentence, Anne called out: "Here we are." She held up a tattered copy of the *Globe*. Half the front page was a photograph of a man kissing a girl in what looked like a park. Its headline was in bold black letters: 'WHO'S A NAUGHTY BOY?'

• • • • •

They sat in the saloon on *Sally Ann*, as they had sat together over a convivial meal so many times. Marnie had made a cheese soufflé to which Anne had added a mixed salad of lettuce, chopped spring onions and diced red peppers, sprinkled all over with thyme and marjoram. Ralph had brought a bottle of red Rioja and a watermelon. The difference was that on that evening, the proximity of Anthony Leyton-Brown MP was uppermost in their minds, and it left a strange taste. Ralph had not seen him again that afternoon, respecting his need for privacy.

Their thoughts drifted off to the lurid photographs in the newspaper. The *Globe* had run articles for four days that week, releasing more photos each day to keep the story alive. It seemed to have fizzled out by Saturday, probably because Leyton-Brown himself had vanished, and his wife had shut herself into the family home. She was receiving deliveries of supplies from relatives brave enough to drive through the besieging paparazzi camped outside.

Cutting off a piece of baguette, Ralph suddenly said, "This is absurd. Here we are on a beautiful spring evening, having a super meal … "

"With an excellent wine … " Marnie chipped in.

"Yes, that too … and anyone would think we were at a *wake*."

"What's a wake?" Anne asked.

"It's a sort of party before a funeral, where the dead person lies in their coffin and friends and family mill around, eating, drinking and talking about them."

Anne grimaced. "Ugh!"

"Got it in one," said Marnie. "The only difference is we haven't got a body." She quickly raised a hand to her mouth. "Oh God … I wish I hadn't said that … "

"Is that what you were thinking, then?" said Anne. "That he might have … you know … ?" Her eyes were enormous in her thin face.

"No, of course not … well yes, actually … I suppose it wasn't in the front of my mind, but maybe niggling away in the background."

"Do you want me to go over and check he's all right?" Ralph offered.

"I don't know. Part of me wants to give him space, but part of me worries he might do something desperate. What do you think? You at least have seen him today."

"I feel torn, same as you. And to be honest, I'm rather reluctant to get you both involved in all this."

"Do *you* feel involved?" said Marnie.

"Only in a remote sense. I told you, I don't know him personally all that well. But on the basis of long acquaintance, I don't like to turn my back on him."

"You don't need to worry about us, Ralph. I don't see us getting involved."

"Famous last words ... " Anne muttered, looking pointedly at the newspapers on the galley workbench.

Marnie leaned over and picked up one of them, flicking through the pages. On the first day, the *Globe* had published a four-page spread. There was Leyton-Brown locked in unambiguous embraces with a girl who looked very young. Some of the photos had black bands across them to cover up the position of his hands, presumably to protect the innocence of the readers. The bands were positioned in the most suggestive way possible. Marnie shook her head, muttering that she felt like a voyeur just by holding the paper in her hands. And so it surprised her when Anne began studying the pictures intensely. Marnie wondered what experience of sex Anne might have had. It was not a subject they had ever broached.

"This is quite interesting," Anne muttered.

"Really?" Marnie could hardly believe it.

"Yes. I only spotted it when you were holding the paper and I saw the pictures from this angle. I could see a kind of pattern." She turned the paper round to face them. "Look at those top photos there. What do you see?"

"Anthony holding hands with a girl young enough to be his daughter," Marnie said flatly. "They're not as clear as the others because there are bushes in the way."

"That's *right*."

"What are you getting at?" said Ralph.

Anne pointed. "Look at the angle of their arms."

Marnie and Ralph leaned forward. "What about it?" said Marnie.

"Ah," said Ralph. "Do you mean ... ?"

"Yes," said Anne. "I think she's *pulling* him by the hand, not just *holding* his hand."

Marnie looked puzzled. "Pulling him where?"

"There." Anne held up the next series of photos. The two people were much clearer, neatly framed by trees and bushes around them but not concealing them.

"I think you may have a point, Anne." Ralph pushed the paper closer to Marnie. "If you go from here to here, you could imagine that the girl is, well, *luring* Anthony to this place where the camera has a better view."

"You think it was planned that way?" Marnie said almost in disbelief. "Entrapment ... like his wife said?"

"Could be. And her hand on his wrist there. Look. We're supposed to think that she's trying to remove it from her ... well, from where it is. But if you looked at it in a different way, you could almost imagine that she's holding it there."

"I suppose that's possible," Marnie conceded. "But there's still all this detail about his private life ... pornographic magazines and prostitutes. And the girl is only supposed to be fifteen years old."

"It doesn't produce evidence about any of that," Anne said. "It only reports *reliable sources* as saying that."

Ralph pulled the article closer. "The girl is *alleged* to be a minor and is *believed* to be in hiding. They don't seem to know anything reliable about her, except that she's disappeared. The accusations are all innuendo in the headlines. This *reliable sources* stuff is just put in to overcome legal problems."

"So he could sue them if the report isn't true?" Marnie said. "If they can't produce evidence, he could get substantial damages?"

Ralph looked sceptical. "Unlikely, I would've thought. What chance would he have of winning once the jury saw those pictures?"

"Zilch," said Anne.

"Quite."

# Part 6

It was mid-morning on the following day when they had a visit from an old acquaintance. Marnie and Anne were working through their lists of phone calls. Replacing the receiver, Marnie noticed that Anne was fiddling with a small package.

"How's it going, Anne?"

"Is that a subtle way of asking if I'm making coffee?"

"Of course not. Are you?" Anne flashed her the Death Stare. "What have you got there?"

Anne held up a mobile phone. "Ralph's new toy. Same make as ours, but look how small it is. I think it's shrunk. He must have dropped it in the canal."

"I didn't know Ralph had entered the world of high tech. That's amazing."

"He hasn't," said Anne. "He's got no idea how it works ... says he's suffering from *technology fatigue* ... wants me to get it working, then show him how to use it."

Marnie laughed. "He had to go on a course to operate his electric kettle."

Anne got up and went over to the kitchen area. "Like I said ... subtle."

Marnie smiled to herself, picked up the phone and dialled a frequent number of her own. She brought her sister up to date on events at Glebe Farm.

"Are you *kidding?*" said Beth.

"About something like that?" Marnie said. "Of course I'm not kidding."

"And he's actually staying at *your* place? I can't believe it."

"Sure. I've let him shack up with Anne in her room over the office here. It seemed the logical thing to do with a man accused of serial sex offences involving young girls."

In the background Anne shrieked in mock horror.

"Marnie!" Beth exclaimed.

"Well, honestly ... Can you really imagine us accommodating him *here*? He's come on a boat and he's staying on it down by *Thyrsis*."

"Now I know you're winding me up. Anthony Leyton-Brown, *Mister Smoothie*, on a narrowboat? That is not believable."

"Believe it or not, it's the truth. And it's also a secret. The last thing we need is the press descending on us."

"How long's he been there? On the news it said he'd disappeared a week or two ago."

"He's just arrived ... a couple of days, that's all."

"What are you going to do with him?"

Marnie became aware that Anne was making gestures, pointing towards the window. She glanced up and saw a grey car pulling into the yard. "We've got visitors," she said to Beth. "And I think I know who it is." She watched two men get out of the car. "Just what I need: Chief Inspector Bartlett and Sergeant Marriner. I'd better go. If you don't hear from me later today, get in touch with Amnesty International, Torture Department. Tell them to organise a search party." She ended the conversation and hung up.

"Shall I make extra coffee?" Anne asked.

Marnie shook her head. "They never accept. They'll only stay long enough to make me incriminate myself, as usual."

She watched the detectives cross the yard. It was a path they knew well. When Marnie was involved in the enquiry into the murder of Toni Petrie, the first woman vicar of Knightly St John the previous summer, the police had been regular visitors to Glebe Farm. Marnie had had a number of unfortunate interviews with them and had gained the reputation of being unreliable. She thought it was all just a series of misunderstandings. The police thought she was just unco-operative. They must be desperate, she reflected, if they were coming to her for help.

The men walked into the office and were greeted by a smile from Anne in the kitchen and a brave face from Marnie, doing her best to look welcoming. She stood up and offered a hand.

"Would you like tea, perhaps?"

Marriner opened his mouth, but Bartlett spoke first. "No, thank you, Mrs Walker. We can't stay long. We're just making a few enquiries in the area."

"Enquiries," Marnie repeated. She had learnt that the less she said, the less scope there was for being misunderstood.

"Have you noticed anything suspicious or unusual in the area in the last week or so ... any strangers around?"

"Not here," said Marnie.

"On the canal? Any sign of an attempt to get into your boat ... damage to doors or windows?"

"No. None at all."

"And you're sure there's been no one here that you didn't know ... or expect?"

"No one."

"You hesitated there, Mrs Walker. Do you want to reconsider your answer?"

"No. I ... was just thinking."

"About anything or anyone in particular?"

Marnie said slowly, "About you, actually."

This time Bartlett hesitated. He frowned. "What about me?"

"I was wondering why a Detective Chief Inspector should be making enquiries about attempts at pilfering on canal boats. I thought you only handled serious crimes."

"All crime is potentially serious, Mrs Walker. Did you think we'd come about some other matter?"

"You tell me."

During this exchange they had remained standing. Bartlett suddenly surprised Marnie by taking the seat beside her desk, while Marriner stayed where he was near the door. Marnie sat down, and Anne returned to her chair.

"You've heard about the disappearance of the MP, Anthony Leyton-Brown?" Bartlett said. Marnie nodded. "We have reason to believe that a man answering his description has been seen not far from here."

"I see."

"Since this was the last area in which a sighting has been made, we're following up every lead. Have you any ideas as to his whereabouts?"

"I didn't realise he'd committed a crime. I thought he was just accused in a newspaper of some sort of sleazy behaviour."

"What about a man having sex with a minor? Would you regard that as a crime, Mrs Walker? Would that be serious enough for you?"

"Of course it would. But I still didn't think officers of your rank would be directly involved in something like that."

In the background Marriner cleared his throat. Bartlett leaned forward. "Any matter involving an MP with that amount of high profile has to be given priority, Mrs Walker. It's a fact of life."

"I understand."

"And sex with an underage girl is a form of rape and carries severe penalties. As a woman you'd surely agree with that, wouldn't you?"

"Of course."

"Then let me come back to my question. Have you any idea where he might be?"

Looking back later, Marnie realised that that moment was the turning point. She knew that she had only to tell Bartlett that Anthony Leyton-Brown was on a boat fifty metres from where he was sitting, and the law would have taken its course. So why had she held her tongue? If he was innocent, the truth would set him free. Or would it? Was Ralph right about his chances of a fair hearing? She heard Anne's voice in her mind. *Zilch.* Was it the lonely suffering of his wife ... the doubts about the so-called evidence from *reliable sources* ... the convenient disappearance of the star witness? Did the camera lie, she wondered, by only telling part of the story?

"You think his disappearance has something to do with me?" said Marnie.

"I didn't say that, Mrs Walker. I only asked if you'd seen him or knew where he was. Mind you, you do have a funny way of being in the middle of trouble."

"That's honest enough. So this is routine now, is it? You round up the usual suspects? Top of the list, M. Walker, Glebe Farm ... "

"You're very secluded down here, Mrs Walker. If someone wanted to keep out of the public eye, he could do worse than hide himself away in a place like this. Also, he's an MP, and you've had contact with politicians in the past." He was referring to her finding the body of a murdered MP in the Regent's Canal in London during the winter.

"I'm sorry, Inspector, but on this occasion I can't help you."

"So you haven't seen him." Bartlett glanced back at Marriner.

Marnie shook her head. "I can't help you. I'm sorry."

"Will you get in touch with us if you see anything suspicious?" said Marriner. He walked over and handed her his business card. "You've got all my contact numbers there."

"If I see anything suspicious, I will."

"Thank you."

"And if you're worried about him disappearing," Marnie added cheerfully, "why don't you drag the canal round *Sally Ann* just to be on the safe side ... for old time's sake?"

Marriner showed the flicker of a smile. Bartlett stood up. "Nice to see you again, Mrs Walker. You're looking much better – good as new, if I might say so."

"Slightly better circumstances than last time we met," said Marnie.

"At least you're not a murder victim this time."

"No. I must be losing my touch."

• • • • •

It was the setting more than any other factor that had attracted Marnie to Knightly St John and Glebe Farm. The first time she had ever seen the place two summers ago, she was suffering from sunstroke, after steering *Sally Ann* for too long without covering her head.

The following year, on a whim, she had returned for a day with Anne to find the whole place, farmhouse and barns, spinney, boat dock and a few acres of land up for sale. It had been the biggest gamble of her life to give up her job in London, her *secure, well-paid job,* as Beth kept reminding her, sell her flat, her *desirable flat in fashionable Hampstead,* and put everything into a business.

Marnie felt uneasy as she sauntered slowly towards the docking area that morning, uneasy about concealing information from the police, but she had not been able to bring herself to turn him in. It went against all her instincts, and she only hoped that she was not going to find herself in trouble for harbouring a man suspected of a serious crime, the virtual rape of a minor.

Marnie stopped and leaned up against a tree, her head spinning with questions and doubts. She suddenly had a mental image of herself dressed in a loose-fitting white shirt with wide sleeves and black tights, muttering: *To be or not to be* ... A smile spread across her face, and she almost laughed. *Why do I do that?* she thought. *Why do I always have this daft tendency to see a funny side to serious situations? Either I'm going ga-ga or maybe it's just my way of coping.*

The shock at hearing a voice close beside her tore away the smile, and she almost screamed. It was a soft voice, but it came without any warning.

"Penny for your thoughts?"

"Oh, my God!" She put her head back against the tree and drew a deep breath. "I *wish* you hadn't done that."

"So do I now. I am sorry." He certainly sounded sorry. "I didn't mean to alarm you like that."

Marnie breathed out audibly. "It's okay. I'm just feeling edgy, that's all. One of those days."

"Then don't let me intrude. But I would just like to say I'm sorry about the other day ... my rudeness when I was occupying your mooring. My name is Anthony Leyton-Brown." He offered his hand.

"I know."

"Of course you do. But I thought it was time I behaved like a civilised person again."

Marnie took his hand. "Marnie Walker."

"Very glad to meet you, Marnie Walker."

• • • • •

Anne took a fresh cloth out of a drawer in the galley on *Sally Ann* that evening and spread it over the table. "Well, this is a turn-up for the book ... whatever that means."

"How do you mean it?" said Marnie.

"First, we meet this rude man, then we find out he's a child molester and rapist – "

"*Alleged* child molester and rapist," Marnie interjected.

"Okay ... *alleged* child rapist. Then you withhold information about his whereabouts from the police and become his accomplice or accessory or something, and invite him round for supper."

"You see a slight inconsistency of approach there, right?"

"That's one way of looking at it. I suppose something made you change your mind."

"You did."

"*I did?*" Anne look startled.

"When you pointed out what was in the papers."

"But I was just surmising ... guessing, really. I don't know what really happened."

"Exactly. Let me ask you something, Anne. What would you have thought if that had been me?"

"*You?*"

"Yes, me. What would you have thought?"

"I dunno. I would've wondered what was going on, I suppose."

"You would've thought it out of character?"

"Of course."

"You might've given me the benefit of the doubt, at least initially?"

"Sure. You know I would."

"And you'd want to know why I was behaving like that. You couldn't work it out for yourself?"

"How could I? It would be so unlike you, I'd want to find out what was going on."

"Right." Marnie spelled it out slowly. "And yet we look at photographs in a newspaper of a complete stranger and immediately think we can judge him when we know nothing about him."

A slight movement of the boat told them that someone had stepped onto the deck, probably Ralph. There was a rapping of knuckles on the steel door.

Marnie called out. "We're in the galley."

"Hallo. May I come aboard, please?" It was Anthony Leyton-Brown.

"Yes. Come through."

He arrived carrying a bottle of wine. Marnie was surprised; he was over an hour early. He read her expression.

"Sorry to arrive when you're busy, but I've brought this. I couldn't get any flowers, obviously, but I wanted to bring you something. You don't have to open it tonight, of course, but if you did want to, it would need to be opened and kept at room temperature for about an hour before drinking it." He held out the bottle.

Marnie took it. "That's a kind thought, but really not necessary. I'll open it now so it'll be ready for when you come."

"Well, don't feel obliged. But it needs to be drunk in the proper conditions if you wanted to. I couldn't very well arrive with an opened bottle of wine ... and I haven't anything else to give."

"Thank you." Marnie glanced at the label and suddenly added: "Oh, sorry, this is my friend Anne. Anne, this is Mr Leyton-Brown."

He reached over and shook her hand. "Good evening."

"Hallo."

"Er ... you might need to be a bit careful with the cork, by the way. It may be a little fragile … at that age."

"I see. Do you think … I mean … would you like to do the honours? It would be such a shame if I made a mess of it after you'd gone to all this trouble."

"I'd be glad to. But I haven't gone to any trouble. It's only a bottle of wine, after all."

Marnie reached into the drawer and handed him the corkscrew. Anne stood back and watched, turning her head slightly as a shadow passed the window.

"I think someone's coming, Marnie," she said. Leyton-Brown paused momentarily and looked up from his task.

"Ralph, I suppose," Marnie said. "I'm not expecting anyone." She called out: "Come through. We're in here." To Anne she said: "I can't find the red onions. Without them, the red onion flan will be rather deficient."

"I think they're under the workbench at the back."

Marnie opened a cupboard and knelt down to rummage. "Brilliant. Anne, you're a genius."

"Er, hallo."

The man's voice made Marnie twist round in surprise and stand up quickly. For a moment a wave of dizziness swept over her, and she had to steady herself against the workbench.

"Are you all right?" The man reached out a hand and held her arm, aware that two further pairs of eyes were staring at him.

"You surprised me, that's all. I'm fine."

He took his hand away. "You did say to come through."

"I thought you … never mind." She glanced hastily in the direction of Leyton-Brown and decided against introductions. "Actually, I think I could do with some fresh air … to clear my head … "

On the stern deck, Simon turned to face Marnie. "Look, I didn't realise you had someone … someone with you, I mean. You got my messages?"

"Yes. It was still a surprise seeing you just standing there like that." They were both speaking quietly.

"Sure. And I could see it wasn't a good time to turn up. You're obviously in the middle of preparing a meal together."

"You couldn't have known that. Anyway, what brings you here?"

"Believe it or not, I read about you in a newspaper at O'Hare airport, Chicago. I had a wait before my flight, bought a copy of the *Times*, and there you were."

"When was this?"

"February. I was going to San Francisco and then on to Australia. I kept the paper. The article said where you were living. Now that I'm back, I thought I'd come and see if you were all right. You seem to have had a tough time over the past year."

"And you seem to have joined the jet set, Simon."

"My business has taken off, you might say." He smiled.

"I'm glad for you. Really, I am."

"Thanks. But what about you? The paper said you'd been almost killed, then you found a body and got mixed up in some sort of political intrigue."

"Well, life hasn't been dull, that's for sure. But I'm fine now."

"It also said you had your own design firm. Is that right?"

"I'm self-employed."

"And this place ... all yours?" He gestured towards the farm through the spinney. Marnie nodded. "It looks great ... masses of potential." He looked back at her. "Are you sure you're okay? I gather from the paper that you nearly died."

"I've put all that behind me. I try not to think about it now."

"You certainly look terrific, Marnie. That short hairstyle is wonderful ... really suits you."

"Thank you."

Neither spoke for a few seconds.

"Well, look, I'd better be going. You have things to do ... as usual. You're still a very busy lady. I'm glad I've seen you. I was worried." He stepped down onto the bank.

"I'll walk through the spinney with you," Marnie said.

"No. No need. I know the way. Glad to see you settled ... all this ... a new life ... your friend ... Take care of yourself, Marnie."

"Thanks. I'm glad things've worked out well for you, too."

Simon walked a few paces and looked over his shoulder. "Perhaps I might see you again some time ... if it's not ... you know."

Marnie nodded. "I'm in the phone book. Walker and Co."

She went down the steps into the cabin. Anthony was holding the wine bottle, staring at her as she walked through to the galley.

"I wouldn't normally not introduce a guest, but ... well ..."

"That was very considerate of you," said Anthony. "Do you think ...?"

Marnie shook her head. "I'm sure he didn't recognise you. He certainly didn't say anything."

"That's a relief. Well, I've been in the way long enough. The wine's opened; the cork smells fine. It should be drinkable. In about an hour, did you say? Or would you like a little longer ... in view of the interruptions?"

"An hour should be fine."

Marnie and Anne settled down to preparing the meal, quieter than usual. Anne sliced the onions; Marnie made cheese pastry. By the time Marnie was sliding the flan into the oven and reaching for the avocados, hardly two words had been uttered between them. Suddenly, Marnie heard a squeak and looked round.

"It was me," said Anne. "I'm being positively mouse-like to leave you to your private thoughts, so I thought I'd play the part properly."

A smile spread slowly across Marnie's face. "Why do you think I need private thoughts?"

Anne shrugged. "He's very good-looking ... *dishy*. Was he your husband?"

"For a while. How did you know?"

"I saw him in Beth's photos when you were in the hospital. I guessed."

"It was a long time ago."

"And its all over now."

"Yes, of course."

"Now you've got Ralph and a new life."

"That's right. And nothing's going to change that."

• • • • •

All through supper on *Sally Ann,* Ralph felt that Marnie was more tense than usual, and he was determined to get Anthony away from Glebe Farm as soon as he could. He noticed that Anne too was less relaxed, and put it down to her usual sensitivity towards Marnie.

In contrast, Anthony Leyton-Brown seemed much more at ease than Ralph had expected. He praised the meal without exaggerated flattery and, when Marnie protested that it did not do justice to the wine he had brought, he brushed her remarks aside.

"Marnie's got a point," said Ralph. "It really is exceptional."

"Mr Leyton-Brown brought it this evening," Anne said. "He uncorked it early so it would be at its best."

"May I see it?"

Ralph examined the label. "1982. A significant year, in more ways than one." Anthony nodded.

"Was that a really good year?" Anne asked.

"With a wine like that I expect every year's a really good year," Marnie observed.

"True," said Ralph. "But I think that for the best clarets, that year was absolutely outstanding."

He passed the bottle back to Anne, who studied it closely. "Château Lafite-Rothschild," she read. "Clarets are the wines from Bordeaux, aren't they?"

"That's right," said Marnie. "The red ones."

"And that year, they were exceptional?"

"Yes," said Ralph. "I believe it was regarded as the great year of the decade."

"Why did you say *in more ways than one?*"

Ralph looked at Anthony, who hesitated a few moments before replying quietly, "It was the year I entered Parliament." They all fell silent, at least one of them thinking that this would be the year he left Parliament forever. Probably for no better reason than to break the silence, Anthony added, "When I saw your visitor earlier on I wondered if I ought to have brought two bottles."

Anne glanced quickly at Marnie, checked herself and returned to studying the label on the bottle. Ralph noticed this and looked thoughtfully at Marnie. He was surprised that she seemed uneasy.

"Er, no. That was an unexpected visitor."

"You did seem rather taken aback at the time," said Anthony. "I wondered if it was because of my being there."

"No. It was because ... that was my ex-husband."

"Ah," said Ralph. "I can imagine that would be a surprise." He noticed that Anne was trying to look at him without making it obvious. He smiled at her. She made a big effort to smile back and nearly succeeded.

Anthony suddenly grasped the significance of what he had said. "Oh dear ... Have I put my foot in it? I really didn't mean to. I had no idea what your ... circumstances were."

"It's not a problem," Marnie said firmly. "Ralph and I are an item. Simon and I parted company years ago. He read about what had happened to me in the press and decided to look in to see if I was all right. I knew he was around, but I didn't know when he'd turn up. That's why I was surprised.

There's no more to it ... " She paused and narrowed her eyes. *"Your friend,"* she muttered softly.

"Sorry?"

"Just a thought."

"Are you going to share it with us?" said Ralph, who seemed the least troubled of the group.

"Simon said something about *my friend* ... "

"Is that important? He meant Anne, presumably?"

Marnie frowned. "He might have. On the other hand, he might've meant ... "

"Me?" said Anthony.

"It's possible."

"Did you get the impression he'd recognised Anthony?" Ralph asked.

"No. I'm sure he didn't. I don't think he gave him more than a glance."

"He didn't take his eyes off you, Marnie," said Anne in a quiet voice.

"It just goes to show," said Anthony. "Appearances can sometimes be deceptive." He took a sip of wine and gazed pensively at the glass, swirling it gently so that it changed colour, through shades of red to purple.

"How did you introduce Anthony?" Ralph asked.

"I didn't. We went out on deck for a few moments to talk."

"How was he?"

"Okay. It was almost like seeing an old friend again ... but not quite."

"And you think he thought Anthony and you were ... an item? That you didn't introduce him because the situation might have been ... awkward?"

"Could be."

Ralph looked at Anthony. "Well, it seems as if your cover hasn't been blown."

"Maybe not, but I think I've caused you some embarrassment, Marnie."

"It's not a problem. I only took him outside to protect your privacy."

"Thank you for that," said Anthony. "I really had no intention of blundering into your life ... inflicting myself on you."

"You have a point there."

"I can only apologise," said Anthony.

"I didn't mean it that way," Marnie said quickly. "I was thinking about what you said ... that appearances can be deceptive."

•  •  •  •  •

After supper it was still light and they went to sit outside. From the stern deck on *Sally Ann* they could see Anthony's boat tied up alongside *Thyrsis* a few metres away, a marked contrast between the shining green and gold of Ralph's boat – the colours of a Harrods's carrier bag, Anne had called it – and the dull, matt grey of the boat with no name.

"How did you get hold of the boat?" Ralph asked Anthony. "I wouldn't have thought narrowboats were your scene at all."

"Why not? I've always liked boats. I used to live by the Thames, remember?"

"I could imagine you on a floating gin palace all right ... but a narrowboat? Much too plebeian for you, I would've thought."

Anthony laughed. It was a natural, carefree laugh, the first such sound he had made since arriving. "Look who's talking! You're not exactly a horny-handed grease-monkey yourself, Ralph!"

"So … a spur of the moment decision, then?"

"Absolutely. I, er … needed time and space when the balloon went up … grabbed the nearest thing that came to hand. The boat belongs … *belonged*, I should say, to a friend who's also a constituent. It's a sad story. He bought this place in Docklands not far from my office … very nice waterside location in a marina, and thought he'd get himself a boat. Unfortunately, his business partner got involved in some dodgy deals and, to cut a very long story short, they both ended up in prison for fraud. My friend went down for two years as a kind of accessory and his partner for five. Another tribute to British justice."

"You thought your friend was innocent?" said Ralph.

"I'm convinced of it. But there was no way of proving it, so my friend went inside."

"Leaving behind a boat."

"Yes … fitted out internally, but not painted up."

"Conveniently anonymous," said Marnie.

"Quite."

"So why did you come in this direction?" she asked.

Anthony shrugged. "By chance, I suppose. One night I loaded some things onto the boat and set off upstream … found my way into Limehouse Cut … followed my nose round to Bull's Bridge. There seemed little point in heading back down to the Thames, so I came north. And here I am. When I recognised Ralph's boat from the newspaper article, I was amazed."

"You thought this was his home."

"Yes. I never wanted to impose on you, Marnie. But I was feeling desperate after what happened. You know all about that, I suppose."

"We've seen the papers," Marnie said.

"Well, if you believe what they printed, I'm astonished that you invite me on board as a guest."

"You don't think I should believe the articles?" Marnie asked in an even tone.

Anthony grimaced. "No one'll believe my version of events," he said dully. "It's useless trying to explain."

"There is another version?" Ralph asked. Anthony nodded.

"Why don't you try us?" said Marnie.

• • • • •

That night, Marnie patted herself dry after showering, pulled on a dressing gown and walked through to the stern on *Thyrsis*, stepping out in the darkness onto the narrow space for the steerer, known as the counter. She rubbed the back of her hair with a towel and breathed in the cool watery smells, mingled with the scent from the trees and in the background the heavy sweet aroma of oil-seed rape that seemed to hang over the whole countryside at this time of year.

There was no light anywhere, except a faint glow from the portholes on *Thyrsis*. Marnie stood for a minute listening to the sounds of the night: the faint rustling of a nocturnal animal on the move; the plop as a fish jumped.

Closing the hatch behind her, Marnie walked through to the cabin where Ralph was sitting up in bed reading a typescript. He took off his reading glasses when she appeared in the doorway.

"You always do that," he said, smiling.

"Do what?"

"Go outside for a few minutes at night when you've got something on your mind. I used to wonder if you were having to steel yourself to come in here with me."

She laughed. "Don't be so insecure. For all you know, I might be saying my prayers."

They both knew she was an agnostic.

"Would it be ... *For what we are about to receive –* "

"Ralph!"

He laughed out loud. Marnie threw her towel at him, catching him off guard. It wrapped itself round his face. He was still laughing when he removed it. Before handing it back, he sniffed it, closing his eyes and breathing in deeply. "Mm ... this smells of you ... delightful."

"Oh God," she said, in a mock serious tone. "The man's a fetishist. Just my luck to end up with some kind of sexual pervert."

"Back to our theme for the evening," said Ralph. "Did Anthony's version of things influence how you feel about him?"

Marnie sat down on the end of the bed. "It was funny how his story matched up with what Anne said about the photos in the paper."

"Entrapment. Do you believe that was the first time he'd had relations with that girl?"

"How could I know? For a start, the girl's gone missing. And as for his story about them going to a meeting and being offered drinks afterwards ... then the girl getting flirtatious ... I just don't know. Could he be so weak-willed?"

"Marnie, any man could be flattered to receive the attentions of a young woman. You don't have to be weak-willed."

"Would you have behaved in the same way if it happened to you?"

"If you want an honest answer, I'd say it would depend on the circumstances. The way I feel about you, I wouldn't be prepared to let any girl jeopardise the most important relationship in my life."

"There you are, then."

"But I don't think it's always as simple as that. People can be tempted."

"So what he did didn't surprise you?"

"Most men would probably behave in the same way ... in nine cases out of ten."

"And you'd be the one in ten who didn't?"

Ralph smiled. "I always aim to excel."

"Even if he was lured into an ambush by the paper, he can't prove anything," said Marnie. "So his career's finished. The media have seen to that. And there's nothing anyone can do about it."

"There I do agree with you."

"I wish there was some way of helping ... especially for his wife's sake," said Marnie.

"Perhaps I should have a chat with Anthony ... encourage him to return home, issue a statement ... make a new start. I don't think he has much choice."

Marnie pulled a face. "I wonder if he's ready to face all that. He still seems pretty shaky to me."

"He can't stay here in hiding for the rest of his life."

"No ..." Marnie chewed her lower lip.

"Look," said Ralph, "I'll invite him over for a meal and talk things through ... man to man stuff. What do you think?"

"Or we could do it together. It might help him."

"Okay. But don't be surprised if he takes action himself. He is a big grown-up politician, after all. He's probably already making plans of his own."

Marnie stood up. "Good. Well, I've had enough of Anthony Leyton-Brown for one day."

Ralph watched her as she began taking off the dressing gown. "We'll have to think of some way of changing the subject," he said.

Marnie hung the dressing gown on the back of the cabin door and turned round. She was wearing a smile. "What was that you were saying about aiming to excel?"

# Part 7

Anne looked at her watch for the umpteenth time that morning, only a minute since the last time she had checked it. Marnie noticed her while she was on the phone and glanced down at her diary, smiling to herself.

When Marnie put the phone down, Anne called across to her. "Why is it called a 'red letter day'?"

"A red letter day?"

"You know, a special day."

"*Special day*? What's sparked this off?"

"Oh, Marnie, you know what I mean. It's special for me, and I was wondering why people said that."

"Why is it a red letter day for you?"

"Marnie! You're winding me up. Blimey, I'm feeling nervous enough already!"

Marnie laughed. "Sorry. Do you know how many times you've looked at your watch this morning? I think you'll have worn its face out by lunchtime."

Anne sighed. "Are you going to answer my question?"

"Make me a cup of coffee and I'll think about it."

Anne stood up immediately. "Deal. It'll help take my mind off my driving lesson."

"Oh," said Marnie casually. "Is that today?"

Anne made a growling sound and headed for the kitchen area. Within minutes she was setting a mug down on Marnie's desk. "Have you thought about it?"

"I think it must be something to do with those calendars they had years ago. You know, you sometimes see them in old films."

"What were they like?"

"Just a sort of grid with the days of the week and big black numbers for each date. The main holidays like Christmas and Easter had the numbers in red. So they were *red letter* days."

Anne looked thoughtful. "Sounds plausible. But they were numbers not letters. Why didn't they call them red *number* days?"

Marnie's turn to sigh. "I don't know. And I'm only guessing, anyway."

"Well," said Anne, "whatever they are, today's a red letter day for me. My first ever driving lesson. In fact it'll be the first time I ever sit behind the wheel of a car."

"You'll enjoy it," said Marnie. "It'll be good fun. You probably won't have to do much actual driving today, not the first time."

Anne made no reply. She went back to the kitchen area and stood staring into her mug.

"You're not really nervous, are you?"

Anne shrugged.

"You've no reason to be. You've always sailed through every challenge you've faced since I've known you. And you've only got to look at other drivers. Most of them shouldn't be allowed out on the pavement, let alone drive a car. The roads are full of morons. You'll soon be up to their standard."

Anne spluttered with laughter. "That's a great comfort. Something to live up to."

"You'll manage it."

Marnie caught sight of movement and turned her head to see Ralph at the door.

"Am I interrupting a top-level meeting of Walker and Co?" he said.

"You've barged in on our break," said Marnie. Anne reached for another mug.

"I only came out for a breath of air. And to boast that I can now operate the new mobile. Thanks for the lesson, Anne."

"No probs." She brought Ralph coffee and went to sit at her desk.

"Anthony returned the old one this morning," said Ralph.

Anne looked at her watch. "Gosh! I've got to get ready. I'll be late." She raced over to scramble up the wall-ladder to her room.

"You've got ten minutes before we have to go," said Marnie. "There's no rush."

They could hear Anne moving around above them. To Ralph Marnie said, "You've seen Anthony this morning, then?"

"No, he just dropped the mobile in on *Thyrsis*. Left it on the top step, probably when he went jogging."

"So you haven't had a chance to invite him round for supper?"

"Not yet. I'll catch him some time today or tomorrow."

Anne called down from the ladder hole. "Black trousers?"

Marnie called back. "Too formal. Jeans are fine."

When Anne was ready, Ralph had returned to his office on *Thyrsis*. She presented herself for approval and was pleased when Marnie said she looked ready for action. Before leaving, Marnie announced that she would make a quick visit to the loo, a fact that Anne did not divulge when the phone rang in her absence.

"Can I take a message?" she said.

"If you could just say Simon rang and I'll ring back some other time. It's not urgent."

"I saw you yesterday when you came on the boat. My name's Anne. I'm Marnie's assistant."

"So you're holding the fort while she's out."

"Not exactly. She's just getting ready to take me for my first driving lesson. It's a red letter day, as they say."

"A red letter day, indeed. Good luck. I hope it goes well."

• • • • •

The MG had attracted admiring looks all the way from Knightly St John to Northampton. Several cars passing in the opposite direction had flashed their headlights at the sight of the open-top sports car with its antique lines and throaty exhaust note. Marnie waved back gaily, and they sped on their way in spring sunshine. The little car drew up on the forecourt of the driving school.

"Well, this is it," said Anne.

Marnie took hold of her hand. "It'll be fine, you'll see. Enjoy yourself."

"Sure. As long as I get the main things right ... like remembering to breathe. We're not late are we?"

"We're okay."

"You've no idea how nervous I feel about this."

Marnie looked at her. Anne was biting her lip, and deep furrows creased her forehead. If possible, she was even paler than usual. "You hide it very well," Marnie said.

"I wish I could keep cool like you, Marnie."

"You're kidding. I can remember my first driving lesson like it was yesterday. For a start it was pouring with rain, so you're luckier than I was."

"That must have been awful."

"Certainly was." Marnie laughed. "The instructor ... Mr Davies ... stroppy little man with ginger hair ... terrifying ex-Sergeant-Major ... told me to test the indicators. I grabbed the controls ... and the sunroof slid open."

"No!"

"Yep. We were drenched before I could get the bloody thing shut."

As they howled with laughter, neither noticed the man coming out of the office and walking towards them. "Good morning, ladies. You're right on time." They looked up in unison and their smiles vanished. The instructor wore a smart suit and tie. He had red hair surrounding a bald top.

"They must breed them for the job," Marnie muttered under her breath.

• • • • •

Ralph was using the photocopier in the office barn later that afternoon when Anne breezed in. She paused on the threshold and raised her arms in the air, beaming. "I survived!"

"How did it go?"

"Brilliant! I am now an expert on the pedals ... clutch, brake, accelerator." She went over to her desk and reached for the diary.

"I didn't hear the car," said Marnie.

"I got Mr Lawson to let me off at the field gate and walked down ... floated down, actually."

"I take it the lesson went well."

"No probs. I stalled the engine twice before I got the hang of the clutch and accelerator ... made some amazing noises. It was great." She carefully selected a felt-tip pen from the desk-tidy and began shading in part of the desk diary.

"What are you up to?" Marnie asked.

"I'm colouring the whole day in red."

Marnie smiled. Ralph looked puzzled. "I'm missing something here," he said. "Why are you doing that?"

"It's obvious. Wednesday the twelfth of May. From now on this will be my Red Letter Day."

# Part 8

Thursday morning in the office, and it was business as usual. Marnie, engrossed in a design for Willards, looked up at the clock as Dolly walked in to mount guard on the fridge. Exactly break time. The cat was fitted with radar. Anne was deep in concentration on Ralph's phone numbers, entering them into the memory of his new mobile.

"I thought Ralph said he'd mastered that phone."

Anne glanced up. "That means he knew which button to press to switch it on."

"Impressive," said Marnie.

"I showed him how to do it."

Marnie noticed Dolly giving her one of Those Looks. She got up. "I'll make coffee."

"Are you sure it's that time already?" Anne asked without turning round. "I didn't see Dolly come in."

Marnie filled the kettle and switched it on before pouring milk into a saucer on the floor. "I suppose Ralph's taken his other phone now that Anthony's given it back."

Anne shook her head. "Nope. He forgot to put it on charge."

"Typical! So he's gone to his meeting without a mobile. That man is amazing. He is to technology what Mother Teresa is to lap dancing. So what happens if someone tries to ring him?"

"I've taken two messages already this morning," Anne said, waving a slip of paper.

Marnie dried two mugs from the draining board. "Have you seen Anthony today?"

"No. Actually, I haven't seen him since the other night when he came for supper. You?"

"No. Ralph thinks we should respect his privacy, give him time to sort himself out."

"I thought he seemed okay that evening," Anne said. "I expect he's all right." Ralph's mobile rang, and she pressed a button. "Hallo, Professor Lombard's office." Marnie brought over Anne's mug and put it down in front of her. "No. I'm afraid he's out at a meeting at the moment. He'll be back this afternoon. Would you like to leave a message?"

Marnie returned to her desk and was just refocusing on her drawing when she heard Anne scream and looked up to see her friend leap out of the chair. She had spilled the coffee into her lap. Marnie rushed across the office and grabbed a tea towel, quickly running cold water onto it and flying back to Anne, who was in a state of paralysed shock, grimacing with pain. Without hesitating, Marnie unzipped Anne's jeans and pulled them down to apply the cold towel to her thighs. She heard Anne gasp, the breath trembling in her throat. "Oh God!"

"Hold that there for a moment. I'm going to get another one." Anne was breathing unevenly, tears of pain on her cheeks.

Marnie was back almost at once with another tea towel, soaked in water. "Try this." She picked up Anne's chair. "Here. Sit down." Anne staggered back and flopped onto the chair like a puppet whose strings have been cut, the towel in her lap, water dripping down her legs, past the jeans crumpled round her ankles, making a puddle on the carpet. She bent forward, breathing heavily, her face in her hands.

"Oh Marnie. Oh God. Sorry. Sorry." Her voice was barely audible, contorted by pain.

Marnie held Anne in her arms, desperately trying to remember basic first aid for scalds. Carefully she raised the towel to look at the damage. The skin at the top of Anne's thighs was vivid red. Her legs were thin like a child's, and Marnie felt like crying with pity. She was unsure how long she had to keep the cold water treatment going. Somewhere in the first aid box she knew there was a booklet that would help. She turned the towel over to bring the colder side into contact with the skin. "Any better?"

Anne replied in a whisper. "Yes. A bit. Thanks, Marnie."

"Shall I get more cold water?" Anne nodded. Marnie soaked the first tea towel again and was back at her friend's side in moments. Marnie felt Anne's breath on her face as she bent over the injured area. "I think you ought to stay like that for a while. Should I get you to casualty?"

"I just want to sit for a bit. It's sore ... stings like mad ... not as bad as it was."

Marnie squeezed Anne's shoulder and went for the first aid box under the sink. She found the notes on treatment of scalds. ... *keep the air out as much as possible* ... Marnie pulled open the drawers: cutlery, a tea towel, a roll of cling film, paper napkins, food bags, cork mats ... *keep the air out as much as possible* ... not much help there. She picked up the tea towel. It was soft and would be comforting, but never airtight. She stared into the drawer.

Seconds later Marnie was removing the damp cloths to reveal Anne's tortured skin. Looking down, Anne was amazed to see Marnie wrapping one of her legs in transparent cling film. Marnie grabbed the scissors from Anne's desk-tidy and cut across the roll before starting on the other leg. The film gripped her snugly.

"This should keep the air out," Marnie said. "It's what you're supposed to do, apparently."

Anne looked dubious, then smiled weakly at Marnie. "Do you think this counts as another red letter day? Red leg day. I look like the packed meat counter in Waitrose."

Marnie reached for the phone. "I'm going to ring the doctor's and check I've done the right thing."

The receptionist confirmed that Marnie's first aid was satisfactory and offered an emergency appointment with the doctor if Anne could be brought in.

Marnie drove the old MG very carefully, aware of every bump in the field track as the firm sports car suspension coped with the ruts and clumps of grass. She did not speak until they were on the main road.

"How did it happen? One minute you were doing Ralph's phone numbers, the next thing you were leaping in the air like a ... "

"Scalded cat?"

"Exactly. But what caused it?"

"I don't know." She shrugged. "Just an accident."

Marnie glanced sideways at Anne. "Not like you to be clumsy."

Anne stared down at her lap. "I had a shock."

"Go on."

Anne did not look up. "It was really strange ... creepy ... a woman on the phone for Ralph." Marnie drove steadily, avoiding even the cats-eyes in the road surface. "I asked if she wanted to leave a message. I couldn't believe what she said."

"Believe what? You're getting me worried. What did she say?"

"She said to tell him that ... his wife had rung ... and she'd call back later."

• • • • •

When they returned from the surgery, Marnie cancelled her afternoon meeting. Anne had protested that she was fine, but Marnie insisted.

It was just after four when Ralph walked in. He smiled at Marnie who was on the phone to a supplier, and she waved back. He noticed that Anne was wearing a long dress of lightweight Indian cotton instead of her usual jeans and sweatshirt. "Not on the post run, Anne? I thought they set the clocks by you in Knightly."

"Not today." Her tone was subdued.

"What's the matter? Are you all right? No. I can see you're not. What is it, Anne?" Behind him he heard Marnie put the phone down and he turned to her. "Oh God. Is it Anthony? Has something happened to him?"

"No," said Marnie. "We haven't set eyes on him. Anne has had an accident."

Ralph turned back to her and put his hand on her shoulder. "What's happened, darling? What have you done?"

Marnie answered. "She spilled hot coffee in her lap. A whole mug. She's scalded her legs. I had to take her to the doctor's. She didn't want me to phone her parents to let them know."

"I'm so sorry." He leaned forward, careful to keep clear of her legs, and held her gently, kissing the top of her head.

"Actually," Marnie began, "she had a shock when she got a message for you on the phone. It made her jump. That's how it happened."

"A *shock*? How do you mean?"

"It was a *strange* message."

"In what way?"

"From a woman ... saying she'd phone back later. She said to tell you ... it was your wife."

Ralph looked completely bewildered. "My *wife* ..."

"That's what she said."

"Good God. No wonder you were shocked, Anne." Ralph frowned and took a breath. "Well ... let's start from the premise that it couldn't have been my wife because ... obviously, I don't have a wife ... at least not any more. We rule out the spiritualist option, presumably. So, who could it've been?"

"You've no idea," said Marnie. It was a statement, not a question.

Ralph shook his head. "It seems too weird to be a hoax call. That would be rather sick. Anne, can you remember anything about her voice that might help us? Did she sound young ... middle-aged? Anything at all?"

"I think she might've had a slight accent," said Anne.

"Foreign or regional?"

"It might've been sort of ... north country ... just a little ... not a broad accent."

"Still doesn't help much," said Ralph. "And in case you're wondering, Laura came from Canterbury ... and I can assure you she's definitely dead. It's a pity we don't have more to go on."

"I can tell you her phone number," Anne said quietly. Marnie and Ralph stared at her. "I did 1-4-7-1." She held up a note from her pad and handed it to Ralph. "That's it there."

He looked at it and shook his head. "Still a mystery to me." He picked up the phone and pressed three buttons. "Good afternoon. I wonder if you can help me. I have a message left on my answerphone. The number begins with 0115. Can you tell me where that is, please? ... Nottingham. Thank you. Goodbye."

"Does that help?" said Marnie.

"Not really."

"Have you any connections with Nottingham?"

"I used to be an external assessor to a post-grad doing a doctorate there, but that was some years ago."

"And you don't remember getting married while you were on a visit?" Anne said.

Ralph smiled at her. "Not as far as I recall. Or perhaps I'm getting absent-minded now that I'm a professor ... " His expression suddenly changed. "*Nottingham ...* "

"What is it?" said Marnie.

"I was just thinking back to my student days. Good lord ... it couldn't be ... "

"I think we can assume it might be," said Marnie, "whatever it is."

Ralph stared at the number on the note. He stood up. "If you don't mind, I'd like to make a call in private. I'll go back to the boat. It'll be all right." He went to the door and looked back. Anne's eyes had become dinner plates. Marnie was sitting with her chin resting on her hands, her expression calm. "Come for a drink on *Thyrsis* before supper. I'll try and have it sorted out by then."

• • • • •

The three sat in the saloon on *Thyrsis*, quietly pondering Ralph's account of his enquiries. For once their drinks were untouched. Marnie spoke first.

"Why do you think she chose now to get in touch? How did she know how to find you?"

"The consultant said she saw a letter I'd written to *The Times*, giving my address as All Saints College, Oxford. She phoned up and they gave her my mobile number, as instructed. I can't be incommunicado."

"So she just rang out of the blue ... after more than twenty years?"

"Yes. The doctor said she'd got quite excited about it. She only told him after she'd left that message. Of course, he had no idea what she'd actually said until I phoned."

"You didn't speak to her direct?"

"Not at that time. When I rang, I was put through to the unit where she's staying. It's a private clinic on the outskirts of town. I asked for her and got the consultant. She was having treatment, so I couldn't talk to her in person."

"What were they doing to her?" Anne's expression revealed that she imagined the woman covered in electrodes, writhing in a chamber that looked like the set from a Gothick horror film.

"I think he said she was having aromatherapy."

"What is that exactly?" Anne was still suspicious.

Marnie replied. "It's an all-over body massage with essential oils, like lavender, geranium and that sort of thing."

"Oh … It sounds … well, sort of … *nice*." Suspicion had given way to incredulity.

Marnie smiled at her. "It is nice … *very* nice … relaxing and soothing. I've had it a few times at a natural health clinic." She turned to Ralph. "How did you leave it? Are you going to contact her again?"

"The consultant was going to talk to her first to make sure it didn't do more harm than good. She's pretty confused much of the time, but has lucid moments and behaves quite normally. Apparently this is typical for her condition."

"How long has she been like this? Presumably not all the time since she was your girlfriend at college?"

"No. It comes and goes. Obviously the doctor wasn't going to discuss his patient's psychiatric history with a stranger on the phone, but in the circumstances he did say she now realised she wasn't married to me – or to anyone else."

"Why did she imagine that you were married?" Anne said. "Were you going to be?"

Ralph took a sip of his gin and tonic. "Tricia was always keener on the idea than I was. She was keener on the whole relationship, to be honest. Things came to a head when we got to the end of our second year. She was reading Modern Languages – French and Italian – and was due to spend the third year in Montpellier. She'd got upset about us being separated for all that time and made a mess of her second year exams. That's when she had the nervous breakdown. Instead of going to France she went back home to Nottingham."

"Didn't you go to visit her?" Anne asked. "Sorry. I'm just curious … since I spoke to her on the phone."

"That's okay," said Ralph. "This doesn't put me in a very good light, I'm afraid. I wrote of course, but Tricia's family blamed me for her breakdown and made it clear I wasn't welcome. I told myself I accepted their demand to keep a distance for Tricia's own good, but the truth was … I wanted the relationship to end."

"So you never saw her again?" Marnie said.

"No. Never. In my final year I met Laura … fell in love … and that was it."

"And Tricia never tried to contact you?"

Ralph sensed the hint of doubt in the question. "I got one or two letters from her … rather hysterical letters. I replied to the first just before going off to a summer school at Harvard. When I came back from America at the end of the long vacation there were two more and one from her mother telling me to stay away. She said seeing me again would only make things worse."

"You were only trying to do the right thing for her sake," Anne said.

"That was what I told myself at the time, but I think it was really just an excuse."

# Part 9

Marnie and Ralph walked slowly through the spinney holding hands after work on Friday. Ralph had called in at the office barn around five-thirty to meet her, and they finished early to prepare for their meal with Anthony on *Thyrsis*. Anne would be taking things easy in her attic room for the evening.

"What time did you tell Anthony to come?" Marnie said.

"About seven-thirty."

"What have you got planned?"

"*Tomates provençales* to start, red mullet with new potatoes, salad, cheese, fruit. That's it. Simple."

"And perfect," said Marnie. "Did you tell him we wanted to talk about his future?"

"I didn't actually tell him anything. I haven't seen him for a few days. Mind you, that's not surprising. From my study I can only see the canal, and I'm usually boggling at the computer. I just put a message through his hatch inviting him to come for supper and a chat."

"How did he accept?" said Marnie.

"He left his *calling card* while I was out this morning. I came back to find a bottle of that excellent wine by the hatch with a note."

In the galley Marnie took charge of the fish, while Ralph cut the tomatoes in half, big Italian beefsteak 'Brandywines', almost the size of grapefruits. As he chopped cloves of garlic, the pungent aroma mixed with the tang of the tomatoes to fill the galley.

When Marnie returned with herbs from the tub on the roof, she found Ralph pouring Orvieto. They settled into a comfortable routine, side by side, sipping the chilled white wine as they worked.

Marnie patted the fish dry in a paper towel and rinsed her hands. "I wonder if Anthony will have reached any decisions about his life."

"I expect he has by now," said Ralph. "What choice does he have? He's got to make a clean break and start again."

"Is it that simple?" said Marnie. "I can't imagine any of his friends in the City – I assume he's got some – they all seem to have them – I can't see them queuing up to offer him directorships in their companies. Can you?"

"Who knows? He's going to have to do something. The alternative is pretty bleak."

"You think he could do something desperate, don't you? When you came back yesterday and saw Anne looking upset, your first thought was of Anthony."

"It did cross my mind. That's why I think it's important to talk to him, help him sort himself out."

"Do you think the girl in the newspaper photos was underage?" said Marnie.

"There's no actual evidence of that."

"But do you think the newspaper can prove it?"

"They don't have to, Marnie. As far as Anthony's concerned, it doesn't matter now. Just by making the accusation, the damage is done. Anthony's finished ... and he knows it."

• • • • •

When Marnie returned to *Thyrsis* from taking Anne her supper, she heard male voices from the galley as she stepped down into the boat. Ralph was pulling the tomatoes out from under the grill as she shook hands with Anthony.

"Perfect timing," said Ralph. "These are ready to serve. Anne okay?"

"Fine. I said I'd look in at the end of the evening if her light's still on." To Anthony she said, "You heard about her accident?"

"Ralph told me. I'm very sorry."

They moved through to the dining area where Ralph had lit the candles, and Anthony's wine stood in a decanter on the table. During the meal Anthony seemed more subdued than when they had last seen him, and Marnie thought she saw a slight tremble as he raised his glass. She wondered if he was drinking excessively in the lonely hours on his boat.

As they ate they chatted about their various boating experiences, until after the main course, when Ralph brought the cheeseboard to the table.

"This excellent wine ought to go well with these. There's stilton, camembert, smoked cheddar."

"Or do you prefer to eat the English way round," Marnie asked, "with the dessert before the cheese?"

"I don't mind," said Anthony. "At home we ..." His voice faltered. "Sorry. It sometimes gets a bit – "

"That's okay," Ralph said. "We know you've got a lot on your mind just now. If it would help to talk about it ... "

Marnie had the feeling their idea of getting him to focus on the future was going to fail. When Anthony spoke it was almost inaudible. "This bloody business ..."

"And it's probably none of our business," Ralph said, almost as quietly. "But since you chose to come to us, or to me at least, I thought you might be in need of someone to talk to. Maybe now's not the time."

"When would be?"

"Well, sooner or later you've got to come to terms with your situation and decide what to do. This backwater has served a useful purpose, but – "

"I've gone over it again and again," said Anthony. "Every time I think of a way out, I realise the whole thing is hopeless. Nobody's going to believe my side of the story."

"Your side?" said Marnie.

Anthony looked at her. "Yes. You don't think there is another side, do you? If it's in the papers, it has to be true."

"I didn't mean that ..."

Anthony looked desperate. "It's all so unjust ... trial by newspaper. What chance have I got to put my side of the story?"

"Perhaps you could make a statement," said Marnie, "if you thought that would put the record straight."

"But don't you see ... I'd be playing into their hands, prolonging the story. They'd just use me to sell more papers."

"Anthony's right," said Ralph. "It would prolong the agony. And frankly, with those photos, you'd have your work cut out to make any kind of headway."

"That's a polite way of saying no one would believe me. No one *does* believe me."

"Try us," said Marnie.

"Based on what you've seen so far, what do you think happened?" said Anthony.

"I can only go by the newspaper reports and the photos."

"Exactly. What would it take to make you believe that I was set up?"

Marnie hesitated. "It's difficult."

"Because you've seen the evidence with your own eyes. You're convinced I'm as guilty as hell."

"But the photos," said Marnie gently. "It's hard to reject that kind of evidence."

"I know." Anthony put his head in his hands. "And who could believe the photos distorted everything?"

"Anne did," said Ralph.

Anthony looked up. "She did?"

"She thought you were being manoeuvred into position by the girl."

"She was right."

"So it was entrapment?" Marnie said.

Anthony nodded. "Could you believe that?"

Marnie ignored the question. "Was she underage?"

"No. I'm absolutely sure she wasn't."

"So you're not denying that things happened between you," said Marnie. "You're saying that you were tricked. You'd be asking the public to regard you as the victim … rather than the predator. That's a tall order these days, with so much sleaze about."

"All I'm saying is that any man put in my position would have reacted the same way. Don't you agree, Ralph?"

"I suppose so …" Ralph looked uncomfortable. "Probably … in nine cases out of ten."

"*Jesus, Ralph!* The Pope would've had a hard time trying to resist what I faced."

"What did you face exactly?" Marnie said. "What did they do?"

"They got this girl into my office as a researcher – it happens all the time, everybody has them – but she was planted. And she was okay until one evening she had a few drinks at a reception and began getting … well, familiar."

"Couldn't you stop her?" said Marnie.

"I did at first, but she persisted. And I'd had a couple of drinks myself. Anyway, it's not the same for men. We're different." Anthony's speech was becoming staccato and he was breathing erratically. "Now it's come to this …" He leaned on the table, his head in his hands.

"Take it easy," said Ralph quietly. "We didn't mean to upset you. We actually wanted to help."

*But how?* Marnie thought.

• • • • •

After supper Anne took the back copies of the *Globe* from her pending tray and cut out the articles about Anthony. From the bottom drawer of the desk she pulled out a file to hold the cuttings. In the drawer was another file, research papers on the Civil War prepared by Ralph's Oxford colleague Dr.

Fellheimer the previous summer. They had played an important part in resolving the mystery of the death of their friend Toni Petrie, the vicar of Knightly St John. Anne hesitated before reaching down and pulling out the file.

• • • • •

Anthony accepted a glass of Ralph's cognac.

"*Thyrsis* being a trad," said Ralph, "I'm afraid I don't have the luxury of a stern deck."

"Here's as good as anywhere else," Anthony said quietly. "I tend to avoid going out."

Marnie was feeling frustrated that they seemed to be making no progress with Anthony. He was in turns despondent, bemused, despairing, anything but positive or constructive. It was so much against her own nature that she wanted to grab him by the scruff of the neck and shake him till he woke up. "Would you like some cream in your coffee?" she asked. Privately, she thought *God! this is so English!* She wanted to scream. "Look … surely there must be some way out of this situation." She pushed the sugar bowl towards Anthony.

"I'm open to any suggestions," he said.

"You must have some ideas of your own, surely?"

His reply was weary. "Frankly, Marnie, I'm at my wits' end. There are times when I don't even know why I'm here or how I got into this mess in the first place."

Ralph said, "You must've done something to upset Hawksby."

"Hawksby?" said Marnie.

"The editor of the *Globe*."

"How could I upset him?" said Anthony. "I don't even know him."

"What do you mean?" said Ralph. "Of course you know him. He was at our school."

"North London Foundation?" Anthony looked bewildered. "I don't remember him."

"He was in the sixth when you came." Ralph turned to Marnie. "We were the same intake, Anthony and I, transferring at thirteen. Hawksby was in the sixth form, and I knew him because he was head of my house that year."

"So he presumably knows that you were there, too, Anthony," said Marnie. "Your entry in *Who's Who* will show that, won't it?"

"Actually no. I left after two years, so the details just state that I was at Exeter Academy and Oxford."

"You left early?" said Marnie.

Anthony smiled grimly. "I wasn't thrown out for misconduct. My father died suddenly, leaving my mother with two children, a huge mortgage, debts and inadequate life insurance. I had to leave NLF at the end of that term. There was no question about it – it's an expensive public school."

"But Exeter Academy can't have been cheap," said Marnie.

"That's right. But things changed. My mother's uncle had a country house in south Devon. He was widowed, family grown up, successful in business. He invited us to live with him. All perfectly proper, you understand. We had a wing of the house for ourselves. He offered to put my sister and me through school. My mother trained as a teacher. A new start for us all."

"So you could've gone back to NLF, presumably?" said Marnie.

"My mother wanted us to be near her, understandably. She'd lost her husband, wanted her children at home. Uncle Jack suggested Exeter Academy, which was nearby, and that was that."

"And you changed your name," Ralph added.

"Yes. In gratitude to my uncle I added his name, which was my mother's maiden name, to my own. When I first met Ralph I was just plain Tony Brown."

"A memorable meeting, as I recall," said Ralph.

For the first time that evening, Anthony came alive. "Yes. Ralph rescued me from bullying. Some senior boys were about to push my head down the loo and flush the chain – some stupid schoolboy joke about my name and where brown matter usually went – and Ralph suddenly arrived on the scene. He was quite imposing even at thirteen. Knocked a couple of heads together and the rest backed off."

"So you've been in touch ever since then?" said Marnie.

"No," said Ralph. "We lost contact when Anthony moved away. That's how it is when you're young, and ..." He shrugged.

"We were never what you'd call friends," Anthony finished the sentence for him. "Though I always had a high regard for Ralph. We didn't see each other again until I became an MP. One day I was in a committee in the Commons and there, giving evidence, was Ralph."

"And he recognised you?"

"Not immediately. And he'd made no connection with the name Anthony Leyton-Brown, not knowing that I'd changed my name."

"So nor does Hawksby, presumably," said Ralph thoughtfully.

"Would the old school tie make any difference to his moral crusade?" Marnie asked.

Ralph shook his head. "I doubt it." He smiled. "It's rich, actually, coming from Alec Hawksby, to hound Anthony on moral grounds, considering the skeletons *he* has in the cupboard."

"Skeletons?" said Anthony.

"Let's just say that you were lucky I was the one who found you being bullied in the washroom."

"You think Hawksby would've joined in the bullying?" said Marnie.

"Oh no. Quite the reverse. Sorry, I ought to re-phrase that. He might well have wanted to ... console Anthony ... in private."

Anthony looked shocked. "*Really*? You mean he's – "

"AC / DC, I think is the term," said Ralph.

"Bi-sexual?" said Marnie. "Do you have evidence, or was it just schoolboy gossip?"

To her surprise, Anthony reached across the table and put his hand on her arm. "That," he said, "is the most encouraging thing I've heard in weeks."

"In what sense?"

"You suggested that you wouldn't believe it unless you had evidence."

"I suppose that was the implication, yes."

"And you're right. Evidence is the only thing that matters. All the rest is loose change." He withdrew his hand and turned to Ralph. "So what evidence do you have?"

"Well, of course it is mainly circumstantial ..."

"Come on, then," said Anthony.

"Don't you remember the rumours about the girl he's supposed to have made pregnant?"

"Marnie will only be satisfied with facts," said Anthony. "Rumour isn't good enough. Isn't that right, Marnie?"

She felt pinned down, as if under cross-examination. "I was only saying ... well, that it seems wrong to judge a person without something to go on."

"That's the point," said Anthony. "Evidence. Well, Ralph?"

"Naturally, there were no eye witnesses as such, but ... You remember Jenny Poulter, a junior house master's daughter? She became pregnant. The deputy head boy in my house, who knew Hawksby well, said he was absolutely in a blue funk over it. The Headmaster sent for him and he left before the end of term. Luckily for him, it was the last term of the year and his last term of all, so it never came out that he was technically expelled. The whole business was hushed up."

"Is that good enough, Marnie?" said Anthony.

"It's all a bit sketchy. Do you know for sure that Jenny had the baby, Ralph?"

"I heard afterwards that she'd had a child, yes, but I never saw it myself."

"Circumstantial," said Anthony. "Is that reliable evidence or just hearsay?"

• • • • •

Anne had felt restless all evening. She sat on the bed propped up with pillows and tried reading a book, but found her concentration wandering. It was the same when she played a CD. After a few minutes, the music irritated her and she turned it off.

The press cuttings about Anthony lay in a heap on the bedside table, and she picked them up to put them in order in the file. One cutting was upside down, and as she reached for it her eyes were drawn to an article headed 'Mystery muggings – police warning'. Most of the article was intact. Northamptonshire Constabulary had issued a warning to the public following a spate of robberies in the south of the county. The mystery lay in the fact that none of the victims had ever seen the robber who seemed able to operate without leaving any trace. He would strike when least expected, disappearing immediately after committing the crimes. The public was advised to be vigilant.

• • • • •

Ralph was on the point of offering more brandy when Anthony looked at his watch and asked his hosts to excuse him. He seemed to tire easily these days and spent more hours sleeping than at any time in his life.

"It was kind of you to invite me. And you don't need to say it was a pleasure. I'm sure my being here must be a trial for you all ..."

"I had hoped we might've been able to help in some way," said Marnie.

"I know you did and I appreciate it. I only regret that I bring a whiff of unpleasantness to your idyllic little corner of the world. You're very lucky in the life you lead. I envy you both."

"You'll put your life back together sooner or later," said Ralph.

"I'm not so sure. I'll always be tainted from now on with these accusations. My only consolation is knowing that this kind of scandal is everywhere in our society."

"*Everywhere?*" said Marnie. "You really mean that?"

"Oh yes. I don't suppose anyone in public life is blameless. That's why the media set out to expose them ... they're an easy target."

"You don't think that's rather a sweeping generalisation?"

"Sadly," said Anthony, "it's based on experience. I've got the wounds to prove it."

Marnie stood up. "Oh well, if you're right, the media people are just as bad as everybody else."

"Of course they are," said Anthony, getting to his feet. "Why should they be any different?"

"They'd probably say they aren't setting themselves up as paragons and examples to the rest of us," said Marnie

"But they *are*," said Anthony. "In many ways they're much worse. They set themselves up as the guardians of public morals, and against them we have virtually no defence."

● ● ● ● ●

After Anthony went back to his boat, Marnie and Ralph left the dishes in the galley and set off slowly through the spinney. The evening was still warm, and full darkness had not yet come down. Neither spoke. They reached the edge of the spinney where the farm buildings stood solidly around the yard. The windows of the Burton's cottage were lit up. Marnie found the sight reassuringly ordinary and, glancing up, saw Anne's attic light through the narrow slit of its window.

Inside the office barn, Marnie called softly up the wall ladder in case Anne had fallen asleep.

"No, I'm awake. How did it go?"

"Permission to come aboard?" Marnie asked.

"Sure. Come on up."

"Are you decent? I've got Ralph with me."

"I'll just slip into my black lace negligee."

They found her sitting up in bed wearing pale green pyjamas decorated with sheep. She collected together her file of cuttings and put them on the table on top of Dr. Fellheimer's Civil War papers. Marnie sat on the bed, while Ralph opted for the only other seat, a giant bean-bag.

"How did it go? Is he any better?" Anne asked.

"Not much," said Marnie. "He's fallen into a slough of despond and doesn't seem capable of digging himself out."

Marnie outlined the conversation, explained about Ralph and Anthony being at school together, the changes that brought about Anthony's move to Devon to a new life and a new name. Anne listened in silence until Marnie finished.

"Like David Lloyd George," she commented.

"What is?"

"Changing his name. It was the same for Lloyd George. His father died, and he was brought up by an uncle – Richard Lloyd – so he added Lloyd to his own name in gratitude."

"That's right," Ralph said. "Now that I think about it, I recall him making that comparison himself in a magazine interview a few years ago. He said it was a defining moment for him that started him thinking about politics as a career."

"I didn't know that," said Marnie, "about Lloyd George."

"We did it in history," said Anne.

"I must've missed that bit. Anyway, whatever his name is, I don't think there's much we can do to clear it."

"No," said Ralph. "In fact, I doubt there's anything much we or anyone can do to help him. He's going to have to sort things out himself."

"I hear what you say, and you're probably right," said Marnie. "But it's his wife I feel sorry for. I wish we could do something, if only for her sake."

"A daunting prospect," Ralph agreed. He began struggling up from the bean-bag. "I think it's time for bed. That's why we're feeling inadequate."

Marnie kissed Anne on the cheek. "True. The talents of an interior designer don't help the situation much."

"If it's any consolation," said Ralph, now upright, "I think it's fair to say that an academic couldn't do any better."

Anne glanced at Dr. Fellheimer's research papers. "Not necessarily," she said.

# Part 10

Breakfast time on *Sally Ann*. Marnie looked out of the window and thought, *typical!* All week long the sun had shone, then on Saturday morning it was, *cue clouds, stand by rain*. The sky, fields and canal had turned a uniform grey in anticipation.

Marnie seemed unduly affected by the morning gloom. Anne pointed out that they would in any case be in the office until Ralph returned later in the day from collecting books in Oxford, and that the weather forecast was promising another fine day. This failed to lift her spirits. Anne eyed her friend over the top of the cup.

"I know what's bothering you," she said.

"Tell all, O Wise One."

"It's Mr Leyton-Brown. He's like a permanent cloud moored over our heads."

Marnie nodded. "That's how it feels."

Anne took a piece of toast from the basket. "But maybe he gets on with things when we don't see him for days on end. Maybe after last night he's feeling better already."

"Could be," Marnie said and managed a smile.

Anne changed tack. "Marnie, can I ask you something?"

"Sure."

"Do you think Ralph would've done what Mr Leyton-Brown did ... in the same circumstances?"

"We've been talking about that. On balance, no. Perhaps I'm being naive, but Ralph's a different sort of person." She shrugged. "Who can tell?"

"I couldn't imagine Ralph behaving like that," Anne said firmly. "He's always very ... proper."

Marnie agreed. "But what about that business with the old girlfriend in Nottingham? Just goes to show ... anyone can have something lurking in their past."

"Not the same sort of thing, though, is it?" said Anne.

"Course not. Ralph's actually rather reticent with women. You can always tell if a man's a predator. Ralph isn't." She smiled. "Of course, I'm not saying he doesn't have his moments."

Anne laughed at the same time as the mobile started ringing. Even though it was before eight on a Saturday morning, she automatically went into work mode.

"Walker and Co, good morning ... Yes. Who's calling, please? ... One moment." She held the phone out to Marnie. "Simon Walker."

• • • • •

Heads turned as Marnie walked through the pub restaurant that lunchtime. When Simon caught sight of her, he first thought she was dressed for jogging, but close up he saw she was wearing a one-piece costume in light cream cotton, fastened at ankles and wrists, elasticated at the waist. He kissed her on both cheeks, and she took the chair opposite him

"*Très chic*," he said. "You look like those racing-car drivers from the thirties. You ought to be driving a Bentley at Le Mans, or something."

"Good guess. I've come in the MG. This is practical gear for an open sports car."

"The *MG*? You've got it running?"

"Sure. Completely overhauled."

"Great. Pity if it just rotted away."

"No risk of that. It's in good hands."

"Very good hands." He smiled at her across the table. "Very good everything, I'd say."

"You ought to be saying: *What would you like to drink, Marnie?*"

He passed her a menu and, as he did so, a waitress arrived, set two drinks down in front of them, and flashed a smile at Simon. It had real warmth.

"Spritzer with dry white wine and soda water," he said. Marnie nodded, studying the menu.

Simon looked round. Deep-coloured wallpapers, a homely clutter of old fishing rods and baskets high up on shelves, prints of gaily painted boats and hunting scenes. "I don't know this place. Is it any good?"

"It's okay." Marnie raised her eyes. "Apart from the decor."

"I wanted to be able to talk in private. Just the two of us. Hope that's all right."

"No problem. Hardly an assignation ... an early lunch and a walk by the canal. Grilled sole, I think. Mixed salad."

"With an Aussie Chardonnay?"

"I'll stick with the spritzer. The MG attracts enough attention as it is."

Simon walked over to the bar to order. In subtle ways he had changed. Always good-looking, he had kept in shape with a neat butt and a flat stomach, but now he had a more confident bearing. He wore a black shirt and pale grey slacks, with grey slip-ons. His hair had been cut by someone who knew which end of the scissors to hold.

When he returned, Marnie noticed the watch. The Rolex in stainless steel and gold was the only minus. It looked expensive, which it was. Everybody knew that. Marnie preferred understatement to opulence and found it difficult not to wince when she saw the crown on its dial. It made her think, Princess Tina.

"What have you been doing that's made you so well off?" she asked. "There are decent cars cheaper than that watch."

Simon fingered its bracelet. "Not this one, I'm afraid. Strictly non-standard."

Marnie was incredulous. "Don't tell me it's an imitation made in North Korea! Let me see it."

Simon slipped it over his hand and passed it across the table. "No. It's the real thing ... apart from the bracelet."

She examined the band, the links seeming to be made of gold and stainless steel. "It looks authentic ... suitably luxurious."

"It's good, but not genuine Rolex."

Marnie read the name on the inside of the bracelet. "Looks like filofax ... no, fixoflex. Why don't you have a genuine Rolex one?"

"You'll laugh if I tell you, Marnie."

"No I won't."

He shrugged. "I ran over it."

"In your car?"

He nodded. "I was in a hurry, carrying a suitcase to put in the boot. I had the watch in my jacket pocket, carrying it over my shoulder. Must've fallen out when I swung the jacket onto the back seat. When I drove out of the parking space I heard a crunching noise ... thought I'd driven over glass or something ... got out to check ... there it was on the ground."

Marnie laughed. "You drove over your Rolex in your Mercedes? Wow! That must be the ultimate yuppie accident." She gave him back the watch.

"I told you you'd laugh. Anyway, as luck would have it, the tyres only went over the bracelet. I got this temporary one fitted when I got to Boston and ordered a replacement from Rolex. It was all included in the insurance package."

"Good old Rolex," said Marnie.

Simon slid the watch back onto his wrist. "Right. That's enough about me. Now tell me about you."

"You know about me already. I left Everett Parker last year, came up here, started my own show. That's it. Anne's working with me – you saw her on the boat – before continuing her studies."

"And it's going well?"

"So far so good. But I'm not in the Merc-and-Rolex bracket like you. So what happened?"

"It was simple really. The old story: right place at the right time. I got into computer software just as it was taking off and now I run my own firm of consultants."

"Would that be worldwide by any chance?"

"Offices in four countries."

Their food arrived, and during the meal Simon filled in the details. After their split he had picked himself up, retrained in computers and found himself helping harrassed managers in companies sort out their IT problems. Money seemed to be no object, ever.

At the end of the meal, Simon settled the bill with an American Express card, and they went out onto the towpath. He looked across at the car park as they set off along the cut. "I can see the MG. It's parked next to my car. Looks good. Brings back a few memories."

"I started using it when the Rover was blown up."

"Yeah, I read about that in the paper. It doesn't seem to have done you any lasting damage. You're still the same confident you, everything under control."

"It's a case of having to be, Simon. I have things to do, commitments, responsibilities. Same as you. Anyway, what was it you wanted to talk about?"

"I wanted to see that you were all right. See if you were settled."

"You can see that I'm all right. And I am settled, but not in a rut. I've had to take some big decisions since we split up. It's not been easy, but I've done it and now ..."

"You're concentrating on the positive ... looking to the future."

"Exactly."

They walked a few paces before Simon spoke again. "After we split up ... I more or less went to pieces."

"If I remember rightly, Simon, the idea of splitting up came from you."

"Yes. But it was because I couldn't face what was happening to us."

"Okay. We don't need to go over everything again. We've done all that. Look, I think – "

"I was only going to mention that time because it is all past history now. Things have moved on. At that time I imagined that all my life would be like sitting alone in an empty room."

"But it's history, like you said."

"That's right. After lots of moping about, I decided I could do no better than to learn from you."

"From me?"

"Yes. First of all I threw myself into my work … sheer workrate pulled me along."

"You were never lazy."

"No. But now I became almost manic. It wasn't just getting by from day to day. I tried to occupy every minute, use every second."

"That could lead to disaster."

"It nearly did. But I was driven. When I wasn't working, my nightmares kept returning. I had to try to find a way of coping. If I just worked all the time, I ended up exhausted. Then I found a way out."

"Did you go for therapy?"

He laughed. "Sort of. Nothing heavy, just a natural health clinic … for chats. They helped me find a way."

"What did you do?"

"I sublimated myself."

Marnie tried not to smile. "Sounds kinky. How did you do this sublimation exactly … or do I really want to know?"

"You'll only laugh if I tell you."

"I won't laugh, whatever it is. I promise."

He stopped walking and looked at her. "I took up writing poetry."

She did not laugh.

• • • • •

Anne's weather forecast proved to be correct, and the day turned mild with a pleasant breeze, the sun poking holes in the clouds. She sat out in a deck-chair by the office barn with a sandwich for lunch and read a magazine. Wearing shorts to let the air get to her scalded thighs, she hoped no one would come by and see the livid pink patches on her legs. Anne closed her eyes to enjoy the sun's warmth on her face and was dozing when she suddenly became aware of movement nearby. Ronny Cope was looking down at her.

"Hey, what's happened to your legs? Are you all right?"

"This is my lobster imitation. I spilled coffee down me and got scalded."

"I bet it hurts like hell," Ronny said feelingly.

"It's not too bad. Could be worse. The doc said I could get blisters, but I haven't so far."

Ronny knelt down for a closer inspection. "I can't see any."

Anne could feel his breath on the tops of her legs. She lowered the magazine into her lap.

• • • • •

They fell silent as they passed a group of people at a lock on the towpath, chatting in loud voices. Marnie and Simon stood aside to let them go by. One of the women glanced twice at Simon.

A boat was easing its way out of the chamber, and Marnie spoke quietly to a grey-haired woman who was lowering the gate paddle with a windlass. The woman stepped aboard with a smile as the boat edged by. Marnie leaned the small of her back against the massive black and white balance beam and put all her weight on it, walking slowly backwards to close the heavy gate. Simon joined in beside her.

"Struth! What is this thing? It feels like a tree trunk."

"It is ... or was."

They stood up when the gate nudged its partner on the other side of the lock. Simon said, "You really know about all this, don't you? All these locks and things. It seems hard to imagine you handling a boat, doing all this physical stuff. You've always been such a townie."

"I enjoy it ... maybe because it is so different. People change. You've changed. I'm surprised at you writing poetry."

"Why not? I did English at university. It's not so strange. Anyway, I had a lot of time on my hands for quite a while. Eventually I saw a therapist who encouraged me to write ... help get things out of my system."

"What sort of poems do you write?"

"All sorts. Lately I've taken up haiku."

"Haiku? What's that?"

"It's a Japanese form. They're very short poems ... just seventeen syllables in three lines. Five, seven, five. No rhyming. It's not as easy as you'd think. They're very intense. Every word counts."

"When do you find time to write them?"

"Odd moments ... at an airport ... on a plane ... having a drink ... any time. Sometimes they come to me in a flash, other times it's harder. But they've helped me come to terms with things."

The gate they had closed began to swing open. Simon leaned on the balance beam to push it back into place.

"Don't worry about that," said Marnie. "There's nothing you can do about it. Just let it go."

• • • • •

Ronny and Anne were sitting together. They had laughed like children when Ronny had made a dog's breakfast of putting up a deckchair. Now they were drinking chilled fruit juice in the sunshine.

"Haven't you got A Levels some time soon?" said Anne.

Ronny grimaced. "Next week. Don't remind me."

"Er ... "

"I know, I know. Just a short break from revision. Where's Marnie?"

"You're changing the subject."

"I was just curious."

"She's gone for a pub lunch with ... a friend."

"Her ex-husband?"

Anne stared at him. "How did you know that?"

"It's all round the village."

"But he only phoned this morning. Are we wired for sound and hooked up to a loudspeaker in the high street?"

"Everybody knows he's around. He was in the shop a few days ago. It's no secret."

"We're becoming a regular soap opera," said Anne.

Ronny laughed. "That's what my mum says. She reckons the place was boring until you two arrived ... Oh, sorry."

• • • • •

Marnie and Simon strolled back towards the pub and stopped on the bridge spanning the cut. They looked down over the parapet. The sun was shining directly onto the canal, and a shoal of tiny fish was lit up in the cloudy water.

"This is very much your world now, isn't it, Marnie? Are you happy?"

Marnie watched the fish swirling about. "Yes."

"And that was your ... what do you call him ... your *partner*, that I saw on your boat the other day?"

Marnie turned to face Simon. "The man on the boat? No. That wasn't Ralph."

"Ralph" he repeated. "I just assumed ... it looked such a cosy domestic scene."

"You didn't recognise him?"

"Should I have?"

She hesitated. "It's ... confidential ... a secret. You know about Anthony Leyton-Brown?"

Simon thought about it. "The man in the paper ... the MP who's gone missing?"

"Yes."

"You're not involved with him, surely?"

"Not in the way you mean. He's staying on a boat next to Ralph's. We've been trying to persuade him to come out of hiding and go back to his wife. She's having to face everything alone."

"I can't help thinking you were better off with me," Simon said quietly.

"What do you mean?"

"At least you didn't get nearly murdered, go round finding bodies and end up harbouring stray weirdoes. Why did this guy come to you, anyway?"

"He's a friend of Ralph's."

"I see. And Ralph ... he's a permanent fixture?"

"It's a permanent relationship, yes."

"Okay." Simon ran a hand through his hair. Marnie thought she saw a few touches of grey at the temples. He was one of those men who age well. In ten or twenty years he'd still look good. Like Ralph.

"Thank you for lunch, Simon."

"You're welcome." He turned towards the pub car park. Marnie did not move. "You coming?"

"You go ahead. I want to get something from the museum shop over there."

"Okay. See you around. Take care of yourself." He kissed her on both cheeks and went off without looking back.

• • • • •

They both heard the car pull up at the same time. Anne knew at once that it was not Marnie's MG. It had a distinctive growl, and Marnie always blipped the accelerator before switching off the ignition.

"Is that her now?" said Ronny.

"No. It'll be Ralph, I expect."

They heard doors slamming, and Ralph came past carrying a cardboard box that looked heavy. He spotted them and called out cheerfully, asking Anne if she was feeling better..

Ronny watched Ralph head off through the spinney with his load. "Is he really a professor at Oxford? He seems so *normal*."

"Ralph's great," said Anne. She smiled at Ronny. "Another star in the soap opera?"

• • • • •

Marnie admired the MG as she walked back to the pub car park, reaching in her pocket for the keys. She loved driving it in this weather.

She was just musing on the need to find a modern car before the end of summer, when she noticed something attached by an elastic band to the leather sleeve round the base of the gear lever. At first she thought it was one of Anne's interminable lists that she had failed to see when she left the office. *That girl!* She pulled it out from the elastic. It was just three lines. She read it carefully and frowned.

> *Almost bearable*
> *You, heartachingly lovely*
> *One day at a time*

She counted the syllables on her fingertips, like playing a scale on the piano. Five, seven, five. Haiku. *Sayonara, Simon*, she thought. But as things turned out, she was wrong.

• • • • •

This time, Anne knew it was Marnie. She heard the little car roll into the garage barn, waited for the brief growl from the engine and the light clunk from the door. She looked up, expecting Marnie to come round the corner at any minute. There was her light footfall on the gravel and Marnie walked straight towards the spinney in the direction of *Sally Ann*. For a second Anne was going to call after her. But there was something about Marnie's demeanour that made Anne hold back.

"She doesn't know we're here," said Ronny.

"No."

He watched Marnie disappearing into the spinney. "Can we have a look at her car?"

Anne held out a hand. "Help me up, then."

Ronny tried to keep hold of the hand once Anne was on her feet, but she turned to put the magazine on the deckchair and he had to let go. Ronny shook his head as they approached the MG.

"Wicked," he muttered. He ran his hand over the top of the leather driver's seat and on to the four-spoke steering wheel. "You can smell the engine," he said. "It comes through the louvres in the bonnet. It's like hot oil. Brilliant." He was beaming.

Anne leaned forward to sniff near the steering wheel and caught sight of a bag lying on the floor in the passenger's foot well. She reached into the cockpit to pull it out. The bag contained a magazine and a packet of ice creams that were going soft.

"What's that?" said Ronny.

"Just a few things from the shop. Fancy a choc ice?"

"Great."

"Happy, now you've seen the car?"

"Sure. It's not the reason I came, though." He looked at the MG. "It's a bit dusty. Pity."

Anne turned towards the office barn. "I want to get the rest of these into the freezer."

"Tell you what," Ronny began. "Why don't I give the MG a quick clean? Marnie would like that … pay you back for the ice cream."

Ronny rummaged around for cleaning materials in the barn's kitchen area while Anne put the ice creams in the freezer compartment. His thoughts were fixed on British Racing Green bodywork and shiny wire wheels. Anne was wondering what it was that had made Marnie so pre-occupied that she had left her shopping to melt in the car.

• • • • •

It surprised a number of drivers on the main road leading towards the M1 when a Mercedes coupé travelling at high speed suddenly braked heavily and dived into a layby, dust and dirt flying up from its wheels. The car remained stationary for a moment or two before making a U-turn and accelerating hard back in the direction from which it had come.

Minutes later, people turned to look as the silver Mercedes drove through Knightly St John. The few villagers in the high street recognised the car and knew who the driver was, even if they could not see the man behind the tinted windows. Most thought it was going faster than it should, as it sped towards the field track that led down to Glebe Farm.

• • • • •

Ronny could not resist the handles that held the old car's bonnet in place. They were the shape of teardrops, two on each side of the engine. Each had the MG octagon badge moulded into it at the thicker end. He gripped them and turned.

"Surely, you're not going to wash the engine, Ronny," Anne said. She had planned to sit nearby in her deckchair and give him moral support while he worked.

"Just wanted a peek under the bonnet." He lifted the lid and pulled it towards him. It was hinged along its full length for folding flat on top of the engine compartment. Still lifting it, he called out, "Oh, look at that! There's even an MG badge on the top of the dipstick." He let go with one hand and pointed inside at the stubby handle, half-turning to see if Anne was looking. As he did so, he lost his grip and the bonnet fell. Anne winced as the edge of the lid slammed down on the back of Ronny's right hand. She heard him grunt with pain as he struggled to release the pressure.

Anne leapt from the deckchair, forgetting her own discomfort. She seized the bonnet lid and pulled it clear. Ronny grasped his hand to his chest, the colour draining from his face.

"*Shit!*" he muttered. "Oh, sorry." His face was contorted with pain.

Anne held him by the shoulders, her mind racing. What should she do? What if he'd broken his wrist? She had stopped noticing that her legs were stinging. "Can you make it to the office barn?"

"Yeah," he croaked, rubbing the back of his wrist.

"Do you think you've broken anything?"

"Dunno ... hurts like bugg- ... like hell."

Anne sat him down in the office, quickly soaking a tea towel in cold water to wrap round his wrist. *Thank God for tea towels,* she thought. She had an idea that a cold compress was the first treatment for this kind of injury, but had no idea what to do next. She picked up the phone and pressed the button for Marnie's mobile.

A minute later Marnie arrived like the Seventh Cavalry. Anne explained what had happened as she inspected the damage. Ronny was mesmerised at the sight of Marnie's slim tapering fingers delicately probing his wrist. He confirmed that the pain was throbbing but bearable and that he was not going to faint. He did not tell her he was now wishing he had been injured all over.

When asked if he could move his fingers, Ronny wiggled them cautiously. When Marnie asked if he could grip her hand, he managed to squeeze it with moderate firmness and waited until he was asked to let go before relinquishing it. After he had performed a few light wrist movements, Marnie announced that he was likely to survive with nothing worse than bruising. She applied witch hazel from the first aid kit, easing the gel into the damaged area with her fingertips, and rounded off the treatment with a tubigrip bandage.

Finally, she asked if he would like her to drive him home in the MG. To her surprise, he said he would prefer to sit out for a while with Anne.

Marnie muttered, "I think he's on the mend."

• • • • •

Once Ronny and Anne were settled in deckchairs, eating ice creams, Marnie tidied up in the office. Ralph called in and put the kettle on while Marnie told him about the accident.

"I might as well leave the first aid kit on my desk. This place is turning into a field hospital." She sighed. "What a day! I feel like I've been through a shredder."

"That came from the heart," Ralph said. "It was only a minor accident, surely. He'll have a swelling and a bruise. It won't stop him doing his exams."

"I wasn't thinking of Ronny. It was the rest of the day."

"Would it help to talk? Or do you need caffeine first? Perhaps I ought to get you a brandy."

Marnie smiled weakly. "Yes ... it would help ... talking, I mean ... not the brandy. We'll have that later."

"You're on. So what was so bad about your day?"

"Well, I had a phone call this morning ... " Before she could continue, they heard a car approaching fast, sliding on the gravel beside the barn. "That's all I need. I expect this is Inspector Bartlett coming to raid us for protecting a fugitive."

Ralph looked out of the window. "It's not the police ... not unless they have a contract with Mercedes for their cars."

"That'll be Simon," said Marnie. She heard footsteps running across the yard and prepared herself for a dramatic entrance.

"Simon?" said Ralph. "As in ... your ex?"

"The same."

Simon burst into the office. "Marnie, have you heard? It was just on the radio as I was going home."

"What was?"

"On the news bulletin ... " He caught sight of Ralph standing to one side. "Er ... "

"It's all right," said Marnie. "You can talk freely. What was it?"

"It's about your ... visitor ... "

"Leyton-Brown? Go on."

Simon walked over to Marnie. "It was about his wife. She's ... committed suicide."

Marnie put her hands to her mouth. "Oh my God ..."

Ralph said, "You heard this just now?"

"Yes ... just after leaving Marnie. You didn't know?"

"No."

Marnie said to Ralph, "Do you think Anthony knows about this?"

"No idea. I haven't seen him at all today."

"I expect she couldn't take the strain any longer," Marnie said. "Poor soul ... "

"Look," said Ralph. "I'd better go and see if he's all right. I'll break the news to him if he hasn't heard it already."

"Do you want me to come with you?"

Ralph hesitated. "No. I'll go. I'll get down there straight away. I'll keep you posted."

For a few moments Marnie almost forgot that Simon was there. She was thinking about the anguish of Melissa Leyton-Brown, alone and abandoned to face the world with her husband's disgrace ... without her husband.

"So that was Ralph, was it?" said Simon.

• • • • •

Ralph walked quickly through the spinney, not running, keeping himself in check. He did not want to arrive breathless and make a dramatic entrance that would only make matters worse. In his mind he was preparing what to say to Anthony. There was no easy way to do this.

He stepped across the bow of *Thyrsis* and edged his way along the gunwale between the two boats. The central doors in the side of the grey boat were closed, and he moved slowly towards the stern. The hatch over the steerer's door slid silently when he pushed it. Leaning forward, he called out softly into the cabin.

"Anthony?" He waited. "It's Ralph. May I come aboard?"

No reply. He stepped down into the boat and walked past the engine compartment. The sleeping cabin was empty, the bed unmade. He passed the open door of the bathroom and continued on towards the galley and the saloon, calling quietly as he went.

"Anthony?"

The galley was empty, a few dishes drying on the draining board, a smell of something indefinable in the air, alcohol perhaps. Ralph looked through to the saloon. A cup and saucer stood on the table. The name *Marie Celeste* drifted through his mind. On the wall above the workbench was a notepad. He tore off a page and moved into the saloon to write a message. As he began to sit at the table he saw the body lying on the floor.

• • • • •

Marnie and Simon were out of the office barn in a second and raced through the spinney in response to Ralph's call. They clambered onto the grey boat and found Ralph speaking to the emergency operator on the phone. Marnie rushed forward into the saloon. Anthony was on the floor, half curled into a ball. Beside him lay a whisky bottle and two bottles for tablets, all empty. Simon stood over her as she crouched beside the body. She leaned forward and touched Anthony's hand. It was still warm. Pressing her fingers against the side of his neck, trying to find an artery, she looked up suddenly.

"He's alive!"

Simon squatted down, took Anthony's wrist and nodded. "Come on! Let's get him out of here." To Ralph he called out, "Tell them not to bother about the ambulance. No time. We're taking him in to the nearest hospital. It's his only chance."

Unceremoniously, Simon grabbed Anthony, turned him over and pulled him upright, lifting him awkwardly to his feet in the confined space. They looked like drunken dancers as Simon dragged Anthony through to the cabin doors. Ralph brought his conversation with the operator to an end and climbed out ahead of Simon, reaching down to pull Anthony through the doorway, holding him while Simon scrambled out. Together, they manhandled the silent form along the gunwales to the bows where Simon hoisted Anthony over his shoulder in a fireman's lift.

Marnie ran on ahead, shouting over her shoulder. "I'll get the car."

Simon bore his burden swiftly through the trees with Ralph following behind. They reached the garage barn as Marnie arrived from the office clutching a bunch of car keys.

"Where's your car?" Simon yelled, breathlessly.

In her haste she had overlooked an important detail. "Oh ... that's it ... the MG."

"*Christ, woman!* Where's your *other* car?"

"I haven't got another one."

Simon was panting. "That isn't a car, Marnie."

"It's a *classic!*"

"It's a fashion accessory. Take the keys from my pocket. Get him in the Merc."

She reached for Simon's side pocket. "And that *isn't* a fashion statement?"

"Marnie, the man may be *dying.*"

"Let's go," she said." We can have the argument later ... it'll be like old times."

Simon laid Anthony on the back seat, and Marnie climbed in with him, cradling his head in her lap. The silver car turned in a spray of gravel and raced up the track, leaving Ralph standing in the yard beside his aged Volvo, watching their trail of dust. Anne and Ronny came round the corner as the Mercedes was passing out of view up the field.

"Wow!" said Ronny. "Look at that thing move ..."

• • • • •

Simon walked back to where Marnie was sitting, carrying two plastic cups. In the waiting area people were sitting in quiet groups, numbed either by pain or the boredom of waiting.

"I was beginning to wonder where you'd got to." She looked at the dark liquid and tried it tentatively.

"I had to move the car from the ambulance space ... car park's miles away. They asked me to book him in ... wanted his details. What's it like?"

"Hot and wet. His *details?*" She spoke in little more than a whisper. "Oh great ... now we'll have the paparazzi round our necks."

"No we won't."

"What did you tell them?"

"I said he was a visitor on a canal boat ... I didn't know his address."

"What about his name?"

"I said I thought it was Simon Alexander, but I wasn't sure."

Marnie stared at him. "But those are *your* first names."

"So I recall. They were the first names that came into my head. I figured there'd be more fuss if I had no name for him. At least that way they could fill in the boxes on their form. Otherwise they might've involved the police, trying to trace who he is."

"With an attempted suicide they're bound to do that anyway."

"Who said anything about attempted suicide? He smells of alcohol. I said I thought he'd had too much to drink while on medication ... it was an accident."

"Did they swallow that?" Marnie almost laughed. She put it down to stress. "Sorry ... you know what I mean."

"They were more interested in saving him. They didn't want his life story."

"Where is he now?"

"They took him through for treatment." Simon shrugged. "They'll pump him out, I suppose."

Marnie grimaced, thinking of the pump-out machines that suck out the sewage tanks on boats. "Well, I must say they were impressive."

The staff had rushed Anthony into the A and E Unit on a trolley within seconds of arrival.

"That's down to you, Marnie, phoning ahead on the mobile. If he does survive, he'll owe his life to you."

"The question is ... will he thank me for it? What he did was his way out of hell. And we've brought him back."

Simon sipped his drink. "Was this where you came ... when you were ... you know?"

"When I was *murdered*? I suppose so. At the time I didn't know what was happening. When I eventually came round I was on my way out of intensive care."

Simon touched her hand. "I didn't mean to bring back painful memories."

"That's all right. We've got new worries to get on with this year." She smiled grimly. "Aren't we the lucky ones?"

"Seriously, Marnie. I really was concerned about you."

To Marnie the situation seemed bizarre. Here she was sitting with Simon, together again after years apart. He looked no different from when she had last seen him, and they were handling a problem together like any married couple, as they had done so often. It was as if the intervening few years had not happened ... the move from London ... Ralph ... Anne ... *Sally Ann* ... Glebe Farm ... Ralph. Ralph. They had left him behind as if he was irrelevant.

"Simon, I must phone Ralph ... let him know what's happening. Have you got your mobile?"

He reached for his back pocket and sat back. "It's in the car. Other end of the site."

"Damn. I don't suppose you've got any change?"

"I used it for the parking ticket ..." He looked at the dubious liquid in his cup. " ... and the drinks machine."

• • • • •

Ralph walked slowly back to the boats. Something had flashed into his mind when he first found Anthony on the floor, and he was determined to remember what it was. With hindsight he knew Marnie should have taken the empty tablet bottles to hospital so that the medics could identify the drugs. Marnie and Simon.

Everything had happened too fast. He had been trying to be methodical, while they had seen straight away what had to be done and had taken decisive action. They had worked like a team, while he had plodded along doing the Right Thing, ringing the emergency services, reporting the incident. He could have kicked himself for not checking Anthony's pulse. It made him feel a fool. They must have had the same thought.

He stepped down into Anthony's boat and went through to the saloon. All three bottles lay there, and the smell of alcohol was still in the air, though fainter now. He wondered what he should do next; perhaps the police would want to test the medicine bottles for fingerprints. All this was worlds away from his experience. He hesitated. Best to leave things as they were and let the experts do what was necessary.

Anthony must have heard about Melissa on the news and decided there was only one way out. Or perhaps he had decided that anyway. If the doctors saved his life, he may have a grim awakening ahead of him. One tragedy heaped on another.

Ralph squatted down and examined the bottles at close range. The whisky was Glenmorangie, one of the finest single malts. Anthony never stinted himself. Even in suicide, only the best was good enough. While this thought was going through his mind, Ralph remembered what it was that had struck him when he first found Anthony on the cabin floor. He had shared some of the Glenmorangie with Anthony one evening. He was convinced that the bottle was half full when he last saw it. Still squatting, on a whim he opened the cupboard where he knew the drinks were kept. There at the back stood a fresh bottle of the same Scotch, unopened.

He was pondering this when the boat rocked gently. Someone had quietly approached and stepped on board. Ralph waited and listened. Footsteps on the treads down into the cabin.

"Hallo?" It was a familiar voice.

"I'm in the saloon, Anne. Come towards the cratch."

She stopped in the galley and looked down at Ralph. "I thought I'd come and see … Well, I'm not sure what, actually. I just came."

Ralph stood up. He knew why she had come. "Did you think I was feeling abandoned?"

"Of course not." She sounded almost convincing. "Is that where he was?" She stepped forward.

"Down here in the corner. I didn't see him at first … he was behind the bench."

Anne was staring at the bottles when Marnie's mobile suddenly rang on the workbench and she picked it up. "Walker and Co. Good afternoon." It seemed incongruously normal in the place where a man had just tried to kill himself.

"This is Northampton General Hospital, Accident and Emergency. I need to speak to Professor Ralph Lombard. It's very urgent."

"He's here. Hold on, please."

She passed the phone to Ralph, who bent down and picked up the bottles as he spoke. He read out the names on each one, with other details. The call seemed to end abruptly.

"That was quick," said Ralph. "He didn't even give me a chance to ask how Anthony is."

"At least we know he's still alive," said Anne. "Otherwise it wouldn't be urgent."

"The doctor said they needed to know what was in the tablets so that they could deal with them."

Anne took one of the bottles. "What are they for?"

"No idea. Never heard of them. The question is, were they enough to kill a man?"

• • • • •

Marnie and Simon walked out through the automatic doors of the reception area and into the forecourt reserved for emergency ambulances. They had taken only a few steps when they became aware of an argument taking place with raised voices and much gesticulating between a uniformed security guard and a young man. They were standing beside a car in which two dogs were barking noisily, adding to the general commotion.

"I know, I know," the young man was saying. "But what else was I to do? Give me a break! For all I knew he might've been goin' to snuff it."

The guard waved a finger under the man's nose. "First, you are not allowed to park here in *any* circumstances. This is strictly for ambulances only. Can't you read?"

"But my car was being used as an – "

"And second, you do not leave dogs in a car unattended at any time."

"I had other things on – "

"Especially without leaving a window open."

The young man, who sported Elvis Presley sideburns, raised his eyes to heaven. "Give me strength! Look – "

With enough problems of their own to occupy them, Marnie was more than happy to leave the men to their quarrel and she walked ahead of Simon round the men, glancing briefly at the dogs as they passed. When she stopped suddenly, it was all Simon could do to avoid running into her back. Marnie half turned, staring at the dogs, two black labradors. They each wore a collar, one red, one blue.

Ignoring the arm movements, she stepped between the protagonists and spoke to Elvis. "They're not your dogs?"

"No," he retorted. "Look lady, just let us sort it out, right? It's bad enough with him – "

Marnie interrupted. "Do you know whose they are?"

"Please. Just leave it – okay?"

"Do they belong to Frank Day?"

"I don't know who they – " He stared. "Wait a minute. You know these dogs?"

The security guard chimed in. "How do you know them, madam?"

"By their collars."

She stooped forward and put her face near the car's side window. The dogs at once pushed closer, still barking, still agitated.

"Leave it out, love," said Elvis. "You'll make things worse doing that."

Marnie straightened up. "Bruno," she said. "It's on the disc. You'll find the other one – with the red collar – is called Cassius. They belong to a man called Frank Day. What are they doing here in your car?"

He ignored the question. "If you can identify the owner, you'd better come with me."

"*Identify*? Why, what's – "

By now Elvis was already heading towards the entrance, looking over his shoulder for Marnie to follow. She set off at a rapid pace. Reaching the doors, she turned and called out.

"Simon, I'll be as quick as I can. See if you can calm the dogs down." She disappeared back inside the hospital.

Simon and the security guard looked at each other as the dogs leapt about in the car.

• • • • •

The nurse on reception in the A and E Unit looked quizzically at Marnie on seeing her return so soon after leaving. "Forget something?" she said.

"A man has been admitted," Marnie said, pulling Elvis forward to explain.

"I brought him in an hour ago," he said. "This lady thinks she can identify him."

"I think you'd better take her through. You know where to go." She nodded towards a bay. It was different from the area to which they had taken Anthony.

Rounding the corner, Marnie's way was blocked by a police constable in uniform.

"It's me," said Elvis. "I've met this lady who thinks she knows him."

The policeman looked at Marnie. "And you are?"

The answer was *Marnie Walker*, but it was not Marnie who gave the reply. She spun round on hearing a male voice behind her and found herself facing Detective Sergeant Marriner.

"May I ask what brings you here, Mrs Walker?"

"I was just … visiting someone … when I met this man outside. He's got Frank Day's dogs in his car. I recognised them."

Marnie was being truthful, but she felt that what she was saying sounded highly improbable. Marriner looked as if he was in agreement on that score. "So you can identify him," he said quietly.

"What's happened to him?"

"He's been attacked and he's unconscious. Would you wait here a moment, please. I'll see if you can look in."

Marnie turned to Elvis. "Where did this happen? How did you manage to bring the dogs?"

"It was over by Hanford. I stopped in a lay-by … went behind a tree for a Jimmy … er … anyway, I saw these dogs charging about down near the canal. I thought I saw something on the towpath … went and had a look … it was a man. He was out cold – looked as if he'd had a nasty fall – so I carried him to my car to get him here. It was the only thing to do."

"And the dogs?"

He shrugged. "They jumped in with him. Now that bloke's giving me grief because I forgot to open a window. I mean – "

Marriner reappeared and gestured to Marnie to go with him. Elvis stayed behind. Marnie was led through curtains pulled round a cubicle. She looked down at a man who lay silently, tubes connected to his nose, a drip attached to the back of one hand that rested on the bed cover. His face was grey, except for the bruising and grazes on his cheek. A bandage was wrapped round his head like a turban, and his mouth was slightly open.

"Do you know him?"

"It's Frank, Frank Day."

"You're sure?"

"Of course. So do you, Mr Marriner. Don't you remember? He was injured in the church last year, the day I was …"

"I didn't think his own grandmother would recognise him in that state. Do you know where he lives, if he has a wife or family, details like that?"

"Sure. Anything you want. His wife's name is Janet. They live in Yore. I know their phone number."

Marriner keyed it into his mobile. At the sound of voices, Frank stirred and Marnie put her hand on his arm. He made a sound as if trying to clear his throat and blinked, struggling to open his eyes.

"Frank … it's me, Marnie … Marnie Walker … can you hear me?"

He croaked faintly, "Mar–"

"Lie still, Frank. You're okay."

"I … I …" His voice was distant, breathless.

Marnie patted his arm. "Just take it easy." To the nurse, she said, "Can I sit with him for a minute?"

"Yes, it might settle him. But don't try to get him talking, okay?" She went out through a gap in the curtains.

Marnie sat in the only chair, holding Frank's free hand. It was grazed and dark with bruising. Marriner went outside pressing buttons on his mobile and was back in a few minutes, nodding to Marnie, whispering that Janet was on her way. Frank's eyes were focusing now, and he looked from Marnie to Sergeant Marriner and back to Marnie, opening his mouth.

"Shhh ... don't speak," said Marnie gently. "Time for that later. Janet will be here soon. Don't worry."

The curtains swirled, and the nurse returned with another young woman in a white coat who introduced herself as the registrar.

"I'll need some time with him now," she said to Marnie.

"Sure." Marnie squeezed Frank's hand and stood up. She leaned forward to kiss him lightly on his undamaged cheek and was surprised that he pulled her down towards him. She thought he wanted to kiss her in return and turned her own cheek towards his face, but instead he spoke softly into her ear. She listened carefully before straightening up.

Marriner caught her puzzled expression, and they left the bedside together. Outside in the corridor he said, "What was that about?"

Marnie frowned. "I'm not sure. I thought he said ... perfume."

"*Perfume*?" Marriner leaned towards Marnie and sniffed. "I hadn't noticed it before," he muttered.

"You're not meant to ..." She smiled. "That's why it costs so much ... it's meant to be subtle."

The nurse came through the curtains and as she was turning, Marnie said to her, "When you talk to Frank, would you please tell him his dogs are okay. He'll be worried about them."

"Will do." The nurse set off on her mission.

"Do you need me any more, Mr Marriner?" Marnie asked.

"No ... thanks. You've been very helpful ... good job you were here." He smiled.

"I'll be off, then."

"Why were you here, as a matter of interest?"

She waved a hand dismissively. "Oh, just someone on a boat had an accident ... nothing serious. Bye now."

In the ambulance bay outside, Marnie was dismayed to find that Elvis had gone. There was no car, no dogs and no Simon. She was making a three-sixty degree sweep of the area when a voice called her name. Simon and the security guard were standing a short distance away. Beside them in the shade of a tree the labradors were lapping water from dishes made of tin foil. Simon explained that the dishes had previously contained egg custard tarts that had been gratefully devoured by two hungry dogs.

"Were you able to help, then?" said the guard.

"Yes, I was."

Marnie looked at the labradors. Soon Janet would be arriving, which would take care of the dogs, but lead to more enquiries about her presence at the hospital. The longer she stayed, the greater the chance of further police questioning.

The guard followed her gaze. "Fine dogs, those," he said.

"You like dogs?" Marnie asked innocently.

"Love 'em. Always had dogs. We've got a Jack Russell at home. You won't find a more intelligent dog than a Jack Russell. Did you know – "

Marnie suddenly put a hand to her mouth with a gasp. "Oh my goodness ... the parking ticket! We'll be clamped."

"Where's your car?" asked the guard, his professional interest aroused.

"Car park A," said Simon, consulting his Rolex with an exaggerated gesture.

"Ooh, that's Martin's patch ... he's a real stickler. You'd better hurry."

"But what about the dogs?" said Marnie. "Janet will be here in a few minutes. I don't like to abandon them."

"Don't you worry," said the guard. "I'll keep an eye on them till she comes."

With profuse thanks, Marnie and Simon legged it towards the car park.

• • • • •

The silver Mercedes turned out of the hospital driveway and headed south towards the ring road. Fastening the seat belt, Marnie noticed a stain on the leg of her tunic where Anthony had dribbled on her during the journey into town. Simon was chuckling.

"What's funny?" said Marnie.

"You and that security man ..." He put on a squeaky voice like Olive Oyl in the old cartoon films. "Oh my gosh, Popeye, what are we gonna do?"

Marnie laughed out loud. "I couldn't think of how else to get away. I didn't want Sergeant Marriner coming out and asking me exactly what we were doing there again."

"Well it worked," said Simon, chortling. "You deserve an Oscar for that performance."

"You can talk, Simon! What about the theatrical way you looked at your watch ... that was – " She did not finish the sentence.

Simon glanced sideways. "What's up?"

"Your watch," Marnie said thoughtfully.

"What about it?"

"Frank." Marnie felt the back of her own hand. "His wrist and hand ... they were scratched and bruised."

"A result of his accident?"

"I wonder ... I think someone had dragged the watch from his wrist."

"Go on."

"I think he'd been robbed. And the police must think so too. Marriner wouldn't be there just for an accident."

• • • • •

Ralph and Anne drove back from taking Ronny home. He lived in one of the executive houses on a small estate beyond the church. The swelling on his wrist had gone down, and the pain had subsided to a steady throbbing. His only anguish had come from being driven home in a ten year old Volvo instead of a classic sports car. His feeling of demotion had been heightened by the fact that Anne had ridden in front with Ralph, while he had the back seat.

"I'm going to make a pot of our best coffee," Anne announced, as they pulled up beside the garage barn. "And I think you deserve a glass of the brandy that Marnie keeps hidden at the back of the cupboard."

"A secret drinker?" said Ralph.

"For medicinal purposes, according to Marnie. What do you say?"

"Lead on, doctor."

• • • • •

The silver car glided effortlessly along, the engine a gentle hum. Scarcely any sound from the outside world reached the leather and walnut-trimmed interior. Marnie leaned back against the headrest and closed her eyes.

"Life can be so complicated," she breathed.

"You're telling me?" said Simon. "We're certainly complicated."

"This isn't about us."

"I thought everything was about us."

"*Us* isn't complicated … it's simple. I'm talking about Anthony and the police … and Frank and the police … and me and the police."

"So it's about you."

"Simon, it is about me. At least, it's about the questions the police'll be wanting to ask me.`

"But you haven't done anything."

"They won't see it that way. They're looking for someone accused in the press of having sex with an underage girl. I know where he is and I'm concealing the fact."

"Could be tricky," Simon conceded. "Why are you protecting him, actually?"

Marnie's eyes were still closed. "I'd have thought that was obvious. Even if he's guilty, no one deserves what he went through: he lost his career; he was hounded in the press; all the evidence was hearsay and innuendo. Now, his wife's killed herself and he's tried to commit suicide."

"That's true, is it … about there being no real evidence against him?"

"You saw the accusations in the press. There wasn't a single fact, not one piece of hard evidence. And the worst thing is, there's nothing we can do about it."

"Press Complaints Commission?" Simon suggested.

"A joke! What's a slap on the wrist to a media baron like Hawksby? Anyway, all the damage has been done. What would be the point?" As she spoke, Marnie's voice drifted off, as if she was falling asleep.

Simon looked at her profile, the clean features, the smooth complexion. It was only with a great effort that he turned his eyes back to the road. "I know how you feel, but if I was in your place, I'd want to get hold of that editor and rub his nose in his own … dirt."

"Easier said than done," said Marnie, without opening her eyes. She thought it must be the season for clichés.

"Yeah. But if everyone's as immoral as you imagine, Marnie, he must have a secret or two of his own, don't you think? Or is he the only clean one in a dirty world?"

• • • • •

By the time they heard the Mercedes pull up in the yard outside, Anne was drying the cafetière and Ralph was wrestling with the deckchairs. When she looked out to see who was arriving, she had the impression that he was gaining the upper hand. But only just.

Marnie announced at once that she was going to change into clean clothes, and Anne went with her to *Sally Ann* to catch up on the news. This left Simon and Ralph together.

"What's the prognosis?" said Ralph.

"They reckoned his chances were fifty-fifty, more or less. There was no point hanging around, so we came away. They'll phone if there are any developments."

"Right."

"I'm sorry not to have better news. I gather he's a friend of yours."

"Not really a friend," said Ralph. "But I've known him for a long time."

"You were at Oxford together."

"Yes and no. We were both there at about the same time, but we were in different colleges, reading different subjects."

"Marnie tells me you're a professor at All Saints."

"That's right. I'm on sabbatical at the moment ... doing a book."

"Impressive," said Simon.

Ralph shrugged. "It's part of the job."

"She also explained that you two are ... well ... that you're an item."

Ralph smiled. "An *item*. Yes. Curious expression."

"I'd say you've made a good choice," said Simon. "Both of you."

# Part 11

The scene before her was quite surreal. Sunday morning had begun early for Marnie. She had pulled open the stern doors on *Thyrsis* and stood at the foot of the steps looking out over still water. All night she had floated in and out of sleep, and had finally slipped out of bed at six-thirty, grabbing a few things to wear. Ralph had not woken.

The air on her face felt cool and damp. The world was blotted out by a mist that hung over the landscape, merging the sky, the land and the water into one opaque haze. From where she stood, Marnie could see nothing but the cloudy light. She felt suspended between heaven and earth. And then it happened.

The air swirled over the canal. A sound reached her, a steady throbbing, and gradually through the foggy air a shape emerged. Coming towards her were the prows of a pair of working narrowboats, breasted up together, hulls low in the water, the distinctive red and black paintwork of *Totteridge* and her butty, *Shardlow*, familiar from her days in Little Venice.

The pair had slowed to a crawl to pass the moored craft, and Marnie went up two steps to wave at the steerer. He spotted her at once, smiling, turning the engine wheel to reduce speed even further. The boats were hardly moving as he drew near enough to speak.

"Hi Marnie! How're you doing?"

"Great. How about you, Andrew?"

"Fine. This your place?"

She moved further up the steps and pointed through the spinney. "Over there."

"Where's *Sally Ann*? Got rid of her?"

Marnie thumbed over her shoulder. "Got her own dock. This is a friend's boat."

Andrew had brought the pair to a halt alongside, the vintage diesel engine pop-popping quietly, emitting faint grey puffs from the thin exhaust pipe sticking up from the roof. He looked at the anonymous boat without comment.

"Early start, Andrew."

"Yeah. Kate's still asleep. We've got customers in Stoke Bruerne and Braunston. You need anything?"

Marnie agreed to a fill-up of diesel for *Sally Ann* and *Thyrsis* with a load of logs and coal and invited Andrew and Kate to join them for breakfast when Kate was up. She asked if he needed help tying up the pair, and he had winked when he pointed out that she was not quite dressed for the job. Marnie looked down. She was wearing only a shirt and the briefest of pants and she smiled as she retreated down the steps.

• • • • •

The kettle was whistling as Andrew and Kate arrived on *Thyrsis*. Marnie called out to make themselves at home while she finished dressing. Ralph was gradually coming alive under the hot jets of the shower. Minutes later, Marnie emerged into the galley to find Andrew looking out of a porthole at the boat without a name. Kate was at the table holding one of Anne's newspaper cuttings from the *Globe*. Marnie greeted her and set about making breakfast.

"The word was going round," Andrew began, "that that MP who went missing … "

"Leyton-Brown," said Kate, reading from the paper.

"They said he'd gone off on a narrowboat."

"The old bush telegraph?" said Marnie.

"I heard he'd been spotted early one morning, travelling west on the Regent's Canal in London. The boat was painted all over in grey undercoat."

Marnie said quietly, "Did you hear the *latest* news?"

"He's been seen on the Grand Union?" said Andrew.

"His wife has just killed herself."

Kate gasped. "When did this happen?"

"Yesterday."

"We were travelling up from Berko all day," said Andrew. "Didn't hear any news." He glanced towards the porthole. "So what did he think of that?"

"He tried to do the same."

"*Bloody hell!*" said Kate, wide-eyed.

"Took an overdose on top of a bottle of whisky. We rushed him to hospital. I'll be ringing after breakfast to see if there's any news."

"Is he going to make it?" Andrew said.

"Touch and go."

They heard footsteps and Ralph came through to join them. He shook hands with Andrew and saw a tall, lean man of about thirty with short sandy hair and John Lennon glasses, wearing blue jeans and a check shirt. He greeted Kate, wearing a black singlet, her auburn hair pulled back in a ponytail.

"Kate and Andrew know about Anthony," Marnie said. "They worked it out. Apparently he was seen coming through London."

"I see. Have you told them …?"

"Yes."

"It's *terrible*," said Kate. "*Awful*."

"What's going to happen to him," said Andrew, "… assuming he pulls through?"

· · · · ·

Marnie had been expecting the call. Janet Day rang first thing that morning.

"I'm so grateful, Marnie. The policeman told me how helpful you'd been."

"I just happened by. Glad to have been of use. How is Frank?"

"When I rang just now they said he'd had a good night. When the doctor's done her rounds this morning they'll ring to let me know if he can come home."

"Good. Does Frank know who did it? Could he recognise them?"

A hesitation. "How did you know about … you know …?"

"Frank's watch had been snatched," Marnie said. "I saw the grazing."

"The sergeant said I wasn't to tell anybody, Marnie."

"You didn't. Would he recognise whoever attacked him?"

"I didn't ask Frank about that. I just wanted him to be quiet and get better. He gave me a message for you … thank you for looking after the dogs."

"No problem."

"And there's another message. The police sergeant said to tell you he'd be in touch."

"Great."

• • • • •

"That is one smart boat, that *Thyrsis*," Andrew said, rubbing the back of a hand across his forehead. He was loading bags of coal into a wheelbarrow beside the docking area. Marnie and Ralph had left for the hospital leaving Anne to supervise the delivery. "Lovely paint job … reminds me of something."

"Same colours as a Harrods carrier bag?" Anne suggested.

"That's right. Definitely non-standard, that shade of green … and the gold." He returned to his task.

"How did Marnie know how much to pay you?" Anne asked.

"She didn't, actually," said Andrew. "I suppose we were talking of other things."

"I'm afraid I'm not authorised to sign the cheques. And it'll be a while before they get back from the hospital."

"No matter, Anne. We'll be passing this way again in a day or two. I'll collect it then. You can take note of what they've had, if you like."

"Sure. I'll make a list."

• • • • •

Marnie and Ralph arrived in the Intensive Therapy Unit at ten, and a nurse had asked them to sit in the waiting area before going through. It brought back painful memories for Ralph, recalling the previous summer as if it was yesterday, Marnie lying there, hooked up to life-support machines, not expected to live. For Marnie, being back was oddly less disturbing. She had never seen the waiting area and had no memories of the ITU.

"Do you think this means bad news?" Marnie said in a quiet voice.

"Doesn't look good."

They were alone, sitting on plastic chairs with their backs to the windows. Glazed double doors led on to a corridor running down to the end of the building. The ITU was round the corner out of sight.

"It's down there, is it?" Marnie looked towards the doors. "I never wanted to come here again, that's for sure."

"Nor I."

"Here's someone now," said Marnie.

A nurse was walking unhurriedly towards the doors, a diminutive young Chinese woman, calm and professional.

"Would you like to come through? Dr Siddiqui wants a few words with you."

She led them to an office round the corner. The nearest bed was being remade by two nurses. Marnie wondered if Anthony had lain there.

Dr Siddiqui looked up from her paperwork as they entered. In her forties, wearing a white coat, her eyes were dark and serious, giving her face an intense expression. She half rose to shake their hands, as they introduced themselves, and gestured to them to sit. Marnie felt her stomach turn over.

"Thank you for coming in."

"We were anxious to find out about ... your patient," said Ralph. "How is he?"

"He isn't my patient any longer, strictly speaking. He's been moved to another ward."

"So he's all right?"

"He's recovering. He began to improve quite quickly once we'd purged his system and he responded well to treatment."

"That's a relief," said Ralph.

"You both seem very concerned about him. I understood Mr Alexander was unknown to you."

"Well, yes. But in the circumstances ..."

"How did you find him, exactly? He was on a boat, is that correct?"

Ralph answered. "Moored alongside mine. I went on board to see him and found him in the saloon."

Marnie heard the words *Last Chance Saloon* in her head. "Is that important?" she said.

"In a way it is," said Dr Siddiqui. "There are certain rules we have to follow. If this was an accident, we record it as such in our files. If I believe the circumstances were suspicious, we have to inform the police."

"*Suspicious?*" said Ralph. He thought they could be regarded as nothing but suspicious. "Why should they be suspicious?"

"Can you think of any reason why they should not be?" said Dr Siddiqui.

"I hadn't thought about it that way. I just saw him lying on the floor and took action to get him here for treatment."

"But you can see what I'm getting at, Professor Lombard."

Ralph did not like this game of cat-and-mouse. "You must be wondering if this was an attempted suicide, presumably."

"What do you think?"

"To be honest, when I found him I was so shocked I just reacted to get help. On reflection, I must admit it looked like suicide, at least as far as I'm competent to judge."

"But you're uncertain, doctor," Marnie joined in.

"Why do you say that?"

"Why else would you be talking to us about it now, unless you weren't sure? Presumably you could've just notified the police and let them investigate for themselves."

Dr Siddiqui stared at them for a moment. "For a start, police procedure is very time-consuming ... not something one embarks on lightly ... not with our workload. We have enough red tape as it is. And there is something else ..."

"You have doubts?" said Ralph.

"Possibly. How well do you know Mr Alexander?"

"Hardly at all," said Marnie.

"Do you know anything about his state of mind?"

"He's only just arrived on the mooring," she said. "I've only seen him a few times." She was glad to have a chance to say something truthful, even if she was avoiding the question.

"Are you free to tell us about your doubts?" said Ralph.

Dr Siddiqui began slowly. "Suicides are usually clear-cut. Someone slashes their wrists or jumps off a tall building ... not much room for doubt. But overdosing is different. Sometimes it's a cry for help, for attention. But it's always risky ... you can never be quite sure of the reaction of an individual to a particular drug in excess. Many factors can influence the outcome. In this case there are some uncertainties."

Ralph could picture Anthony lying among his empty bottles and thought there was no possibility of doubt. "Uncertainties," he repeated.

"Do you know if he was a heavy drinker?"

"Not really."

"On medication?"

"What kind of medication?" said Marnie.

"A tri-cyclic anti-depressant."

Ralph shook his head. "No idea. Though he did seem rather solitary. Perhaps he drank to combat loneliness."

Dr Siddiqui leaned forward on the desk and rested her chin on her hands. "It's possible that he may have been taking his tablets ... started drinking ... got confused ... took too many. It can happen, but usually to older people living alone."

"You think it might have happened to ... er, Mr Alexander?" said Marnie.

"Hard to tell. The dose may not have been big enough for a suicide attempt. He may not have drunk enough alcohol and may not have taken enough tablets to kill himself. Not quite."

"In which case, it could've been an accident?" said Ralph.

"If you know of no reason why he might've wanted to take his life, it's possible."

• • • • •

Too early for visiting Anthony, they left the hospital just before eleven. Marnie suggested stopping somewhere on the way home. They were sitting in the garden of a hotel in Towcester, where sunshine was breaking through for the first time that day. The other tables were unoccupied.

"What's on your mind?" said Ralph.

"Is it that obvious?"

"Well, when you suggest breaking our journey at a hotel ten minutes from home, it makes me wonder if there's something you want to talk about in private."

"We'll make a detective of you yet."

"Fire away, then." Ralph felt sure he knew what Marnie wanted to talk about.

"I wanted to talk about Anthony and his attempted suicide."

That was not it. "Of course," he said. "You believe that's what it was."

"Don't you?"

"Yes, I do. I'm assuming he heard about Melissa and tried to kill himself. Not surprising."

"He bungled it," said Marnie. "It was lucky for him you turned up, otherwise he might've succeeded."

Ralph smiled ruefully. "I doubt he'll see it that way. He'll be mightily cheesed off when he finds he's been saved."

Marnie frowned. "I saw a film once about the First World War ... French, I think ... there was a soldier badly wounded in a battle ... shell-shocked. He got confused and crawled the wrong way ... accused of desertion ... surgeons struggled to save his life so he could be executed in front of his regiment."

"*Pour encourager les autres*," said Ralph. "We saved him so he can go through hell. But we couldn't choose to let him die. That would be inhuman."

"Of course. But from his point of view he'll end up as the loser however things turn out. If he'd only drunk more Scotch and had more tablets, he might've been better off than facing the future he's got now."

People were beginning to arrive for Sunday lunch, their minds on roast beef and all the trimmings. They scarcely glanced at the quiet couple sitting at the edge of the garden.

"Actually, there was something else on my mind."

"Yes," said Ralph.

"It's about Simon."

"Yes."

"It was only after we set off for the hospital with Anthony that I realised you'd been left behind."

"It was all a great rush."

"But I didn't even discuss it with you."

"You were busy ... discussing it with Simon." Ralph stressed the word discussing. "It was interesting to see you like that." He smiled.

"You must've felt left out."

"Perhaps. But I didn't feel jealous then and I don't feel jealous now."

Marnie smiled. "You don't suffer from insecurity."

"But I know the feeling. Actually, Simon doesn't strike me as insecure either. Very confident ... success written all over him."

"I've told him about us," said Marnie.

"I know. He said you'd told him we were an item."

"Yes, I did. He's another one who's had to come to terms with problems. Mind you, I can't see Anthony solving his difficulties the same way as Simon."

"What did Simon do? He certainly looks as if he does it well ... he's in business, presumably?"

"I didn't mean that. Simon went for therapy. Perhaps that's what Anthony ought to do."

"And he found it helpful?" Ralph asked.

"Simon said he found a way to sublimate himself."

"Hard work? That's what I did after Laura died."

"Partly. But more than that ... he's taken up writing poetry."

"Poetry? That does surprise me. Although, I suppose he does rather have the air of a Romantic poet about him, if appearances are anything to go by."

# Part 12

"I'm going to ring the hospital."

"Now?" said Anne, looking up at the clock.

"It's gone nine," said Marnie. "Anyway, hospitals run all the time."

"Are you still worried about him?"

"I'm just going to check if there's anything he wants us to bring when we visit this evening." Her tone was casual.

"Fine," said Anne. "So you are worried about him."

Marnie reached for the phone and pressed buttons. "The doctor said you can never tell how someone will react to drugs. Though I expect he's walking around already and telling them he wants to go home ... or whatever. Hallo? Good morning. Oliver Kenton ward, please ..." While she waited to be connected, Marnie looked at the desk diary, thinking of visiting times. "Oh, good morning. I'm phoning about Mr Alexander, Simon Alexander ..." She listened. "But I understood he'd been transferred to this ward ... He's *what*? ... When did this happen? ... I see ... No. I had no idea. Thank you." She put the phone down.

Anne was staring at her. "What's happened?"

Marnie shook her head. "I can't believe it. He's discharged himself, left the hospital an hour ago ... put his clothes on and walked out."

"Can he just do that?"

"He just did."

• • • • •

Ralph came as soon as Marnie rang him on *Thyrsis*. He arrived through the office door like a projectile.

"Did they say where he'd gone?"

"No, just that he'd left. He dressed after breakfast, said he was feeling fine, thanked them very politely and walked out. That was it."

"Well ... I wonder what's next on the agenda," said Ralph.

"Do you think he *is* fine?" Anne asked.

"God knows," said Marnie. "He must be a bit shaky. Last time I saw him he looked *dreadful*." She turned to Ralph. "Do you think they knew who he was?"

"It's possible, I suppose."

"What do hospitals do if someone discharges himself like that?" Marnie said.

Ralph shrugged. "Probably write to his GP."

"And if they don't know who the GP is?"

"Ah, yes ... I see what you're getting at. I expect they have two choices. They either do nothing because their patient has gone and they're too busy dealing with the ones who are still there ... "

"I think we can guess the second one," said Marnie.

"Try and trace someone called Simon Alexander?" said Anne.

"No," said Ralph. "Inform the police."

"Great," said Marnie. "Especially if they suspect he might be a potential suicide case. Anne, let me know when Inspector Bartlett arrives. I'll go and run out the red carpet."

• • • • •

The car was heard rolling into the yard an hour later. Marnie and Anne looked at each other across the office and sighed in unison. Anne stood up and looked out.

"It's not their usual car," she said. "The police've got a grey Cavalier like Dad's. This one's a Mondeo, I think."

"Blue light flashing?" said Marnie wearily.

"No, it looks like ... uh-oh ... Guess what? It's him. Mr Thingy-Brown."

Marnie leapt up. "With the police?"

"No ... with a taxi driver."

Anthony came towards them. He still looked sickly pale, but he walked steadily and gave a weak smile when he saw them at the window. The cab driver was standing patiently at the side of his car.

"Marnie, hi! Could you possibly lend me a tenner to pay the driver? My cash is on the boat."

"Sure." Marnie fetched her bag and handed him a note.

Anthony paid and returned, both hands laden with bulging carrier bags. Unlike the police, he accepted the offer of a cup of coffee. Anne pulled up a chair and he lowered himself gently to sit beside Marnie's desk.

"We know about the hospital," said Marnie. "Did you leave because you thought someone had recognised you?"

"No. But I wanted to get out before anyone did."

"You do realise the police'll be arriving any time now? My guess is the hospital will tell them where you were found. Their cars automatically head for here whenever there's any kind of trouble south of John O' Groats."

Anthony closed his eyes. "Oh, God ... " he muttered.

"They can't do anything if you haven't committed a crime." As an afterthought she added, "That girl wasn't under age, was she?"

"I keep telling you, she wasn't even a minor. She was eighteen. Definitely. But don't you see? The word'll get round. The press will find out I'm here. It'll be awful ... "

"Tell me, Anthony ... was it an accident? The doctors thought it could've been. Was it a mistake with your pills?"

"What do you think?"

"Well," she said. "They can't prove anything."

"They don't need to."

Marnie reached for the phone.

"What are you doing?" He looked panic-stricken.

"I'm going to tell Ralph you're here. Believe it or not, people have been worrying about you."

• • • • •

The three of them had trudged through the spinney, Marnie and Ralph carrying the shopping, Anthony dragging himself. They dropped the carrier bags in the anonymous boat and went on board *Thyrsis*.

"How did you manage to get all that shopping?" said Ralph.

"Easy. I had an emergency fifty quid note in my back pocket. Old habit."

"And just as easy to get out of hospital too, it seems."

"Yes. Once I was outside, I walked to a shop, bought cheap sunglasses and got a taxi to Towcester. Found a supermarket. Got a minicab to bring me here. Voilà."

"Which brings us back to the eternal question," said Ralph. "You're going to have to face facts, Anthony. You can't keep running for the rest of your life."

"Ralph, I can't face the media right now. I'm regarded as a national disgrace, my wife has killed herself and I've just tried to commit suicide." He laughed without humour. "I couldn't even manage that properly … The papers'd have a field day. Look at me … do you think I'm capable of handling all that?"

He was a pathetic sight, unshaven, wearing a grubby shirt and crumpled trousers, a man on the run.

"We must get you away from here," Marnie said. "You and the boat."

"What do you have in mind?" said Ralph.

"A quick getaway at four miles an hour?" said Anthony with a gallows smile.

"Old Chinese proverb," Marnie said. "If you want to hide a leaf, put it on a tree."

• • • • •

The Queen Eleanor fleet was one of the smallest on the canal system, but it had a good reputation. It had been founded twenty years ago by a retired naval officer who could not imagine life away from water and invested everything he had in a modest boat repair yard on the Grand Union Canal near Blisworth.

Among its assets was a thirty-foot narrowboat that was hired out to visitors for short trips, and it gave him the idea of fitting out a bigger boat for holidays. It became the first in a series, the fleet taking its name from the Queen of England, Eleanor of Castile, whose body had rested in Northampton on its way back to London in 1290 for burial. Her grieving husband, King Edward I, had paid for stone crosses to be erected at every place where her body had stopped overnight, twelve in all, the most famous being at Charing Cross in London. Three of the crosses survived, two of them in Northamptonshire. Each boat in the fleet bore the name of a Queen Eleanor Cross.

After fifteen years, the naval officer retired for a second time on reaching his 'three score years and ten', and handed the business over to his son and daughter, who had proved in their five years in charge that their father's faith in them was well justified.

It was late in the afternoon when a boat painted all over in grey undercoat and bearing no name slipped quietly into the Queen Eleanor boatyard alongside another boat primed all over in dark red. No one paid any attention to the boat or to the woman at the tiller who brought her in single-handed.

• • • • •

"Walker and Co, good afternoon."

"It's me. Any visitors?"

"Not so far. All quiet on the western front. Package safely delivered?"

"Yes. He's going to have an early night. Have you seen Ralph?"

"He's here. Hang on." Anne passed the phone.

"Hallo, Marnie. I'll come straight away."

"Great. Listen, can you bring my briefcase with you? It's on the floor by the desk. And my filofax. Oh yes, and there's a set of rolled-up plans. Better bring them, too."

"What are we doing?"

"Just ... keeping up appearances."

•　•　•　•　•

When Ralph drove in to the Queen Eleanor boatyard he saw Marnie speaking into her mobile by the back door. She finished the call as he drew up beside her. He recognised the determined look in her eyes; she was in decisive mood. She slipped into the front passenger seat and leaned over to kiss him.

"I've got your things in the back," he said, reversing into a three-point turn.

"Slight change of plan," said Marnie. "Can we go to Yore first? I want to look in on Frank Day."

"Marnie, there's something that's slightly bothering me," Ralph said, as they drove out of the boatyard.

"Would that be the idea of leaving a man who's recently attempted suicide all alone on a boat?"

"You don't think that's a tiny bit risky?"

Marnie looked out at the fields they were passing. "No."

"Any particular reason why not?"

"First, he seemed willing enough to agree to the plan. I think he wanted to be helped."

"Okay. And second?"

"Second ... if he's going to do himself in, he'll do it no matter where he is. If he's going to stand any chance of getting over this business, he has to see that we trust him." She thought fleetingly of Simon's haiku. "He'll have to take one day at a time."

"Okay. If you're sure. I hope you're right."

"It's his life, Ralph."

"So, problem solved, then ... for the time being at any rate."

"I give it a day," said Marnie.

"A *day*? Is that all?"

"One day max. With the police breathing down our neck, not to mention the press, a day's not bad going. What we do next is the question."

Ralph glanced quickly sideways at Marnie. "You're about to tell me you've got that figured out, too?"

"No. I haven't a clue. But at least we've bought a day to work it out."

"We'd better have a talk with Anthony tomorrow ... see what he has in mind."

"I don't think so."

Ralph was surprised. "You don't?"

"He's not been too successful so far, has he? Time someone else had a go."

"And that someone is you?"

"It's us. Come on, Ralph, you're the brainbox. What's the logical thing to do? What's your *key factor*, or whatever you call it?"

"You're much better at handling this kind of thing than I am," said Ralph, accelerating through Towcester past the town hall. "It was your idea to hide him and his boat in a boatyard. Brilliant. No one'll know he's there. I don't see why he can't stay there for a good while."

"Simple. Because the boatyard people will know he's there, and the word will get out. We can leave him there for a day, but no longer. The press'll be on to him in a flash. Just you wait."

"Yes ... the damn paparazzi!"

"Exactly," she sighed. "Simon was right about that."

"You talked about it with Simon?"

"Of course. He said he'd like to rub the editor's nose in the dirt. I know just how he feels."

Ralph frowned. "Maybe, but I don't see how that'll help Anthony."

"What will?" said Marnie. "That's the question."

For the final mile or two of their journey they retreated into their private thoughts. Ralph was pondering the possibility of letting Anthony stay at his Oxfordshire cottage. It could be a practical expedient and buy more time. Marnie's thoughts involved piranhas and pushing newspaper editors into the canal on a dark night.

• • • • •

Frank and Janet Day lived in a traditional Northamptonshire long house, about two hundred years old, built of the local stone, set back from the road in the middle of the high street. Yore was a smaller village than Knightly St John, laid out on gently sloping land that ran down towards the canal. Janet answered the doorbell and led them through to the sitting room, where Frank was sitting on a sofa, a newspaper folded beside him. The room was spacious, comfortable and homely. Frank looked drawn and grey.

"Good of you to come," he said, smiling weakly, gesturing to two armchairs. "Forgive me if I don't get up."

Janet left the room. Marnie was shocked at Frank's appearance.

"So, how are you feeling?" she said cheerfully.

"Still got the headache." He raised a hand to the back of his head and ran it slowly down to his collar. "Concussion. Could've been worse."

"Have the police any idea who attacked you?"

Frank began to shake his head and winced. Marnie and Ralph could almost feel the pain. "Don't think so."

Janet reappeared with a tray laden with crockery. She set it down on a low table and began pouring tea.

"Help yourselves to biscuits," she said. "When you rang, I thought you might be the police. They said they'd be coming to take a statement later today if he was feeling all right."

A phone began ringing somewhere in the house and Janet got up.

"If it's Jeff," Frank said. "It'll most likely be about that estimate I promised for today."

"Well, they're going to have to do without you for once," said Janet firmly. "Jeff can deal with it ... he's supposed to be the office manager. Today he's got to *manage*."

After she had gone, Frank sighed. "Janet doesn't realise how complicated it is, running a business."

"She's more concerned with looking after you," said Marnie. "And you're not a hundred per cent after what's happened. It's not surprising. What did happen, actually? Or would you rather not talk about it?"

"There's not much to talk about, Marnie. I took the dogs to one of our regular walks – you know, over by Hanford, near the clumps. There are no cattle in it at this time of year, so I left the car in the lay-by, walked them down the slope and let 'em off the lead. Next thing I knew was this smash on the head, and out I went."

"What was that about perfume?" said Marnie. "You were trying to tell me about it when I saw you in hospital."

"Just as I was going down ... someone grabbed my wrist ... must've bent over me. Last thing I remember was this smell like perfume."

"Was it like mine?" said Marnie.

"Not really ... yours just gave me the idea."

"Could it have been aftershave?"

"I don't know ... yes. I'm not sure. It was just an impression ... a sweet sort of smell ... then I was out."

"Why didn't the dogs do anything?" Ralph asked.

Frank made a gesture with his hand. "Oh, they were off. You know what they're like ... charging through the trees ... lolloping great things ... useless." He smiled indulgently. "Mind you, they went mad when they ran back and found me lying there ... barked their whiskers off, apparently. That's what made that chap come and look ... the one who found me and took me to hospital."

"Up until then, you'd not been aware of anyone else near you?" said Ralph.

"No one at all. I keep going over it in my mind. Nothing."

"Did you notice any other car in the lay-by?"

Frank shrugged. "I don't think so. Nothing that I can remember."

"He can't have sprung up from nowhere," said Marnie. "Weren't you in open country?"

"There are trees and bushes down there. He must have been hiding behind them. I just came along and that was it."

• • • • •

Marnie gave Ralph directions to the lay-by where Frank had parked on the day he was mugged. As the Volvo stopped, less than five miles away, an unmarked police Cavalier was pulling into the yard at Glebe Farm.

Marnie pointed down the slope beyond the lay-by. "It must've been about there, by those trees. Would you mind if we had a quick look, Ralph?"

"You want to go down there?"

"I'm just curious," Marnie said, pushing the door open. "After hearing what Frank said, and seeing him in hospital, I want to get the full picture. You know what I'm like."

"Yes, I know," Ralph muttered, following her.

They climbed over the stile, walked down to stand roughly where Frank must have unleashed the labradors, and surveyed the scene. There was nothing visible to suggest that an attack had occurred in that place; no marks on the ground, no damage to branches. Marnie gazed into the distance where the trees stood closer together, forming a small copse bounded by meadowland and the canal. She turned to speak to Ralph but he was nowhere to be seen.

"Ralph?" she called.

He stepped out from behind a cluster of trees. "I could see you through the foliage," he said. "But obviously you couldn't see me."

"Not at all." She looked beyond him. Extending to the horizon, only meadows and fields were visible. Away off at the edge of vision, a solitary church steeple rose up between trees like a tiny pin. They were about twenty metres from the canal bank. Joining Ralph, Marnie squatted for a closer look at the ground.

"Pity we left the magnifying glasses and deerstalkers behind," Ralph observed.

"Mm."

"It's probably the way I tell them." He squatted beside her. "What are you looking for?"

"Sex."

He grinned. "What now?"

"Ralph, you're not taking this seriously." She stood up, still staring at the grass, and shook her head.

"Sorry. It's just that there's nothing at all to be seen."

"That's the point, isn't it? Come on, then. We'd better go home."

Walking hand in hand up to the lay-by, Ralph left Marnie to her thoughts. When they drove off he said, "You were being very enigmatic, Marnie. What did you mean back there ... all that Sherlock Holmes stuff?"

"Are you making fun of me?"

He looked serious. "No. Of course not. But you seemed to be looking for things that weren't there."

"I was. Got it in one."

"I was rather hoping you'd become less enigmatic."

"But you were right," said Marnie. "I was trying to see what wasn't there."

"And what did you see ... or what didn't you see? Whichever of those is appropriate."

"Not sure. I've got to get things sorted out in my mind. It's complicated."

Ralph glanced across, saw that Marnie was frowning and judged it best to let her cogitate. He turned off the main road towards the village, along the high street and through the farm gate onto the field track.

"Have you time to talk about things now?" he asked.

"It'll have to be later, probably this evening."

"Okay. I guess we've both got plenty of work to do."

"Partly that and ..." The sentence was left unfinished. She had caught sight of the police car standing in the farmyard.

• • • • •

Anne was feeling desperate. She had already asked DCI Bartlett and DS Marriner at least three times if they were sure they would not like a cup of anything. It was clear that Marriner would have gladly accepted, but his boss was adamant. She was feeling ready to confess all and be carted off to the cells when Marnie breezed into the office, briefcase in one hand, filofax in the other, a roll of plans tucked under her arm, car keys dangling from a finger.

"What a day! You wouldn't believe the traffic on the ... oh, Inspector Bartlett, Sergeant Marriner. Is that your car outside?" She laid her bits and pieces on the desk. "Has Anne offered you refreshment? Would you like something?"

"Mrs Walker, good afternoon." Bartlett looked less than cordial. "I understand we have reason to be grateful for your help at the hospital on Saturday."

"There was no reason to come all this way to thank me," said Marnie.

"We didn't. But I do thank you all the same."

"My pleasure. Was it the mugger you told me about?"

"It looks like it. Mr Day couldn't identify anyone, unfortunately. He just had a vague impression."

"The *perfume*," said Marnie.

"Quite," said Bartlett.

Marnie snorted. "Do I need an alibi?"

"That won't be necessary."

"Are you able to tell us what happened?"

Bartlett outlined the events surrounding the attack. His version matched the story told by Frank.

"And they took his watch," said Marnie.

"Very observant," said Bartlett. "And his wallet."

"Strange that the dogs didn't come to help him," Marnie observed. "Do you have any views on that?"

Bartlett did not like it when someone else asked the questions. "They were too far away at the time. And he didn't make a sound. It was all very quick ... very professional."

"But afterwards ... surely the dogs would've seen the attackers making their getaway."

"If they did, they're not telling us," said Marriner dryly.

"I meant, they must've been confident they could get away quickly. Otherwise, why would they go for someone with two big dogs?"

"We're still working on that one," said Bartlett. "What interests us more at the moment is how you came to be at the hospital when Mr Day was admitted."

"I told Mr Marriner. I was just visiting someone."

"Oh, I think it was more than just visiting, Mrs Walker. I understand one of your fellow boaters was rushed to hospital – by you – suspected of having attempted to commit suicide."

Marnie crossed to the kitchen area and filled the kettle. Anne got up and joined her, muttering about making the coffee.

"*Suicide*? I suppose that's one way of looking at it."

"How would you look at it, Mrs Walker?"

"The man wasn't actually one of *my boaters*, as you put it. He was on a visitor's mooring. He appears to have had a drop too much to drink and taken more of his anti-depression tablets than he should. They seem to have disagreed with him."

Bartlett looked bewildered. "*Anti-depression tablets?*"

"I think that's what the doctor said. She didn't assume it was suicide."

"That has yet to be decided. We're keeping an open mind on that score."

"There was no suicide note," said Marnie. "I thought people usually left a note behind."

"There are no set rules in these things, Mrs Walker. Tell me, have you been to visit this Mr Alexander in hospital?"

"No. I've been working." She nodded towards her desk. "As you can see."

"Did you know he'd discharged himself this morning?"

Marnie accepted a cup from Anne. The detectives would know that a woman had phoned the ward sister that morning. They would know it was her. "Are you sure you wouldn't like some refreshment, gentlemen?"

"Quite sure. Would you answer the question, please?"

"Yes. I did know. I phoned to see if he needed anything, and the sister said he was better and had left."

"*Better?* Are you sure that's what you were told?"

"I think so. That is the situation, isn't it?"

"He discharged himself and seems to have disappeared. Have you any ideas as to his whereabouts, Mrs Walker?"

"Probably gone back to his boat, I expect. Unless he's gone home, of course. I've no idea where that is."

"You indicated his boat was moored near here," said Bartlett.

"Through the spinney." She indicated the direction with a nod.

"Could I ask you to accompany us and identify the boat?"

Marnie got up. "Sure."

• • • • •

Ralph had to admit Marnie was a cool customer. As soon as they had seen the policemen's car, she had rattled off a series of orders. He was to get to *Thyrsis* by skirting round the back of the barns out of sight. Once on board, he was to switch on his electric kettle and his computer, surround himself at his desk with books and papers, making sure they were exactly relevant to the program on the screen in case anyone had a close look. He was to make a cup of coffee and pour more than half of it into the sink, rinsing away the remains so as not to leave a stain. To the rest, he had to add a little cold water, so that it was lukewarm. Knowing that he often worked with music playing softly in the background, he was to put on a CD as soon as he sat at his desk. Then, he was to start working as normal.

It was the last part that he found hardest to follow. His thoughts kept returning to the sight of Marnie and Simon dealing with Anthony. They worked well together. There was an understanding between them that was intuitive. Even their argument about the cars did not seem to get in the way of their effectiveness. It just seemed to underline their wholeness, that they could keep up the banter without being diverted from the matter in hand. And they looked so good together.

Ralph had felt middle-aged just watching them. His life was spent analysing data, devising theories, advising people. They may have been Very Important People: presidents, ministers, chairmen. But he advised and they took the decisions. Marnie and Simon had not even waited for his views. They had read the situation and leapt into action. It had been impressive.

He heard the knock on the porthole behind him and went to open the side doors, reminding himself to focus on his story. Marnie and the two detectives were standing on the bank.

"Mr Lombard," said Bartlett, who looked far from happy. "Can we ask you a few questions, sir?"

"Er, yes ... come aboard." Ralph sounded distracted.

"We're obviously disturbing your work. It shouldn't take a minute."

Ralph went through to the study, not the saloon, as Marnie had told him. He offered his visitors the sofa. Marnie sat on the floor and waved aside their protests. Ralph turned down the music and swivelled his chair to face them.

"What can I do for you?" His face was serious as if he had been concentrating and was making an effort to change direction.

"You discovered the man we know to be Mr Simon Alexander unconscious on his boat. It appeared that he had attempted to commit suicide."

"Has that now been established, Chief Inspector?"

"Isn't that what *you* thought at the time?"

"I didn't have much time for thoughts. We had to move fast. I suppose suicide is a reasonable assumption, though I don't think the doctors would necessarily agree with you."

Bartlett glanced fleetingly at Marnie. "Tell me, sir, did you see a note or an envelope near Mr Alexander when you found him?"

"A note?" He reached for his coffee, took a sip and winced. "No ... nothing like that. I'm sure I would've noticed if there had been. Can't stand lukewarm coffee. May I offer you something?"

"No thank you, sir. Are you aware that Mr Alexander's boat has left?"

Ralph gave every impression of not quite relating to his surroundings. "Left?"

"I understand it was tied alongside your own boat. It isn't there now."

"I can't say I've been paying much attention to the canal today." Ralph's computer screen was covered in figures, a graph and a pie chart.

"But you would notice if a boat alongside you moved away? You'd hear the engine presumably ... see it go past ... feel it bump against your boat, perhaps?"

"Oh yes. All of those are possible. But there's movement all the time on canals ... boats coming and going. That's one reason I use music to filter out the sounds. With my work, I rarely have time to sit and stare out of the window."

"Isn't it likely that a man whose life you saved would come to say goodbye if he was leaving?"

"Yes, of course. But if he knocked on the doors, for example, I might well not hear. And I spend a fair amount of time on the phone. It would be quite easy to miss him."

"That's why I tapped on the porthole," said Marnie helpfully.

• • • • •

Bartlett and Marriner maintained a gruff silence on the walk back through the spinney. Marnie thought it best to keep quiet herself. All her objectives had been achieved, and Ralph had played his part with great success. He was a surprisingly good actor.

They stopped at the door to the office barn. "Is that it? Can I carry on with work now, inspector?"

"What was Mr Alexander's boat called? Can you describe it for us?"

"I don't remember seeing its name," she said truthfully. "It was grey all over, I think."

"Have you any idea where it went? Had Mr Alexander mentioned where he was going?"

Marnie shook her head. "If I had to guess, I'd say it probably went south."

"Why south?"

"It was pointing in that direction. That's usually a clue." Bartlett's expression began turning hostile. "No. I'm not being facetious, inspector. Turning round isn't easy for a boat that length. It would need a winding hole. He'd have to go south for about three quarters of an hour before finding one. Then why would he want to return here when his boat had already been going south, anyway? I'd suggest you look in that direction."

• • • • •

Anne looked round the corner of the office barn as the police car disappeared up the field track. Her legs were still tender but no longer painful, and she was walking normally.

"All clear," she said. "How did it go?"

"Fine, I think. I tried to persuade them the boat was going in the opposite direction."

"And they actually believed you?"

"I think so."

Anne feigned shock and put a hand on her heart. "It's gotta be a first!"

"Ralph was great," said Marnie. "You can never quite be sure with the police. They always know more about what's going on than they tell you."

"You were gone for ages. I thought you'd be back sooner."

"I should've phoned to let you know, but I got sidetracked. We called in on Frank."

"And how was he?"

"Awful. I'll tell you about it later."

"Okay. It's a good job you went to the boat just now. Anthony rang. He said the batteries in his razor have packed up and he wants you to get him some new ones or a pack of disposable razors."

"Right. He'll have them tomorrow. I've got a pile of work to get through. Anything else?"

"Yes. Simon rang."

"Did he leave a message?"

"Not as such. Actually, we had a chat. He's got a very good telephone voice, hasn't he?"

Marnie heard his voice in her mind, *Very good everything, I'd say.* She said, "I suppose so. What did you chat about?"

"This and that ... everything, really. I told him about Mr Leyton-Brown leaving hospital, the police coming here, you hiding the grey boat, that sort of thing. He wanted to know about our life, the building works. I even told him about how we use *Sally Ann* and *Thyrsis*, and how we get supplies delivered by Andrew and his working boats."

"My, my, you seem to have had quite a cosy chat."

Anne looked concerned. "You don't mind, do you, Marnie? I mean, I wasn't indiscreet about ... well, you and Ralph or anything personal like that."

"Of course not. It's fine. So he didn't leave a message."

"Well, not a serious message. He just said we should tie Anthony to the mast on Andrew's boat and send him off to the furthest point on the waterways."

"What *mast*?"

"That's what he said."

Marnie laughed. "And hope for a hurricane on the way. Good idea."

• • • • •

The three of them had baked trout for supper on *Sally Ann*'s stern deck, enjoying the mild spring evening. Ralph brought along a crisp white sauvignon from the Périgord, and for the first time that day Marnie felt content. In the galley, Dolly was enjoying a share of the fish in her bowl, and Marnie felt like purring in unison as she walked through to the deck with a dish of steaming Jersey royales and a crock of Cornish butter. She sat at the table, sipped the chilled wine and sighed.

Anne chuckled. "I could almost taste that with you, Marnie."

Ralph smiled. "What a wonderful idea."

"I'm way beyond having ideas," said Marnie. "Let's just eat."

A narrowboat slipped past as they began the meal, and the steerer called out an envious greeting. Three glasses were raised in reply. The silence was broken after a while by Anne asking about the visit to Frank, and Marnie outlined their conversation and the subsequent detour to see where he had been robbed.

"Did you see anything there?" Anne asked.

"Not a sausage."

"Must be funny muggers," said Anne. "Who'd think of lying in wait in a place like that? Doesn't make much sense."

"Marnie was trying to see what wasn't there," said Ralph and quickly added, "If you see what I mean."

"Oh yes," said Anne. "I know just what you mean."

Ralph looked suspicious. "You do? Then can someone please explain it to me?"

"Do you want to try, Anne?" said Marnie.

"Well ... if it's an odd place for robbers to wait for victims ... then maybe that isn't what it's about. Right?"

Marnie nodded. Ralph said, "Go on."

"So maybe what you're looking for isn't what you'd expect to find ... and he was mugged for some other reason ... that isn't obvious ... that you can't see. Perhaps he wasn't mugged at all."

"That's what I was wondering," said Marnie. "And that's what wasn't there ... the reason for the attack."

"What was it, if not a mugging?" Ralph asked. "After all, he was hit on the head and robbed."

"It could be he was attacked to camouflage something else that was going on."

"And that's where sex comes into it?" said Ralph.

"*Sex?*" Anne looked thoughtful. "Oh ... I see ... yes. You mean some people might've been having ... you know ... Are there bushes and things round there?"

"Yes. I looked for traces of rolling around on the grass ... and any less savoury clues, but there was nothing to see."

Ralph said, "So you think he might've been attacked to stop him seeing people involved in an illicit relationship?"

"That's what I was wondering," said Marnie.

"But why attack him? Why not just let him get on with his walk?"

"The dogs," said Anne.

"That's right." Marnie continued. "They would've hit him because at any minute the dogs might come running back and pick up the scent – literally in this case. The last thing they'd want was two large canines bouncing all over the place, drawing attention to them."

Anne laughed. "Probably sticking their noses in where they're not wanted!"

Marnie gave her a school-ma'am look, but ruined its impact by laughing herself.

Ralph smiled. "And you worked all that out from looking at a clump of trees and bushes? Amazing."

"And completely wrong," Marnie said.

"Why wrong?"

"Because there was no evidence of any kind, not a single sign. Without that, it's just an idea, a theory with no proof ... useless."

"Not necessarily, Marnie. You might just've been looking in the wrong place, and – "

Before he could finish, Anne burst out laughing. "You might've been barking up the wrong tree!"

• • • • •

They had stayed out until the light faded and the evening cooled. Anne had excused herself, and Marnie had walked back with her to the office barn while Ralph took his shower.

When Marnie's turn came to shower, she was thinking about Ralph. When she had dried herself, she slipped along to their cabin and through the gap in the door saw Ralph sitting up in bed, reading as usual. What was unusual was that he was wearing a T-shirt. She turned back and went to the second sleeping cabin, pulled on a T-shirt from the wardrobe and went back to join him.

Sliding in under the duvet, she said quietly, "Your performance this afternoon was brilliant."

"Mm?"

"When Bartlett and Marriner came to see you."

"Good."

"You really looked as if you had a lot on your mind and couldn't quite get your thoughts back to Anthony. It was a great performance. The police were totally convinced."

"It wasn't difficult, in the circumstances. And I had my orders."

"Ralph, I'm sorry if I was a bit ... dogmatic ... or ... you know."

"You weren't. It was fine. You and Simon are much better at that sort of thing than I am, Marnie."

"*Simon?*"

"Yes. He's very much like you ... acts decisively, takes the initiative."

Marnie lifted herself up onto one elbow. "*Simon ... decisive?*"

"I saw the two of you working together ... the way you dealt with Anthony."

"Ralph, I took my cue from you. You were calling for medical help. I just tried to back you up, to see if first aid might work. Simon lifted Anthony because he's stronger than I am. Also, he had a better car. That's all it was."

"I thought Simon was rather impressive."

"We all did what we could, Ralph."

Ralph smiled. "Don't think I don't know what you're up to ... trying not to make me feel inadequate."

"Of course you're not inadequate. And I can prove it."

"My new role ... character actor ... playing the dotty professor?"

Marnie sat up and began pulling the T-shirt over her head. "That isn't what I had in mind. Can't we just get on with being the two of us? There isn't any room for Anthony or Simon in our lives. Things are complicated enough as it is. Why are you wearing that T-shirt?"

# Part 13

"Amazingly, things aren't looking too bad," said Marnie.

Tuesday morning, and it was staff conference time at Walker and Co. They had missed the regular Monday session because of the hospital visit. Now, with Anthony away, Marnie was getting the firm back on track.

Anne looked concerned. "Why *amazingly*? Things are all right, aren't they?"

"I mean, despite all the upheaval with Anthony."

Anne ran her eyes down the list of projects, most of them for Willards Brewery. Everything was on target, all the designs completed, and briefing on the next phase programmed for the coming month. Work on the cottages was more or less on time, though they were still waiting for the joiner, delayed on another job, to finish work in cottage number three. The timing was not critical, and Marnie was not worried.

Anne, always anxious to keep the operations of the firm running smoothly, knew they were susceptible to peaks and troughs in the work pattern and it no longer worried her. She accepted that they could do nothing to even out the timing and knew they were approaching a period of reduced pressure. When that came they could concentrate on completing the cottages for letting. Marnie assured her they would not starve.

The phone rang. Anne transferred Simon to Marnie.

"Hi! what's new?" He sounded cheerful.

"No change since yesterday. Anthony's safely ensconced up the canal."

"Good. How did you get on with the police?"

"Fine. Ralph handled them brilliantly. The perfect impression of the absent-minded professor. They don't have any problems with him."

"Good. Look, I'm on the road just now. Could I call by in about hour ... just for a short time? Is that okay?"

"That's okay."

• • • • •

Marnie spent half an hour on the building site with Bob the foreman going over the jobs list. When she returned to the office barn, Anne had several messages waiting for her. The final one was from Andrew arranging to call in for payment.

"Did he say where he was?" Marnie asked.

"North of the Blisworth tunnel."

Marnie stood for some moments looking out of the window across the yard towards the cottages. Suddenly, she went to her desk, flicked open the address section of the filofax and picked up the phone. When Andrew answered, in the background was the steady beat of the engine.

"Andrew, it's Marnie. Where are you right now?"

"Just leaving Blisworth. I've got some more customers to see ... be with you some time this afternoon. That all right?"

"We'll be here. Any chance of you picking up a cargo for me?"

"A *cargo*? Sure. What kind of cargo? Where from?"

"Queen Eleanor boatyard. Can you collect Anthony and bring him with you?"

"*Anthony*? Okay. I'll be there in about a quarter of an hour."

Anne looked across at Marnie who was pressing the buttons for her next call. When Marnie noticed her, Anne raised an eyebrow. It rang several times before Anthony answered.

"It's Marnie. Listen, have you got some jeans and a sweatshirt? You've got to be ready to leave in the next few minutes."

• • • • •

Anthony sat on the first step down from the steerer's counter inside the grey boat, waiting. He did not have long to wait. When the working pair eased alongside, he jumped out beside Andrew and immediately dived below into the cabin. He spent the journey to Knightly St John out of sight.

• • • • •

Marnie and Simon sat on the stern deck of *Sally Ann*. Simon came straight to the point.

"I've been worrying, Marnie, thinking about you having this Leyton-Brown guy here. It could bring you no end of problems, the longer he stays. You really can't afford to get associated with him. It could do you a lot of harm. You've got to get rid of him."

"You've got contacts in Chicago or Palermo?"

"I mean it; it's not a joke. His reputation could stick to you. Whether he's guilty or not, he could damage everything you're working for."

"I know," said Marnie. "It's on my mind all the time. But I keep thinking, what if I sent him away and he killed himself?"

Simon shook his head. "I don't think he'd do that. I really don't. That failed suicide attempt will've made him see things differently. He'll be looking for a new way forward now."

"Maybe. But if he did try again and succeed, how would I feel about it?"

"Marnie, there's nothing you can do to help him out of this mess. Have you thought you could even make it worse?"

"*Worse?*"

"You're making it easy for him. If he didn't have you, he'd *have* to work things out."

"I know. That's why I've decided to follow your advice."

Simon blinked. "*My* advice? Can you remind me what it was?"

"I'm packing him off with Andrew, lashed to the mast."

"Marnie, I was only chatting with Anne. That was meant to be a joke."

"Many a true word," said Marnie.

• • • • •

When they walked back to the office barn, Anne was ready with more messages.

"Beth rang. Could you ring her back. And Mr Jeffries from Willards. Also the builders' merchants in Buckingham. Oh ... and there was a message for Ralph ... from a Dr Greenman in Nottingham. He said he'd ring back later. I think it's about ... you know ..."

Simon said, "Well, I can see you've got a lot on. I'd better be going."

"I'll walk out with you," said Marnie.

In the yard, Simon smiled at the MG standing in its barn. "Isn't it about time you got a more *normal* car?" He touched her arm. "Sorry, you've had enough of my opinions for one day, I expect."

"No, I appreciate your coming, Simon, and what you said. You were right. That's why I'm taking action."

"I'll be careful about making jokes in future. I know it's none of my business, but … well …" He pressed a button on his car key, and the boot of the Mercedes sprang open.

"I don't have to do that with the MG," said Marnie light-heartedly. "No boot to open."

Simon began fiddling with something out of sight in the boot.

"What are you doing?"

"Loading the auto-changer. It's built-in. Then I can select any of the CDs from inside the car."

"Another thing less to worry about in the MG," said Marnie triumphantly. "If I want in-car entertainment, I just sing my old favourite songs." She eyed the Mercedes while Simon rummaged. "This is a seriously smart car. And understated. I like that."

"You'd love the technical bits too, Marnie." He closed the boot lid, and Marnie heard faint sounds as electromagnetic catches fastened themselves. "Did you know they can adjust the running of the engine through its computer by satellite from a control centre near London?"

"You're kidding!" She peered inside through tinted glass. "I expect you've got satellite navigation, too. Or is that old-fashioned these days? Do you just tell the car where to go?"

"No. You still have to turn the steering wheel from time to time, but it does have satnav, and it's part of the security system. They can pinpoint almost exactly where the car is at any given time."

"How does that work?"

"The satellite can spot it anywhere it goes, so if thieves can beat the security systems – crane it onto a lorry, for instance – Mercedes can tell where it is. No hiding place."

Marnie shook her head. "Are you serious, or did you just make that up?"

"It's the truth, Marnie."

"And that bit about adjusting the engine by satellite? What about that?"

"It's all true, really. Here." He opened the door and reached across to the glovebox, pulling out the driver's manual. "You can borrow this if you want … bedtime reading. You'll enjoy it. You always did like fancy cars."

Marnie took the book and glanced down at the three-pointed star emblem on the cover. "Great, though I expect it'll turn me green. Can I try the driving position?"

"Sure. Help yourself."

Marnie slipped into the driver's seat and pulled the door shut, letting the cockpit wrap itself around her. The interior had cream upholstery and shiny walnut trim; it smelled of new leather. The instrument panel had been borrowed from Concorde. A cradle stood ready for the mobile. It was an executive express with all the trimmings. Her gaze fell on a notepad attached to the fascia beside the wheel. A few words were written on it and, without thinking, she read them. Haiku.

> *That face in repose*
> *Serene beyond all measure*
> *A haunting beauty*

The door opened, taking her by surprise. There must have been something in her expression; Simon glanced down at the pad. Marnie slid out from behind the wheel.

"Lovely car," she said.

. . . . .

The Volvo ended its stately progress down the dual carriageway and prepared to take the turning to Knightly St John. As Ralph changed down for the corner, a silver Mercedes reached the junction approaching from the village. The driver quickly assessed the traffic situation and pulled decisively out ahead of him, accelerating rapidly away.

. . . . .

"Hi, Ralph! It's great to have you back." Anne beamed at him as he came through the office door.

"That," said Ralph, "is what I call a welcome."

"You deserve it. I've missed you." She looked across to where the large black cat was sitting single-mindedly beside the fridge. "So has Dolly."

"Er … am I missing something here? Has some disaster happened while I've been out?"

"Of course not. Simon's been here… not that he's a disaster … well, not really."

Ralph smiled. "I thought you liked him. You said, as I recall, that he was … what was the term … *dishy?*"

"He's not like you."

"Thank you for that."

"I mean … he's not *special* like you"

"Stop there, while I'm ahead. Where's Marnie?"

"She's gone to make lunch. She rang Beth and then announced she was going to do something exceptional. She raided the freezer and put a bottle of wine in to chill."

. . . . .

The spinney echoed to the sound of Vivaldi, appropriately the *Primavera* movement of the Four Seasons. Marnie had all the windows open on *Sally Ann*, and Ralph could hear the sound of pans clanking in the galley.

He went down into the cabin, and Marnie caught sight of him. She put down the grill pan and hugged him tightly, finishing off with a kiss that registered six-point-nine on the Richter scale. Ralph blinked in astonishment.

"Good afternoon, madam," he said. "I've come to read the gas meter."

. . . . .

Lunch started with grilled tiger prawns in a coulis of red pepper and cayenne, followed by an asparagus and lemon risotto that looked bland but tasted superb. The wine was Sancerre, the dessert fresh pineapple. An unspoken question hung over the table throughout the meal.

"I expect you're both wondering what's come over me ... producing something like this for a Tuesday lunch. Anyone care to guess?" There were no takers. "Well, I've decided what needs to be done with Anthony."

"Does it involve a phone call to Sicily?" said Ralph.

Anne sniggered. "We've got bags of cement in the yard." She caught Marnie's expression. "Sorry."

Marnie smiled to reassure them. "Simon put an idea into my head, so I explained it to Beth on the phone."

"She thought it was a good idea?" said Ralph.

"No. She said she thought it was rather crazy ... well, actually ... *completely* crazy ... so I knew it had to be all right."

"So what is this good-if-rather-completely-crazy idea?" said Ralph.

"Well, it's obvious that Anthony can't stay here any longer and he has to go." Anne and Ralph nodded. "The question is ... where to?"

"Seems reasonable so far," said Ralph.

At that moment the mobile rang. It was Dr Greenman from Nottingham.

Ralph took the call outside, walking up and down on the bank for some minutes. While he was away, Marnie and Anne cleared the table and washed the dishes. Marnie outlined her idea to Anne.

Ralph was still talking to Dr Greenman when he walked over to *Sally Ann* and tapped on the galley window, pointing down the canal. Marnie came up onto the stern deck to see *Totteridge* and *Shardlow* approaching in line astern.

• • • • •

The council of war was held in the saloon on *Sally Ann*. The participants were the home crew of Marnie, Ralph and Anne, plus Anthony, Andrew and Kate, all bunched together in the cramped space.

Marnie began. "Sorry there's not much room, but I wanted us to have privacy. The fact is – and we all know this – the present situation can't go on any longer. I want to suggest a way out. It's quite simple – even rather obvious – but we've got to do it now." While she was speaking, she picked up her mobile phone and switched it off.

"My idea depends on the goodwill of more than just myself and my immediate friends. I have a favour to ask of you, Andrew and Kate ... a big favour."

Andrew's eyes flickered towards Kate and then back to Marnie. "How long would it be for?" he said.

Marnie shrugged. "That's hard to say just now. A few weeks, maybe."

Anthony looked confused. "How long would *what* be, exactly?" he said, sitting upright in the chair.

It was Andrew who replied. "Does it matter where we take him?"

"Just your normal itinerary," said Marnie.

"Take him?" said Anthony. "You mean *me*?"

"What do you think, love?" Andrew said to Kate.

"Up to you," she replied quietly. "I'll go along with whatever you want."

"Hang on," Anthony said, agitated. "You're talking about me here. What about *my* opinion?"

"I think," said Marnie, "we've got beyond that point now. It's more than just about *you*. You've found it hard to make up *your* mind. Now it's *our* turn."

Anthony sat back in the chair. "So what are you saying?"

"Let me spell it out for you," Marnie began. "The plan is to get you out of the way ... to where your privacy will be safeguarded. My idea is that you travel with Andrew and Kate for a while. It'll get you out of our way, which is a selfish motive I know. But sooner or later the police will come back, and we can't guarantee they won't find you. They've been once; they'll come again. The press could do the same."

"So ... I've got to go into hiding and be confined in that cabin for several weeks. Is that your plan ... a sort of floating prison?"

"Not at all."

"No?" said Andrew.

"No. Anthony will become a member of your crew. He'll work with you, doing the things you normally do. In return, you'll provide him with a place to stay. He can contribute towards food and so on. I'll leave the details for you to work out ... if you can agree to the plan, that is. Remember, it is only an idea. If you don't want to do it, Andrew, then that's fair enough."

"Wait a minute," said Anthony. "If I'm working on a boat delivering coal and so on, people will see me. I'll be recognised."

"I don't think so," Ralph joined in. "Marnie's got a point. People will see you, yes. Or rather, they'll see a man working on a boat. They won't be expecting to see Anthony Leyton-Brown MP."

"Whether they're expecting it or not, they'll see me, and chances are, someone will recognise me sooner or later. It's inevitable."

"Not with a beard, they won't," said Marnie. "Not when you're wearing scruffy jeans and an old jumper."

"*Beard*? I've never had a beard in my life and I don't – "

"You've got one now," Kate pointed out. "Almost." Anthony ran a hand over his face, where three days' growth was already stubbling his jawline.

They digested the plan in silence. Anne pulled one of the newspapers towards her and studied the face in the photos, comparing it with the man sitting opposite her.

"You think this could work?" said Anthony. He was more subdued than before.

"Got any better ideas?" said Marnie.

"Actually," Ralph began. "I was going to make a suggestion ... in some ways similar. I was going to offer my cottage in Murton, near Oxford, as a refuge. It's quite secluded."

"That sounds like a good idea," said Anthony.

Ralph shook his head. "Marnie's plan is better. As soon as the press realise I'm in the frame, someone might use their initiative and track you down. These people are tenacious and desperate to get their teeth into you. Don't underestimate them."

"What happens to my boat?" said Anthony.

Marnie nodded. "I'll check with Queen Eleanor. But I don't think that'll be a problem ... at least not while their boats are out on hire over the summer. We'll worry about that later."

"I don't quite know what to say." Anthony sounded as if he meant it.

Marnie said, "Don't think about it. It isn't your call."

• • • • •

While Ralph drove to Queen Eleanor boatyard to collect some of Anthony's belongings, the crew of *Totteridge* and *Shardlow* took it in turns to use the shower in the office barn.

Marnie and Anne tried to get back to work, but concentration was difficult with so much else to plan. Eventually they gave up in the office and turned on the answerphone. Marnie filled the water tanks on both boats from the tap in *Sally Ann*'s docking area. Anne helped Kate to clear out the cabin on *Totteridge* to make room for Anthony.

Leaving Kate to finish off, Anne walked over to Marnie, "I think he's really lucky to have you planning this for him."

"He's more lucky that Andrew's willing to go along with the idea. There's no reason why he should, after all. It's quite an imposition."

"I suppose so. Marnie, I've had a thought … about Anthony's appearance."

• • • • •

That evening, the docking area of Glebe Farm looked like a wharf from times past. Ralph and Andrew had made several trips through the spinney, carrying Anthony's belongings from the Volvo. He stowed them in the boatman's cabin on *Totteridge*. The supplies included two cases of wine. Meanwhile, Marnie prepared a supper of hot soup and a buffet of cold meats and cheeses that they ate sitting at tables on the bank. There was an almost festive air, and the backdrop of boats, canal and trees, with candles in glass jars, brought a theatrical atmosphere to the scene.

Anthony donated two bottles of Burgundy to the meal. It was like a celebration on the eve of a pleasant voyage. For the first time in weeks, Anthony was out in the open, visible to anyone who passed by on the canal. Shortly before eating, he had changed into a collarless denim shirt and dark blue jeans and disappeared with Marnie to the office barn. He emerged twenty minutes later as a new man, his hair very short, a number one crop all over. Towelling it dry, Anthony appeared before them as almost a skinhead. Kate completed the effect by tying a red neckerchief round his throat. A total transformation.

During the meal, they laid their plans. Marnie insisted that Anthony leave his mobile behind, and she removed the sim-card to prevent it being traced to Knightly St John. He would now be known simply as *Tony*, with no surname and no explanations. None would be expected on the waterways.

Gradually, the group became more relaxed and Anthony – *Tony* – settled comfortably into his new persona. To the few boats that passed that evening, they looked like a group of old friends. The surprise of the evening was Kate. Ralph brought her into the conversation out of politeness, asking about her interests. She muttered about helping Andrew, but he replied, with a degree of pride in his voice, that she was an artist, a graduate of the Royal College of Art no less, and a specialist in portrait painting.

"She's too modest to admit it, but I reckon she's a genius," he declared.

• • • • •

As night came down, the docking area at the edge of the spinney had returned to normal. Looking out from the stern doors on *Thyrsis*, Marnie wondered whether normality had featured on the Glebe Farm agenda since her arrival. But for now at least they looked set for a period of relative calm.

*Sally Ann* lay snug in her dock, and the working pair had vacated the bank beyond. It had been Marnie's idea that they should set off after supper and aim to tie up for the night below the lock at Cosgrove, close to the Iron Trunk Aqueduct over the River Ouse.

When Ralph came out of the shower room, he smiled at Marnie.

"I know," she said. "I always do this ... look out at the canal when I've got something to think about. You don't have to remind me."

"I wasn't going to. I was just thinking how gorgeous you looked standing there framed in the doorway." He came to stand beside her, slipped an arm round her waist and kissed her gently. "It's good to have the place to ourselves again."

Marnie wondered if he was referring to the absence of Anthony or Simon. "Yes ... for a while at least."

"Is that why you suggested that Andrew and co went off tonight?"

"Not actually, no," she replied. "I figured they could get through Cosgrove ready for an early start tomorrow. It takes hours to get round Milton Keynes ... an easy beginning to their life afloat."

"And a chance for Anthony's beard to grow a bit more," Ralph added.

"It all helps," said Marnie.

Ralph moved closer and touched her forehead with his lips. "Would I be right in thinking there's more to your master plan than we've yet been told?" he said softly.

"Whatever gave you that idea?"

# Part 14

It was breakfast time on *Sally Ann*, and rain was pounding steadily on the steel roof. Anne removed mud-spattered trainers by the stern doors after a quick trot through the spinney. Padding through to the galley, she was met by the smell of toast and coffee. She stared at Marnie in surprise.

"You're here."

"Why shouldn't I be?" said Marnie. "Here is where I do breakfast."

"But ... that's odd ... it must've been Ralph. But then where would he be going? It's too wet for his walk."

"Explain, O Mysterious One."

"I thought I caught sight of you in the spinney just now. I thought perhaps you were going to the office after looking in on Ralph. I didn't stop 'cos of the rain."

Marnie picked up the mobile and pressed buttons. "Ralph, hi. Where are you at the moment?"

"In the saloon, putting my shoes on. Why?"

"So you weren't outside just now?"

"No. Is anything the matter?"

"Anne thought she saw someone in the spinney."

"Really?"

"I was just thinking ... after what happened to Frank ..."

"I'll check."

Through the galley windows Marnie and Anne looked out on both sides of *Sally Ann*. The downpour was falling vertically like a silver curtain, making it difficult to see through the trees. Water was dripping from the branches, and raindrops were splattering among the tussocks of grass in open ground. They scanned the spinney. Ralph appeared from *Thyrsis*, criss-crossing between the tree-trunks. Anne giggled at the sight of him, an improbable sleuth carrying his umbrella. Eventually he came on board.

"Nothing?" said Marnie.

"Not that I could see. And I looked carefully at the ground for footprints. Everywhere's just mud."

Marnie turned to Anne. "How sure are you that you saw somebody?"

"Well ... obviously ... I thought I did at the time."

"Clothes?"

Anne shrugged. "Dark things ... in amongst the trees. You're thinking it was a trick of the light and the rain?"

"Possibly."

"I suppose ..."

They sat pondering over breakfast, half listening to *Today* on Radio 4. Even Ralph, an avid consumer of news programmes, was thinking of other things. When the sports report came on, Marnie got up to make more toast.

"Do you think it might've been a reporter?" she said.

"Why should it be?" said Ralph. "They surely couldn't connect us with Anthony ... unless they've been asking questions all along the canal, of course. Seems unlikely. We're a long way from London."

"The local police were asking about him," said Anne.

Marnie leaned against the galley workbench. "Mmm ... what are the alternatives?"

"What about ..." Ralph began. His eyes flickered towards Anne, and he stopped.

"The mugger?" said Marnie. "I wonder ..."

• • • • •

During working hours they were normally independent, but that miserable day with rain still falling intermittently from a leaden sky, Marnie rang Ralph and asked if he wanted to join them at break time, while Anne boiled the kettle and sorted mugs.

Bringing the tray to her desk, she said, "So what did Ralph say about Dr Greenman?"

"Dr Greenman?" said Marnie vaguely.

"You know, you were going to talk about Tricia last night. Remember?"

Marnie had vivid memories of the night before when she and Ralph retired to *Thyrsis*, but Dr Greenman and Tricia did not feature in them. "I forgot. We chatted about other things in the end."

Ralph came into the office backwards, flapping his umbrella. "What a morning! Still at least it'll be an advantage for Anthony. He'll be out of sight all day."

Anne handed a mug to Ralph. "I was asking Marnie about your phone call with Dr Greenman. She said she forgot to ask you about it last night. You had other things to ... er, chat about, she said."

"That's right," said Ralph. "We got rather engrossed in the economic recession in the Far East, I seem to recall."

"Right." Anne's expression remained inscrutable. "So how was it for you? ... the call with Dr Greenman, I mean."

Ralph twinkled the briefest of smiles at Anne. "He said Tricia's a very confused lady ... good days ... not-so-good days. Sometimes she actually believes we got married."

Marnie took her mug from Anne. "Is it some form of schizophrenia?"

"Greenman said it was one of the main types of personality disorder. She probably never quite recovered from her breakdown at university. I think her relationship with me was a disaster for the rest of her life."

"Did he say that?"

"Not in those terms, exactly."

"Ralph, you're not going to go blaming yourself for everything, are you? I don't think that would do anyone any good. It certainly won't help Tricia. I doubt anything could."

"No. I did offer to go and see her ... try to help her to get things straight."

"What did he say? Don't tell me, I can guess."

"He said it could possibly make things worse ... seeing me would be like opening up an old wound."

• • • • •

Andrew was running *Totteridge* and *Shardlow* in line astern that morning, with Kate at the tiller on the butty and Anthony out of sight in the cabin as they chugged for hours round the northern and eastern edges of Milton

Keynes through a landscape that varied continuously between urban and rural.

It was late in the morning when a shout from a solitary boat tied up at the bank signalled a customer. Andrew brought Totteridge over to the moored craft, and Shardlow slipped gently alongside.

The customer asked for a fill-up of diesel and a few bags of coal, wanting to cheer up the cabin on a dismal morning. It surprised Andrew when Anthony suddenly appeared from the cabin, wearing a cagoule with hood up, to heave the coal into the customer's cratch well. Without a word, he began filling the tank with fuel, while the rain got in under his hood and ran down his sprouting beard.

"Didn't know you had staff, Andrew," said the customer.

"That's Tony. He's a mate ... helping out for a bit."

"Right."

The customer paid no more attention to the newcomer and settled the bill with Andrew, waving thanks to Tony as Totteridge moved off into the mist and drizzle. The water under the stern boiled as the two seventy-footers pulled away. A movement in the cabin caught Andrew's attention, and he glanced down. Looking up from below, Anthony raised a tentative thumb. Andrew nodded.

• • • • •

The rain was easing off when Ralph took Anne for her driving lesson leaving Marnie alone in the office, working on the scheme for a Willards canalside pub. She was trying to get away from the traditional mixture of dark Victorian colours and old framed photographs, introducing murals to give a more exciting style. She badly needed an uninterrupted hour or two to work out the design. When the phone rang she wished Anne had been there to take the call.

"Marnie Walker, good morning."

"Marnie, it's Frank." He sounded agitated. "Look, the police've been here asking about the mugging."

"Are they making any progress?"

"I don't think so. They've got this strange idea that you know something about it."

"*Me*? Frank, let me assure you I don't know any more than you do ... well, obviously less, in fact. I'm sorry if you're concerned about that."

"I'm not ... really I'm not. The thing is, I didn't seem able to persuade them that you couldn't have known more than you said."

"I'm not sure I follow."

"They don't believe you, Marnie. When they were talking to me they got a call from the station. I'm sure it was about the man you were supposed to be visiting in hospital the other day. I didn't get all the details, but the inspector said something about him not existing."

"Of course he exists! We brought him in to casualty. Was it Inspector Bartlett, by any chance?"

"That was the one, yes. Like I said, Marnie, I didn't hear all the conversation, but I think they might be coming to see you. I wanted to let you know."

"Coming to see me *now*?"

"I think so."

"Great. Okay thanks, Frank. But don't be in any doubt, they're making a mistake."

●　●　●　●　●

Who were you visiting that day in hospital, Mrs Walker? What was his name? Why had you brought him in? Why were you involved? How long had you known him? Why was he at your mooring, on your property? What aren't you telling us, Mrs Walker? Do we have to beat it out of you?

Marnie hung suspended from chains in flickering torchlight in a dungeon deep in the bowels of police headquarters. In the shadows of the dungeon, torturers were lurking menacingly, clutching sharp instruments as Bartlett leaned towards her. She could feel his hot breath on her cheek, as a trickle of sweat rolled down her face into her eyes. She shook her head to clear it, and her desk came back into focus. The vision passed and she was sitting in the office barn, waiting for the police car to drive into the yard. Her mind settled on the questions, and gradually things became clear. She had to stick to her story, keep it simple, be consistent.

Why did Bartlett think Simon Alexander did not exist? It was true that he did not exist, but how did Bartlett know that? What had he found out? Not for the first time she asked herself why she had got involved with Anthony Leyton-Brown, but she knew it was too late now to change tack. They had to hold on and give Anthony a chance to defend himself.

●　●　●　●　●

Marnie did not have long to wait before the familiar grey Cavalier arrived. Bartlett was out of the car before it stopped, striding across the yard while Marriner was still opening the driver's door. The DCI swept into the office, and Marnie stood up.

"Good morning, Mrs Walker," said Bartlett briskly. "You look surprised to see us."

"Always a pleasure, though," she said.

Marriner followed his boss and closed the door behind them, nodding at Marnie. "We're in our usual parking space."

"And I usually offer you coffee and you refuse, but I'm making one for myself. Will you join me?"

To her dismay, they accepted. With coffee and a plate of biscuits giving the meeting a cosy atmosphere that Marnie felt it did not merit, she braced herself for the questions about the man she and Simon had been visiting in hospital.

Bartlett dunked a biscuit, ate it and looked up. "You recently visited the place where Mr Day was attacked. Why was that, Mrs Walker?"

Marnie was taken off-guard. "The place where …?"

"You were seen walking down from the lay-by and searching around where he was robbed. You do remember that, don't you?"

"Of course." Bells were clanging in her head. They would ask what was her husband's name, so as to check his version of the story. It would take only the simplest of enquiries to find out he was not just Simon Walker, but

Simon Alexander Walker, and she would be in trouble with the police again. Damn! she thought.

"Did my question surprise you?"

"I just didn't realise anyone else was there," Marnie said feebly.

"One of my officers in an unmarked car saw you walking down the field. You went off in a blue Volvo. That would be Professor Lombard's car, would it?"

"Yes," said Marnie.

"So I come back to my question: why were you visiting the scene of the attack on Mr Day?"

"We were curious, that's all," said Marnie. "Frank's a friend … I was going past … it was an impulse. We didn't touch anything. Anyway, there wasn't anything to see."

"Just curiosity, then," said Bartlett. "Very well. And was it curiosity that brought you to the hospital on the day of the attack?"

"No, of course not. I told you, we were there with a boater who'd had an accident."

"Ah yes, the disappearing boater … and the disappearing boat. Very appropriate. How well did you know him. Mrs Walker?"

"I thought I'd told you that already; I didn't know him."

"Yet you'd rushed him into hospital and were concerned enough to ring up about his condition and check on his needs."

"Naturally. Anyone would do as much. And boat people in particular never pass another boat or boater in trouble. It's a sort of unwritten code of conduct."

"Would it surprise you to learn that he doesn't exist?" said Bartlett.

Marnie was ready for this. She raised an eyebrow. "If he doesn't exist, then how did he manage to discharge himself from hospital?" She was tempted to ask if he walked out through the wall, but restrained herself.

"There's no record of any Simon Alexander owning a boat," said Bartlett. "We checked registrations with British Waterways."

It was the glance from Bartlett to Marriner that alerted her.

"There is something I want to say," she said. "Simon Alexander are the first names of my former husband. I think he may have given them to the man we took in to casualty just so the medics would have a way of referring to him."

Bartlett nodded slowly. "Just … for convenience."

"I suppose so. The man was unconscious, after all."

Bartlett drained his cup and stood up. Marriner followed him to the door.

"We knew about your ex-husband, Mrs Walker … his names. Can you tell us where we can find him?"

Marnie looked blank. It occurred to her for the first time that she had no idea where Simon lived. "Inspector, you're not going to believe this …"

"Amaze me, Mrs Walker."

● ● ● ● ●

The grey Cavalier groped its way over slippery grass and muddy ground up the field track, Sergeant Marriner steering carefully past the bumps, trying not to make his boss's mood even worse.

"Here we go again," Bartlett said irritably.

Marriner grunted, not sure whether the object of wrath was Marnie Walker's testimony or his driving.

"That bloody Marnie Walker!" Bartlett exclaimed. "Why's she always trying to hide something from us?"

"You think she is?" said Marriner.

"Don't you, Ted?"

Marriner gave exaggerated concentration to his driving. "She does seem to be holding something back."

"Too bloody right! She knows something about the bloke who took the overdose. I bet she knows who he is. Did you show the staff in casualty the photo of Leyton-Brown?"

"Yes. They didn't recognise him."

"Probably too rushed off their feet, poor sods. Simon Alexander ... huh!"

They reached the top of the track, and Marriner turned onto the road. "At least she came clean about the name."

"Don't make me laugh, Ted. She only admitted that because she guessed we knew about him. I don't know how she guessed, but she did. I could practically hear her brain working. What do they know? she was thinking. What should I say? She's too clever by half, that one. It nearly got her killed last year. You'd think she'd have learnt a lesson from that experience."

"You don't think she's just trying to protect another boater from having to face questions from the police?" Marriner ventured.

"The so-called unwritten code of conduct?" Bartlett hunched into his jacket as another shower began hitting the window. "D'you know what I think, Ted? I think you fancy Marnie Walker, and it's warped your judgment."

"I'm only trying to be objective, sir."

"Then why d'you reckon she went to see the place where Frank Day was attacked? What's your objective view on that?"

"I think you're right about her not knowing when to keep her nose out of things. She should've learnt that from last year at least."

"So just morbid curiosity?" said Bartlett.

"I suppose so. What else could it be? You don't think she's in any way connected with the mugging. She'd hardly protect someone who'd attacked a friend of hers, would she?"

"I think my judgment's getting warped as well," Bartlett muttered gloomily.

"How come?" said Marriner. "Don't tell me you fancy Marnie Walker!" He almost added as well, but stopped just in time.

"Very funny, Ted. No, she gets under my skin so much that it puts me off my stroke. I should've pressed her harder about why she went to the scene of the crime and what she saw there."

"You think she might have ideas about that?"

"Dunno. But she worked out who killed the vicar last year ... You never know with that one."

• • • • •

110

When Ralph returned, Marnie filled him in on the police visit.

"It's happening again," she said. "I'm getting myself into deep water with the police. It's just like last year. I told myself to give them all the information I could and now I'm making the same mistakes over again. It's no wonder they don't trust me."

"Do you think you ought to tell them about Anthony?" said Ralph. "About him being here ... what really happened?"

"I don't know what's best. All I'm trying to do is give Anthony a chance to clear things up."

"Well, you promised to get Simon to contact them when he's next around. You can agree your line with him when he comes."

Marnie frowned. "Why should I wait for Simon?"

"I thought you might want to talk things over together."

Marnie said slowly, "Ralph, why do you keep talking about Simon?"

"I suppose ... I thought you were following a course of action that you'd agreed together. Didn't you talk things over with him yesterday morning?"

"No. Whatever gave you that idea?"

"I had the notion it was something he said that made you act in that way."

"Simon? No. He just said he thought I had to get Anthony away from here ... which was fairly obvious. And it only buys a little more time."

"It certainly achieves the object of the exercise," said Ralph.

"Not really. It's only a short-term expedient. I'm hoping it'll kick-start Anthony into deciding on his future and doing something about it. Actually, Ralph, there is something that's been going through my mind. For some reason, I feel hesitant about telling you."

"Why's that?"

"I'm not sure. To someone like you, someone with your straight way of looking at things, it would probably seem a bit crazy."

"Have you thought of talking it over — "

"Ralph," Marnie said quickly. "I'm talking it over with you."

"Okay."

Marnie took a long breath. "It's just ... well, do you remember I told you Simon said he felt so angry about what the papers had done ... you know, especially on account of Melissa ... that he wanted to rub the editor's nose in the dirt?"

"Yes, I remember. And how would he do that, exactly?"

"By giving him some of his own medicine?" Marnie suggested.

"But how could Simon do that?"

"Oh, he wouldn't," said Marnie.

"But I thought this was a plan you'd concocted together."

"No. Simon just started me thinking along those lines. It's up to us now ... you and me."

• • • • •

For the rest of the morning Ralph found it almost impossible to concentrate on his work. For years he had managed a busy life of lecturing and research, writing and examining, interspersed with consultancy tours. He advised people at senior levels in governments and major institutions around the world. It was challenging and fulfilling. It brought him occasional large sums of money and an international reputation in his field.

But since meeting Marnie, he had seen another side of life. Here was someone who handled matters that were out of his normal range, someone who had no fear of unorthodox approaches to problems. She took risks, even risking her life at times. It was not unusual for her to do the opposite to what anyone might expect. In fact, on reflection, it was her normal response. You want to conceal a boat ... send it off up the canal where anyone might see it; you want to hide a man ... thrust him out into a conspicuous job where he will meet people every day; you find yourself hunted by one of the most powerful newspaper editors in the country ... He shuddered mentally.

He heard a tap on the window and saw Anne's face in the porthole.

"Ready for a sandwich?" she called.

They strolled together to *Sally Ann*. Ralph only now noticed that the rain had stopped. Anne seemed to have brought her sparkle into his life again. Breaks were appearing in the clouds, and patches of blue were showing. A wave of sunlight flowed over the canal and into the fields beyond. It was going to be one of those days when the country was scrubbed clean, and all around would smell of new growth ... fresh blossom ... Anne's optimism.

Ralph smiled at her. "So how did the driving lesson go?"

"Great! My clutch pedal technique's coming on a treat. I managed to make a *very* interesting noise with the gearbox before I got used to pressing the pedal right down. Hey, the sun's come out ... it's going to be a lovely day. Perfect."

• • • • •

"You can *not* be *serious!*"

"Beth – for goodness' sake! Why must you always sound like John McEnroe when you get all ... *aerated* like that?"

"Marnie, have you gone out of your miniscule mind? I really mean it. What you're planning to do is crazy. Have you talked this over with Ralph?"

"Sort of."

"Meaning?"

"I've ... sort of ... broached the subject."

"But you've not gone into detail?"

"No. I've told Anne, though."

"And her reaction was the same as mine, I bet. She's sensible, that girl. What did she think of your plan?"

Marnie sighed. "Modified rapture, on the whole. She didn't actually say much ... her mouth was hanging open. She's got over it now ... I think."

"Marnie, you're rambling. When are you going to tell Ralph? You are going to tell him, aren't you? You're not just going to let him read about it in the papers one morning, wondering why he hasn't seen you around the place for a day or two?"

"I thought I'd tell him at supper time."

"What about Simon? Is he still around?"

"No ... only from time to time. He thinks it'd be a good idea to rub the editor's nose in the dirt. His words, not mine."

"I guessed. You'd be more graphic. Was this partly his plan?"

"No. It's all my idea ... and it's not properly formed yet. I'm still working out the details."

"Really? I see Simon's hand in this. I can just imagine him swanning in and out, putting crazy ideas into your head. You know he was never heavily into sound judgment."

"I told you it wasn't his idea, Beth. Anyway, Simon's changed a lot. He's into other things these days."

"Like what?"

Marnie hesitated. "Like ... well ... poetry."

"*Poetry? Simon?*"

"Sure. He writes ... haiku ... that's a kind of short Japanese poem."

"I had no idea he spoke Japanese."

"Beth, he ... oh, never mind. Anyway, that's what he does. There's no harm in it."

"No ... not unless he's writing them to you, there isn't."

• • • • •

When Marnie finished talking, there was silence. Ralph sat at the lunch table contemplating a few crumbs of bread remaining on his plate, chewing his lower lip. It was a habit he had developed since meeting Marnie. Anne pushed her plate to one side so that she could scribble a few notes.

"Right," said Ralph eventually. "Presumably this follows on from what Simon said about wanting to rub Hawksby's nose in it?"

"No," said Marnie. "Everyone seems to think this all came from Simon. I can't understand it."

"Maybe because it seems so ... improbable," Ralph suggested.

"Well, whatever it may be, it's *my* idea ... though I suppose what he said might've lodged in the back of my mind. It struck a sympathetic chord, I expect."

"Mm ..." Ralph was chewing his lip again.

Marnie said, "Tell me it's crazy and I must be mad."

"Marnie, it's crazy and – "

"I didn't mean that literally!"

"Well, it does seem rather ... Run it past us again."

"It's simple ... at least the idea is. First we find the girl who had Hawksby's baby when he was in the sixth form, to make sure of our facts. Then we write and tell him we know all about it and won't hesitate to make the information public if he persists in hounding Anthony in his paper. We'll confront him head-on."

Ralph was shaking his head, another habit he had acquired since knowing Marnie. "You're talking about trying to blackmail the editor of a national newspaper."

"Of course I'm not."

"Marnie, that's how he'll see it and, more to the point, it's what his lawyers will be telling the judge – when he gets an injunction slapped on you – or the police before they cart you off to the nick."

"Oh Ralph, don't exaggerate. It won't come to that ... will it?"

"And there's another small consideration," said Ralph. "The girl, even if you can find her, won't want to be thrust into the limelight. Nor will her child, who's grown-up by now."

"There's no reason for her to be thrust into the limelight. Hawksby won't let it get that far. He wouldn't dare call our bluff. We'd only need to contact her to make sure we were on firm ground."

"Even so ..."

Marnie shrugged. "Then we'll find some other way of checking the facts. You can probably come up with the details if you think hard enough about it. If *you're* convinced it's the truth, Ralph, it *must* be okay. I can't think of anyone more reliable than you."

"Then maybe you should try listening to what I'm saying. Didn't it occur to you that Hawksby could go to the police and accuse you of trying to blackmail him?"

"Hardly. I'd not be demanding anything but an end to his hypocrisy. I've already worked out how to do it ... I'd write a letter to the editors of all the national dailies."

"Marnie, are you ready to face the consequences of what you're proposing? Do you really want all the media attention? This isn't a simple matter of kiss and tell. You'd be playing with fire."

Marnie grimaced. "So we just sit back and do nothing? Anthony's wife can commit suicide, he can try to kill himself and fail – at least at the *first* attempt – and we can do nothing about it. That's it? We give up? End of story?"

"Do I tear up my list?" said Anne.

Ralph looked out of the window. When he spoke, his voice came from far away. "Not necessarily. There might be other ways of looking at it."

• • • • •

"Hi Marnie, it's me."

"Hi Beth." Her voice was as flat as a polder.

"So you've told him. What did he think? Or do you need to tell me?"

"He thought it was probably the worst idea since the invention of athlete's foot. But he let me down gently ... said he'd think it over. Save your breath. I'm feeling deflated enough."

"Oh, Marnie ... I just wanted to say I was sorry. I think I may have over-reacted."

"No kidding," said Marnie. She paused. When there was no reaction, she said, "No, you were probably right. Ralph agreed with you about this one."

"You mustn't go blaming him. He only has your interests at heart."

"I know. But it'll amount to the same thing in the end."

• • • • •

Ralph had suggested they talk before supper so that the meal would not go as unnoticed as lunch. The three of them sat in the study on *Thyrsis*, each holding a white wine spritzer. While Ralph spoke, Marnie and Anne listened in silence.

When he finished, Marnie said, "I don't get it. What you're saying is, you basically agree with me? Have I got that right?"

"I'd say I'm sympathetic in principle to what you want to achieve, yes. But I think your tactics are too risky. Too much of the risk would fall on you. I want to avoid that at all costs. Knowing you as I do, I suspect you'll go ahead anyway. I'm looking at damage limitation."

"So you don't object to our trying to establish what happened to the girl who had the baby – if she did – and you're convinced she did – as long as we don't try to force her into anything against her will. Right?"

"I think that has to be the bottom line. If she can't face it, then the whole thing would have to be dropped. There's a limit to how many people have to suffer to help Anthony sort himself out."

"Right," said Marnie. "I agree."

"Good," said Ralph. "And what do you think of the rest of my views?"

"What you're basically saying is that we follow my plan but with different people taking the action."

"Yes. It's no good you going after Hawksby. That could rebound on you, which would be very unfortunate. I know how you feel about Anthony's wife, and I understand that's your reason for wanting to do something, but Anthony has to take that responsibility on himself."

"Always assuming he'll do it," said Marnie.

"That's the other half of my bottom line. If Anthony won't play his part, the whole thing is off."

"Do you think he will?"

"Frankly, I don't know. In it's favour is that it at least offers him some form of action, and I doubt if he'll think of anything better. He might just think he's got nothing to lose."

"He can hardly sink any further than he has already," said Marnie.

"Well, that's up to him. These are desperate measures to meet a desperate situation, as you might say. We're dealing with the Rottweiler British press, one of the fiercest in the world."

Anne laughed. Marnie and Ralph stared at her.

"Sorry," she said. "I know it's very serious and all that, and the whole thing scares me to death, but I just thought of something I read about the press for our current affairs module at school. It said, 'Dog bites man ... no news. Man bites dog ... that's news.'"

Ralph smiled. "That's right. It's an old saying in journalism."

"What about 'Man bites Rottweiler'?" said Anne. "That would be news, wouldn't it?"

# Part 15

The next day, Thursday morning, Marnie interrupted her concentration to take a policy decision: her hair needed a trim. She made a call to Joanne at the salon in London for an appointment the following week. She had hardly replaced the receiver when the phone rang.

"Marnie, it's Stevie from Queen Eleanor boatyard. Are you selling the boat you left here? You didn't say anything about that when you brought it." Her tone was bordering on a reproach.

"*Selling* it? No. It isn't mine to sell. I'm just – "

"Look, is there any chance you could call in?"

Marnie paused. "Is everything all right, Stevie?"

"I'll be in all morning if you can make it."

Bewildered, Marnie said, "Okay. I'll come over now ... give the MG an outing."

"Come in by the delivery gates. Okay?"

How strange, Marnie thought. Could Stevie really be miffed that Marnie might be selling the boat without using her as agent? And what was that about coming in by the delivery gates? ... *the delivery gates* ... Less conspicuous, less public. She thought about cars ... the MG ... a 1930s sports car ... very rare these days, even in this area near the Silverstone racing circuit that attracted enthusiasts in unusual cars from all over the world to its events. She thought about Ralph's Volvo, ten years old. Stevie had joked about it in the past when she had seen it ... said it was ... *built like a truck ...*

"What was that about?" said Anne.

"Stevie wants me to go round."

"What for?"

"Didn't say. I expect the boat's in the way and she wants me to help move it. Must be short-handed this morning."

"You sounded surprised."

"It was just her tone. I think she's under stress. I'll just pop over and sort it out. Won't be long."

"Nice morning for a drive in the MG with the top down," Anne observed, looking towards the window.

Marnie stood up, grabbing her shoulder bag. "That reminds me, we haven't seen Ronny since he injured his hand on the MG that day. I hope his accident hasn't ruined a beautiful friendship."

Anne smiled. "Er ... well ... I do hear from him ... he gives me a ring some evenings when he's finished his homework. I think he's still keen to get the MG shining for you. He said he'd come down at the weekend."

"Okay, but you keep an eye on him. I don't want him hurting himself again."

"Sure. I'll tell him. Don't worry. He'd do anything for me."

"Really? Well, I hope you don't take him for granted." Marnie picked up the phone. "Ralph, it's me. Do you think I could borrow the Volvo for an hour or so?"

• • • • •

Marnie drove past the regular boatyard entrance, swung in through the tall black delivery gates and parked at the back of the workshops. She walked through to the office along a narrow corridor with no windows, that smelled of oil and machinery. At the far end she found Stevie leaning on the reception counter, checking documents. She looked uneasy.

"Marnie, I'm sorry to have to call you out like this, but something strange is going on."

"What's the problem?"

"Your boat. Someone's been here looking at it."

"When was this?"

"Yesterday. I spotted this bloke in the yard … asked him if he wanted something. He said was the boat for sale. You haven't advertised it anywhere have you, Marnie?"

"No."

"But could the owner have advertised it? The man said he understood it was on the market."

"Wrong boat. He probably just turned up on spec."

Stevie shook her head. "Not this one. I get enquirers all the time. I know when someone's genuine. This man wasn't serious about wanting to buy, but he wasn't just passing time, either."

"How can you be so sure?"

"There was something about him. He was really fixed on that boat. He took photos of the boat … the yard … I even thought he was going to take one of me, but then Gus turned up. That put the wind up him. One look at Gus — all tattoos and arms like tree-trunks — and he backed off."

"Have you seen him since?"

"Not sure. We're always getting people in and out of the office, and I can't be here the whole time. I did think I saw movement on the towpath side opposite the yard, but it could just've been kids, I suppose."

Stevie led Marnie out onto the wharf and pointed across the canal. The towpath was bordered by a hedge, with a field beyond. They stood thinking in silence beside the few Queen Eleanor boats that were not out on hire. The grey anonymous boat rested alongside them.

"Odd," Stevie said quietly.

"I'm sorry about this," said Marnie.

Stevie shook her head. "He didn't ask any of the questions people always ask when they're looking at a boat. That man was more interested in the owner, if you ask me."

• • • • •

Marnie parked the Volvo beside the barn and went straight to see Ralph on *Thyrsis*. She outlined her talk with Stevie.

"It's started," Ralph said. "I don't want to sound alarmist, but they're on to him. The question is … are they on to us?"

"You think they could be?"

"What else could it be? We know he was spotted on his way through London. It was only a matter of time before they worked their way up here."

"Are they so determined?"

"Newspapers are always under pressure to keep up their circulation.

They'll do everything they can to track him down and they seem to know what they're looking for. We can't just airbrush him out of the picture now."

Marnie stared at Ralph.

"What?" he said. "Marnie?"

• • • • •

A thick tattooed arm pushed open the door to Stevie's office. She was sitting at her desk going through VAT returns.

"What's up, Gus?"

"Your boyfriend might be back."

"My boyfr- ... oh, right. Where is he?"

"I think I just saw the slippery little sod on the bridge."

"Coming this way?"

"No. Going over."

"You're sure it was him?"

"Think so."

"Okay. Well if he comes back – "

"Don't worry, Stevie. I'll know what to do."

• • • • •

Marnie was thumbing through the address book section of her filofax in the saloon when Ralph went on board *Sally Ann* for lunch. "Anne, what's the name of that engineer up by Blisworth ... the one with the crane on the wharf? Something like Pillock."

Anne was at the workbench in the galley washing tomatoes. She laughed. "Sounds promising."

Marnie ploughed on through the P section. "It's here somewhere ... Got it! ... Pinkerton." She hit buttons on the phone.

Ralph picked up plates and set them out on the table while Marnie was talking.

"Are you sure about that?" she was saying. "You've got that quantity in stock? ... Right. And the guns? I'll need three ... Good. If you can put them aside, I'll call by this afternoon ... That's definite. See you later."

Marnie pressed more buttons and had to wait a while before getting a reply. Ralph raised an eyebrow at Anne, who shrugged.

"Hi Andrew. It's Marnie. How's it going? ... Right. Listen, tell Anthony someone's snooping around up here, could be a reporter ... Yes, around the boat ... I'm getting it sorted. Tell him to be vigilant. ... I'll keep in touch. Thanks for all you're doing. Bye now."

Anne put the cheeseboard on the table. "Did you say guns, Marnie?"

"No need to be so surprised. Desperate situations call for desperate measures." She smiled sweetly.

"You are going to share this with us, presumably?" said Ralph.

"Share it? Absolutely. We're all in this together up to our necks." It was not the last time she was going to say those words in the days to come.

"Why doesn't that bring me any comfort?" said Ralph.

They took their seats at the table. The picnic lunch looked inviting, but they ignored it.

Marnie took a sip of mineral water. "Are you sitting comfortably? Then I'll begin."

• • • • •

While they unloaded the materials from the boot of the Volvo, Ralph found himself thinking that his next car would be the estate version. It had been a busy day, and it would be an even busier night. They arrived at the Queen Eleanor boatyard by arrangement with Stevie as darkness was falling, and locked the gates behind them.

Marnie wanted to cross the canal bridge and check the bank on the opposite side. The village was deserted as they slipped over in silence and took the steps down onto the towpath. The three of them squatted at the foot of the hedge and shone torches through.

Anne pointed and whispered. "Look at that ... It's been disturbed. Someone's definitely been standing here."

Marnie tried parting the hedge, but it was too dense to pull open. She tried getting her head through a gap, but it was too tight and she had to resort to pushing her torch between the branches. She strained forward. "You're right ... but they weren't just standing."

"What do you mean?" Ralph said in her ear.

"Have a look. The ground's all churned up."

"More than one of them?" said Ralph.

"That's what I was wondering. There's been a lot of movement here."

Anne had walked further along the path. She knelt down, her face close to the ground, peering through. "Here as well. The footprints come as far as this."

Ralph was leaning over the hedge, hoping for a better view. "This wasn't caused by just one person," he said in a low voice, quieter than a whisper. "There's been a group here, I'm sure of it."

"Ow!" Marnie stood up, rubbing her cheek where twigs had scraped her face, her mind filled with images of newspaper photographers in a posse, blazing away at celebrities. "Paparazzi?"

"Could be."

"Surely not. Stevie would've seen them."

"Maybe not, if they were determined to stay hidden," said Ralph.

"I wonder where they are now," Anne muttered. "Maybe someone's watching us at this very minute."

"Come on," said Marnie. "We've got work to do."

Back in the boatyard they unloaded their supplies onto the grey boat in the dark without speaking. When everything was on board, Marnie pressed the starter button, and the noise from the engine was horrendous after their efforts at silent running.

She pointed the boat up-channel and settled down for a nocturnal journey, her eyes gradually adjusting to the darkness. In half an hour they reached their goal, turning off the main line to pull in at a secluded spot a fair distance from any habitation, between weeping willows either side of the docking area of Guy Pinkerton, boat engineer. As Marnie brought the anonymous craft in to the wharfside, she was thankful that it was a still night. No breeze ruffled the branches of the willows trailing in the water. It was perfect for what she had planned.

Marnie went below quickly to slip overalls on top of the dark clothes she had worn for the journey. The three of them unpacked their materials and equipment, attaching extension cables to a bank of power sockets to which Marnie found the key.

"I think that's everything," said Ralph.

Marnie nodded. "Good. Okay. Let's get on with it."

• • • • •

The dawn chorus began just before five. Marnie's eyelids had been replaced by strips of lead and her mouth had been re-programmed to the yawn function. The sky had turned from dark blue to grey to pink, and it was bright enough to make out the branches on the trees and reveal the buildings beside them. It was also bright enough to show the colour of Anthony's anonymous boat. No longer grey, it had been transformed by their efforts with paint and spray-guns. They had not done a bad job. The paint was drying quickly to give an all-over coating of red oxide. It now looked like any one of a hundred boats along the canal, waiting to be given its final topcoats of paint. Anyone looking for a grey boat would have to look elsewhere.

They cleaned up every trace of their presence that night. Not a splash of paint on the dockside revealed that they had been there. The newspapers and tape used to cover the widows were bundled into a rubbish sack and dropped into the bin. When they were satisfied that they had covered their tracks, they trooped below to flop down on bunks and couches for as much sleep as they could squeeze in before eight o'clock.

"Ronny's father knows where to find this place?" said Ralph, spreading himself out on a sofa.

Marnie stretched her limbs on a bunk and closed her eyes. "I gave him precise directions. He said he'd arrive at eight sharp."

"It's good of him to offer to do this," Ralph said.

"I know." Anne smiled and yawned at the same time, closing her eyes. "I told you … Ronny would do anything for me."

# Part 16

They crashed out as soon as Ronny's father dropped them off at Glebe Farm, Marnie and Ralph on *Thyrsis*, Anne in her loft. With the answerphone fielding calls, Marnie hoped for at least four hours sleep. They managed three before the mobile rang. To her surprise, it was Anne.

"Sorry, Marnie, but the phone's gone berserk. For the last half hour it's been ringing every few minutes."

Her mind fuzzy from sleep, Marnie propped herself up on one elbow and blinked. "Have you heard the messages?"

"I caught part of the last one. It was Stevie from the boatyard. You'll never guess what ..."

"Try me."

"She said something about the police being there."

"The *police*? Anything else?"

"She wants you to ring her as soon as you can."

Marnie swung her legs out of bed and ran a hand through her hair, her mind racing. "Are you dressed, Anne?"

"T-shirt and knickers."

"You'd better get some clothes on. First, switch everything on in the office, including the kettle. I'll be with you in a minute."

"Expecting visitors?"

"Guess who."

•  •  •  •  •

Marnie was towelling her hair while she jogged through the spinney. Ablutions had consisted of a splash of water on the face, followed by running wet hands over her head. A dab of foundation and a touch of eye pencil completed the picture in thirty seconds flat. Only the builder's van stood in the yard, as she raced into the office to find Anne pouring coffee into mugs. Satisfied that it looked and smelled like a working office, she grabbed the phone and rang Stevie.

"Where've you *been*, Marnie? I've been going *frantic*."

"Talk to me. What's up?"

"I've had the police here ... asking about anything strange going on ... any visitors ... anything at all out of the ordinary. Had I seen anyone hanging about? That sort of stuff."

"What did you tell them?"

"I didn't know what to say, but I thought I'd better mention the man who was here with the camera the other day."

"And?"

"They wanted to know all about him. What did he ask me, what did he want, what was he looking for?"

"Did you mention my name?"

A pause. "Oh, Marnie ..."

"How did it crop up?"

"They asked me for the names of every visitor to the yard on business or otherwise in the past few days. I didn't know what to tell them, but I thought it might look bad if they found out you'd been here and I hadn't said anything."

"Good thinking."

"As soon as I mentioned your name, the man was on the phone like a shot. In minutes another one came in – said he was a sergeant – ten minutes later their boss arrived by car from HQ."

"DCI Bartlett, by any chance?"

"Could be ... Anyway, he got me to tell him all over again ... exactly when and why you were here, what was your business with the yard, everything ..."

"What did you say?"

"That you'd brought a boat in and left it here for a day or two. That's all." Marnie groaned.

"Sorry, Marnie, but what could I do? They were talking to all the staff, and I couldn't warn them. And I didn't know what to warn them about, anyway."

"It's okay, Stevie. Really ... it's fine. I'm sorry to have put you in that position."

"Marnie, what *is* actually going on? I can't believe you're involved in something *dodgy*."

"Thank you."

"I mean it. But you haven't told me anything and ..."

"And you feel I've used you in a way that might cause you trouble."

"Well ... No. I don't mean it like that."

"I promise I'll explain one day and you'll understand. Listen, I'm not involved in anything illegal. Quite the opposite in a way." A tapping sound alerted Marnie, and she looked up. Anne was pointing towards the window. Outside, a car was drawing up in the yard. "Stevie, I've gotta go. They're here. Talk to you soon."

As Marnie put the phone down, she cursed. *Damn!* She had not asked Stevie what the police were investigating. No doubt she would soon find out.

"Anne, quick. Go up to your room and ring Ralph. Tell him the police are here. Prepare for a visit."

Marnie was alone in the office when Bartlett and Marriner came in. It was Marriner's grim expression that worried her most. Bartlett looked as severe as usual. She stood up, trying to compose her features.

"Good morning, gentlemen."

"Mrs Walker, good morning," said Bartlett.

"What can I do for you?"

"Can you tell me where you were yesterday evening between eight and ten?"

"Eight and ten?" The unexpected part of the question made her fatigued mind go blank.

"You can surely remember that, Mrs Walker."

"I was ... here ... well, on the boat to be precise, having supper."

"You're sure about that? Were you alone?"

"No. I was with Ralph and Anne."

"Does the name Gary Rawlings mean anything to you?"

Marnie felt strangely disconnected from the line of questioning, as if the police were using the wrong script. "Gary Rawlings?" she repeated slowly. "Never heard of him."

"Have you been to Blisworth in the past few days?"

"Yes."

"Where exactly did you go and for what purpose?"

"I was at the Queen Eleanor boatyard on business. I wanted to park a boat there – it was to be redecorated – on the way to another yard that had the facilities for the work to be done."

"I'll be wanting details of the boat, Mrs Walker. When exactly were you there?"

"I took the boat there a few days ago." *This was it,* she thought. *They'll work out that I moved Anthony's boat and I'm in deep trouble.*

"And last evening? You're sure you don't want to change your mind about where you were?"

"No. It was just as I told you. Between eight and ten, I was here."

"With Mr Lombard and Anne," said Bartlett.

"Yes."

"Where are they now?"

"Anne's up in her room. I'm not sure about Ralph."

"I'd like to speak to them."

Marnie was relieved to move her limbs; tension was making her feel stiff all over. She crossed to the foot of the wall ladder and called up. "Anne! Can you come down, please. Mr Bartlett's here."

Anne descended the ladder and greeted the detectives. She looked attentive and calm. Marnie gestured towards the chairs and sat at her desk. Bartlett stepped forward, pulling a chair into the middle of the room and sat down, while Marriner moved to the side of the office and took a chair by the wall. Despite asking for Anne, Bartlett took no notice of her.

"I want to talk about your movements," he said facing Marnie. "And I don't want anything concealed, omitted or misrepresented. Do you understand?"

Marnie knew the game was up, and she was too tired to offer any resistance. It was too bad about Melissa and tough on Anthony, but she had simply run out of energy. She had done everything she could, but now saw it had been a waste of time trying to pull off some master stroke. Inwardly she gave up and decided to tell the police the whole story.

"Inspector Bartlett," she began. "I'm going to explain why I was at the hospital the other day. We weren't doing anything wrong, but – "

"Please don't waste my time, Mrs Walker," Bartlett snapped. He leaned forward, smashing a fist into the palm of his other hand.

Marnie jerked upright in her seat. Across the room she could see Anne's eyes widen in shock. "Waste your – "

Bartlett did not let her go on. "I'm not interested in some nondescript boater." He was speaking fast with an edge of menace to his voice. "I'm dealing with violent crime here, and you're not going to fob me off."

Marnie was speechless. Her mind took in what Bartlett was saying, but she could make no sense of it, and words failed her.

He continued. "You're going to tell me when was the last time you were at Blisworth and what you did there ... now."

"Last night," Marnie croaked. She cleared her throat and swallowed.

Anne stood up and walked towards the rear of the office.

"What are you doing?" Bartlett said.

In a matter-of-fact tone, Anne replied without stopping. "Getting some water for Marnie."

Bartlett resumed. "Last night. You said you were here."

"At the times you asked about, I was here. I went out afterwards."

"To Blisworth?"

"Yes."

"What were you doing there?"

"I had to see to the boat."

Anne came back with a glass and handed it to Marnie. Taking a sip of water, she reached out and lightly squeezed Anne's fingers.

"You went alone to see to the boat?" Bartlett said.

"No," said Anne. "We went with her."

"Presumably Mr Lombard will be able to vouch for that," Bartlett said. "When we find him, of course."

"He's *Professor* Lombard," Anne said. She sounded like a schoolgirl answering a question in class. "Or doctor, but not mister."

"And there's no need to try and find him." The voice came from the doorway. Ralph walked into the office. "Good morning, gentlemen. What do you need me to vouch for?"

"I was saying – " Marnie began, but she was silenced by Bartlett raising a hand as he stood up.

"You were with Mrs Walker last evening, sir?"

"Yes. All evening."

"Did you go out at any time?"

Ralph did not look in Marnie's direction. "Yes."

"When exactly?"

"I'm not sure *exactly* … some time after ten, I suppose. Ten fifteen, perhaps."

"And where did you go?"

"To Blisworth … to the Queen Eleanor boatyard."

Bartlett turned towards Marnie. "Why did you cross over to the towpath on the opposite side to the boatyard, Mrs Walker?"

If the question was intended to surprise, it succeeded.

"The towpath …?" Marnie's voice faded away.

Bartlett persisted. "You were on that side of the canal, weren't you?"

"I …"

"Are you missing any personal items, Mrs Walker?"

"What kind of items?"

"Do you wear ear-rings?"

Marnie's hand moved to touch her right ear. "Quite often, yes."

Bartlett quickly rose and stepped towards Marnie, bending to look at her face. "You seem to have a slight scratch on your cheek, Mrs Walker. I hope it isn't too sore."

Marnie could feel her face reddening. "No, it's fine."

"How did you do that? If I didn't know you better, I'd almost think you'd been in a fight."

"I don't really remember."

Bartlett lowered his voice. "I think you do. And I think you ought to tell me."

"Chief Inspector," Ralph cut in. "You may find this hard to believe, but your line of questioning is mystifying us all." Bartlett raised a hand in Ralph's direction, but Ralph shook his head. "No. Just a moment. You obviously have a very definite idea in your mind, and you're hinting that we know about it – whatever it is – but we don't. And we'd stand a better chance of helping you, if we knew what you were talking about."

"Well let me help you," said Bartlett. "I'm talking about a violent assault that was carried out in a place where you have admitted to being last evening. And I'm not hinting at anything. I have evidence that you were there – or rather that Mrs Walker was there ... the same Mrs Walker who now has a scratch on her face that was not there when we last saw her two days ago."

Bartlett looked satisfied at the impact of his words on the three apparent suspects. Ralph, Marnie and Anne all wore expressions combining surprise and bewilderment. None spoke.

Bartlett took his seat. "Well, *Professor* Lombard, it's your turn now. How are you going to help me, now that you know what I'm talking about?"

Ralph perched on the corner of Marnie's desk. He spoke slowly. "You're saying ... there was a fight of some sort last night ... and you think Marnie was involved in it? Or presumably all of us took part since we've told you we were together? Correct?"

"You tell me about it, professor. I've told you what I meant."

"Who else was involved in this fight?" Marnie asked.

"Mrs Walker, I'm not interested in playing games. You'll tell me what you know – everything you know – about the incident, and if I'm not satisfied, you'll come to the station to be interviewed, all of you. And you may be charged."

"But Mr Bartlett, I don't know what you're getting at."

Bartlett rolled his eyes. As he opened his mouth, Anne spoke. "I do. At least ... I think I do."

"Yes," said Ralph. "I'm getting the picture too."

"Something happened opposite the boatyard, didn't it?" said Anne. "Where we saw the footprints. That's what it must've been."

"Footprints?" said Bartlett.

"Oh," said Marnie. "My ear-ring ..."

"And you scratched your face in the hedge," Anne added.

"Yes."

"So," Ralph said to Bartlett. "you've found Marnie's ear-ring at the scene of some sort of fight, and your conclusion is that she took part in it, the ear-ring and the scratch being the evidence." He shrugged. "It seems circumstantial to me, I must say, though I can see why you're treating us with suspicion."

"Very generous of you," said Bartlett. "So what's your explanation of events?"

"We've told you," said Marnie. "We were there. We took a look at the other side of the canal ... I looked through the hedge and scratched my face on the branches ... it must've pulled my ear-ring out ... it was just a gold stud, actually. Is that good enough?"

"Why did you cross over the canal? Who – or what – did you see?"

"The owner of the yard told me she'd seen something odd – maybe someone doing something suspicious over there earlier in the day. I was curious, that's all. You know what I'm like when I get an idea in my head."

Bartlett stood up and walked to the door. Marnie thought the interview was at an end, and her shoulders relaxed. Marriner rose slowly, looking at Bartlett. The Chief Inspector nodded.

"Marnie Walker," Marriner began, "I must ask you to accompany us to the station for questioning. We've applied for a warrant to search your premises – including your boat – and we'll want to remove items of clothing and shoes. During the interview you're entitled to have your solicitor present."

Marnie, Ralph and Anne stood up, aghast.

"I don't understand," Marnie said. "I don't understand any of this. We've told you what happened – "

"No, Mrs Walker," said Bartlett. "You haven't told us anything. You've made up a story to fit the facts."

"We've told you the truth."

"Chief Inspector," said Ralph. "I don't think you've been entirely candid with us. What Marnie said is right. Look at us … can you seriously imagine us being involved in some kind of fracas? Apart from that tiny scratch – which we've explained – we're none of us marked in any way. You can't possibly have any evidence to support that accusation."

Bartlett walked into the middle of the office to face them. "Yesterday evening a journalist called Gary Rawlings was seriously assaulted by the canal towpath at Blisworth. His camera was stolen and he was badly beaten. He was found by the farmer who owns the field and taken to hospital where he was diagnosed as having a fractured skull and collarbone. He may also lose the sight in one eye."

"*What*? " said Marnie in disbelief. "You can't *possibly* think that – "

"When he regained consciousness in the early hours of this morning, he was asked if he knew who his assailant was. He told my officer that he was attacked by a man and a woman. He identified the woman as you, Mrs Walker."

• • • • •

"What is going on here, Marnie?"

"Roger, you're my solicitor. I thought you were meant at least to *sound* as if you were on my side. Someone's got to believe me."

There was a silence at the other end of the phone. Marnie could hear Roger Broadbent breathing.

"You're not actually under arrest?" he said.

"I'm apparently going to give a voluntary statement."

"And what's happening now?"

"Marriner's collecting some of my things to take away for examination. Bartlett's with him. They said I could phone you."

"So they've got a search warrant?"

"No. They said they'd be getting one. I just told them to take what they like. I've got nothing to hide."

"Marnie, you've got to be careful. You should've spoken to me first. This is a very serious charge, and you've got to treat it seriously."

"It's bloody nonsense, Roger!" Marnie almost shouted down the phone. "They won't find evidence from any of my clothing for the simple reason that *I wasn't there* – at least not where the man was assaulted."

"What about this ear-ring?"

"It must've got pulled out when I was looking through the hedge, which is where they'll have found it. It doesn't prove I was in the field behind the hedge."

"It's near enough, Marnie. Things get thrown about during a fight. You've got to see it from their point of view."

"Roger!"

"I'm trying to help you, Marnie."

"But I've *done* nothing, so the police can *prove* nothing."

"You've admitted to being at the scene at about the right time. Your alibi is from two people also implicated by their own admission. Your ear-ring was found there. Your face is scratched. The victim has positively identified you as his attacker, with another man. How much more do you think they need to regard you as a suspect?"

Another silence. Roger could hear Marnie breathing.

"Oh, God ..." she muttered.

"Have they told you how bad the victim is?"

"Fractured skull, broken – "

"No, I mean the prognosis."

"That's bad enough, isn't it?"

"Believe it or not, Marnie, it could be worse. If he were to die, you'd be in deep schtuck ... with that ID. Though actually, things could be worse in another way."

"You're really cheering me up, Roger. Do go on. I'm so glad you're there for me."

"They haven't actually arrested you."

"Yet."

"Could be significant."

"How?"

"Where did the attack take place, precisely?"

"Over the hedge in a field beside the towpath. I told you."

"Did you go over the hedge at any time, even briefly?"

"No."

"Did Ralph or Anne?"

"Course not. It's too high and too dense."

"So you won't have left any footprints on that side, and forensic won't have a match with the field soil on the soles of your shoes."

"Obviously not. That's why I've not been arrested?"

"Could be. They're still gathering evidence. Time's on their side."

"So what do we do?"

"Where's Bartlett at the moment?"

"Just outside the office in the yard. He's been talking on his mobile."

"Can you ask him if he'll speak to me."

Marnie opened the door and went out. "Mr Bartlett, my solicitor would like a word with you, if that's possible." He held out his hand. "It's Roger Broadbent ... you've met before."

Bartlett took the phone. "On several occasions," he muttered.

Marnie made a diplomatic retreat into the office, where Anne was tidying the kitchen area ready for departure. She cast a rueful glance at Marnie.

"It's all ridiculous," Marnie murmured, collecting the papers on her desk and putting them in the pending tray. "There's obviously been a serious crime committed, and all they can do is – "

Marnie stopped abruptly as Anne nodded in the direction of the door. Bartlett was coming in. He handed the phone back to Marnie and went out without speaking.

"Hallo, Roger?"

"Right, well you'll be pleased to know you're not going to the station, at least not today."

"What's happened?"

"I've got Bartlett to agree that as you've been so co-operative – letting him have your things without the need for a warrant – he'll have tests carried out on whatever he takes away before further questioning."

"Great! So we're not being dragged off to the cells." Marnie was elated.

"Marnie!"

"Sorry." More contrite. "Thanks, Roger. What now?"

"We wait till they contact you. Because I'm down here in London, he'll give me warning in good time if he wants me to come up."

"That's good. Well done."

"He's a reasonable man, Marnie. If you treat him fairly, he'll be the same with you. You'd do well to remember that. And wait till I'm there before you make any further statements. Ralph and Anne the same. Just keep everything cool."

• • • • •

The strain was too much. After Bartlett and Marriner left – taking with them half of the entire wardrobes of the three suspects – Marnie announced that she felt ready to collapse and suggested taking the rest of the morning off. They sat out beside *Sally Ann* in deckchairs under the garden parasol and drifted into sleep. Dolly made Anne scream when she leapt into her lap, but eventually settled under Anne's deckchair, curled up in a ball.

It was early afternoon before they returned to consciousness, Ralph's nostrils twitching at that most English of smells, bacon sizzling under the grill. He opened one eye and saw that Anne's deckchair was empty; Dolly was also absent. He could guess why and had a shrewd idea where the cat was. The smell was emanating from the window of the galley on *Sally Ann*. Ralph stretched his long limbs and yawned.

No breakfast ever tasted so good. They ate egg-and-bacon sandwiches by the waterside, to the accompaniment of birdsong. Anne the vegetarian enjoyed the baconless variety, to the delight of one contented black cat who crunched her share from a saucer on the grass beside the table. When they had finished they returned to their deckchairs and sat back.

With his eyes closed, Ralph said, "Anyone else feel like a zombie?"

"Trying to give'em up," Marnie muttered in a dreamy voice.

Ralph glanced across at Anne, who was dozing with the cat in her lap.

"How are you feeling, Anne? You've done wonders. That breakfast was brilliant."

"Mmm ... Actually I don't feel bad ... considering. I think it was relief at not being hauled down to the 87$^{th}$ Precinct for the Third Degree."

"Good old Roger," Marnie murmured.

"Yes," said Anne. "It was Roger who gave me the idea for the late breakfast. I kept saying to myself he'd *saved our bacon*, and that did it. Then I got thinking ..."

"Oh yes?" Marnie recognised the signs. "About what?"

"Well ... I've sort of had an idea ... it first came to me during the night while we were spraying the boat. I don't think you'll like it."

• • • • •

On arrival back at the station, Bartlett had a message to contact Chief Superintendent Scutt. He made the call, left DS Marriner dealing with forensic and went along to see the Head of CID.

Scutt was an old hand, tough and shrewd, good at handling the politics. He waved Bartlett to a chair. "Did you bring her in, Jack?"

"Not this time, sir."

"I see. And your reasoning?"

"I didn't want to rush it. We've got an ID from a semi-conscious victim with serious head injuries. No formal statement as yet. I wanted firm evidence to go with the ear stud."

"So you'll be getting a warrant. She won't be able to get out of that."

"No need, sir. Walker offered to let us take anything we wanted from all three of them. She seemed almost pleased to co-operate."

"Co-operate? Walker? The words don't even sound right together."

"Her actual words were, *You can take the bloody lot as long as you leave us something to wear tomorrow*. We came away with shoes, clothing by the armful. And that's part of my reason for not bringing her in."

Scutt looked steadily at Bartlett without comment. He nodded for him to continue.

"Either she's very convincing or she didn't know what I was talking about. She acted as if she really had nothing to hide. We seemed to be on different wavelengths."

"What's new? So where are we on the assault?"

"I've got her solicitor ready to come up from London as soon as I've got the report from Forensic."

"You want to confront them with as much evidence as you can. Play it by the book."

Bartlett frowned. "Ye-e-s."

"Nothing wrong with that, Jack. Get all the ammo you can. We've got to be copper-bottomed on this. National press are going to take a big interest. We want it sorted, quick and clean. No balls-ups."

"I know that, sir, but ..."

"But what? You know Walker was at the scene ... the victim named her ... you've got her ear-ring. What more do you want?"

Bartlett shook his head. "It's just ... You never know where you are with Walker or what's going on in the background. She never gives anything away. You never know what she's up to."

"You're saying you believe her because she withholds information?" Scutt snorted.

"No, sir. I'm just saying she's very deep, that one. And also ... I just don't see her – or them – being caught up in violence. The professor ... the girl ... it doesn't add up."

"The photographer might've started it, Jack. They might've tried to take his camera away, and it all got out of hand."

Bartlett shook his head. "Another thing that doesn't add up. A photographer from a national daily taking shots at a canal boatyard at that time of night."

"No great mystery there," said Scutt. "We know his paper's looking for the vanishing MP ... probably photographing anything that looks in the least unusual. Some people moving a boat after dark ... could be worth following up. Why were they moving it at that hour, anyway?"

"Walker said it was the only time they had free. They were going to paint it for a client. The boatyard woman corroborated their story. Walker's name's up on the jobs board in the office. It all looks straightforward."

Scutt narrowed his eyes. "You know Walker. Is she the sort to take offence at someone filming her activities?"

"She's the sort who wouldn't be able to keep her nose out," said Bartlett. "I could imagine her asking him what he thought he was doing."

"And he being a cocky sod up from London giving her a stroppy answer ..." Scutt surmised.

"Could've been something like that. It's why I wanted more evidence, sir."

"All right. Keep me posted every step of the way on this one, Jack."

Bartlett began to rise from his seat. "Yes, sir. I'll be back in a few days."

"Not good enough."

"I need a reply from Forensic, sir."

"Tomorrow," said Scutt.

"Tomorrow's Saturday."

"I don't care if it's Christmas, Yom Kippur or Red Nose Day. I'll authorise the overtime. You tell Forensic I want that report PDQ. And if they don't know what those initials mean, tell them to talk to me."

· · · · ·

The short afternoon passed quickly, with Ralph back on *Thyrsis*, allegedly working on his new book, and Anne reviewing progress on Walker and Co's current projects. Marnie spent an hour on the phone to Roger explaining everything frankly. Nearly everything. She did not tell him about Anne's latest brainwave. She talked about Anthony Leyton-Brown and explained about Melissa. She told him about the snooping photographer and why they had crossed over the canal to check Stevie's story. Roger listened patiently without interrupting and finally told Marnie that her best course of action was to tell everything to the police, just as she had told him.

"Thanks for your advice, Roger. I know you're wanting to protect my interests, but there's more to it than that. If I tell Bartlett the whole story, he'll track down Anthony, and we'll have no chance of getting at the truth."

"Marnie, that's not your problem. You've got to proceed with caution here.

Listen to me. My concern is to prevent you getting arrested on a GBH charge. Nothing gets the police more lively than a crime involving violence. And don't go underestimating how bad things are looking for you. The facts are not on your side."

"But I didn't do anything."

"How are you going to prove that, Marnie? If it comes to trial, what evidence are you going to offer? The best defence barrister in the world can't work miracles."

"So what are you saying?"

"Forget trying to sort out Anthony Leyton-Brown's affairs. You've got enough problems of your own to worry about. Talk to Bartlett and hope he accepts your story. That's what I'm saying."

After hanging up, Marnie checked the other messages. Most were from Stevie. One was from Simon telling her to keep in touch, especially if she needed any help. Two were from clients. One was a familiar voice from London.

"Hallo, Marnie. Are you there? Can you hear me? Oh dear, this is one of those answering things. Well, I just thought I'd give you a ring to see how you are. I expect your life has settled down to a comfortable routine now. I hope so, anyway. Perhaps I might see you and Anne some time if you're coming this way? Keep in touch, my dear. Lots of love to you and your friends. Oh, yes, I forgot to say … it's Mrs Jolly, of course. Bye, dear."

*"Comfortable routine,"* Marnie repeated, looking up Mrs Jolly's number. "Some hopes … "

• • • • •

Marnie enjoyed cooking. She found it a relaxing distraction from the issues that confronted her at work. Best of all, she liked preparing the meal with someone else, so that the whole process became a social occasion. It also had other advantages. It meant she could talk about plans without having to look that other someone in the eyes. At the end of the working day she found herself in the kitchen with Ralph and Anne, relating her conversation with Roger.

"Good advice," said Ralph, dicing a cucumber.

"But it's *your* friend – *almost* friend – that we're trying to help," Marnie protested, peeling spring onions.

"Of course, but you've got to draw a line somewhere. Roger's right to advise you to concentrate on getting your own problems sorted out. And even that's not going to be easy."

"Whatever Roger says, I'm innocent and the police can't alter that."

"Ever heard of miscarriages of justice? We could end up as the Blisworth Three."

Marnie grabbed a little gem lettuce and began cutting it into wedges. "I still think we shouldn't give up on Anthony, if only for Melissa's sake. She's dead because of what the newspaper people did. *There's* a miscarriage of justice for you."

Ralph shook his head. "I respect you for what you're trying to do, Marnie. You know that. But your time would be better spent clearing up this matter with the police."

Marnie sighed over her chopping board. "Well, nothing's going to happen on that front over the weekend, so we can use the time as breathing space."

Anne collected the cucumber and onions and put them beside the bowl of quartered tomatoes on her part of the workbench. It was her job to organise the ingredients for the *salade niçoise* and arrange them in the bowl. She handed out cooled salad potatoes and a green pepper to the production line and drained a tin of tuna into the sink. "What did Roger think about my idea?"

"Er ... well ..." Marnie began. She concentrated on cutting the potatoes.

"You didn't tell him." Anne took a hard-boiled egg and began shelling it. "Did you?"

"Not in so many words," Marnie admitted without looking up.

Anne cut the egg lengthways into quarters and tipped it onto a saucer. "Because ...?"

"I thought ... well ... it seemed to me ..."

"The worst idea since the invention of gunpowder?" Anne suggested.

"I just wondered how practical it was."

"So you think it's crazy."

Marnie frowned. "I think it'd be risky and it could well be dangerous."

"Not bad reasons for turning it down," Ralph muttered, trying to be helpful.

Marnie reached for a jar of olives. "Oh, I didn't say we should turn it down. I just didn't want to talk to Roger about it."

"Because he'd think it was crazy," Anne said.

"Yes – I mean no! He'd just object on the grounds that ... you know ..."

"Using myself as a decoy could be the most stupid plan he'd ever heard."

"At the risk of repeating myself ..." Ralph began. "Not bad reasons – "

"You've got a point there," said Marnie.

"Thank you," said Ralph.

"No. I meant Anne has a point. It completes the circle ... makes good the weakness in my own plan. It probably won't work out – and it's not without risks – but Anne's the right age to be a ... contact, and might be our only chance of finding the girl in the newspaper photos."

• • • • •

They sat round the table after an early supper feeling listless and unsettled. Anti-climax hung in the air. Anne offered cognac, but there were no takers, though Dolly expressed interest in a drop more milk, and Anne was glad to have something to do.

"We ought to take stock of where we are," said Marnie. Ralph agreed.

"And what we do next," Anne added, closing the fridge door.

"Is there any brandy in the cupboard?" Marnie asked.

Anne put the bottle and two cognac glasses on the table. Ralph poured.

"The press are onto us," Marnie said. "Or onto me, at least. I don't know how, but they certainly know my name. Unless ... do you think Bartlett just made that up to see how we'd react?"

"I don't think so," said Ralph. "The fact that the victim named you was what brought him here."

"Well, Bartlett can do what he likes, but he can't find anything firm to implicate me in the attack. He's not going to find a trace of my skin under the man's fingernails, or anything else. He's got nothing but the name to go on. It's my word against his."

"And ours," said Anne.

"Quite. So what's our next move?"

"Wait for further contact from Bartlett, presumably," said Ralph.

"I mean with Anthony."

"I would've thought he's safely out of the way."

"I don't think we can assume that. We mustn't underestimate them. I'd never have guessed they knew about me, but that man was able to tell the police my name. We're going to have to move quickly again."

"No one's going to recognise his boat," said Ralph. "Not after the repaint. And Anthony's well away by now."

"Not so sure," said Marnie. "They're watching us and probably watching the canal. As soon as the man in hospital can talk to his colleagues, they'll be homing in. They'll ask everyone about us and about boat movements around us."

"You think they could trace the boat after what we've done to it?" Ralph said.

"You bet," said Marnie. "If they're as persistent as you say – and all the evidence so far suggests they *are* – they won't be fobbed off by a change of colour. We're going to have to move fast to keep ahead of the game."

"What do you have in mind?"

Marnie eased back in the chair, staring in front of her. Ralph thought how tired she looked. "I think Mrs Jolly was right," she muttered. "When I spoke to her on the phone she asked if we were going to be in London. I told her about my hair appointment next week, and she said to look in on her. That set me thinking. Why not go down in Anthony's boat?"

"What about your work? Surely you can't go traipsing off on Anthony's account when you've got a business to run."

"Okay, but at the moment we've got a lull and the weekend's coming. If I don't get the Anthony business sorted out now, things are going to get worse. Hawksby won't expect us to go on the offensive. He thinks he's calling the shots."

"So what's the master plan?"

"It's quite straightforward. We need to get the boat out of the way and agree action with Anthony. First I'd better find out where he is."

Marnie rang Andrew and told him what she wanted to do. They agreed to meet on Sunday evening to agree a plan of action somewhere in the long pound between Bulbourne and Cowroast on the Tring summit.

"Will it be a summit conference?" said Anne, yawning.

Marnie gave her an old-fashioned look. "It's secluded up there, not easily reached by road ... nice and private."

"Marnie?" Ralph began.

"Ye-e-s?"

"No need to sound suspicious. I was just wondering whether it would be a good idea if I stayed on here."

"Of course. You've got work to do for your lecture tour. I do understand."

"Well yes, but also it might be better for me to hold the fort. If we all suddenly went off it would look odd ... or so the police would think. You can't just take off without checking with Bartlett."

"I can ring him on Monday and tell him where we are. By then he'll probably know he's on a wild goose chase."

"I think you should leave a message at the station tomorrow and give him the mobile number. Let's not make things worse than they are already."

Marnie nodded. "Okay. That seems reasonable." She yawned. "Tomorrow will be another long day. We all deserve an early night."

Ralph looked at his watch. "It's barely eight o'clock, but it can't be too early for some." He nodded across the table.

Anne was asleep in the chair with Dolly curled up on her lap.

# Part 17

They were up after a solid eight hours of sleep as the sky was brightening in the west. After a hasty breakfast, they set off in the cool half-light for Pinkerton's wharf and took charge of Anthony's boat. Ralph waved them off and returned to Glebe Farm.

Ahead of Marnie and Anne lay a long journey through gently rolling countryside, their route punctuated by locks at steady intervals, and they alternated every hour at steering and working the locks. It was a fair day, with a breeze that ruffled the canal's surface but caused them no problems in manoeuvring. As many times before, Marnie revelled in the freedom of the waterways. The two of them standing together at the tiller, she put an arm round Anne's shoulders, setting aside their problems to enjoy the rhythm of the boat and the beauty that surrounded them.

· · · · ·

Chief Superintendent Scutt told his wife he would ring her later in the morning to pick up any messages, particularly the one he was expecting from Bartlett. He was not like those men who took their mobiles onto the golf course, even on a Saturday morning, to remind people how indispensable they were.

After packing his clubs in the car, he paused in the hall by the full-length mirror, wondering whether his new sweater in a blue and pale yellow diamond pattern looked effeminate. The phone rang on the hall table beside him, and he picked it up immediately.

At the other end of the line DCI Bartlett was impressed. He had not even heard the first ringing tone. He imagined Scutt sitting at the desk in his study catching up on office work in his own time.

"Scutt."

"Morning, sir. It's Jack Bartlett."

"You've heard from Forensic?"

"They've just phoned with the results."

"And?"

"Nothing, sir."

"Go on."

"No trace of any soil from the field on any of their shoes. Likewise, nothing on any of their clothes to connect them with the victim. They can only prove they were on the towpath."

"What about the ear-stud?"

"Inconclusive so far: minute scratches on the surface that could've been caused by a branch scraping against it, and that's how it got pulled off."

Scutt sighed in exasperation. *"Bugger!"*

"Yes, sir. I've been onto the hospital. Rawlings is making good progress, and they're going to move him out of Intensive Care."

"Has he said anything else about his attackers?"

"Not so far."

"You'd better get over there and question him as soon as the medics give the go-ahead. Looks like he's the only lead we've got. Keep me posted."

Bang goes my Saturday morning, thought Bartlett, putting the phone down. We're not all workaholics, like you … sir. He grabbed his car keys and headed for the door.

Several miles away in a superior suburb of Northampton, the disgruntled Scutt decided to change out of the pale sweater, preferring darker shades, before setting off for the golf course.

• • • • •

Progress on the anonymous red oxide boat was slow but unrelenting and, though they were travelling at no more than walking pace, they could maintain their momentum without stopping for as long as the journey took, day and night if necessary, like the fly boats of old. For cover they relied on the secrecy of the canal network, passing unseen through hidden landscapes.

Mid-morning, Anne came up to take her turn as steerer. Marnie handed over the tiller and leaned against the hatch looking back at the last receding sector of the Grand Union in Northamptonshire.

"Marnie, I've been thinking," Anne said slowly. "Nobody in the world knows exactly where we are at this moment, do they? That's what you're hoping, isn't it?"

"I'm counting on it."

"Are you going to leave a message for Inspector Bartlett, like you said you were?"

"No."

"You think he'd tell you to stay at Glebe Farm?"

"Either that or come and arrest me. Why stir up trouble?"

"He'd be annoyed if he knew what we were doing, wouldn't he? I mean, *seriously* annoyed. You don't think it might be better to clear it with him … just to be on the safe side?"

Marnie shrugged. "It's easier to ask for forgiveness than to ask for permission."

Anne smiled. "I suppose it'll be okay if your plan works out."

"That's a big *if*," said Marnie.

Anne pointed. "There's a lock up ahead." In the distance they could see the familiar black and white paint of the balance beams. "Do you think we will be able to keep ahead of the *Globe*, Marnie?"

"No guarantees. For now, we have the advantage. We're invisible, and they don't know about the change of colour, unless that journalist ran into someone who saw us at Guy Pinkerton's place. That would really be bad luck."

"I've been wondering why the man who was attacked said it was you … and how did he know your name, Marnie?"

"That's been on my mind, too."

Anne eased back the accelerator and brought the boat in towards the bank. "It's all such a sordid mess. When we did the module about the media and communications at school, nobody said how cynical it all was."

"Didn't your teachers talk about the 'gutter press' … 'chequebook journalism' …all that side of things?"

"I suppose so. I did hear terms like that, but nobody made it seem real. It feels real enough now."

"I think this must be a pretty extreme case," said Marnie.

Anne put the engine into reverse to slow the boat against the side. "I've learnt something from this experience."

"What's that?"

As the boat nudged the bank and stopped, they both stepped down onto the path, Marnie carrying the windlass to work the lock paddles, Anne to grab the centre rope to hold the boat steady.

"Bad news *is* good news ... good for selling papers. It's *kiss and tell*, like Ralph said."

"Oh, it's much worse than that," said Marnie. "This time the paper set it all up. Anthony cracked under the strain, and his wife picked up the tab. That's what makes it all so bloody."

# Part 18

On Sunday evening with dusk falling they reached the final phase of their journey and motored out of the last of the Marsworth locks by Bulbourne junction, past the entrance to the Wendover Arm. Marnie took the tiller while Anne went forward to the cratch. They cruised past the Bulbourne workshops and entered the long pound of the Tring summit level, where wooded banks gradually began to rise on either side of the cut. The sky was heavily overcast now, cloud cover adding to the twilight, ideal for their purposes.

Marnie had no hesitation in switching on the headlamp. It would really be bad luck if they had been followed this far or were under surveillance now, so far from home. The instrument panel glowed, and the engine rumbled softly as they edged forward searching for *Totteridge* and *Shardlow*. She had pointed the headlamp down so that it lit up only the area a short distance ahead of the boat and left her night vision almost intact.

Marnie leaned forward at the sight of boats tied up on the towpath side, pale slits of light showing round the edge of their curtains. Leisure craft. She relaxed and her thoughts wandered as minutes passed.

She thought of Simon and how much he had changed. The poetry thing was unexpected. Simon had never written before, as far as she knew, but he certainly had a *romantic* side to his character. It had been one of the qualities that had first attracted her to him, when other boyfriends had little more than sex on their minds. Simon's approach to their relationship had excited her more.

The first time they had gone away together, it was to a small hotel in Brittany, with a room overlooking islands in a bay on the north coast. On their first night, Simon had suggested they undress each other with the lights out and the curtains open. As their garments fell away, the only sounds were the waves running onto the shore and their own breathing. Before they slipped into bed, he had opened the French windows wide *so that the moonlight could step in from the balcony during the night*. In the morning she had woken to find him stroking her hair on the pillow. At nineteen years old it was a far cry from the fumbled smash-and-grab raids of other boyfriends she had known. Marnie felt the corners of her mouth forming a smile.

By now the sky was darkening. Trees on the bank were no more than shadowy shapes. A sudden movement from below brought her back to the present as Anne bustled up through the hatch.

"It's them. They're up ahead. Twenty metres. Towpath side."

· · · · ·

It was a tight squeeze. Fitting five people into the cabin on the butty *Shardlow* was no easy matter. Marnie slid in beside Kate, and Anne eased in next, with Anthony and Andrew opposite on the bed, and the door left ajar for ventilation. The cabin was lit by a single fitment in the ceiling, not much brighter than a candle.

While Marnie found space for her legs under the table, in the background came the sound of a cork being drawn, as Anthony opened a bottle of claret to celebrate their arrival. Kate twisted in her place and from the cupboard behind her head withdrew their full complement of three glasses, plus two mugs.

Marnie looked at Anthony as he poured the wine. He was scarcely recognisable with a neat beard, now well established, and his cropped haircut.

"So, what news?" said Andrew. "Why the clandestine meeting?"

"There've been developments," said Marnie. "I thought we should meet and talk them over in person."

"What kind of developments?" said Anthony.

"Your pursuers have found out about the grey boat. They've obviously been asking questions, and we know you were spotted in London."

"We already knew that," said Andrew. "That's why you got it away from Knightly."

"It must be safe there for a while, surely," said Anthony.

"It isn't there any more," said Marnie. "People came asking questions, so we moved it to another yard, then moved it again."

"You have been busy. So where is it now?"

"Tied up behind us. We came in it."

Anthony was incredulous. "You've brought it *here*? Wasn't that risky ... I mean, when I know they're looking for a boat in grey undercoat?"

"It isn't grey any more. We've painted it in red oxide primer."

Anthony's mouth fell open, as Anne suppressed a grin. Abstractedly, he slowly muttered, "I thought primer came before undercoat."

"That's the point," said Marnie. "Or one of them."

"*Struth!*" Anthony exclaimed, raising himself as much as he could in the cramped quarters to squint out of the door. "You *painted* the whole frigging boat?" He laughed. "Just like that? Didn't anyone see you do it?"

"No. We did it through the night, a couple of days ago. Now we're taking her south out of the way."

"*Bloody hell!*" He stared at her. "I didn't think you could paint at night. Didn't it go blotchy?"

"It's only primer, Anthony, not a refit of the *QE2*."

Andrew said, "You didn't get us here just to tell us about the new colour scheme, did you, Marnie?"

"No. We've got to agree on what to do next."

"In regard to ... me?" said Anthony.

"Unless you intend working for Andrew for the rest of your life, yes."

"What do you have in mind?" said Anthony.

"What do *you* have in mind?" said Marnie.

Anthony took a sip from his wine. "Last time we talked about it, you seemed to imply that my opinion wasn't the only one."

"That was then. This is now. You've had plenty of time to think things over. If you have a plan, we ought to know what it is."

"You think I should come out of hiding and face the press. But you wouldn't come all this way after doing what you've done just to ask my opinion. I'm guessing you have something up your sleeve, Marnie."

"I've talked it over with Ralph and Anne. To be honest, I'm not sure yet how we begin, but that's where you come in, Anthony. That's why we've travelled here."

"What do you want me to do?"

"I think there may be two ways to advance. First, we exploit the editor's own weak points. We go public about his indiscretion while at school … the girl he made pregnant and abandoned."

"I can't imagine him being too worried about that," said Anthony. "This isn't Victorian England. And how would you use the information, anyway? I wouldn't want you leaving yourself open to charges of blackmail on my account."

"Sure. But I said there are probably two ways forward. That's just to soften him up. The second is to discredit the story about you and the girl."

Anthony sipped his wine. "And how do we make all this happen, Marnie?" The weak point … *how do you make it happen?*

"That's easy," she said softly. "You do."

• • • • •

Ralph had spent Sunday on *Thyrsis* making preparations for his lecture tour, filled with misgivings about going away, but having no choice. This was the pattern that their life together would follow. At intervals he left the boat to check on Glebe Farm and its surroundings, but all day long saw no one but the occasional walker or jogger on the towpath opposite. If anyone was watching the property, they were well camouflaged.

It was in the evening while he was packing a case, thinking of supper when the call came. He expected it to be Marnie touching base, but he was wrong.

"Ah … is that Ralph? It's Simon."

"I'm afraid Marnie isn't here at the moment. She's gone to London. Can I get her to ring you when she returns?"

"Any idea when that might be?"

"Not exactly. She's gone down by boat, so it'll be a few days before she even arrives."

"I was just ringing to see how things are working out with your friend. I'm going off for a business trip … thought I'd catch up on progress before I leave."

"I'll get her to phone you. She has your number?"

"I'm at home in London – in Docklands – if she has time to get in touch." He gave the number.

"I'm sure she will."

• • • • •

Andrew pushed the doors wider open to let some air into the stuffy cabin on *Shardlow*. The night seemed to have closed in around them. No stars were visible and no other craft had passed them all evening. Marnie had chosen the ideal place for their rendez-vous.

"Our aim is to find two people," she began. "We have to track down the girl who had Hawksby's baby, assuming she did go ahead with it."

"Ralph believes she did," Anthony commented.

"We can't keep on calling her *the girl*," Marnie said. "Can you remember her name?"

Anthony closed his eyes in thought. "She was the daughter of the Deputy Head of one of the Houses … Poulter … Jenny Poulter."

"Okay. The other one we have to trace is the girl in the photos. I assume you had papers when you employed her … National Insurance … that sort of thing?"

"No idea."

"Then, who was it who introduced her to you?"

He shrugged. "Marnie, we'll *never* find her. It was just a set-up. And even if we can find Jenny and the girl in the photos, what can we do about it?" He stared into his empty cup.

Marnie sighed. "I need some fresh air."

• • • • •

Ralph was standing at the stern door of *Thyrsis*, looking out at the still black waters of the canal. The cordless phone was in his back pocket, and he fumbled to extract it when it began ringing.

"Hallo?"

"It's me. Hi."

"Marnie, I was just thinking about you. How are things going?"

"Anthony's got cold feet. He won't go along with the plan."

"Why not?"

"Says it's too risky … too far-fetched … Need I go on?"

"I get the picture. How do you feel about it, Marnie?"

"Thwarted. It may not be a brilliant plan, but at least it's better than just accepting defeat and giving up. Anyway, it looks as if he's going to have to make his own way from now on."

"Is that how have you've left it?"

"I've come out for a walk on the towpath with Anne. The others are in the butty."

"Do you want me to come and fetch you?"

"No. I want to come home, but it's been a tiring few days and I need some sleep."

"Can you do one thing before you turn in? Simon rang. He's about to leave on a business trip. Could you call him and bring him up-to-date? He lives in Docklands, apparently."

"Okay. Have you got the number?"

Anne wandered back to *Shardlow* while Marnie rang Simon who was packing for his trip. She explained the situation, and he listened without comment while she spoke.

At the end of her narrative, he said, "So, the end of the road. Oh well … you did your best, and he's probably right. But I know you, Marnie, probably better than anyone else, and I guess you'll be feeling miffed that he isn't following your plan."

"I'm not miffed."

"But you are sorry he's not going ahead with what you intended, aren't you?"

"Only because I'd gone to a lot of trouble to work it all out."

"It sounded a half-arsed scheme to me."

"Thank you. Well, I'm dropping with tiredness and ready for bed. You've got packing to do, so I'll say good night."

"Look, I didn't mean to pour cold water on things. Get some rest. I'll phone you when I get back ... if that's all right with you."

Marnie hesitated. "Sure."

•  •  •  •  •

As Marnie walked slowly back along the towpath, she could see Anne perched in the entrance to the cabin, waving to her. She quickened her pace. Anne stepped onto the bank and took her by the arm to whisper in her ear.

"Anthony may have changed his mind."

Marnie nodded and made to return to the boat, but Anne kept hold of her arm to hold her back.

"You haven't said anything about the police suspecting you – us – of assaulting that photographer and trying to get evidence to incriminate us."

"Things are complicated enough as it is, Anne."

"Don't you think they ought to know we might get arrested at any minute?"

Marnie smiled. "The police aren't going to find any evidence to link us with the attack. Don't worry."

Anne shrugged. "Sure. After all, they're only detectives from the CID. What chance do they stand against an interior designer?"

She pulled a face and they linked arms. They walked back to the butty and slid into their places.

"So," said Marnie. "What's new?"

"Perhaps," said Anthony, "I've been a little hasty in my judgment. No one seems able to come up with a better idea than yours, Marnie. I'm sure I can't ... apart from surrender. I know I'm supposed to be a hard-nosed politician, but believe me you can't imagine what it's like to be attacked in public in a national newspaper."

"Okay. Go on."

"Andrew and Kate have said they're willing to keep me on, while we see how your plan shapes up. So tell me what you want me to do."

"For starters, talk to me about the girl ... how you met her ... what happened that evening ... where she is now ... everything you know."

Anthony sat back in his seat. "I haven't been totally truthful with you."

"Just tell us about the girl ... her name ... her background ... who introduced her to you."

"It wasn't really like that. She was planted. It was that very wet spell back in March ... "

They settled back as comfortably as they could in the cramped cabin to listen to the story.

The first encounter was on a rainy Friday afternoon. Anthony left his car in a secure parking lot to walk to his constituency office round the corner from the old Limehouse Town Hall in East London for the regular weekly meeting with his agent, Reg Haslam. The traffic between Putney and Docklands had been even heavier than usual, and he was running late. Walking the familiar route on auto-pilot, he almost tripped over the girl as he rounded the corner. She was sitting with her back against the wall, a cardboard box lying on the pavement. The box contained a sprinkling of coins, mostly copper. She did not look up as he checked himself from stumbling and skirted round her. He hated to see beggars in the streets. They could get work if they wanted it. There were hostels. He knew they only begged to get money for drugs.

The second encounter came the next morning, Saturday, while he was on the way to his surgery to meet a list of constituents with problems. This time the girl was in conversation with a man. She had pulled up the hood on her cagoule against the drizzle, and Anthony could guess what kind of conversation she was having. She was trying to look away, trying to get away from the man. As Anthony approached, she bent down to pick up her begging box and was gathering the mat that she had laid on the ground. The man made a grab at her, and she shook her arm irritably away from his grasp. Anthony heard her exclaim, wondering if he should intervene.

When Anthony was only a few metres away from them, the man suddenly noticed him, growled something indistinct at the girl and made off in the opposite direction, pulling up the collar of his raincoat as he went. Anthony acted as if nothing had happened. The girl gave him half a glance as he passed her.

The third encounter was on the following Friday. It was raining again, and this time it was Reg Haslam's turn to be late. He rang to say he was stuck in a traffic jam the other side of Tower Bridge. A lorry was blocking the road.

There she was, standing on the corner, hood up, as the rain began to ease off. It was the first time he spoke to her, and that was how it all started. They went to his office ... he eventually gave her a job ... "The rest you know from the papers. That's it."

"No it isn't," said Marnie. "It's not even a beginning. All you've told us is that you met her in the street. You've told us nothing about *her*, what she was like, how you came to offer her a job ... anything."

"I thought you knew the basic details from the press," said Anthony.

"And I thought you said it was all lies. Anyway, I want to know more about the girl as a person ... and more about the story from your angle."

"Okay. Where shall I begin?"

"She was standing on the pavement in the rain ... your agent was held up in traffic. Take it from there."

Anthony leaned forward, elbows on the table, eyes half closed.

• • • • •

*As Anthony drew level, the girl put out a hand without looking at him, asking for some change. She had a pleasant voice with a hint of north country. Her outstretched hand had long fingers, gently tapering. He had an umbrella in one hand and a briefcase in the other. The girl noticed, too.*

*"Oh, it's all right," she muttered. "Sorry ... I shouldn't have troubled you."*

*"No, no," he stammered. "It's just that I'm rather ... "*

*"Yes, I can see that. Please don't worry."*

*She was almost as tall as he was. Green eyes, a pleasant face framed by the hood of her yellow cagoule and wisps of corn-coloured hair.*

*"Look," he began. "It's none of my business, of course, but do you have to*

*do this? I mean … isn't there a better way of earning a living?"*

*To his surprise, she smiled. "A thousand better ways. I don't do this through choice … it's not a soft option."*

*On an impulse he said, "Look, why don't you come in out of this rain?"*

*She became wary.*

*"Don't get me wrong. I'm the local Member of Parliament … here for a meeting with my agent. My office is just down the road … number thirty-four … blue front door … of course."*

*He tucked the briefcase under his arm, reached in his pocket and took out a business card. "I might be able to help you."*

• • • • •

"So you did make the first move," said Marnie.

"I took the bait. They made the first move by setting the trap."

"How could *they* – assuming it was a *they* – know your routine?"

"Easy. It wouldn't take the CIA or MI5 to find out when I see my agent. Everyone knows MPs go back to their constituencies on Fridays and take surgeries on Saturday mornings, usually once a fortnight … the conscientious ones, at least. You'd have no problem knowing where I park the car and the route I take to the office."

"Did you often see beggars on your walk to the office?"

"Not usually round there. It wasn't what I'd call a regular pitch. But there are homeless people all over London, so it didn't surprise me."

"You refer to *homeless people*. I find that interesting."

"Getting to know her made me see them in a different light. I got to know how they lived."

"What was she called?"

• • • • •

*"My name's Marlene," she said, standing in the office while Anthony fiddled with the venetian blind to let more light into the room. She pronounced the name so that the ending rhymed with 'lane', not 'lean'.*

*"Nice name," Anthony said without looking round. He pulled on the strings and adjusted the slats. "That's better. Let me take your … er … jacket."*

*"Cagoule."*

*"Cagoule." She pulled it over her head. Underneath she was wearing a red sweatshirt and jeans. Her trainers looked sodden. He hung the cagoule on a coat stand together with his raincoat. "Coffee?"*

*She nodded. "Where's your agent?"*

*"He's on his way … held up in traffic near Tower Bridge. He rang me on the mobile to tell me. He'll be here soon. Have a seat. I'll do the coffee." He went out and she heard him clinking cups in the kitchen.*

*Marlene slipped off the trainers and laid them upside down under the coat stand. On the wall hung a row of portrait photographs: the Queen, Margaret Thatcher, John Major. She walked to the window and looked out over the back garden. It had been paved over, and there were flower pots standing in clusters. After a minute or two Anthony appeared carrying two mugs.*

*"My agent will be here soon … any minute."*

• • • • •

Marnie frowned. "But I heard your agent in that interview on the radio. I thought he said he'd never met her."

"That's right. He never did turn up. After a while he rang and said it was a waste of time trying to reach the office, and we were going to see each other anyway the next morning."

"So you were alone together, you and the girl."

"Yes, but it was all completely innocuous. I actually did want to help her, if I could."

"If she'd been knock-kneed, flat-chested with a squint, would you have felt the same?"

Anthony smiled. "I had no ulterior motive. Until the ... incident in my garden took place, I did not entertain inappropriate intentions towards Marlene ... and I didn't initiate them even then."

"All right. So how did you get into that mess?"

• • • • •

"So how did you get into this mess, Marlene?"

"It really is a mess. I hardly know where to begin. And don't think I'm expecting you to be able to do anything about it. Nobody's helped in the past ... well, nobody from your side of the fence, at any rate."

"You think the Opposition would do better? Don't count on it. They're all talk, believe me."

"I don't mean them. I mean the sort of ... official side of the fence. They've never been any good to me."

"Well, when I know some details, perhaps I can help."

"I come from Leeds. Dad's an accountant ... got his own firm ... Mum's a teacher. We live in a big house in the suburbs. I wanted to go to drama school ... in London, where all the action is."

"And that's what brought you here?"

"No. Failure brought me here."

"I don't follow."

"You interrupted."

"Sorry."

"I was in the sixth form doing A levels when it happened. I'd always been self-conscious about my height. I'm five foot ten and I worried about getting too big to be an actor. You'd probably think of that as an actress."

"You're assuming I'm a dinosaur."

"Definitely."

"Thank you."

"So ... I worried about my size ... became obsessed with my dimensions."

"They look great to me." He noticed her expression. "Do go on."

"You've already guessed. I became anorexic ... almost starved myself. When I'd lost two stone in a couple of weeks, my mum took me to the doctor. He prescribed some tablets, but because of all that, I made a mess of my studies and left school last year without completing the course."

"How old are you?"

"Eighteen."

"How did your parents feel about you giving up your studies?"

"Good question. My mum was supportive ... sympathetic. Dad went *ballistic. Said I was wasting my life, throwing my chances away, ought to get down to some hard work, never did him any harm, bla-bla-bla."*

*"You didn't get on well with your father."*

*"Wrong. I'd always been daddy's girl. Funny, isn't it? That's what made it harder to handle. So ... blazing row ... I stormed out."*

*"They expected you to go back."*

*"I suppose so. But I had a friend who was doing a secretarial course in London. She offered me her floor for a few nights, and I stayed for a month. I trailed round all the agencies."*

*"Secretarial?"*

*"Modelling. My dad had said I was all skin and bones, so I figured I could try to be a model. That's what they look like."*

*"How'd you get on?"*

*"Not bad. One or two single shoots: hairspray, sandals ... I've got good feet, they said. My left armpit even featured on a poster for underarm deodorant in Boots. I thought the armpit stood a good chance of making a solo career."*

*"You were hoping for the big break."*

*"I got it ... or I thought I got it. I'd met this photographer ... it was doing the sandals shoot. He gave me his card ... said keep in touch. I gave him my phone number. One day he rang me, said he had a job where he needed a model quick ... beachwear ... not bad money. I went round to his place ... he had a studio all set up ... "*

*"You had a few drinks," Anthony joined in.*

*"Yeah. Glass of wine while he set up the lighting. There was music playing. It was just like that old film, where the photographer moves around shooting different angles, saying yes! yes! all the time. Then he had to put more film in the camera ... poured me some more wine. It seemed great, like proper modelling for a magazine. I knew the wine was going to my head and I was worried my nose might be going pink. All the time there was the music and the lights ... it was great. Then he just said ... all sort of casual ... to slip the bikini top off. I thought I'd not heard him right. Then he said, just like people do on the beach ... this is swimwear ... All reasonable, like. And there were so many lights shining on me ... he seemed a long way off. There was just me and the music and the lights ... and my head going round. I thought so what ... he's just being creative and artistic ..."*

*"Was that all?"*

*"Course not. It sort of ... went on from there ..."*

*"And he filmed it ... everything."*

*"Yeah. I didn't even know he had a video camera running. He kept saying don't move away ... stay here ... turn round this way ... that sort of thing."*

*"You're telling me that you were being set up ..."*

• • • • •

"You're saying that you were set up just as she'd been?" said Marnie.

"Of course. That's where she got her first lesson. I must've been stupid not to realise at the time what was going on."

"You'd only just met her."

"Not then. I meant when they took the photos in the garden."

"But why did they pick on you?"

"The tabloids are always on the lookout for scandal."

Anthony shrugged. "But they must've got you marked down as a target for a reason."

"There was a rumour I was having an affair – untrue as it happens – and the paper kept tabs on anyone in that position – must've been a very big file."

"Hardly earth-shattering these days," Marnie interjected.

"True. But hypocrisy is *the* British malaise ... our national sport."

"All this aggro just because they thought you were having an affair?"

"Well, no. There was more. I'd made outspoken comments about inaccurate and unfair reporting. That didn't endear me to them. Also I'd been involved in drafting a policy document on family values ... 'Back to basics'. It kept us backbenchers occupied and gave us a chance to get noticed. It also gave the tabloids a field day trying to expose our weaknesses. They got their fingers burnt trying to prove one member of the Cabinet was a serial womaniser – hilarious ... he was actually a raving woofter!"

"Let's get back to the girl," Marnie said. "What happened to her?"

• • • • •

*"What happened to you next?" said Anthony.*

*"My friend where I was staying wanted her boyfriend to move in ... I'd be in the way. She didn't say it, but I knew how she felt. I told Bruno – the photographer – and he said I could move in with him."*

*"So you moved in and everything was hunky dory ... until ... "*

*"He asked me ... " Her voice tailed off.*

*"Don't tell me. Another shoot? Something creative and artistic?"*

*Marlene nodded, fighting back tears. "I wouldn't do it. We had a row. I walked out."*

*"Why didn't you go back to your parents?"*

*"I was too ashamed, I suppose. I knew they'd ask all sorts of questions. I figured they'd end up sending me away ... just as you will."*

*"I said I wanted to help you if I could. Tell me, do you live round here?"*

*"I'm not telling you my address."*

*"If you're a constituent, I could do more to help you."*

*"I've had enough of people trying to help me."*

*"It would make it easier for me. Don't you see? It would make it different than if I just ... picked you up off the street. Did you get GCSEs at school?"*

*"Yes. So what?"*

*"And you do live in this part of London?"*

*"In a hostel ... not far away."*

*"Right. If you came to work for me, you could put that down as a reference in future. A job in an MP's office. It could help you. You could earn some money, get your A levels and go to drama school or something. What do you think?"*

• • • • •

"What did she think of that?" Marnie shifted in her seat. She was numb.

"She seemed undecided for a while, but gradually came round to the idea."

"And you really could get her into your office, just like that? Don't staff in Parliament have to go through all sorts of security checks?"

"Normally, yes. And I set that in motion. But she wasn't there long enough for me to get her cleared. She'd only been with me for two weeks when the garden thing happened."

"You said she'd egged you on after a reception when you'd both had a few drinks."

"And that's exactly what happened. That's the honest truth. I swear to you."

"Yes. I believe you."

"Good. Now let me ask you something, Marnie. What do you really think you can do about it?"

"What I've said all along. We get the evidence from the girl back at school, confront Jeremy Hawksby, find Marlene and get her to admit in public that she was a set-up. Then you contact the Press Complaints Commission."

Anthony smiled. "It doesn't sound too bad if you say it quickly like that."

"Ralph says that behind every complex idea lies a simple proposition. That's my plan. Undermine Hawksby ... expose him in public as a hypocrite and a crook. It's the best I can do."

"Ralph may be right about that, but he's not infallible, you know. Frankly, Marnie – with the greatest respect – I don't think you're proposition adds up to much by itself."

Marnie sighed. "What else can we do?"

Anthony leaned forward. "You need to land a big hit. What if we outed him as gay at the same time?"

# Part 19

Sunday morning, quiet as a graveyard. They slipped their moorings and set off in convoy, the three boats in line astern pushing through early mist floating on the water, hulls and topsides sweating with dew. As the sky brightened and brought light to the deep cutting, they breakfasted while they travelled, chewing toast at the tiller, gulping down hot coffee that helped kick-start the day. They were soon upon the first lock and began working their way down from the Tring summit level in the Chiltern Hills on the long descent that led ultimately to the Thames in London.

Waiting at the lockside while the red boat slowly descended in the chamber, and the working pair pulled away in the next pound, Marnie rang Ralph to outline the plan.

"Anthony's boat is going to Andrew's boatyard in Hemel Hempstead. It'll look like any other craft being worked on. Anne and I will leave them there and get a train back. I'll fix another time to see Mrs Jolly."

"I see."

"What's the matter?" said Marnie. "You don't sound very keen,"

"Well ... is it wise to let Anthony take the boat on by himself? They're looking for a man on an unmarked boat."

"A *grey* unmarked boat," Marnie reminded him.

"Yes, but if you can envisage it changing colour, perhaps they could too."

"You really think they're watching the canals that closely?"

"Of course they are. Where else?"

"You think we should take the red boat on to Andrew's boatyard ourselves?"

"It'd be a pity to blow it when you've gone so far. Does it really matter to you for the sake of a slightly longer journey?"

"I suppose not. I was just wanting to get back as quickly as possible. I wanted everything to seem normal if anyone turns up in the office on Monday morning."

"No one's going to turn up in the office on Monday morning, Marnie."

"How can you be so certain?"

"It's a bank holiday. They won't expect you to be at work."

"A bank ... Ah ... " She held the phone away and called down to Anne at the tiller, "Did you realise it was a bank holiday tomorrow?" Anne shrugged. Returning to Ralph, Marnie said, "I'd lost track of that."

"Well, our so-called 'victim' is in Intensive Care and presumably your friend Bartlett will still be waiting for his test results."

Marnie was frowning. "I'll get back to you."

Weighing up the implications, she pulled on the heavy balance beam to open the lock gate and waited while the red boat eased out. Shutting the gate and going down the steps to re-board, her mind was elsewhere.

"I hadn't thought about Monday," Anne said, looking perplexed. "So much seems to have been happening lately, I've hardly looked beyond the next few hours."

"One day at a time, I know," Marnie muttered. Somewhere at the back of her mind she could hear Simon saying the same words. She wished she couldn't.

"Everything keeps changing all the time." Anne looked downcast. "I hate being caught off-guard."

"It's okay." Marnie smiled at her friend. "You're not responsible. The point is, what do we do about it?"

"Does it make a big difference?"

"Everything makes a difference. We may've just gained an extra day. And Ralph doesn't like my plan to let Anthony take the boat on. I've got to work it out all over again." She pointed ahead. "There's the next lock coming up. Pull over just before it. I'm going back to talk to the others."

They tied up at the bank and Anne watched Marnie jog back down the towpath, off to marshal her troops, tugging the mobile out of her back pocket.

• • • • •

"You've been busy!"

Marnie slithered the last metre or two down the bank from the lockside, scattering pebbles under her feet. She was breathing heavily, a pink flush in her cheeks, and smiling. Anne had the red boat tied up below the lock. She had taken it through by herself and refilled the lock, opening the gates ready for *Totteridge* and *Shardlow* to make their approach.

Anne pushed the red boat's nose out and stepped onto the gunwale as Marnie pressed on the accelerator and they moved away. The new plan was simple. They would take Anthony's boat to Hemel and leave it at Andrew's yard before continuing on to London to visit Mrs Jolly and have a talk with Jane Rutherford. Jane was an old friend and a well-known boat signwriter. She and her husband kept their own boat in Little Venice and, more importantly for Marnie, they had a daughter who worked in the media. Anthony would stay on with Andrew and Kate for a while longer, safely out of the way. Marnie and Anne would return home that evening.

Mid-morning, chugging through Berkhamstead, Anne said, "That was a bombshell, wasn't it? The editor bloke being ... well, *gay* ... as well as making that girl pregnant. What did you make of all that?"

"Well ... it's unusual ... but not impossible." Marnie smiled. "I suppose it's what the tabloids are for."

"But seriously, Marnie. I thought people were either one way or the other."

"It's probably more complicated than that. You can find some people who are inclined in both directions – unfortunate choice of words! – but it's hard to judge how common it is."

"How do you know about that sort of thing?"

"Oh ... reading books, magazines ... in films ... in conversation ..."

"But ... you've never ... "

Marnie was startled. "*Me?* Blimey, no! Boringly normal, I am. What gave you that idea?"

"I didn't mean *that* ... I just meant ... have you ever *known* people who were like that?"

"AC/DC? By the law of averages, I suppose I must have. Never given it much thought. For some people, life can certainly be complicated."

Anne frowned.

"We've never talked about things like this before, have we?" said Marnie

Anne shook her head. "Never come up before."

"No. Well … after Simon and I split up, I went off relationships in a big way, including sex. I did have a kind of affair after a couple of years, but it was unsatisfactory and in the end it just sort of … fizzled out. Then nothing … until I met Ralph."

"Marnie, I didn't mean to pry into your personal life."

"You weren't prying. I just thought it might help to make things clear."

"But if people accept that things can be … *complicated* … why does Anthony think we can use that against Hawksby? It's no real ammunition, is it?"

"Ah. That's different. We're back to what Anthony called the *British national sport* … good old hypocrisy. If Hawksby was open about it, then it probably doesn't matter a great deal. For some people it'll be a problem, but society as a whole is reasonably tolerant about unorthodox relationships these days. They see them on TV the whole time and they've grown used to them, I suppose."

"But the hypocrisy?"

"Simple. If Hawksby uses his paper to attack people for their morals – or lack of them – but has an exotic private life of his own – or a murky past – he'd be seen to have double standards. Publicly attacking gay people while being gay, and condemning immorality having left a girl pregnant as a teenager, could just be regarded as a tad inconsistent."

"Why does he do all that?"

Marnie shrugged. "Smokescreen? It sells papers?"

"He must be really horrible."

"But that's not the worst part, don't forget. Think of the collateral damage, the consequences of what he's done. Melissa Leyton-Brown paid the price. Who knows who else has suffered because of Jeremy Hawksby?"

• • • • •

Chief Superintendent Scutt and DCI Bartlett met for a drink that Sunday morning at a pub by the canal in Stoke Bruerne. They ordered non-alcoholic lager and took a table on the terrace near the water. At the first sip of the uninspiring drinks Bartlett wanted to remark that sometimes it was a bugger being in the police, but he thought better of it. Scutt was wearing a three-piece suit and looked as if he had just been to church.

"So how do things stand, Jack?"

"Not looking too good, I'm afraid, sir."

"But I thought you had things pretty well sewn up. You know Walker was there at about the right time. It was late in the evening – very odd for them both to be on a canal towpath at that time, but they were; she doesn't deny it. You've got an ear-ring found at the scene; she admits it's hers. There must've been a fight or a struggle; Walker's got a scratch on her face. The victim regains consciousness and you ask who attacked him; he puts the finger on Marnie Walker."

"And she shows no concern at all," said Bartlett. "Treats the whole affair as if she has other things on her mind and just discounts everything we've got on her."

"What about her solicitor?"

"He said she maintains she's completely innocent and will give us full co-operation. He says he believes her. I think he does."

"What do you think, Jack?"

"Bugg- ... blowed if I know, sir. Forensic can give us nothing to show she was in that field behind the hedge. Same goes for her professor bloke and the girl who works with her."

"But all three of them were there."

"They admit it."

"At that time."

"That evening, sir, yes. They say it was later."

"So what was going on? And why did this Rawlings say it was Walker?"

Bartlett shook his head. "Something was going on. I wondered if he was following her, she thought he was a stalker and decided to confront him."

"How?" said Scutt. "Clobber him with a golf club from the other side of the hedge? In which case, how did her ear-ring get pulled off ... and what about the scratch on her face? And why didn't she *say* she thought he was a stalker ... argue it was a matter of self-defence?"

"And why is she so relaxed and confident about the whole thing?" said Bartlett.

"Jack, you're supposed to be coming up with the answers, not the questions."

"I know, sir, but she's hardly a master criminal, is she? She's just a bloody interior designer. Most people at least get a bit nervous when they're under investigation by the police. This one's far too cool."

"So ... what's your point?"

"Could it be she knows we've got no evidence to go on because she didn't do it? We've been wrong about her before, sir. Maybe we're just not on her wavelength. Maybe she does have some bigger problem on her mind and isn't taking our charges seriously because of that."

"Then she could be making a big mistake, Jack. If that photographer swears she was the one who attacked him – and nearly killed him – she's going to have to come up with something more than being too busy to take the accusation seriously."

"I know, I know." Bartlett sipped his lager and grimaced. "I'll talk to Rawlings as soon as he's fit to be questioned. The medics want us to give him another day or two ... till he's out of Intensive Care."

"Cheer up, Jack. You've got a cast-iron witness there. Play it by the book. Talk to Rawlings as soon as the doc says he's up to it. No rush. He's not going anywhere."

• • • • •

Marnie and Anne subsided gratefully onto cream and blue chintz loose covers in Mrs Jolly's house overlooking the canal in Little Venice. The old lady had answered the door wiping flour from her hands on a National Trust apron. She had a friend coming to stay for a few days that evening and, true countrywoman that she was, she was busy baking bread. Instantly assessing that they were gasping for a cup of tea, she had ushered them into the front sitting room, leaving their bags in the hall, and was now tinkling tea-cups in the kitchen.

The room was furnished in antiques of polished mahogany, with family photos in silver frames on the mantelpiece and two table lights with gold shades casting a pleasing glow. A tray loaded with scones and biscuits was already waiting for them on a low table, the lamplight reflecting off a Georgian silver milk jug.

Marnie sat back in the armchair and stretched her long legs in front of her. "This house always makes me feel I've arrived at an oasis of peace in a crazy world."

"It's wonderful," said Anne. "Mrs Jolly's like a favourite aunt or a granny."

The favourite aunt-granny bustled in carrying a teapot, with the offer of milk, lemon or sugar in various combinations. "It's lovely to see you both. You must tell me all your news."

It seemed a thousand miles away from the sordid gossip in the newspaper and the paparazzi hunting them down at every turn. Over Darjeeling with lemon Marnie outlined Anthony's story, giving just enough detail to let Mrs Jolly understand the situation.

"And you want to expose this … Hawksby. My goodness, you do get into some scrapes, the pair of you. Do have another scone, Anne. They're never as good the next day. I know what you're thinking … I'm just an old biddy who'd have a seat-belt fitted to a Stannah stairlift." Marnie and Anne laughed. "So, what next?"

"That's the problem," said Marnie. "We've got to find the two women and the man involved."

"And you think it would be helpful to have contacts in the press and media," said Mrs Jolly. "Such a pity Jane couldn't be here."

Marnie sat up. "*What?* I thought you said she was coming round."

"She rang to say she won't be back till late and had to send her apologies. Oh dear … I can see you're more than disappointed."

"We *desperately* need contacts in the media," said Marnie. "Jane's daughter works for a TV company. I thought she might be able to help us."

Mrs Jolly looked anxious. "Perhaps you can talk about it on the phone … or see her some other time."

• • • • •

The three boats travelling in convoy reached Andrew's base near Hemel after an easy journey. Andrew showed Anthony round the boatyard in under five minutes and offered him the use of the shower in the small cottage where he and Kate lived when not on their travels.

Anthony would continue to sleep on *Totteridge* as the cottage had no spare room and he went to collect his sponge bag and toiletries from the tiny cupboard above his bunk. He was just emerging through the stern doors, when he caught sight of Andrew talking to a man at the far side of the yard. Instinctively he pulled back. A movement in the cottage caught his eye, and he looked out to see Kate at an upstairs window, waving at him to retreat into the cabin. After a few minutes sitting on the bunk, he heard footsteps approaching, followed by a tap on the hatch.

"That was close." Andrew slipped in and pulled the doors shut behind him.

"Who was it?"

"Said he was looking for a boat. Wanted something fitted out but not painted, so he could do his own colour scheme."

"Oh, good." said Anthony, relieved. "Just a customer."

"Doubt it. He said he was interested in a boat painted in grey undercoat. Did I know of anyone who had one?"

*"Damn!"*

"I told him there were loads of boats like that. He asked what colour they were painted *after* the grey. He pointed at your boat and asked how long it had been red."

*"Bugger!"*

"That's what I thought. I told him red primer came first, then undercoat, often grey. But he wouldn't be shaken off … said as he was here he just wanted to go on board and have a look round … out of interest. I told him we were closed for the weekend and were tired after a long journey. He said he'd come back tomorrow. I put him off till Tuesday."

"Can we be away by then?"

Andrew shrugged. "I've got things to do, a business to run. I'll do what I can."

"I'll call Marnie," said Anthony. "You've bought us some time. At least we've got tomorrow."

• • • • •

Marnie sat on the stairs and phoned Jane, who offered to see her at nine the next morning before leaving to spend the day cooing over her new grandson. This was at least something, but it left Marnie with a problem. There seemed little point in travelling back to Knightly St John for the night. With no chance of staying over with Mrs Jolly, Marnie thought through the options. Beth and Paul were away for the weekend and she did not have their door key with her. She pressed the buttons for Faye Summers. Answerphone. Bank holiday weekend, of course.

Marnie got up and opened the front door to look down the line of moored boats. There was a gap where Roger kept *Rumpole*, so that chance was ruled out. Pulling the front door closed, she was starting to resign herself to another dash and early getaway when an idea formed in her mind. If Simon had not already left, perhaps … She checked the number in her notebook and pressed the buttons. It rang half a dozen times.

"Simon Walker."

"It's Marnie, hi. Listen … I've got a big favour to ask."

"Ask away."

"Is it right you live in Docklands?"

"Yes, by Tower Bridge … I've got a flat."

"I don't suppose I could possibly use it as a base … just for a day or two?"

"Of course. Why not move in permanently?" There was a smile in his voice.

"One night – possibly two – would be fine."

"Oh well … it's a start. Seriously, though, feel free to make yourself at home. I'll leave a key at the lodge."

• • • • •

Marnie saw Anne off at Euston – she did not feel she could invite Anne to stay at Simon's – and rang Ralph to give him the arrival time for picking her up from MK Central. She took a black cab and made good time through the City of London, crossing Tower Bridge and diving into the back streets that ran parallel with the Thames. The old wharf buildings were now among the smartest residential addresses in the capital, rising above narrow cobbled lanes lined with boutiques, restaurants and bistros.

Marnie got out at the corner of the main block and walked through to the centre of the building to find the porter's lodge where Simon had left his key for collection. It turned out to be a piece of grey plastic like a credit card. The porter directed her to the end of the block where she would find the entrance lobby and the lift up to Simon's flat.

She found the entrance to the lobby and stood in the doorway pressing three of the buttons on the panel by the glazed door, using the sequence given her by Simon. Problem: what to do with the security card? She knew she had to use it to gain admittance but could not find a slot for it. She ran her fingers over the display panel like a blind person reading Braille. In tiredness and frustration she wanted to kick the door in and was turning to go back to the porter for help, when a voice behind made her jump.

"I think it's probably my fault."

She spun round. *"Simon!"*

"I think I forgot to explain the system properly. Here." He took the card from her, pressed the three-number code and held the card flat against the panel under the keypad. With his other hand he pulled on the door handle and it swung smoothly open. He kissed her on the cheek and guided her through the entrance hall to the lift.

"You said you were going away."

"I am." He pressed the button for the lift.

"Then why are you here?"

"I'm going a little later than planned. Something came up." The doors slid open, and Simon ushered Marnie inside. "Don't look so worried. It's a nice flat. You'll like it." The lift ascended without a sound.

He was right. The flat was spacious with a large living area, mahogany wood-strip flooring, scattered with oriental carpets. The walls were in pale honey, the wall-lights and table lamps in brass with cream shades. Three sofas covered in an ivory fabric were grouped around a low, glass-topped table. The walls were hung with large oil paintings, abstracts on the theme of London's riverside. Opposite, by the wide expanse of windows looking down the Thames towards the Isle of Dogs, was a dining area. Drawn by the view, Marnie crossed the room.

They were four or five floors above ground level, and no sounds penetrated from outside. The view was bounded by a horizon of low hills. Here and there high-rise blocks of flats jutted up, and away over to the left, beyond the choppy waters of the river, the bulk of Canary Wharf dominated the landscape, its pyramid roof touching clouds, flashing like a lighthouse in the evening sky. Simon spoke from the other side of the room.

"You look just right standing there, Marnie. It looks like your kind of place. What do you think of it?"

"It's as I expected." Remembering that she was accepting Simon's hospitality, she politely added, "It's beautiful … great view … very stylish …

goes well with your car."

"My *car*?"

Still looking out of the window, she laughed gently. "It wouldn't surprise me if you brought it up here at night ... probably has its own room."

"Not a bad idea," said Simon. "I'll bear it in mind. Though actually there's a snag."

"You haven't got a bed big enough for it?"

"Good guess. In fact I've got three bedrooms, but two are set up as an office and a junk room. Perhaps I should've mentioned that only one bedroom's functional. I hope you won't mind sharing my bed."

# Part 20

Marnie yawned on the train. She had been yawning on and off all morning after a night with little sleep. As the miles rolled past the window, she watched for the canal cutting its way through the counties north of London, neglecting the cappuccino she had bought at a kiosk, while she relived her conversation with Jane Rutherford. She wished she had not stayed the night.

The conductor came through the carriage, a West Indian with a cheerful face.

"Good morning, madam."

Marnie held up her ticket and asked what time they were due to arrive.

"That'll be ... sixteen minutes past eleven."

"Thank you."

"And we're running right on time."

"Amazing."

The conductor laughed, a rich warm chuckle. "Don't be like that!" He flashed a smile of gleaming white teeth in a mahogany face. Marnie smiled back. He added, "That's why we're called *Virgin Trains*, you know."

*All right, I'll buy it,* she thought. "Why's that?" she said.

"Because there's a first time for everything!"

Infectious laughter broke out around them and, surrounded by an aura of good humour, the conductor continued on his way. Feeling a little more cheered, Marnie took a sip of her cooling cappuccino and made a quick call to Ralph to let him know her ETA.

• • • • •

At about the time Marnie was speaking to Ralph, DCI Bartlett received a call from Sergeant Marriner at the hospital. Bartlett had sent him to check on the condition of Gary Rawlings in Intensive Care. It was bad news.

• • • • •

The conductor was right. The train pulled in at MK Central as the platform clocks recorded eleven-sixteen precisely. Marnie walked out through the station's glazed facade and spotted the Volvo in the car park. Ralph waved as he and Anne came to meet her ... good, dependable Ralph.

After hugs all round, they travelled the familiar route to Knightly St John. It felt marvellous to be coming home, and Marnie relaxed in the front seat.

"I hope you're hungry," said Anne. "Ralph and I have been slaving away in the galley on *Thyrsis* all morning."

Marnie had eaten nothing since the previous day, apart from a biscuit at Jane's, but had no appetite. "Great," she lied.

"How did you get on with Jane?" said Ralph. "Are you seeing her daughter?"

Marnie sighed. "It was all rather unsatisfactory. Rachel's away on business."

"For how long?"

"Jane didn't know. It's a nuisance ... just when I wanted to press on and get things sorted."

"Oh dear," Anne chimed in. "There's another hold-up … Andrew phoned. They can't leave the boatyard till tomorrow because of work." She laughed. "He asked did you have any orders for him."

"*Orders?*"

"I think he feels part of a military operation," said Ralph.

"What did you tell him?" Her voice sounded sharper than Marnie intended.

"In your absence I used my initiative, of course." Ralph seemed slightly offended by the question.

"And?"

"I … er, told him I'd get you to ring when you got in."

Marnie laughed. "I don't think I have any *orders* … apart from get the hell out of there as quickly as possible." She looked down at the by-pass as Ralph swung the big car over the roundabout. "On second thoughts … yes I have."

• • • • •

Marriner was not looking forward to his meeting with Bartlett. He knocked on the door and went in. The DCI looked up from his desk, exasperated.

"What the bloody hell's going on, Ted?" he exploded.

Not the most cordial greeting, but it could have been worse. With an impatient gesture Bartlett waved him to a chair.

"Why didn't anybody tell us what was happening?" he barked. "It's not as if they didn't know he was involved in a crime investigation!"

Marriner shook his head. "I think it was a mix-up when they transferred him out of Intensive Care. They moved him to this room and next thing, a colleague of his from the *Globe* turned up with two paramedics in uniform and an ambulance. Rawlings discharged himself, and before anyone knew what was going on, he'd left."

"*Jesus!*" Bartlett banged the desk with his fist. "How could the hospital just let them do that? Didn't it occur to anyone to inform us?"

"Like I said, sir, it was when he was transferred."

"I heard you the first time. So what?"

"Intensive Care transferred him out, and he'd left before the consultant even had a chance to see him on the new ward. The ward manager was told Rawlings was being transferred to another establishment. She rang the consultant, but they had no authority to stop him. He signed a disclaimer. I arrived ten minutes after he'd gone."

"Where did they take him?"

"The nurse said they had a private ambulance from somewhere outside London … near St. Albans, she thought."

"*She thought?* Didn't she frigging *know?*"

"It all happened so quickly …" Marriner raised his hands palms upward.

Bartlett stared down at the desk, his brow furrowed, two clenched fists resting on the blotter. "What are they playing at?" he muttered.

There was a knock on the door, and a young woman looked in.

"Not now, Cathy," said Bartlett.

"It's about the hospitals, sir," she said. "Sergeant Marriner phoned in asking me to run a check and report here immediately."

"Go on, then."

"There are several private hospitals in the St. Albans area and quite a lot of clinics and nursing homes. You're looking at around twenty places, I reckon."

"We can ring round to see if Rawlings has been moved to one of them, sir," said Marriner.

Bartlett nodded. "Get started, Cathy."

The door clicked shut, and Marriner made to get up. Bartlett looked at his sergeant. "The whole bloody thing's fallen apart, Ted … just like that. One minute we've got a case … suspects at the scene … evidence … identification … Now, we haven't even got a victim, and all the evidence has evaporated."

"You know what I think, sir? I was going over it in the car just now. I think we're on the wrong track. We thought Walker was up to something and was trying to stop this photographer finding out what it was, so she tried to clobber him."

"What else could it be, Ted?"

"It did occur to me … well, other people've been attacked round here by our phantom mugger, who just pops up and then disappears …"

"Doesn't make sense," said Bartlett.

"But Walker did visit the place where Frank Day was attacked. There's some sort of connection."

"You seriously think she was involved in the assault on Day?"

"No, not really. But something else is going on … it must be. Marnie Walker's not violent, and as for her professor … he couldn't hurt a fly … nor could the girl, Anne. There's got to be something we don't know about."

"Rawlings is involved with Walker," said Bartlett emphatically. "He didn't say anything about muggers or anyone else. He accused her. And we've got proof she was at the scene."

"But the rest of the evidence – "

"It's a start. We may not have everything we need right now, but we'll keep looking."

"We've searched every inch of the crime scene, sir. There's nothing to link Marnie Walker with the victim … except that he named her, I grant you that. But we're missing something important."

"You're right there, Ted. We're missing our key witness … the victim. Get out there and find him."

Marriner got up. "Okay, sir. We'll trace the hospital all right."

"Let Cathy follow that up," said Bartlett. "You get on to his paper. Find out what they're playing at."

• • • • •

It was mild enough to eat outdoors. As soon as Marnie saw the table and parasol that Anne had set up on the bank, she realised how hungry she was and allowed herself to be pampered by the 'galley slaves'. With a flourish, Ralph served asparagus with hollandaise sauce, followed by aubergine parmesan and a salad of tomato and basil in balsamic vinaigrette. He produced a bottle of Chianti, and Marnie felt more relaxed than she had in a long time.

As usual, they planned as they ate, and Ralph's insistence that they take the day off met no opposition. He proposed either a walk in the country or a 'tootle' on one of their boats. Marnie opted for the boat trip, reasoning that if they were being watched, it might be a good idea to let themselves be seen on their own boat in home waters, if they were suspected of being on a different boat a long way to the south.

Anne had the table cleared in two minutes while Marnie made her phone call to Andrew.

· · · · ·

They slipped gently along, the sun dodging in and out of light clouds, a cool edge to the breeze, and lambs playing in the fields. The three friends stood together on the stern deck of *Sally Ann*, with Marnie at the tiller. She yawned, and Ralph put his arm round her.

Seconds later, Anne yawned too. "I'm going to need an early night," she said. "I hardly slept at all last night."

"Why? What was the matter?"

"I kept thinking about you in Simon's flat. It seemed so strange."

"It felt strange. Anyway, it's not as if Simon was there ... except at the beginning."

"Oh?" said Anne.

"Fortunately for me, he was still there when I arrived ... showed me how to get in. The security arrangements are impressive ... it's Fort Knox. No one could enter without a degree in electronics. Actually, I didn't sleep much either."

"Worried you might not be able to get out?" Ralph suggested.

"Too much on my mind ... thinking about the newspapers."

"So was I," said Anne. "Really depressing. I got up in the middle of the night and made a cup of tea."

"It's not too late to change your mind," said Marnie.

"No, I was just feeling gloomy about the papers ... the tabloids ... they're so *stupid*. They've got so much influence, and they're always so *negative*, as if the public only wants to read about bad news. Why don't they ever write about good things?"

"Talking of bad news ..." said Ralph, pointing forward.

They were rounding a bend and ahead of them about fifty metres further on, a boat was lying across the canal, completely blocking the way. Marnie throttled back and put *Sally Ann* into reverse gear, and they drifted slowly up towards it. They could see the name *High Jinx* painted on the side of the boat, framed by a pattern of roses in bright colours.

The boat itself was in a livery of green and red, with yellow lining and a faded black hull. It was about forty-five feet long, like as *Sally Ann*, and on this stretch of water it could almost touch both sides of the canal at bow and stern. As they drew nearer they saw it was attached to the bank by a rope at the stern. The rope in the bows hung straight down into the water.

Ralph went forward along the gunwale, grabbing the pole from the roof as he went, and stood in the bows, signalling to Marnie when she should bring *Sally Ann* to a complete halt. They eased forward until their nose button was within a metre of *High Jinx*. Anne went down through the cabin to help Ralph. When she stepped into the cratch she found they were almost nudging the bank. Ralph was holding their mooring rope, signalling to Marnie to ease forward.

"Are we going to pull them off?" said Anne.

Ralph nodded. "I'm going to attach this to their nose. When I throw it back to you, will you fasten it to our T-stud?"

Anne clambered out of the cratch onto the prow, while Ralph stepped carefully across to the other boat. He tied the rope firmly and passed it back to Anne, who wound it in a figure-of-eight round the stud. Ralph signalled to go into reverse and poled off against the bank so that both boats began moving as one across the canal. Marnie soon had *Sally Ann* and *High Jinx* pulled over to the opposite bank.

Anne went back through the cabin to pick up mooring stakes to hold *Sally Ann* securely while they dealt with the other boat.

"How do we tie this one up?" she said to Ralph. "There's nothing we can fasten it to here."

Ralph reached out to *High Jinx* and pulled on the forward mooring rope that hung down into the water. He could feel the weight of something on the end and had a fair idea what it was. Sure enough, a mooring stake broke the surface. It was made of steel with a loop near the top forming a letter P, and the rope was fastened through the loop. Ralph took hold of it, feeling slimy mud where it had dragged in the canal bottom. He knelt down on the bank and swirled it in the water to wash it clean and wiped it, and his hands, on the grass. Marnie came up to join them. In the field sloping down from the canal behind them, several cows were staring curiously in their direction, chewing the grass.

"The stake must've worked itself loose," Marnie observed.

"Looks like it," said Ralph. He took the hammer from Anne and secured the mooring stake firmly. He knocked it into the ground so that only the loop at the head was visible with the rope still in place. "The soil's not very firm here. It probably got loosened by boats going by without slowing down."

Marnie walked along the bank inspecting the boat. The curtains were drawn, and there was no sign of occupancy. Now that they had made it secure there was nothing left to do, so they untied *Sally Ann* and pushed her off.

"That's better," said Marnie. "A bit of action to clear the cobwebs ... take our mind off things, even if only for a few minutes."

Ralph nodded vaguely. He had a serious expression on his face and was looking back down the canal towards the boat they had tied up.

"What's up?" Marnie asked.

"That boat. Did anything strike you as odd about it?"

"Apart from it blocking the whole canal, you mean?"

"It looked abandoned," Anne suggested. "Like the *Marie Celeste*. Someone had left it there and gone off without making sure it was safe."

"Gone off where?" said Ralph.

Anne shrugged. "Dunno."

"I see what you mean," said Marnie. "It wasn't tied up on the towpath side. So where had the people gone ... across the field of cows?"

# Part 21

Next morning, Marnie was braced for the arrival of the paparazzi at any time, but all was quiet on the Knightly St John front. Every few minutes she would look towards the window expecting to see strangers charging about outside, clutching notebooks and cameras. But by mid-morning nothing had disturbed the peace of Glebe Farm. Anne got up to put the kettle on and went over to look out of the window.

"Any sign of the Apaches?" Marnie asked.

"Not yet." Anne cocked her head on one side. "But I think ... ah, yes. Not the Apaches, Marnie. It's the Seventh Cavalry."

Marnie walked over to join her. "Sergeant Marriner ... but no Bartlett. Interesting."

Marriner got out of the car and opened the boot. He was accompanied by a young woman, and together they approached the office barn, each carrying black plastic sacks. Marnie opened the door to let them in, and they set the sacks down on the floor by her desk.

"Good morning, Sergeant Marriner and ... it's Cathy, isn't it?"

"Well remembered," said the young woman brightly. She extended a hand. "Cathy Lamb. I haven't seen you since ..."

"Since a time we try not to think about too much. Can I offer you both coffee?"

"That'd be very welcome," said Marriner.

Anne immediately headed for the kitchen area while Marnie looked in the sacks. They contained the clothes that had been taken away for examination, everything carefully folded and stacked in neat piles.

"Thank you for taking so much trouble with them."

"That was Cathy," said Marriner, taking a seat.

"So you found nothing, just like I said. Have you brought everything back?"

"All but the ear-ring. Forensic wanted to hang onto it a bit longer."

"Fine. It won't incriminate me. You know that, don't you? I had nothing whatever to do with the attack on that man."

"How did he know your name?" said Cathy Lamb.

Marnie shook her head. "It's a mystery to me. But most people on the canal round here know me for one reason or another. Perhaps he'd seen me before in connection with the murder last year. The whole place was crawling with media people then. You'll have to ask him."

"We will," said Marriner, " ... when we catch up with him."

"What do you mean ... *catch up with him*?"

"He's gone," said Lamb.

"Where?"

"To a private hospital in another area."

"You've *lost* him?" said Marnie. "You've let him *go*?"

Marriner accepted a mug from Anne. "He wasn't a suspect. His bosses moved him as soon as he came out of Intensive Care."

"So what happens now?"

"As far as you're concerned, nothing. We've been told he's not pressing any charges against you."

"But if it's a criminal matter, surely it doesn't depend on him pressing charges."

"Marnie!" Anne exclaimed. "Whose side are you on?"

"That's true," said Marriner. "But if he now says he was confused because of his head injury, there's not much we can do about his testimony."

They all fell into a thoughtful silence.

"Well if it's any consolation," Marnie began, "I didn't assault him, neither did my friends. You can be sure of that."

"But why were you there at that time?" Lamb asked, as if making casual conversation.

"I told Mr Bartlett. We were at the boatyard on legitimate business ... a project we're working on. They'll confirm that at the yard. Ask Stevie, she'll tell you. We heard a noise on the opposite side of the canal and went over to check it out. There was no one there, nothing to see. That's the truth."

Marnie felt relieved at telling them such a good story, almost the whole truth, but giving nothing away. Convincing.

"Give me a break, Marnie," Marriner said, looking at her over his mug.

"You're getting to be as bad as your boss. Why don't you believe me?"

"You don't need me to answer that. Just tell me what's really going on." He sounded weary.

Any minute now, he would be asking for details of her whereabouts over the last few days.

"Look, Mr Marriner ... Cathy ..." She looked at them each in turn, with her most sincere expression. "I promise there's nothing illegal going on, but it is private and confidential. You're going to have to trust me."

Marriner drained his coffee and stood up. "The DCI will be delighted when I report that back to him. It'll make his day."

"It's the best I can do. It's all I can do."

"Okay, but if it turns out that something's happening that you should have divulged ... you could end up in deep trouble."

Marnie watched the car reverse out of the yard and heard it move off up the track. Relieved at no questions being asked about their absence over the weekend, she turned to Anne. "That I should have *divulged* ... Only the police talk like that, surely."

• • • • •

"You don't believe her, do you sarge?" Cathy was holding on to the grab handle as the police Cavalier bumped up the track.

Marriner steered round the ruts. "I'll swear she leaves the track like this to put us off coming down here. She'll be getting a Land Rover next ... or a tank. And I expect you think she's telling the truth."

"Of course she is."

"Is that female intuition ... or solidarity?" He jerked the steering wheel to miss a pothole, and they both swayed in their seats.

"No. She is telling the truth."

Marriner grunted. "Perhaps I am getting as bad as Bartlett."

"It's what she's not telling us that bothers me," said Cathy. "She's definitely up to something."

Marriner looked sideways at her. "So that makes two of us getting like the boss." He smiled and immediately swore as the car caught a bump and he hit his head against the roof.

• • • • •

Minutes later, the phone rang in the office barn. Andrew was reporting in to HQ. He sounded deflated.

"Hi, Marnie. We've had quite a morning."

"Paparazzi?"

"What's the singular of paparazzi?"

"One too many. What's happened?"

"Our visitor came back ... just by himself."

"Tell me about it."

• • • • •

They had tried to make the yard look like normal in case anyone was watching them. Business as usual. Andrew and Cliff, the engineer, were conferring on a customer's boat, squatting in its engine room. Anthony was tucked away in the cabin, and Kate was on the wharfside perched on a folding chair, sketching the bridge, her bag lying on the ground at her feet. A car pulled up and a man walked over to where she was sitting. Andrew, his head upside down examining the gearbox, did not see him arrive. Kate looked up from the sketchpad as he approached.

"Good morning. I've come about the boat."

"Which one was that?"

"I saw the man here on Saturday. We were talking about that red one. I understand it's for sale. I'd like to look over it."

"For sale?" Kate looked confused. "I didn't realise we'd had instructions from the owner."

"Well, as I'm here, I may as well have a look ... I've come all this way to see it. It won't take long."

Kate looked over to where Andrew and Cliff were working, but they were both out of sight. "Just a moment, please. I'll get the key."

Kate shouldered her bag and went to the cottage, returning a minute later to find the visitor already standing on the red oxide boat's counter by the door. She opened up and led the way into the cabin, leaving her bag hanging on the tiller.

The man looked surprised; the boat was totally empty. Not a dish in a cupboard, not a towel in the bathroom, stripped bare, the whole thing, just as Marnie had told them to do on the phone the day before. The visitor walked through the boat, quickly opening every drawer and cupboard. Without comment he turned and walked out. Kate paused to close cupboard doors and straighten the bed cover.

She emerged to find the man standing on the bank examining a sketchbook that he had taken from her bag. Before she could protest, he handed it back, complimenting Kate on her skill. He strode across the yard, climbed into the car and drove off, as Andrew climbed out from the engine room and hurried across to where Kate was standing.

They opened the sketchbook, page after page of drawings of their last journey. Prominent among them were studies of a man working the boat and locks, handling sacks of coal, dispensing diesel. One drawing was a portrait. It was very lifelike, the detailing of the bone structure and eyes, excellent. In the bottom right-hand corner Kate had written one word. *Tony*.

· · · · ·

It was no use. Marnie felt hot, and even though she pushed the light-weight duvet away from her, she knew she would find it virtually impossible to get back to sleep. She lay for several minutes in the darkness, hoping that Ralph's quiet breathing would help her to relax. It was a vain hope.

She remembered Anne getting up on Sunday night to make a cup of tea. It seemed a good idea. Marnie slid quietly out from under the cover, grabbed the dressing gown from the foot of the bed and made her way along the passage to the galley. Just before switching on the light, she heard a sound that surprised her. She pricked up her ears as it grew louder and unmistakable. A boat was passing, and even at low revs Marnie recognised the familiar chugging of a Lister diesel, like the engine on *Sally Ann*.

Parting the curtain with a finger, Marnie was able to make out the shape slipping by, but the night was too dark for her to recognise the boat if she had known it. At the tiller she could not see clearly who was steering. Only a tiny red lamp glowed on the control panel. The boat was motoring without headlight or running lights, the steerer relying on night vision to guide the boat on its way.

Marnie hurried forward to the cratch through Ralph's study. Noiselessly she fiddled with the bolts on the glazed doors and pushed her way out. Standing in the cratch well, she found her view no better. There was no moonlight to help her, and the sound of the engine receded, increasing briefly as the steerer accelerated to normal cruising speed. Marnie made her way back to the galley, now more wide awake than ever.

Stirring her tea at the galley table, Marnie looked up at the clock and wondered why anyone would need to be navigating on the canal at three in the morning.

# Part 22

"Are you all sorted out for your driving lesson … flat shoes, clothes you're wearing?"

Anne looked up from her computer. "Yes. I'm going like this. Jeans are fine for the lessons. I'm keeping the mini-skirt for the actual test."

Marnie smiled across the office. "You haven't got a mini-skirt, have you?"

"I'm saving up."

"Oh well … shouldn't take long. Mini-skirts don't cost much."

"I know. It's the legs I'm saving up for."

Marnie laughed. It took an effort of will. Her mind was with Andrew and Kate plus their crewman, whose cover was almost certainly blown. Over breakfast they had begun discussing tactics. It was a short conversation. Their plan was now reduced to the working boats scuttling away at four miles per hour with the paparazzi probably not far behind them.

Anne yawned. "Oh dear … this is becoming a habit … this not sleeping."

"Not sleeping? Why not?"

"I seem to have too many things running round inside my head. I'd better not fall asleep during my driving lesson."

Marnie was worried. They were all feeling the strain, and she was the one forcing the pace. The last thing she wanted was to make Anne suffer.

"I didn't sleep much either," she said. "I was too hot, though I expect that wasn't the only reason. I followed your advice and got up to make some tea."

"Me too," said Anne.

"*Again*? How often are you doing this?"

"That was just the second time … last night and Sunday."

"Something strange happened when I got up," Marnie began.

Anne's eyes widened. "A boat went by," she said. "In the dark … without any lights on."

"That's right! How on earth did you know that, Anne?"

"I saw it too."

"How? You can't see the canal from your loft …"

"I … er … got up and went for a walk."

Marnie looked horrified. "In the middle of the night … in the *pitch dark* … all by yourself?"

Anne's expression changed to a smile. "I only walked through the spinney to the canalside over by *Sally*. I was probably standing just a few metres from where you were when the boat passed."

"Did you see which boat it was?"

"Not really. There wasn't any light to go by, not even starlight. I had the impression it might've been that boat we tied up the other day."

"*High Jinx*?"

"Like I said … I couldn't be sure. But I did notice it sounded like *Sally Ann*."

"Lister engine," Marnie agreed. "Anne, you've really got to be more careful. I don't think you should wander around alone in the dark. It might not be safe."

"Why not?"

"Well … for a start there are muggers about. Look what happened to Frank Day."

"*Muggers*? Marnie, I don't think muggers lurk in the spinney at night-time."

"Then ... mad axe-murderers and rapists ..."

Anne laughed. "Marnie, this is Glebe Farm. It's the safest place in the world. What harm could anyone possibly come to here?"

• • • • •

An hour later, soon after nine, Marnie walked quickly through the spinney. She wanted to talk with Ralph about his arrangements at Oxford. His post as Professor at All Saints College and his sabbatical were almost over, and she wanted to know his plans for the next few days. She tried to imagine the spinney as it had been during the night when Anne came that way. Anne was right. It seemed hard to imagine this quiet place holding any dangers.

• • • • •

Just after Marnie went out, Anne heard tyres crunching on the gravel in the yard. She glanced at the window, expecting to see the red post van, but it was an unfamiliar car that drew up. She ran to the door to call Marnie, but she was well into the spinney, and Anne did not want to shout after her. By the time the visitor opened the office door, Anne was sitting at her desk engrossed in the data on her computer screen.

"Oh ... good morning. Can I help you?"

Tallish, dark slicked-back hair, black leather jacket. *Designer* black leather jacket.

"I'm interested in a boat." No preamble. A clipped London accent.

"A *boat*? I'm afraid we don't normally do designs for boat interiors." She pointed to a display screen covered in photographs and drawings of their designs.

"I wasn't looking for a design. I'm interested in *buying* a boat."

Anne looked confused. "We are interior designers," she said slowly.

"But you've got a boat."

"Yes. But we live on it ... temporarily. It's not for sale."

"Look ... is there anyone I can talk to about this?" His tone was becoming impatient faced with this thick office junior.

"I'm the only one in the office this morning."

"All right. Let me start again. You have a boat here, right?"

"Yes."

"And there was another boat ... a grey one."

"Green," said Anne.

"*Green?*"

"Our other boat's green ... sage green with gold lettering."

"No. This was grey."

"We only have two boats: dark blue and cream; green and gold."

"This was another boat ... a grey one. Did you see it? Try to remember."

She paused. "I may have done."

"*May have done?* Aren't you sure?"

She shrugged. "Boats are coming and going all the time. A lot of them are grey. It's one of the standard undercoats," she explained helpfully.

"Yes. I know." *Christ Almighty!* he thought. "Look ... this other boat ... the *grey* one ... can you remember seeing it in the past couple of weeks?"

"Yes. I think I can."

"You mean that?"

"Yes. I'm sure I saw it." She looked as if she was thinking hard. "It was moored near here for a few days."

"Do you know who owned it? Did you see him? Think carefully."

She really was thinking carefully. *What do I say that will mislead him most?* "I'm trying hard to think."

"Good girl."

*Yuck!* "No, it's no good. I can't remember seeing anyone on board. Sorry."

"Can you remember which way it was travelling?"

She thought carefully again. *They took it south.* "North."

"You're certain?"

"Well, it was pointing that way at its mooring."

"Okay. And what colour was it?"

"The *grey* boat? It was ... grey."

"You're sure about that?"

"Definite. Grey ... and it was pointing that way." She raised her arm.

He turned to leave and hesitated in the doorway. "Do you know a pair of barges that go along selling coal and stuff ... sometimes tied together? *Totteridge* and *Shardlow*."

"Not barges," said Anne. "Narrowboats. They're sometimes *breasted up*."

"That's them. Good. Do you know the people who run them?"

"Yes."

"How many are there? Do you know what they're called?"

"There's Andrew and Kate."

"Ah ..." The stranger narrowed his eyes.

"They're on *Shardlow*, the butty. And the other one's Tony. He's on *Totteridge*."

"Tony? You mean there are three of them? You're sure about that?"

Anne nodded. She looked as innocent as a schoolgirl. The man frowned.

"How long has he been with them, this Tony?"

Anne shrugged. "As long as I've known them. Ages."

The man opened the door and walked quickly away. Anne waited till he had turned the car and driven off up the field track before ringing Marnie's mobile.

• • • • •

The consensus of opinion was that the paparazzi – or at least their local representative – might leave them in peace for a while. Anne's performance might just have done enough to earn them a brief respite from outside attention. Marnie rang Andrew who confirmed that *Totteridge* and *Shardlow* had set off from the boatyard early that morning and were heading towards London. Moving targets. Anthony's boat was moored at the boatyard in its red undercoat, its contents stacked in the box room of Andrew's cottage.

They had done everything they could to withstand attack. Now, all they could do was wait for Rachel to be in touch for the next stage.

Marnie took Anne to her driving lesson in the MG. There was a warmth in the air, and they revelled in running on the open road with the hood down, the little car growling gamely along despite its advanced age. When Marnie returned to the office there were no strange cars waiting for her in the farmyard, but the red light glowed on the answerphone. She pressed the button.

"This is Rachel Rutherford. My mother asked me to ring you. I'm back for a couple of days. I'm not sure if I can help, but let's have a chat. I'll give you my mobile number. Ring any time you want. See you!"

Marnie scribbled down the number. In one way she felt exhilarated; things were falling into place. In another way she felt anxious; things would be getting tricky from now on. This was the hardest part.

• • • • •

Anne was disappointed. She drove slowly along the village high street with no one to see her at the wheel. But then, she thought, arriving in a Metro covered in red letter Ls was hardly the ultimate in cool. She pulled over at the gate by the field track, thanked her instructor for the lesson, waved him off and turned down the slope to home.

After a minute the buildings came into view and she branched off from the main track to walk across the field and approach the complex from behind the outer barns. This route gave her a clear view of the yard, and she was relieved that no cars were parked outside the farm. As she drew nearer she saw Ralph's Volvo standing with the boot open. Inside was Marnie's overnight bag. Anne walked round to the office.

Marnie looked up from writing on a pad. "How did the lesson go?"

"Okay. I've been doing three-point turns — well seven-point actually — and reversing round corners ... nearly. Shall I pack?"

"You've seen Ralph?"

"No. But I've seen your bag in the boot of the car. You don't normally have to stay overnight for a hair appointment ... or are you having a general anaesthetic this time?"

Marnie outlined the plan. She was seeing Rachel the next morning. Ralph would drop her off at the station on his way to Oxford and collect her the next evening after a meeting in London. Anne could choose whether to stay on at Glebe Farm, promising to take no nocturnal strolls, or go with Marnie and stay in Simon's flat in Docklands. It was no contest.

• • • • •

They dined out that evening and spoiled themselves. Marnie wanted to give her haircut an outing in polite society and chose a smart restaurant at the other end of the block from Simon's flat. They had a table by the window with a view of Tower Bridge and across the Thames to Saint Katharine Docks.

It rekindled Anne's enthusiasm for interior design, and she was enchanted. The decor was restrained, the service calm and efficient, the food traditional but imaginative. She loved this way of life and she loved Marnie for giving her the chance to embrace it.

They took a walk after dinner in the gentle spring evening, looking at the galleries and boutiques, boggling at the property prices in estate agents' windows. They wandered along the river promenade and saw the lights coming on like a theatre backdrop. For a few minutes they leaned on the railings and watched pleasure boats go by.

"Marnie? I don't want to spoil things ..."

"Good idea."

"But ... you remember that boat that went past during the night? Do you think it could've had anything to do with the newspaper people?"

"What makes you say that?"

"Well ... it was very odd, wasn't it?"

"Some people travel at night if they've got a long way to go in a limited time."

"Without lights on? Don't you find that strange?"

"People do strange things, Anne. That summer two years ago when I went off on my first solo journey ..." She smiled at the memory. "One night I couldn't sleep and I just set off in the dark. It was wonderful ... the water ... the peace ... the sun coming up ... Waterways can be magic."

As they stood together in silence, a Victorian Thames barge glided upstream, red sails furled, leeboard stowed clear of the water against its dark hull.

Anne sighed. "Isn't this gorgeous!"

Marnie nodded. She decided not to tell Anne that where they were standing was the place where in centuries past they hanged river pirates and left their bodies to rot on the gibbets.

They turned to walk back, and Anne said, with urgency in her voice, "Wouldn't it be good if we could find somewhere like this on a canal somewhere and create a Mini-Docklands of our own?" Her eyes were sparkling.

"Why not?" said Marnie. "But shall we get Glebe Farm finished first?"

"Oh yes. That's wonderful too. That's *home*."

"I take it you won't mind being in the flat by yourself tomorrow until I get back from seeing Rachel?"

"No probs. I might just go out for a little walk." She saw Marnie's expression. "In broad daylight."

# Part 23

Halfway across Tower Bridge Anne stopped and looked down river. She was on her way back to Simon's place from seeing Marnie off on her journey to west London to meet Rachel. Although buffeted by the turbulence thrown up by lorries and buses, nothing was going to spoil this for her.

This was London Docklands, providing *des res* for the capital's fashionable classes. Converted Regency and Victorian warehouses interspersed with new blocks had created a city within a city, offices, plazas, lofts and penthouses scattered over a vast area, bounded by the river and the broad sky. It had brought employment and prosperity to hundreds of thousands of Londoners, untold wealth to speculators and builders and international reputations to architects and designers. Standing on the most distinctive bridge in Europe, Anne looked down at the wide river bending away to the left, the great tower of Canary Wharf rising up on the horizon.

It suddenly occurred to her that she was looking at the parliamentary constituency of Docklands West, whose representative was Anthony Leyton-Brown MP. Momentarily she shuddered, though whether it was from that thought or the blast of air whirling round her, she could not tell.

• • • • •

Marnie sat in Rachel's living room surrounded by the chaos of homecoming. The flat was virtually one large room with a kitchen, bedroom and bathroom attached. The living room contained a double futon, a scrubbed pine dining table and bentwood chairs, with a small desk in a corner on which stood a laptop computer in its carrying case. On a low table a mound of mail had been dumped.

Occasional cries came from the kitchen where Rachel was battling with an espresso machine, a flat-warming present when she had moved in a year ago. This was its maiden outing. "You do like espresso, don't you Marnie? ... I don't seem to have any sugar ... Oh, yes I do. Panic over ... Biscuits ... biscuits ... now, where ... ?"

Marnie could see the resemblance to her mother as Rachel bustled in carrying a tray. She turned round in a circle like a cat preparing to sit and, finding no clear surface big enough for it, she squatted down and laid the tray on the floor. She sat cross-legged beside it, and Marnie slid down from her chair to join Rachel on the carpet.

"How very Japanese," Rachel said in a cheerful voice and poured thick murky liquid into tiny cups of dark blue with a gold rim.

Rachel had the pleasing looks of her mother, but her features were less fine. Like Jane, she conveyed the impression of being arty and more than a little disorganised, her curly hair pulled back into a loose bun. She listened quietly while Marnie outlined the problem. Once again Marnie found herself dreading the reaction of another person to her improbable plan. But strangely, she found that she was starting to believe in it herself.

"So where do I come in, Marnie?"

"You'd be willing to help?"

"If I could ... if I can."

Marnie smiled with relief. "Most people who know about this – and there aren't many – think the whole idea is completely far-fetched. It's comforting to hear you say you're willing to help."

Rachel laughed. "Oh, I think the whole thing sounds *unbelievable*, but I just figured you had it all worked out and knew what you were doing." Seeing Marnie's expression she added, "You do know what you're doing ... don't you?"

• • • • •

Anne was at heart a practical person, but that breezy spring morning, as she turned into Butlers wharf, her imagination permitted her a small indulgence.

She walked between the renovated wharf blocks, stepping lightly on the cobbles between the converted warehouses in the yellow brickwork so common in London, that had been scrubbed and repointed to look as good as new. In her imagination, Anne saw herself as a new Terence Conran, designer of lifestyles. She pressed *her* code on the security keypad, took the lift to *her* floor. She opened *her* front door as the phone began ringing – *Simon's* phone – and instantly felt like an intruder.

Anne looked down at the answerphone and paused. Simon's voice invited callers to leave a message after the long tone.

"Ah ... " said a familiar voice, hesitant.

Anne grabbed the phone. "Ralph! It's Anne."

"Good. I was in two minds about – "

"Yes. I understand. But I'm here. Marnie's gone off to see Rachel."

"Already?"

"She had to see her first thing. She'll almost be there by now." Anne could hear traffic noise in the back ground. "Where are you?"

"In a queue of cars stuck behind a delivery van somewhere in the City. I think I'm not far from Tower Bridge. Can you give me directions ... assuming I ever get out of this jam?"

"It's easy. Just come over the bridge and take the first left. Look out for me. I'll be waiting for you there."

"I'll be as quick as I can."

"Ralph?"

"Yes?"

"Have you got plans for this morning?"

"I think I'm about to get some."

• • • • •

Rachel thumbed through her address book. They were still sitting cross-legged on the floor.

"Trouble is ... most of my contacts are in drama or documentaries. The news and current affairs people tend to be a little world apart." Rachel shook her head slowly.

"I suppose it was just a long shot," said Marnie.

Rachel turned more pages, muttering. "I did have a friend who used to work on *Panorama* ... no ... She went back to Scotland ... works with the

Beeb in Inverness now. Ah … I wonder if Judith … Judith Wilkins … "

"Is she at the BBC?"

"Not any more. She left to have a baby and get married."

"The other way round, presumably," Marnie suggested lightly.

"Well no, not actually."

"I'm being old-fashioned," Marnie said. "So … Judith married her baby's father … and is now living somewhere nearer than Inverness, hopefully?"

"No."

"She's moved to Shetland?"

"She didn't marry the baby's father. That was rather the point. Actually, the whole business was a bit odd."

"After what I've been experiencing lately, anything goes."

"It's a long story," Rachel began, "and I don't have a lot of time this morning. Also, I don't know *all* the details. But the basic facts are … Judith worked on the *Today* programme as a researcher. Actually, she handled the piece about you when you were interviewed a couple of years back. She had an affair with one of the producers, Tim Rodgers. You've probably never heard of him, but you'll probably know his partner … Sue Groves?"

"The newsreader on TV?"

"Correct. Sue and Tim have been together for yonks and they've got two kids. But the rumour was that Tim had a fling with Judith, and she got pregnant."

"Not uncommon," said Marnie. "And not without a number of possible solutions."

"For some of us perhaps … but tricky for Judith … she's RC. Anyway, Judith had had a boyfriend who was mad about her … I gather she went to cry on his shoulder, and out of the blue he proposed to her. Just like that!"

"She had to leave her job?"

"Not much choice in the circumstances."

"Tim Rodgers is still there, presumably?"

"Senior Producer."

"You don't think Judith will be out of touch with the current scene?"

"She'll know more news people than I do."

"That's assuming she'll want to help me," said Marnie. "Or even talk to me."

"Yes. I don't know about that. Tread carefully. You see, Marnie, I think it's possible that she still … Anyway, the other thing is Sue, Tim's partner. She's not the forgiving kind, and he really loves their kids. She could make his life hell if it all got raked up again."

• • • • •

Ralph spotted Anne waiting on the pavement after crossing Tower Bridge. She climbed in beside him.

"Taxi?" she said.

"Where to, guv'nor?" It was as close to a Cockney accent as Ralph could manage, and it made Anne laugh.

"To the other side."

The *other side* was where it had all begun. Anne navigated a route back across the bridge using Ralph's *A to Z* street atlas. Near the old Limehouse

Town Hall they took a left and pulled up outside a modern block of council flats.

"This is it." He pointed across the street. "If I understood the story correctly, that's where Anthony met Marlene."

There were few people to be seen. Anne wound down the window, and the noise of the heavy traffic on the main road poured in, even though it was more than fifty metres away.

"The constituency office must be down that street."

Anne nodded. She was trying to bring up the scene, those rainy days when Anthony had encountered the girl who was to change his life. The area was the usual mixture: blocks of flats built after the war between terraces of houses up to two hundred years old.

Something was bothering Anne. She tried studying the street to see if it clarified the problem. On the opposite side stood a newsagent's and a fish-and-chip shop. The other houses were residential. On the next corner was a phonebox, of the new grey variety, open on one side, and beyond that, a pillar box, its vivid red paintwork bringing life to dull surroundings.

"No girl," Anne murmured.

"Did you expect her to be there?"

"No. Not really. I'm not sure what I expected. But whatever it was ..." She shook her head. "I wonder what Marnie would do."

"She'd offer me a cup of something after my drive from Oxford."

Anne smiled and reached in her back pocket to pull out a small wallet of black leather. It contained some of Marnie's business cards.

"Can you wait while I give these to the people in the shops? I'll ask them to ring us if they see the girl back again."

Ralph looked doubtful. "It might be worth a try, I suppose, as we've come this far already."

Anne quickly ran across to the shops and was soon back in the car.

"What did they say?"

"They just said okay ... didn't ask any questions ... didn't say anything. I expect the cards are already in the bin." She pulled on the seat belt. "Oh well ... at least I tried."

She turned her head to look over at the shops. Beside her, Ralph stirred.

"Something's bothering you," he said.

"Sort of." She bit her lip.

He started the engine. "Come on. There's something I want to show you."

• • • • •

On the way from Rachel's flat to the tube station, Marnie rang Judith Wilkins. It was the inevitable answerphone. There were no real people left on the planet. She recorded a brief message that she would ring again later and disconnected.

• • • • •

"There." Ralph stopped the car on double yellow lines and looked down the road ahead of them.

"What is it?"

They were looking at a modern development of offices several storeys high, with a wide drive into which an articulated lorry was turning. It was carrying enormous rolls covered in plastic material, like the round bales of hay in the fields after harvest.

"Do you see the name on the building? There's a signboard over there."

Anne read it out loud. "Global House - home of Global Communications International."

Below the heading, in smaller letters, were the names of publications: *The Globe, The Sunday Globe, Global Market Review.*

"That," said Ralph, "is their headquarters."

"Hawksby's office?"

Ralph nodded. "Top floor, I believe, though I've never been there myself."

Anne looked at the enormous complex. It seemed to fill the whole road; the hub of a news empire that had almost a quarter of the UK newspaper market covered. This was the power-base of Jeremy Hawksby, the organisation they had decided to fight.

"Blimey," she muttered.

• • • • •

The lack of positive progress was getting through to Marnie. She sat on the tube train rattling across the city back to Simon's place and felt frustrated and depressed. Looking round the compartment, she noticed that quite a few of the other passengers were reading the *Globe*. Feeling cornered, surrounded, claustrophobic, she stood up and went to stand facing the doors, watching the black walls of the tunnel flash past in a blur.

• • • • •

"Got it! I know what it was."

Anne leaned earnestly across the table. They were sitting in a bistro in Butlers Wharf.

"Go on," said Ralph.

"I know what was odd back there ... that street where Anthony met Marlene."

"Yes. I think I know what you're going to say."

"It was a hopeless place for begging. It wasn't really a through route to anywhere. What do you think?"

"Certainly a strange place for beggars ... assuming she *was* just begging."

"Yes. It was just a side street. And if she was ... you know ... a *hooker* ... I can't imagine she'd do much trade with people popping out to buy cod and chips and the *Evening Standard*."

Ralph smiled. "No. I agree with you."

"So it *could've* been a set-up," Anne said firmly.

"Looks like it."

"Good," said Anne. "At least we can tell Marnie we've got that sorted out."

"Yes. But maybe *good* isn't quite the right word, Anne. You do realise that means we're back to square one? Let's hope Marnie's had better luck this morning."

• • • • •

Marnie stared half-heartedly at the menu. Ralph reached across to touch her hand, and her fingers closed around his. Anne sat fingering the book of matches in the ash tray, wishing she could do something to improve things. Anything. She read the name of the restaurant on the cover of the matches: The Tower Quay. She flipped it open; the matches were tipped in bright blue. A waiter appeared at their table.

"Have you chosen?"

Marnie had barely focused on the print. "Not quite," she said.

He bowed slightly and withdrew.

"Would you prefer to go somewhere else?" Ralph said quietly.

"No. This is a really good restaurant, and I ought to jolly well buck up and stop spoiling it for you."

"Don't worry about that. It's not as if we've got much to celebrate."

"Oh, what the hell! I'll have tiger prawns followed by rack of lamb. Okay?"

Ralph gestured towards the waiter who took their order and was back in two minutes with a bottle of Chilean red. He poured three glasses. Anne stopped fiddling with the matches and slipped them into her back pocket.

Marnie picked up her glass and admired the colour of the wine. "Sorry to be a wet blanket, but we're getting nowhere and not very fast. I can't get hold of Judith Wilkins, and you don't think we stand any chance of finding Marlene over the river. *And* they may be onto Anthony hiding on Andrew's boat."

Ralph raised his glass. "To absent friends." They drank.

Marnie said, "This is rather adventurous for you, Ralph. Very fruity. It's good."

"I thought it might make a change. Anyway, in these surroundings I wanted to do something fashionable."

"Why not ... you trendy. Would you mind if I just checked the answerphone for messages?"

She pressed the buttons to interrogate the machine. There were several routine messages on the Glebe Farm number, nothing urgent. She saved them for later and continued listening.

"Andrew," she muttered, pressing the phone close to her ear. "Engine noise ... "

When the message ended, she put the mobile on the table and stared at it.

"Amaze us," said Ralph.

"Yeah, make our day," Anne joined in.

"He sounded agitated. Wants me to ring him urgently."

"You've got time to phone him before the first course arrives."

• • • • •

Not being one of those who entertained other people in restaurants with their telephone conversations, Marnie stood outside on the terrace overlooking the river to phone Andrew.

"Marnie, thank goodness! I'm really sorry about this." There was no sound of the boat's engine running.

"Why should you be sorry? What's happened?"

"Apparently, not long after we left the yard, this journalist turned up with a photographer. Cliff said they were really annoyed that we'd gone … kept saying he knew there were three of us and wanted to know who the other man was. Cliff couldn't think what to say. He told them he didn't know Tony and had never seen him before. Also I think he accidentally gave away which direction we'd gone in."

Marnie kept her voice calm and even. "Where are you now?"

"We've turned up the Wendover Arm, gone round the bend after the first bridge. I figured they might not know about the canal up that way, and if they asked anyone they'd be told it was only passable by small boats."

"Good idea. But you're going to have a hard time getting your pair out of there when the time comes."

"We'll manage. I just wish I was a quick thinker like you, Marnie. I'm not used to this kind of thing. Apart from hiding out, I couldn't think what to do next."

"Your instincts were right, Andrew. Now, I suppose the important thing is to get Anthony out of the way. Let me think it over. I'll ring you in the morning."

"I'm really sorry I've blown it, Marnie."

"No. You've done well … And thanks for everything. I don't know what we'd have done without you."

*But we're about to find out,* she thought, as she turned to go back into the restaurant. Before she had gone two paces, the mobile rang.

• • • • •

"You know that silly question: *do you want the good news or the bad news?*"

Ralph and Anne nodded, neither convinced that the good news part was about to apply. Marnie rejoined them at the table, where the first course had just arrived.

"You mean there *is* good news?" said Ralph.

"Judith Wilkins rang. I can see her tomorrow." Marnie unfolded the napkin and spread it on her lap.

"That's good."

"In fact, it gets slightly better before the bad news kicks in. Judith lives in St. Albans and, being just north of London, not too far from the Grand Union, it means I can collect Anthony without going too far out of the way."

"*Collect Anthony?*" Ralph echoed.

"That's the bad news."

Marnie explained the situation while they ate their starters.

Ralph said, "Is this where you tell us, as usual, that you've worked out what to do next?"

Marnie ate a forkful of grilled tiger prawns served in a piquant sauce for which the chef was renowned. His efforts, on this occasion, went largely unnoticed.

"That's the other bit of bad news."

# Part 24

On Friday morning the phone was ringing when Marnie and Anne unlocked the door of the office barn. It was becoming a habit, and Marnie approached the phone with apprehension. But it was only the builders' merchant with a problem, and to Marnie it was light relief compared with her recent worries.

"So how long will the roof slates be delayed?" she asked.

"Could be a month, maybe six weeks."

"*What?* Where are they coming from ... *Scotland?*"

"Tarragona."

"The only Tarragona I know of is in *Spain*," she said sarcastically.

"That's right."

"Look ... the planning regs state they have to be *local*, to match the existing ones. Where does Spain come into the *local* category ... or have some Tectonic plates moved while my back's been turned?"

"Eh? You can't get grey slates in Britain any more, me dook ... only Spain has the right colour."

"Then get Welsh blues. They'll match the ones on the other cottages."

"Can't do that. Planning said they have to be grey. They've got to be local."

Marnie put her hand over the mouthpiece and sighed to Anne across the room. "I don't believe I'm having this conversation."

But Anne was not paying attention. She was rising from her seat, straining to hear a sound from outside, crossing quickly to the window.

"We've got a visitor. Don't know the car."

Marnie said into the phone, "Gotta go. I'll get back to you. Don't order any slates at all – grey, pink or orange – till I've talked to you again, okay? Bye!"

She joined Anne at the window in time to see the driver step out into the yard. There were no tape recorders or cameras, just a grey dress and a dog collar. The vicar had come to call. Marnie and Anne had never seen Angela Hemingway before. Marnie thought she looked like her name. It seemed to her a *tall* name, and she was long and thin with mousy hair and a horsy, not unpleasant face. She caught sight of them at the window and the face lit up into a friendly smile.

Marnie pulled the door open. "Hallo."

"Hi! This is my third attempt to meet you. I've heard such a lot about you both."

They shook hands and ushered her in, offering a seat.

"I think Mr Fowey told you I'd be coming to see you."

"Yes. He popped in for coffee one day."

"He praises your coffee to heaven."

"How appropriate," said Marnie. Anne took the hint and had the kettle filled in seconds.

"Did Mr Fowey also tell you we were Zen-Buddhist-Jewish-Hindu-Catholics?" Marnie enquired in a matter-of-fact tone.

"He did ... and therefore ripe for conversion!" The smile again. It transformed her.

As they drank they made polite small talk about settling into the village, taking on a new job – a *first parish* – and moving into the rectory. Sooner or later they all knew the conversation would turn to Toni Petrie, Angela's dead predecessor. Marnie decided to take the lead.

"You'll know that Toni became a friend of ours ... in her short time here."

"Yes." No smile this time.

"Did you know her?"

"Only slightly. I saw her at the patronal festival in the cathedral once. She sang a solo introit with the choir. It was marvellous."

Anne said, "I remember the first time I heard her singing in the church. I thought she sang like an angel." She looked down as her voice faded.

"Quite a contrast with Randall, *her* predecessor," Marnie said cheerfully. "But both very nice in their different ways. How do you like the decor in the rectory? That was all Randall's work."

"*Was it?* I didn't know that. It's quite ... well ... "

"Yes it is," Marnie agreed.

"Certainly is," said Anne.

"I was going to say ... *lively* ..." The smile returned.

"Oh yes. That's Randall, all right. I think he's enjoying his new job."

"Rural Dean suits him," said Angela. "He's full of ideas."

"Yeah. We've been over to see his drop-in centre."

"For drop-outs," Anne added.

"I was there last week," said Angela. "It was thriving ... if you can say that about that sort of hostel."

"We visited at Christmas," said Marnie. "There was a really good atmosphere ... easy-going ... welcoming."

Angela took a sip from her cup. "I think it's because the ... what does Randall call them ... the *guests* ... they feel relaxed because no one pries into their lives ... no questions asked ... all very private. Mr Fowey was right ... this is *excellent* coffee. I'll have to think of all sorts of excuses to come visiting you."

She took another sip. It seemed like the cue for a response, but none came. When she put the cup down, Angela looked at Marnie who was staring at her. Marnie turned quickly to Anne.

Anne had the same expression on her face as Marnie. She nodded. "Got it," she said.

• • • • •

There were times that spring when Marnie felt she had become a perpetual motion machine. The end of every journey only seemed like a pit stop before the next stage began. On that Friday morning they were going to split forces. Ralph had meetings at his college in Oxford. Marnie would travel down to St Albans to meet Judith Wilkins and go on to pick up Anthony. Anne would hold the fort in the office.

It was when Marnie put the phone down after speaking with Randall Hughes that Anne pointed out a snag.

"Good," said Marnie. "That's all arranged. We can go to Randall's this afternoon. No problem."

"Except for one small detail," said Anne, looking up from her notepad.

"Detail?"

"You haven't got a car ... I mean a *proper* car."

Marnie was about to protest on behalf of the MG when the reality of the situation struck her. "You've got a point there. I keep forgetting."

"Didn't Ralph say he had to go to Oxford?"

Marnie sat pondering. "I think we need a democratic decision. I'd better go and tell ... I mean, discuss it ... with Ralph."

"In that case, we need two democratic decisions," said Anne. "I'm coming with you."

"Who's going to run the office?"

"Dolly ... and the answerphone."

• • • • •

By the time they had reached the outskirts of St Albans, Marnie was glad she had relented and taken Anne with her. Leaving Dolly in charge of a substantial bowl of milk, and with instructions from Anne to keep the place clear of mice, they had set off on a circuit that Anne traced on the road atlas like a stage in a car rally. They dropped Ralph at the bus station to catch the Oxford coach. On the road to St Albans, Anne monitored their answerphone with the mobile and took occasional notes.

"We follow signs to the abbey and hang a right at the first set of traffic lights. There's a Shell garage on the corner."

"Okay."

"Marnie, do you want to drop me off somewhere before we get there? I can wander round the cathedral or something. She might be more willing to talk if there are just the two of you."

"I was wondering about that. Let's play it by ear."

"Fine. Her road's coming up on the left."

Marnie turned into a pretty tree-lined street of Victorian terraced cottages, most of which had been renovated, their front doors gleaming with bright paintwork, behind tiny neat front gardens. She pulled up opposite number twenty and looked at its white window frames, its dark green door already flanked by yellow roses climbing up a trellis.

The door was answered by a woman of about thirty. She did not look happy. Clinging tightly round her neck was a small child with a sullen expression. It shot the visitors a grumpy look and pushed its face into Judith's neck.

"Come in. Rosie's had to leave early from playgroup. She's been sick. I've only just got back. It was too late to tell you not to come."

The narrow hallway was half blocked by a push-chair, and they stepped round it. The little girl made whimpering sounds in her mother's arms, aware that she would not be receiving undivided attention. The ground floor had been converted to one all-through living room, and the floor nearest to the front window was littered with toys and books. Judith offered chairs to her visitors and settled herself carefully on the sofa with her burden. She did not offer refreshment, and Marnie had the feeling their meeting was going to be brief.

"It's nice of you to see us, but I can see it isn't a good time."

"Well, it's like that with kids, especially little ones. You can never be quite sure what's going to happen next."

"How old is Rosie?"

"Three and a half." She stroked the back of Rosie's head.

"She's your only child?"

"Yes, the one you've come to talk about ... by implication at least."

"She's a sweetie."

"She's also a constant reminder of her father ... looks just like him."

"Do you know what made her sick?"

"Could be anything." Judith shrugged, and Rosie tightened her grip. "Not so tight, poppet. Mummy can't breathe if you do that. Do you want some juice? Eh?"

The little girl made no reply but clung on, turning to eye the intruders with curiosity and suspicion. Marnie could see this was going to be a waste of time.

"Oh, sorry. I didn't introduce Anne. She works with me ... training to be a designer."

"Hi," said Judith.

"Hallo."

Anne slipped down from the armchair and moved across the floor to where the toys were strewn. She picked up a bear and examined it.

"Good morning, bear. What's your name?"

From the other side of the room came an indistinct murmur.

"Pardon?" said Anne to the bear. "You'll have to speak up. I couldn't hear you."

Another murmur that dissolved into a giggle. Judith and Marnie watched Anne as she picked up a ragdoll.

"Good morning, ragdoll. What's your name?"

This time the reply was clearer. "Rosie."

"*Rosie?*" Anne echoed. "I know a little girl called Rosie. Have you got a friend called Jim?"

"No, silly!" A short laugh this time.

Rosie let go of her mother and stood uncertainly beside her for a few seconds, contemplating Anne who was now picking up all the dolls and teddies and asking them their names. It proved irresistible. Rosie walked across and sat down beside her new friend. A big girl. Together they began lining the toys up in a row, Anne asking questions about them in a quiet voice.

"She's a treasure," Judith said under her breath.

"Yes. She's a lovely little girl."

"No, I mean your ... er ... "

"Anne," said Marnie. "Anne with an 'e'."

• • • • •

Ralph had the laptop on his knee as the coach trundled steadily through the countryside towards Oxford. He worked through the address book, systematically selecting every person who had any connection with the news media: journalists, broadcasters, writers and academic colleagues who might have useful links of their own.

As he cut and pasted to set up a new list, he tried to work out how he might approach them to elicite the kind of information he needed without revealing his intentions. He tried various possible lines.

*In my new role as Visiting Professor I'm needing to build up my contacts in the media …*

*I thought it would make sense if I put together a directory of press officers, PR people, maybe even journalists and editors …*

My publisher wants to set up a media and PR database for issuing press notices about my new book and it seemed like a good time to revise the whole thing …

The tricky part was managing to include the *Globe* in his line-up. None of this was easy. He looked out of the window and thought he caught a glimpse of a canal in the distance, the tell-tale black and white paint of the balance beams of a lock beside a small cottage in the middle of nowhere. He had to force into the back of his mind the heretical idea that Marnie's plan was not going to succeed. Even Marnie could not work miracles.

• • • • •

The tea party was going well. All the bears were lined up on one side of the 'table', with the dolls facing them. Anne was getting to know their names, but each time she made a mistake Rosie laughed out loud.

Marnie had declined the offer of tea and encouraged Judith to talk, fearing that the interview might be terminated prematurely if Rosie's sickness suddenly returned. Judith had been sorry to give up her job with the BBC, and had settled into a pleasant if humdrum existence. Her husband lectured in media studies at a college and was a 'wonderful father.' But Marnie sensed a regret in her and had a fair idea of its cause. She wondered if it would be a problem.

"Do you feel able to speak about … what happened?" she said in a low voice.

Judith laughed gently. "You make it sound like I'm some kind of Victorian fallen woman. Mind you, I suppose that's what I was." She laughed again. "Do you know those women who always go for the wrong man? Well, guess what!"

"Tell me about it," said Marnie dryly.

"You too? Well, I bet your judgment of men isn't as bad as mine. I'm hopeless. Would you believe I used to have a thing about Paul Pinder?"

"The journalist on the radio?"

"It was when he was doing spots on news programmes. I was a researcher, he was an investigative journalist and I knew he'd go far. I had a real crush. It was stupid … so adolescent."

"I've seen pictures of him. He's really good-looking … charming, too. Who could blame you for that?"

Judith stared at Marnie. "You don't know."

"Obviously not. What don't I know?"

"He's very good-looking, very charming … and very *gay*."

"Ah … difficult," Marnie conceded. "Wait a minute … he can't be."

"Believe me, Marnie. I've been there … got the ungroped T-shirt."

"But didn't he do that programme about closet gays? Wasn't that him?"

"He'd say he was just doing his job. Anyway, attack's always the best form of defence, isn't it?"

"You're sure about that, Judith?" Marnie was sceptical. "You don't think he was just fobbing you off?"

"Because he thought I had thick ankles or my boobs were too small? No. He's a regular at the Pink Flamingo. You must've heard of it."

"Gay club in Soho?"

"That's the one. He looks great in make-up."

"I see."

Judith looked across at Rosie. "Still, at least there was no risk of an accident happening."

"No," Marnie agreed. "Rather unlikely in the circumstances."

"I'm sure you know I had this thing with Tim ... another example of my lack of judgment with men. I thought it was going somewhere ... had my little accident ..." She nodded in the direction of Rosie. "You know the rest, I presume. Martin came along on his white charger and whisked me off to the altar ... made an honest woman of me ... almost. But then you're not really here to talk about me, are you?"

"I need contacts," Marnie said simply. "I don't want to go into the details, but I have to be able to get through to people in the news business in senior positions."

"Like Tim Rodgers?"

"I'm mainly interested in the newspapers, though you've made me think I ought to look further afield. Obviously I wouldn't cause any ... awkwardness ... for you ... or any of your friends .. present or past. I promise you that."

"If by *friends* you mean Tim ..."

"The people I want to approach are big fish in the national press. I need to get through to them so they'll take me seriously and not just ignore what I have to say."

"You'd need some pretty big bait to lure them, Marnie. Contrary to popular opinion, a lot of the news people *are* pretty decent. But there are some tough cookies, too, and they won't let themselves be used. You don't stand a chance unless you've got a big story. What *have* you got?"

"It's about political sleaze."

"It'd have to be very high level to be newsworthy."

"High enough to make the front page, I think. It'd be a scoop. I'm pretty sure of that."

"Are you trying to expose someone in the government?"

"It's not as straightforward as that. I'm trying to fight back for someone who's been damaged ... whose family's been damaged."

"How badly?"

"Fatally."

"So who's your target?"

Marnie looked across the room at the child pouring an imaginary cup of tea for a teddy bear, asking if it wanted a cake or a biscuit. The bear, supported by Anne, was making comical efforts to pick up its cup and drink. The little girl giggled contentedly.

Marnie said quietly, "I'm not sure I want to get you involved in all this."

"Are you scared of the consequences?" Judith said.

"Yes."

"Who for?"

"All of us, I think. But at least I've made a choice. If I get really scared, I can back out. If I get you involved … it could harm you as well. I wouldn't want that, obviously."

Judith looked her steadily in the eye. "Who are you going after, Marnie?"

"Do you know … Jeremy Hawksby?"

"The *Globe*? *Christ!*"

"Look, I'd understand if you – "

"This is the Leyton-Brown thing, isn't it?"

"If I said yes?"

"You want to *defend* him?" She paused. "So there's more to it."

"I think there could be," said Marnie.

Judith nodded. "There usually is. The news distorts everything one way or another. But how did you get involved with him?"

"By chance. It's a long story."

"What do you plan to do about Hawksby?"

"I've already told you more than I intended, Judith."

"Does it involve a woman … or a man?"

"What do you mean?"

"I just want to know how much you know about Hawksby … and how you think you can use it."

"It's a woman."

Across the room, Rosie staggered to her feet and ran to her mother. "Potty!"

Judith smiled wearily and got up. "Here we go. I'll have to deal with this before we have an accident. She's just getting the hang of it."

"Of course." Marnie was reluctant to leave, but she stood up and knew the conversation would go no further that day.

"Potty, Mummy!"

"Come on, darling." To Marnie she said, "Let me have a think about what you've told me. I'll try to help you … but I hope you know what you're doing."

• • • • •

They set off for their rendez-vous with Andrew at the Wendover junction, Anne navigating for Marnie through the St. Albans one-way system in the lunchtime traffic.

"How much of the conversation did you manage to hear, Anne?"

"Not a lot. The bears kept asking for more tea and biscuits."

Marnie smiled. "That was brilliant. Well, I think Judith might help. At least she seemed willing enough … which surprised me in a way."

"Why?"

"She's still carrying a torch for Rosie's father."

"For Tim Rodgers?"

"I'm almost certain of it. And I'm sure she regards us at best as bloody fools, at worst as amateurs in a tough world."

"Well, Marnie …"

"I know, don't say it."

They picked up the road signs to Tring, and on arrival there Marnie pulled over to phone Ralph and put him in the picture. They completed their run up to Marsworth and walked the towpath until they located the boats. Andrew was polishing a brass mushroom vent on *Totteridge*, keeping a lookout. He renewed his apologies, but Marnie waved them aside.

Anthony dropped a bag into the boot of the car. He seemed a different man, moving confidently, playing his role with conviction. And he certainly looked the part in his jeans and sweatshirt, his cropped hair and beard.

When they were ready to leave, Marnie hugged Andrew and Kate tightly.

"What about Tony's boat?" said Andrew.

"Good question."

"You're welcome to leave it at the yard, if you like."

Marnie preferred moving targets. "Thanks, but I think I'd better shift it. The question is ... where? And when? Can I get back to you on that?"

"Why don't we move it for you?" said Kate. "We're more flexible than you are."

"Oh, I don't like to – "

"No trouble," said Andrew. "Least we can do. We'll load everything on board again and get it to ... where do you want it?"

"Well ... back to Knightly, I suppose."

"How soon?"

"Doesn't matter. Whenever you could manage it."

"Leave it to us, Marnie. We won't let you down."

• • • • •

Finding the right road cross-country back to Northamptonshire took up all the attention of Marnie and Anne, as they headed north. There was little scope for conversation, and Anthony sat in the back letting his companions take the lead. He had learnt that new habit in recent weeks, though it still seemed strange. They pulled into a garage for fuel before rejoining the motorway, and Marnie came back to the car carrying sandwiches and cold drinks. They ate as they travelled.

Cruising on a main road, Anthony asked where they were going. "Or is that on a need-to-know basis?"

"We're going to a safe house," Marnie called over her shoulder.

"MI5 or KGB?" Anthony asked flippantly.

"Ne nado gavarit nepravdu dietiam, tovarich," came the reply.

"Dasvidanya," Anne added, trying to keep a straight face and nearly choking on her sandwich.

There was silence from the back seat. Marnie looked in the rear-view mirror and smiled.

"You should see your face, Anthony."

"*Jesus* ... I never know what to expect from you two. Nothing would surprise me."

"Sit back and enjoy the ride, and I'll tell you where we're taking you. I guarantee you won't believe it." *And you won't much like it, either,* she thought.

• • • • •

For the last few miles they travelled almost in silence, and Marnie could guess why. The only sounds came from Anne.

"Main road up ahead ... T-junction ... go left."

"Turning off to the right ... probably marked 'town centre' ... about two miles."

"It's after the traffic lights, first or second on the right."

Marnie parked opposite Randall's drop-in centre. Behind her, Anthony said nothing. They got out and took his bag from the boot. He was so pre-occupied he let Marnie carry it across the road. On the doorstep she turned to him.

"Okay?"

"It's a doss house, isn't it?"

"It's a *safe house*, like I said. Just think of it like that."

"Has it really come to this?" His face looked blank.

"It's because it's what it is that makes it perfect, Anthony, but if you've got any better ideas, tell me now."

He cleared his throat. "No. Let's ... get on with it."

Randall was already waiting for them in the reception area. Anthony blinked at the bright cream walls and glossy white paintwork. Randall held out a hand to his new guest. "Glad to have you here ... er, what do we call you?"

"Ant – "

"Tony," Marnie interjected.

"Yes," said Anthony Leyton-Brown MP. "Tony will do fine."

He could not help turning his head to take in the spacious hallway and the staircase curving away with a polished mahogany banister. Over the door to the reception office hung a sign in bold letters: WELCOME.

On the wall beside the office was a framed print of Holman Hunt's painting, *The Light of the World*, above it another sign, a quotation:

> *Jesus said*
> *Behold I stand at the door and knock*
> *If any man hear my voice and open the door*
> *I will come in to him and will sup with him and he with me*

Anthony half opened his mouth as if to speak, but only drew in some short breaths. He blinked several times. Randall put a hand on his shoulder and guided him towards the stairs, picking up the overnight bag as he went.

"Let's get you settled in. We can save the guided tour till later."

Marnie and Anne watched him go, walking slowly beside Randall, like a wounded man being led away from a battlefield.

Mounting the stairs, Randall called back to them. "Why don't you get a cup of tea in the sitting room? We'll join you shortly."

*Thriving* had been the word used by Angela Hemingway, and they saw what she meant. The *sitting room*, the size of a small hall, was almost full, with most low chairs occupied, and one or two tables free. At others, *guests* were sitting chatting or playing board games. Marnie found a table in the corner and went to get tea, leaving Anne to mind their places.

Anne became aware that a girl was looking at her, not much older than herself, sitting alone at the next table. She smiled and nodded at her, and the girl nodded back.

"We're visiting Randall," Anne volunteered. "Er ... Mr Hughes ... the Rural Dean."

"Randall," the girl said. She had a small crescent-shaped scar on her chin. "You coming to stay?"

"No. We've ... got a friend who's here for a bit. Temporary."

"We're all temporary."

"Yes."

"Haven't got a fag, have you?"

Anne shook her head. "Sorry. I don't smoke."

"I'm down to me last one ... been saving it."

Anne glanced up at the No Smoking signs on the wall, and the girl read her mind.

"You have to go outside. They're very strict here."

"*Strict?*" Anne said. "I thought they were easy-going about most things."

"Yeah. It's okay. But not smoking ... smoke alarms everywhere. One night one old bloke nearly burned himself alive having a secret fag in bed. The alarms went off and we was out on the pavement in two minutes."

"Did he get hurt?"

"No ... well, not much. He got a fright, though."

"Did he get into trouble?"

"Nah. He should've got chucked out, but Randall's soft. He lined us all up and gave us a lecture on what could've happened ... as if we didn't know."

"Better than waking up dead, I suppose," said Anne.

"Yeah." The girl began to get up. "Not much point asking you for a light, is there?"

"No. Sorry." An afterthought came to her. "Hey! ... wait a minute." She reached into her back pocket and pulled out the matches that she had picked up in the restaurant by Tower Bridge. "I've got these. You can have them if you want."

The girl took the book of matches. She turned them over to read the address on the flip side, and sat down again, looking appraisingly at Anne.

"You from London, then?" She looked significantly at the cover on the matches.

Anne paused before replying, sensing that the atmosphere across the table had changed. The girl took her hesitation for reluctance to answer.

"I'm not snooping."

"Just curious?" said Anne.

"I know that part of London," the girl said.

"I was down there looking for someone." Anne kept her voice matter-of-fact. "A friend of mine. She's sort of ... living away from home at the moment." At the other end of the room she could see Marnie chatting by the trolley with the tea lady and hoped she would not return too soon and scare the girl away.

"On the street?"

"Probably."

"On the game?"

"I don't know. I heard she's been hanging out over by Commercial Road ... up one of those streets ... near the old Town Hall."

The girl shook her head. "No. No one hangs out over there."

"No?"

"No way. Wouldn't be no point ... no one goes looking round there ... wrong part. You've been wasting your time."

"I know." Anne was aching to ask where she should look, but knew she had to avoid a direct question. From the corner of her eye she saw Randall arrive in the doorway in his distinctive long black cassock. He went over to Marnie and joined in her chat with the tea lady, who was patting the urn. "I'll just have to keep looking. I might be going back there tomorrow."

"Well don't go over Commercial Road."

"No?"

"No. You want to try round there." She held up the matches.

"Round *Butlers Wharf?*" Anne sounded as if she did not believe it. It seemed highly improbable.

"*No.*" The girl was emphatic. "It's posh round there ... further back, *away* from the river."

"Thanks. I'll give it a try."

The girl got up and picked her way through the tables, passing Marnie and Randall as they came over with cups of tea.

"Had to wait for the water to boil," Marnie said in explanation as she sat down.

"I'm glad you did," said Anne.

· · · · ·

The Volvo turned off the high street in Brackley and headed towards the main road south. Anne calculated no more than thirty minutes before they reached Oxford city centre unless the early evening rush hour thwarted them. There was little need of map-reading as the road ran direct to their goal.

"You did well getting the information out of that girl, Anne."

"She seemed to know the area, and I'm sure she was right about there being no point hanging around where Ralph took me."

"No. So ... back to Simon's, I suppose."

"Do you really think there's any point, Marnie? I mean, do you think we'll ever find her? Surely, she'll be miles away by now."

"What choice do we have? I reckon we've got to keep plugging away at everything we can." Marnie turned onto the motorway and pushed the big car up to cruising speed. "What did you make of Anthony?"

Anne thought for a few seconds. "Somehow different. What do you think?"

"Outwardly he was calmer ... more composed. It may have been the effect of the shower and the change of clothes. Just that simple white shirt and the black trousers ... and he'd trimmed the beard ... I thought he looked nice. But it was his manner ... I'm sure Randall had spoken to him."

"That girl in the hostel said Randall was soft."

"Then she was mistaken. Randall is *not soft*. But he is careful about how he uses his authority. My guess is he told Anthony things could only get better from now on. Extraordinary."

"What is?"

"I think Anthony actually believed him."

"Don't *you* believe him, Marnie?"

"Not sure. We've been having a tough time lately. And it could get tougher once we come out and attack Jeremy Hawksby in public. Still, at least for the moment, Anthony's in the *safe house.*"

"Do you remember when you spoke Russian to Anthony after he asked if you were the KGB?" Anne shrieked with laughter and added, "Was it really Russian?"

"Yes, though I can't vouch for my pronunciation."

"It sounded good to me. What did it mean?"

"It meant ... *you shouldn't tell lies to children* ... or something like that."

"Why did you say that?"

"It's the only Russian I know ... from a poem by Yevtuschenko. I saw him years ago on one of his tours. I liked the poem and the way he performed it. I memorised the first line."

"And you went to see him performing in Russian?"

"Yes. It was a big arts festival in London. I went with Simon when I was a student. It was the first time we ever went out together."

# Part 25

Mid-morning on Saturday, the three of them back in London in the Volvo. Over Tower Bridge, turn off the main road, down to the underground car park. Marnie took the overnight bag up to Simon's flat while Ralph went off with Anne. There had been a major economic initiative announced in Tokyo, and he needed to find a newsagent.

They were in luck. Anne waited outside reading the postcards on the notice board in the shop window, while Ralph went in to buy papers. She scanned the cards: mainly advertising second-hand computers and CD players, interspersed with offers of top rates for cleaners and domestic help. One or two offered unspecified personal services. A sudden tug on her elbow made Anne turn round. She was confronted by a young woman with attitude in a tank top, *very* brief skirt and white ankle boots. The attitude was not friendly.

"Here, what's your game?" she said in a menacing whisper. "What are you up to?"

"Nothing. I'm just waiting for a friend."

"This is *my* pitch so *you* can sod off."

"I don't understand." Anne looked at the woman. She was pretty underneath a layer of make-up that had been applied with a trowel. "Oh, yes ... I *do* understand. And it's not what you're thinking."

"Don't give me that."

Just then Ralph came out of the shop. "Hallo. You seem to have found a friend, Anne. Or do we have a problem?"

"Don't worry, Ralph. I can handle this."

"You reckon?" said the woman.

"Listen." She stepped closer to the woman who backed up against the wall, and spoke looking her straight in the eye. "My name's Anne ... Anne Price. I'm not on the game or anything else, okay? But I am looking for a friend of mine who may have been ... *working* round here. Her name's Marlene. Do you know her?"

"No." There was no hesitation.

"She's tall and slim, slight north country accent, wears a yellow cagoule. Ring any bells?"

The woman said nothing. Anne continued. "She's not in any trouble ... as far as I know ... not from me at any rate. I just want to find her and talk to her. I want to know she's all right."

"*You* haven't got a north country accent."

"Leighton Buzzard isn't up north, that's why. It's where I come from."

"So how do you know your *friend*'s round here?"

"Another girl told me."

"What other girl?"

"Someone I met in a hostel. I don't know her name."

"What a surprise."

"It's the truth."

The woman turned on her heel and began walking away. Over her shoulder she called out, "Just watch yourself ... and keep away ... for your own good."

Anne watched her go, feeling desperate. From behind her Ralph said, "Well, at least you tried."

Ignoring him, Anne chased after the woman and caught her by the arm. "The girl who told me about Marlene ... she had a small scar on her chin." Anne pointed at her own face. "Here ... like a new moon ... tiny ..."

• • • • •

Simon's cleaning lady had done a good job. No doubt he paid top rates. Everything was neat and tidy, fresh towels in the bathroom, clean tea-towels in the kitchen, sheets changed on the bed. Mrs Hedges was a treasure.

Marnie hunted for any clue as to when Simon was returning. There was a note from Mrs Hedges: she would be coming in the afternoon the following week, rather than the morning; she had to take her mother to the clinic again. Passing the answerphone, she noticed the number 4 glowing in the messages window. *That's odd*, she thought, convinced that it had previously been a 5. So ... Simon had been checking his messages from wherever he was. She wished she had asked him exactly when he was planning to come back. The last thing she wanted was for him to get in very late to find her in his bed.

The phone rang, a gentle hi-tech warble. It had a device for vetting incoming calls. In its window was a single word: *Simon*. Marnie grabbed the phone before he could start checking the messages.

"Hi! It's me."

"Oh! Still there?"

"No, just got back, actually. When are you returning?"

"Do you want to stay on?"

"Please."

"Fine. Make yourself at home."

"Thanks. Would you mind if Anne slept on a sofa?"

"You'll find a fold-up bed in the glory hole. She'll probably be more comfortable on that. Sheets and things are in the airing cupboard."

"Great."

"Any progress with your boating visitor?"

"Only very slow."

"Well, watch out."

"I will. You've got four messages on the machine here, by the way."

"I'll get'em later. Gotta go ... just having a break from a meeting."

"Okay. And thanks, Simon."

"No problem. You take care of yourself."

Good, that was sorted. Marnie was turning to fetch the spare bed when the phone rang again, Simon having an afterthought, perhaps. But there was a number in the window that seemed familiar. It took Marnie a second or two to realise it was her own mobile.

"Hallo, Anne. Everything all right?"

"How did you ... Look, I've met someone ... you ought to see her. Are you ready to come down?"

"Where are you?"

"We can meet you by the entrance to the car park."

"Give me two minutes."

· · · · ·

On her way down in the lift, Marnie had entertained thoughts of taking the new person for a drink at one of the bistros in Butlers Wharf, but one look put her off the idea. She only lacked a flashing neon sign reading: *I am a hooker*, to complete the ensemble.

Anne introduced the woman, who had not given her name, explaining that this was her boss and they were all *legit*. She had remembered that word from television dramas set in the underworld. Marnie confirmed that they just wanted to speak with Marlene and introduced Ralph, *Professor Ralph Lombard of Oxford*, as further corroboration of their credentials. The woman looked at them suspiciously.

"So you aren't from Social Services," she said. "Or the law."

Marnie reached into her shoulder bag, pulled out a business card and handed it to the woman.

"That's who I am. Anne's my assistant. Ralph is my partner."

The woman read the card. "Where is this place?"

"It's a village, about fifty miles north of London. Look, we're just worried about Marlene. Do you know where she is? Do you really know her?"

"Avril."

"That's your name?"

"That's the girl you're looking for."

"No," said Marnie. "She's called Marlene."

"It's Avril. Take my word for it."

"Well, whatever it is, we'd like to talk to her."

"Maybe she doesn't want to talk to you."

Marnie knew the woman was only stalling. If she was not prepared to talk, why was she still there? "We can't talk out here on the street." She wondered where they could possibly go with a woman dressed to catch the eye of kerb crawlers.

"There's a caff round the corner," said the woman.

The improbable group arrived at the *caff* in two minutes. In any guide to the watering holes of the capital it looked from outside as if it would have merited three crossed greasy spoons.

· · · · ·

The inside of the café surprised them. From the street it had been obscured by condensation on the windows, and although it belonged to the neo-Formica school of interior design, with PVC chairs and tomato-shaped plastic ketchup bottles on every table, it was clean and only lightly scented with the tang of fried breakfasts. The place was run by a jovial Greek and bore his name, Asterios, in green neon letters over the door.

They sat at a table away from the picture windows, and Ralph bought them cappuccinos which he and Anne ferried back from the counter.

"What do we call you?" Marnie asked to open the conversation.

The woman stirred sugar into her cup and took a sip. Eventually she said, "Fran."

"Well, Fran, I'm going to be absolutely honest with you. We believe this girl Marlene – or Avril – has got mixed up with some very dodgy people. We're worried about her and we – "

"So you keep saying. Why should *you* be worried? How well do you know her?"

"Not very well. But we know she could be in trouble."

"From the law?"

"No ... from the people she's got involved with."

"What people?"

"The people who got her picture in the papers."

"How much?" said Fran. "What are you offering?"

Anne butted in. "We're not offering anything ... not money. It's not like that. We just want to see her. We want her help so that no one else gets hurt. That's all it is."

Fran took a mouthful of cappuccino, pushed the chair back and stood up. The eyes of other patrons focused on her thighs as she straightened the tiny skirt with the palms of her hands.

"Tomorrow morning. Eleven o'clock. Here."

• • • • •

That evening, after Ralph set off for home, they put up the folding bed in Simon's living room. Anne put on sheets and a blanket while Marnie rang the office to check the answerphone. It was the usual collection, including a call from Mrs Jolly ... *just wanting to keep in touch, my dear* ... and a surprise.

"Hallo, this is Judith. I'm ringing at seven-thirty on Saturday evening. I've had some ideas about one or two other people to contact. One in particular could be interesting. You've got my number. Bye!"

Marnie wrote notes on the other messages, disconnected and rang Judith. Ann sat beside her at the dining table looking out at the Thames and the skyline.

A man's voice, friendly. "Sure. I'll get her for you. She's just looking in on Rosie. Won't be a mo'."

Seconds later Judith arrived. "You got my message?"

"Yes. You've had some ideas."

"One of my friends is a researcher. She may have something that could interest you."

"Can you give me a rough idea?"

"Not ... easily. She's called Becky Thornton. I'll give you her mobile number. It's a bit of a long shot, and she's in a difficult position, *very* difficult, but ... well, see how you get on. Marnie, I would just say ... don't push her too far. Her job could be on the line."

"Okay. This is all very mysterious, Judith."

"You should be used to that by now."

"True. Did you say there was someone else?"

"Yes. Even more of a long shot, I'm afraid. He may phone you ... or he may not."

"*He*? This is the man from Hawksby's past?"

"Could be. I can't promise anything, but he may contact you."

"Where does he fit in?"

"It's hard to tell. He might not. He wants to think it over." Judith laughed. "I can tell you, Marnie, this is quite a change from my usual daily life. It's a far cry from potty training and the Teletubbies!"

"But not too much of a nuisance, I hope."

"No, not at all. I said I wanted to help you. It just reminds me of what it's like working on *Panorama* sometimes ... informants, leaks, inside information. You wouldn't believe it."

"Sounds intriguing. And this mystery man, what's he called?"

"I'll let him tell you that ... if he gets in touch."

"How will I know who it is?"

"You'll know."

· · · · ·

Ralph, driving solo, turned off the high street at Knightly St John and steered the Volvo onto the field track. In the headlights, a sudden mass of movement, dozens of rabbits diving for cover, white tails like raindrops bouncing off the ground.

Everything was quiet down at Glebe Farm, lights shining in the windows of the cottage where Jill and Alex Burton were leading normal lives. He walked by torchlight through the spinney and was joined by Dolly on her night prowl. He bent down and picked her up, and she settled herself over his shoulder, purring, the cool fur gradually warming against his ear. He knew how to make a girl happy. This one, at least.

· · · · ·

Anne had been in bed for twenty minutes, lying awake in the darkness, her head spinning with a thousand thoughts, when she heard a sound from the other side of the room.

"Is that you, Marnie?" Her voice came out as a whispered croak.

"Have I woken you up?"

"No. I'm wide awake."

"Me too. Do you think Simon's got any cigarettes hidden away?"

"*Cigarettes*? Marnie! You gave up years ago."

Marnie sighed in the darkness. "I know. Every now and then I get a need for a puff or two."

"You can put the light on and search around if you like."

"You sound as if you don't approve." There was no reply. "You don't approve."

"I don't think Simon would like it. I'm sure he doesn't smoke. It doesn't smell of cigarettes in the flat. But if you found any, you could always stick your head out of the window."

Marnie laughed. "Thank you for that practical suggestion."

She walked over to the window and drew back the curtain. The moon was reflecting off the river, lights from the streets and buildings shining from all directions. It looked like a scene from a film, and Marnie half expected Tinkerbell the fairy to fly past with Peter Pan and the Lost Boys on their way to Never Never Land. She became aware of Anne at her side in the darkened room.

"Some of those lights must belong to the *Globe* offices and printing works over there."

"I suppose so," said Marnie. "This must be when they work ... in the night. It's strange to think they're beavering away on the Sunday papers on that side of the river and we're hunting them down from over here."

"They're hunting us down, too, don't forget."

"No. Not quite. They're hunting Anthony. They probably don't think we're worth hunting ... with any luck."

"You don't think so? Really?"

"I don't think they know we're on to them. We're safe for the moment. We're certainly out of their reach up here. This place is like Fort Knox. It's impregnable."

# Part 26

There is something about the quiet of a Sunday morning in London that is like no other time. It was a thought that had only occurred to Marnie since she had been living in the country.

She much preferred rural Sundays, especially in the morning. There was a sense of calm in the air. Church bells rang like wind chimes in a garden, and even though Marnie was an agnostic and never went to services, she liked to hear the peals as a backdrop to planting tubs of flowers in the courtyard or polishing brass on *Sally Ann*.

In London she had always felt an unease, as if her neighbours were frantically devouring the newspapers behind their net curtains, trying to gen up on style in the colour supplements, competing for knowledge about what was in and what was cool, another part of the rat race that consumed them the rest of the week.

Things had changed now. Marnie believed one day soon their current problem would be left behind them and everything would be rolling forward just as she had planned, even though there could still be a bumpy ride ahead.

That Sunday morning, looking down on Docklands from Simon's flat, she felt immune from the competitive pressures of London. She felt safe, if only for a while from the battle with the *Globe* and its empire, cocooned up there in the fortress protected by state-of-the-art security systems. Fort Knox.

She found instant coffee and powdered milk in the kitchen and heated water while Anne stowed the folding bed back in the glory hole.

Marnie called out, "Can you make do with coffee and a couple of shortbread biscuits, Anne? That's all I can find. We can get a croissant or something when we go out."

She found mugs in a cupboard and sniffed the coffee in the jar. It smelled fresh enough. Anne had obviously not heard her. She called out again.

"Is that all right for you, Anne?"

Still no reply. Odd. Marnie walked towards the arch leading into the living area and met Anne coming towards her across the room. There was something strange about her expression. She was clutching a slip of paper which she held out to Marnie without a word. It was a note, handwritten.

> *Marnie Walker*
> *Change of plan.*
> *Meet me half past ten at the cafe.*
> *Fran*

Fran? *Fran!*

"Where did you get this?" Marnie said. Her head was buzzing. Alarm bells were clanging.

"It had been pushed under the door."

"It can't have been. Are you sure? Show me where."

Anne led Marnie to the door and pointed at the ground. Marnie looked through the security peephole into the hallway. It was deserted. She pulled open the front door. Nothing and no one. She closed the door.

"So much for Fort Knox," she muttered.

• • • • •

Their first stop was the porter's lodge. They pushed open the glass door and found a young man sitting behind the counter writing on a notepad. He had fine features and a pale brown skin that glowed against his very white shirt.

"Good morning, madam."

"Good morning. Can you tell me, is it possible for anyone to gain access to the flats from outside?"

"Only with a security card."

"But what I mean is … could anyone be given a card to let them in if, for example, they said they wanted to put a note under someone's door?"

"No, madam. That is quite impossible. If you wish to pass on a message I can take it from you – "

"No, it's not that. I'm already staying here … in a friend's flat. But if someone wanted to give me a message, how could they do it?"

"They could leave it with me and you could collect it from here."

"How would I know it was here?"

"The porter on duty would phone you and tell you."

"The porter might bring it up and deliver it in person?"

"I'm afraid not, madam. We never leave the lodge unmanned."

"Not in any circumstances?"

"Not in any circumstances, no."

• • • • •

The café was closed when they arrived a few minutes early, so they waited outside the newsagent's across the street, mulling over how someone might be able to penetrate the outer defences of Simon's flat.

"I don't get it," said Anne. "Unless it was one of the neighbours."

"Too great a coincidence, surely."

"Not if Fran waited outside until someone came along. She could've asked them to drop it in at Simon's flat."

"How could she know we were there? And which flat we were in?"

"I don't know, but she did. We got the message, didn't we?"

"But how did she know where to come at all?" Before Anne could speak, Marnie answered her own question. "She must've followed us. That's the only way."

"Up to the flat?" said Anne. "I don't get it."

Marnie shuddered. "It's creepy. And I thought we were secure up there."

"Oh well … Fran will know the answer, so we'll soon find out," said Anne.

Marnie checked her watch. Ten minutes to go. She looked up and down the street and realised how exposed they were, standing out on the pavement in full view of passing cars and pedestrians. The words *drive-by shooting* came into her mind.

Another glance at the watch. She was growing nervous. They were dealing with hookers, and hookers were run by pimps and crooks. They were part of the underworld of organised crime. Marnie looked at Anne standing beside her, young and defenceless, and a decision formed in her mind. The odds were too great; they had to get away. Before she could move, she felt a hand on her shoulder and heard a voice behind her.

"Marnie Walker?"

She spun round to find a girl standing there. It was not Fran. The same tarty style, but not Fran.

"Yes."

"And who's this?"

"This is Anne, my friend."

"I've got a message from Fran."

"Where is she?"

"Not your concern. She says be here tomorrow, same time. Got it?"

"Yes, but I don't know – "

"Take it or leave it."

• • • • •

That Sunday morning did not feel like a day of rest for Marnie and Anne. They converted Simon's living area into their operations room. It felt like RAF Fighter Command, vintage 1940. Each of them had a list of phone calls to make to reorganise the start to the week.

On the way back from the aborted rendez-vous with Fran, they had agreed to make one final effort in the Docklands campaign. If that came to nothing, they would give up. It would be disappointing after all they had done, but it would be no disgrace. They divided up the tasks. Marnie handled strategy, while Anne dealt with the tactical issues.

On the phone Marnie outlined progress – the lack of it – to Ralph and told him of her decision to give it one more go. He agreed to stay at Knightly and man the office till they returned.

After hanging up, Marnie said to Anne, "Poor Ralph! He's really finding out what he's taken on with me."

"He knows what he's doing," said Anne. "He wouldn't want you any other way."

Marnie laughed lightly. "Well, at least he knows exactly what he's getting, no illusions, no secrets. I think that's important."

"Huh!" said Anne.

"*Huh?* What does *Huh* mean?"

"You know what it means." Anne gave her an indulgent look, complete with heavy eyelids.

"No I don't," Marnie said indignantly, but sensing she was about to lose the argument.

"If it's important not to have any secrets, why didn't you tell Ralph about the phantom message coming in under the door?"

"Ah, yes ..."

"Quite. You didn't want to worry him, I suppose."

"I didn't want to worry him. No."

More heavy eyelids from Anne. "Okay, well, I've done all my calls." She ticked them off her fingers. "I've left messages for the builders, the electrician and a reminder not to go ahead with the grey roof slates."

"Great. I was going to ring Randall to check up on Anthony, but it's Sunday and he'll be busy."

Anne went off to the kitchen while Marnie rang Simon on his mobile to check it was okay for them to stay on. He answered immediately. In the background Marnie could hear music playing softly and the sound of voices.

"Am I phoning at a bad time?"

"No, it's fine. Everything okay?"

"We've got to go back to meet the girl tomorrow ... the one in the photos. Is it convenient for us to stay one more night?"

There was the briefest hesitation. "Sure."

"When are you coming back, Simon?"

"Soon."

"The truth."

A pause. "I am back. I was at the airport when you picked up my call yesterday ... with some associates."

"So where did you go last night?"

"I stayed at their hotel. It seemed the best thing to do in the circumstances."

"Oh ..."

"It's okay ... not a problem."

"But if you're here, you ought to have your flat back. You shouldn't have to pay for a hotel room."

"It's all covered by the contract I'm working on. Forget it."

"What about mail and things?"

"Don't worry about that. I dropped by and picked it up. I only had to come over from City Airport."

"When was this?"

"Last night. I called in and collected it from the porter's lodge. Did you see the message I left you, by the way?"

"*You* left it?"

"Yes. It was in my pigeonhole, so I nipped up and pushed it under the door. It seemed to be a note about a meeting, so I thought you ought to have it straight away."

"Oh my God," Marnie sighed.

"What?"

"I am *so* relieved. I thought ... well ... I didn't know what to think, actually. I couldn't work out how it had got there."

"I suppose I should've written a message on it, but it was late and I didn't have a pen."

"So it was you all the time. I didn't know about the pigeonholes."

"It just goes to show," said Simon. "There can be some advantage in having my surname, after all."

"Look, you must come back tomorrow. We'll be gone in the morning. And thanks again."

"Okay. I'll come over some time. But don't rush off. I can't be sure when my meetings will end. You know what it's like."

When Marnie hung up she smiled at the simple explanation of how the message had penetrated Fort Knox. The smile lasted only long enough for her to realise that Fran and her associates knew exactly where she was staying and how to reach her.

# Part 27

Dark clouds were scudding over Docklands the next morning. The hills on the horizon had vanished when Marnie and Anne took their first look at the pouring rain from Simon's flat. Armed with a golf umbrella in rainbow colours from the glory hole, the two set off for their meeting. They had their first surprise of the day. Fran was waiting for them in a car parked outside the newsagent's.

"Change of plan," she said through the half-open driver's window, blinking as raindrops splattered against her face.

"Oh yes?" said Marnie.

"Avril's coming, but she won't be here for half an hour."

"Are you wasting our time?"

"Got anything better to do?"

"Plenty."

Fran began winding up the window. Marnie put a restraining hand on it.

"Will you be bringing her?"

"No. She's coming separate."

"Half an hour, then," Marnie said. "We'll wait in the *caff* over the road."

Fran wound up the window and drove away.

• • • • •

They were still waiting for the cappuccino to cool, when Marnie's mobile vibrated and warbled. She pressed the buttons and a text message came up on the tiny screen.

*Please move your car from car park – space needed.*

"Simon," she muttered. "He must be back … needs to park his car. I hadn't thought of that. He must've given my number to the porter." She grabbed the umbrella and slipped on her jacket. "I'll be five minutes, Anne … I hope … have to find somewhere else to park. Sit back and relax. I'll be as quick as I can."

Anne looked anything but relaxed. Marnie winked at her and made for the door. She put up the umbrella, stepping round puddles, walking fast. At the approach to the car park entrance, she pulled out the security card and pressed it against the metal plate. She tapped three numbers on the keypad, and the shutter slid upwards. To reach Simon's space she had to go down two levels and she found the Volvo in slot two-o-eight. She had half-expected to find Simon sitting there in his Mercedes, but the place was deserted.

Driving into the street, she looked up and down to see if the distinctive silver car was visible. It was not. She uttered an apology to Simon under her breath at the thought of him having to walk a long way in the rain to retrieve his car and felt even more guilty when she quickly found a space along by Butlers Wharf at the end of a row. It offered two hours' free parking. Perfect.

Marnie's estimate of five minutes' absence proved to be accurate. She pushed the café door open with her back, pulled down the umbrella and turned to look triumphantly across at Anne. Her smile was returned, if rather quizzically, by a large man with a moustache and a bald head.

• • • • •

Anne watched Marnie pass the window and looked at the cappuccino. She realised that she had grown accustomed to the finer things of life and, hoping she was not becoming a snob, she raised the cup to her lips. Through the steam she spotted a familiar face at the door. Fran waved at her and disappeared outside into the rain.

Anne pulled her bag over her shoulder and moved round the tables towards the entrance. Nobody spared her a glance as she edged her way to the door. At first she could not see where Fran had gone. A short beep from a horn attracted her attention to the car that she had seen earlier. Anne walked over as Fran pushed open the front passenger's door. Anne shook her head, spraying raindrops.

"I'm not getting in the car," she said.

"You'll get soaked out there."

"I don't care."

Fran stared at her for several seconds, sighed impatiently and pushed her own door open. She climbed out and got in the back, leaning over to open the window. "That better? Happy now?"

Anne hesitated, feeling her shoulders getting cold and wet. She looked up the road, but Marnie was nowhere in sight. Hesitantly, she pulled the car door open and got in, so that the two of them were sitting in the rear seats.

"Where's Marlene ... Avril?"

"She's coming, I told you. She won't be long."

"Why have you come, then?"

"We just want to know why you want to see her ... why you *really* want to see her."

"I told you."

"We want the truth this time. Avril doesn't know anyone from Leighton Buzzard. She doesn't even know where it is. And she's never heard of you."

Before Anne could answer, the driver's door swung open and a man jumped in behind the wheel. He had the engine running and was shifting into first gear when Anne seized the door handle and pulled hard. Nothing happened.

The man called over his shoulder as the car moved off. "Childproof locks. Great safety feature. We wouldn't want you to come to any harm."

• • • • •

Marnie walked over to the table where she had left Anne. The man sitting in her place was still smiling, but his expression was changing to puzzlement. He studied the woman approaching him and reached two immediate conclusions: he did not know who she was; she did not look like a hooker. For both reasons, he could not understand why she had smiled or why she was now closing in.

"I'm sorry to trouble you," Marnie began, "But when you came in here, did you see a girl sitting at this table, or perhaps leaving it? My height, thin, very short blond hair, grey sweatshirt."

"No. It was empty. No one was here."

Marnie thanked him and went to the counter. Asterios looked up from cutting sandwiches and smiled at her. She asked about Anne, and he looked over her shoulder towards their table.

He shook his head. "I'm getting ready for the lunchtime rush, love. No way I can notice everyone who comes and goes." He smiled again. "I remember *you*, though."

"It's my friend I'm concerned about."

"Sorry."

• • • • •

The car hit a hole in the road and bounced, water splashing the windscreen like spray over the bows of a boat. Anne lurched into Fran who hit her head against the window and pushed her away.

"*Get off*, will you!"

Anne steadied herself against the front seat. "It's not my fault. I didn't ask to be here." She thought she sounded braver than she felt.

The driver pulled round a corner into an alley and stopped the car. He turned to look back with an expression not designed to put his reluctant passenger at ease.

"I'm bloody sick of you," he said thickly to Anne.

"Why are you b-bloody sick of me? I haven't done anything to you ... or anybody."

"Messing Avril about, that's why. Tell me ... why do you want to see her?"

"We want to ask her about that MP ... Anthony Leyton-Brown."

"You're a friend of his, are you? I might've known it."

"*No!*" Anne protested. "I just want to find out why he was set up and who by."

"What's it to do with you?"

"He knows someone we know – a friend – and he came to us for help. Then his wife killed herself and ... we figured Avril could help us find out what was going on ... and maybe do something about it."

"*Do something*? Like what?"

"I'm not sure. It depends on what she can tell us. That's all it is."

The man stared without blinking. Anne did not like the idea that he was taking decisions about her.

"Look," she said. "Do I look like some kind of informer or whatever you think I am? I'm seventeen years old. My friend Marnie wants to talk to Avril. You met her, Fran. You could tell Marnie's a good person just by looking at her. She'd never do anything to hurt Avril ... or anyone else."

"What is she wanting to do, then?" said Fran.

"Get at the truth and expose the newspaper editor."

"By getting at Avril," said the man at the wheel.

"No. She could just make a statement or something."

"And land herself in trouble? You must be joking!"

"Not at all," said Anne. "We don't think she's committed any crime. It's not her fault she was used like that. But she could help put it right."

Fran said, "Why are you doing this? What do you get out of it?"

Anne shrugged. She looked unhappy. "We just somehow got dragged into it. I wish we hadn't. It's taken over our whole lives."

The driver said, "Listen to me. If you're telling the truth … fine. If you're not, darlin' … I'm your worst nightmare."

●　●　●　●　●

Marnie ordered another cappuccino and found a seat by the window, her mind racing with possibilities. She had checked the loos and found them empty. She could see that Anne was not in the newsagent's. There was no way Anne could get into the flat. This was the nightmare scenario.

How could they get Anne away without anybody noticing? Anne would not just let herself be abducted. She was not a fool. But she was young and inexperienced. *Oh God* … Marnie did not dare let herself think about Anne's parents and what she might have to tell them. They had allowed their daughter – a *minor* – to go and live with Marnie to learn about interior design. Tackling the underworld and going off on crazy missions had definitely not been part of the deal.

Marnie forced herself to think logically. The text message about the parking space. Who could have sent it? The porter in the lodge? Not Simon. He would just have phoned. Marnie had to talk to him urgently. She hit the buttons on the mobile. Two rings. A woman's voice: *Welcome to the Network answerphone service. To leave a message, please speak after the tone …* beep.

"Simon, it's Marnie. Please call me on my mobile as soon as possible. It's urgent."

She knew he would know nothing about the message or the car park. It had been a trick. The options were closing down. Maybe it was time to call the police. She decided on one last shot. At the counter Asterios looked up at her apprehensively. No smile this time.

"I'm going out to look for my friend, but I'll be back soon. If she comes in, you know what she looks like: thin with short blond – "

"Sure. I know."

"Okay. Would you let her use your phone to ring me on the mobile? Here's a pound to cover the call."

"No. It's okay." He pushed the coin back. Marnie left it.

"I insist. Please. Will you let her use your phone? I'm worried about her."

"No problem."

"Thank you. She should wait here till I return."

"That's fine."

For the second time that morning Marnie left a full cup of cappuccino going cold and went out into the rain.

●　●　●　●　●

They drove without speaking over Tower Bridge and up through the City of London away from the river, passing sky-scrapers that gradually gave way to avenues of offices, then parades of shops with residential side streets and deserted parks looking miserable and abandoned in the rain. The grim driver made a succession of turns among terraces of houses that estate agents would have described as having 'scope for modernisation'.

They drew to a halt outside a two-storey house as the rain eased off for the first time that day. The driver took her firmly by the arm and ushered her into the house, leading her through to a back kitchen and sat her in a wooden chair by the table.

Anne took it as a good sign that no attempt had been made to prevent her from seeing where they were going, but she did not know London well enough to guess the district, and had not had the presence of mind to try to read signs or street names.

"Where is this?" she asked Fran.

"Never you mind," said the driver.

• • • • •

The porter was involved in a complicated discussion with a woman with a strong French accent and limited English. At any other time Marnie would have joined in to help, but that day she was close to panic and needed all her reserves of mental energy to keep focused. She walked up and down in the lodge until the woman finished her conversation and went out.

Marnie approached the porter's desk. "Could you tell me if you've sent me a text message this morning?"

The porter looked blank. "Sorry, madam?"

"Have you sent me a message … on my mobile … a text message about the underground car park? You wanted me to vacate a parking space."

"No, madam."

"Has anyone told you they needed their space back? Mr Walker?"

"Mr Walker is out." He glanced over his shoulder at the pigeonholes. "His mail hasn't been collected this morning."

Marnie clenched her fists in front of her, resting them on the counter. "His space is two-o-eight, level minus two. Ring any bells?"

"I'm afraid not."

She felt like screaming.

• • • • •

They left Anne alone in the kitchen. She got up and peered out of the window in the back door. There was a yard, cracked concrete, a few flower pots with dead twigs and a grimy yellow bucket filled with rain water. She knew she ought to be frightened and part of her was, but she was more worried about Marnie. They had tricked her into going away with them, and Marnie would be frantic. No. Marnie would be trying to work out all the possibilities. She would guess who had abducted her, but not how or where.

At that moment no one in the world knew where she was, except her abductors. How long would it be before Marnie contacted the police? Or her parents? *O God!* Her family would be distraught. They might be so upset they would want her back home, living with them, instead of working at Glebe Farm with Marnie. Always assuming that she actually *got back*. She told herself to keep calm, try to think what Marnie would do in this situation.

Should she try to escape? At the end of the yard was a brick wall. If she was desperate enough, she could climb over it. Part of her was desperate enough. But then what? She would be in another back yard like this one, enclosed on all sides by walls and buildings. She would have to go through every yard in the street to get out, by which time she would be exhausted.

Meanwhile the gang – she had begun thinking of them as a *gang* when she was in the car – would be waiting for her at the end of the street and would just catch her as she scrambled over the wall and bring her back to this kitchen. Square one. But with one important difference: they would be feeling angry with her for escaping. They might have imaginative ways of showing their displeasure.

Anne cocked her head on one side and listened. She could hear nothing, but sensed that the house was not empty. Out of curiosity she put her hand on the knob of the back door and turned it. Locked. Of course. No key visible. End of tentative plan. Unless she wanted to break the glass and climb out. That would make it easier to track her down. The gang would just follow the trail of blood from the multiple lacerations. Great.

And did she really want to escape? Apart from the risk of bleeding to death in a back yard somewhere in north London, Anne was where she wanted to be, possibly. She was near Marlene-Avril, or so she hoped. For a second or two she wondered what her *worst nightmare* might be, but quickly pushed the thought out of her mind. This was the moment of truth, the meeting they had been planning for so long, and it was almost incredible that she had been able to come this far. If Marnie was in her place she would keep a cool head and see it through. That was what she must do.

The handle on the kitchen door turned slowly, and Anne felt her cheeks tingling, a cold flush sweeping over her. The door eased open and a face appeared. A girl. Anne suddenly had the impression that they were in a competition to see which of them was more frightened. She also knew who the girl was.

"You're ..." she began.

The girl came in and shut the door behind her. Immediately there were rapid footsteps outside and the door burst open. Fran pushed her way into the room.

"You said you were – "

"It's all right, Fran. I'm here now. Don't worry. I just wanted to see her."

"You don't know her, do you?" said Fran.

"No. But she doesn't look dangerous to me." To Anne she said, "Who are you?"

"I'm who I told Fran I am. My name's Anne Price."

She held out her hand without thinking. For both of them it was an unexpected gesture. The girl looked at it and then shook it.

"What do I call you?" said Anne.

"Avril, they call me ... but I prefer Marlene."

"Marlene, then." She attempted a smile. "It's good to meet you."

• • • • •

Marnie rang Ralph as she walked back to the café. A woman's voice came on the line, calm and beautifully modulated.

*The mobile phone you are ringing is currently switched off. Please try again later.*

*Ralph!* Marnie was exasperated. *Doesn't he realise how important it is to keep the lines open at a time like this?* She forced herself to keep cool. She only wanted to talk to him because he would be a rational influence, a friendly voice to commiserate. No point getting angry.

The mobile rang a minute later. "It's Ralph."

"Where are you? I've been trying to call you."

"I'm in the office, holding the fort. Remember? I'm obeying orders."

"Your mobile's switched off." She did not mean it to sound like an accusation.

"It's on charge. But I don't need it. I'm sitting next to the office phone. Everything okay?"

"No. It's not okay at all. Anne's gone missing." Silence at the other end of the line. "I know what you're going to say."

"No you don't. You can't. I don't know myself yet."

"I left her in the café while we waited for Avril. I had a message to move the car. It was a trick. When I got back she'd gone."

"When was this?"

"Nearly two hours ago. You're going to say I should've reported her missing to the police."

"Not necessarily."

"No?"

"Marnie, I doubt the police would count two hours as *missing*."

"No. I think that's why I've been holding back. But I'm really getting worried now. What do you think I should do?"

"Sit tight for a little longer. Are you in the café?"

"On my way."

"I can't believe anyone would want to harm Anne," said Ralph. "They couldn't regard her as a threat."

"They could regard her as a hostage," said Marnie.

"Not really likely, I'd have thought. What would be the point?"

"What else?"

"Marnie, all you can do is hang on and wait to be contacted. Give it a bit longer. I don't think you've got any choice."

*Where have I heard that before?* Marnie thought, when she hung up.

• • • • •

Marlene made Anne a cheese sandwich and she realised she was hungry. They sat and ate together, the two of them alone in the kitchen, while Marlene told her story. It was all familiar, almost identical to the version that Anthony had told them. Anne watched Marlene closely and was convinced she was telling the truth. When Marlene came to the end, she shrugged and bit into her sandwich at the point when Anthony was photographed with her in his garden and she had run off to a waiting car.

"So are you living with your boyfriend, then?" said Anne.

"No. That *creep*. I never want to see him again after what he made me do."

"He's not living here?"

"No. He's miles away. He's no idea where I am. None of them know."

"None of who?"

"All that lot … from the newspaper. I *hate* them … and him. They used me."

Anne was confused. "What are you doing here, then?"

"I got away from my so-called boyfriend but I had nowhere to go ... just wandering the streets in a daze ... no clothes, no money, nothing. Then I ran into Cheryl. She thought I was trying to work her pitch."

"On the game?"

"No ... begging."

"Beggars have a pitch?" Anne felt naive in asking.

"They're organised ... well, sort of."

"And this is their base?"

"It's Mick's house. He drove you here. Cheryl rents it."

"And they're beggars?"

"Keep your voice down!" Marlene muttered softly. "They're a mixed bunch. Fran's on the game. Cheryl's got a pitch in Docklands by Tower Bridge." She lowered her voice to a whisper. "They don't reckon she'd earn enough to survive if she went on the game."

They smiled together. For a moment it was almost like girl talk.

"What about Mick?"

Marlene reached across the table and grabbed Anne by the hand, shaking her head. "He's into all sorts ..."

It was a crazy thought and it made Anne want to laugh, the idea that a tough character like Mick might be running a liquorice racket. Taking Anne's expression for levity, Marlene frowned at her.

She whispered, "Seriously ... Mick's into drugs and stuff like that. It's not a joke."

"And *you're* involved in all this, with Mick?"

"No. *God*, no. It's Cheryl lets me stay here. Mick's with Fran ... and the others."

"So what do you do?"

"Nothing. I don't even go out most of the time."

"Is the *Globe* looking for you?"

"I dunno. I hope they think I'm history. But I can't go home ... they'd find me if I did."

"You can't stay here all your life."

"I haven't got a life."

"You know what I mean."

"This is where I am for now. I just get by from one day to the next."

Somewhere in the house a phone rang. It stopped. Seconds later they heard footsteps on the stairs. The door opened and Mick pushed his way in. Behind him, Anne could see Fran loitering in the narrow hallway. Without a word Mick walked up to Anne, seized her by the shoulders and slammed her backwards against the wall. She could feel a nightmare scenario coming on, Mick's breath in her face, his hand on her throat.

"Did you bring the fuzz here?" he growled, showing his teeth like an angry dog.

It was all Anne could do to speak in a hoarse whisper. "You brought *me* here." She sensed that she had not answered the question. "I don't even know where here is."

Mick looked into her eyes at point blank range, and Anne braced herself for violence, scarcely breathing.

"Mick!" Fran's voice from the hall.

His gripped tightened round Anne's throat, and she was willing herself to have the courage to bring her knee up sharply into his groin as a last resort, when he released her and rushed out of the room. The front door opened and slammed shut. Alone in the quiet house, the two girls stared at each other, wide-eyed, Anne breathing heavily, rubbing her neck. Faintly came the sound of a car engine starting and a screech of tyres.

"What was that about the fuzz?" said Anne.

"Mick's paranoid ... always thinking the police have got him under surveillance. Are you all right?"

"Yeah, I think so."

"You didn't lead anyone here, did you?"

Anne shook her head. "Course not. No one knows I'm here ... not the police or anyone else. Where are we actually?"

"Stoke Newington ... Hackney."

"Marlene, we've got to get away from here."

"We?"

"This isn't a safe place. God knows what might happen to you if you stay much longer. Come with me. We'll take care of you."

"Why should you?"

"That's not the right question. You ought to be asking what've you got to lose. The answer is zilch. Get your things and we'll go ... and be quick about it. Mick left in a hurry ... he must've had a reason. Come on!"

Marlene hesitated. "I don't know ..."

"Oh, Marlene ..." Anne sounded weary. "Don't think about it, just get going. You fetch your things, I'll check if the coast is clear. *Please!*"

They walked out into the passage, Marlene taking the stairs, Anne going to the front door. She put her head out. There was a short approach to the house, three paces to a low coping wall and the pavement. No one in sight, she walked out and looked along the quiet street. She turned to go back into the house to find herself confronted by three men, two of them in police uniform.

The third was a tough-looking man in a suit. He stared at Anne for some seconds, his expression changing from belligerence to bewilderment to recognition.

"Well, well, well," he said slowly. "Now here's a face we've seen before."

"Good afternoon," said Anne. "Good afternoon ... Inspector Bruere."

• • • • •

Asterios looked up and shook his head at Marnie when she opened the café door. She had not really expected good news, but was still disappointed. It was lunchtime and all the tables were occupied. Marnie found a stool at the counter and felt obliged to order something. She waited while Asterios finished making up an order behind the counter. He passed her a sandwich and a cappuccino. She looked at him in surprise.

"Is for you."

"But I didn't – "

"Is all right ... on the house. Please." He nodded. The decision was final.

Marnie reached into her bag. "You must let me – "

"No. You are worried about your friend. You aren't hungry, right? So I give you this so you have something ... to keep your strength up. Take it."

Marnie had often travelled to Greece on holiday and knew well the generosity of the people. Even so, she felt her eyes prickle at this act of kindness in a bad time.

"Evcharisto," she muttered, dragging out some of her tourist Greek. "Evcharisto poli. Thank you very much." Her voice was barely a whisper. She reached across the counter and touched Asterios lightly on the hand. He turned his hand over and squeezed her fingers firmly but gently.

"Parakalo," he said formally. "You're welcome."

Marnie smiled, her eyes moist. "This must be the only café in London where the owner tips the customers."

Asterios laughed softly, turning his head towards the door at a flash of colour ... mixed colours, outside in the street. A car had drawn up, white with a red stripe on the side, a black-and-white chequered band and blue lights rotating on the roof. Half the clientele of the café suddenly looked nervous. Marnie stifled a gasp and almost slipped from the stool as the door of the police car opened and Anne climbed out. Her joy was modified when from the front passenger door appeared Detective Chief Inspector Bruere.

• • • • •

Marnie watched the lift doors close and exhaled slowly. She was relieved that DCI Bruere and his side-kick were heading down for the exit. Back in Simon's living room, Anne was lying on a sofa, hand trailing to the floor, pretending to have passed out. Or was she pretending? Marnie leaned back against the door to the flat after closing it.

"Why do the police never seem to believe me?"

"Probably because – " the reclining shape began.

"That was a rhetorical question, Anne. You're not meant to supply an answer."

Anne swung her legs round and sat up. "Do you think it was a good idea letting Mr Bruere smoke in here? I don't expect Simon would be very happy."

"I hoped it might make Bruere feel relaxed."

"Good," said Anne. "Somebody had to be."

"What do you mean? I thought I was very convincing as being perfectly at ease."

"Well, don't hold your breath for the Oscar nomination."

"Thank you."

They looked at each other and smiles slowly spread across their faces. Marnie crossed the floor and hugged her friend, kissing her on the forehead.

"Do you think you ought to ring Ralph and let him know I'm back?"

"I already have. I phoned him from the bathroom. I was only pretending I had to go to the loo."

Anne laughed. "You're like a real spy, Marnie!"

"I also checked our answerphone. Guess what? We've got Anthony's boat back at home."

"Andrew and Kate have delivered it?"

"Yeah. They didn't waste any time. I can't blame them wanting it out of the way. They've moored up just beyond *Thyrsis*."

Anne collected the cups and saucers, including the one that Marnie had offered Bruere as an ashtray. They cleared everything into the kitchen and began washing up.

"So, go on ... tell me what happened. Where did they take you? How did they get you to go with them? And what was Marlene like? Everything."

Anne told her story while drying the dishes. It differed markedly from the version she had given to DCI Bruere. As far as he was concerned, Anne had simply been visiting a friend for a sandwich lunch. They had been astonished to find the house being watched by the police. A search of the premises from loft to cellar had revealed nothing. While the search was carried out, Bruere had hooked up to the central police computer but could find no information on Avril. When Anne had stated that she was staying with Marnie in Docklands, they insisted on driving her back to check she was telling the truth. Bruere was openly suspicious, but despite all his efforts could find no evidence of wrong-doing on the part of anyone in sight, and reluctantly let matters drop.

"What next?" said Anne.

"Well ... Bruere will be wearing out the phone line between his office and Bartlett's, comparing notes about my nefarious activities. That's guaranteed."

"Will that mean trouble for us ... more trouble?"

"I don't see how it could. We're not breaking any law ... at least, I think we aren't."

"What are we going to do?"

"I want to go down and get some flowers to put in the flat ... to thank Simon for letting us stay."

"I mean, what are we going to do next about Marlene?"

Marnie perched on the arm of a sofa. "Frankly, Anne, after what happened today, I feel like dropping the whole business. I nearly died worrying about you."

"But just before the police put me in their car, I got her to promise to keep in touch. It was the last thing I said to her ... phone us tomorrow. She said she would. At least I think she did. She sort of muttered it."

"You really think she'll help us ... or more to the point, Anthony? She was part of the plot against him, remember. I'd be very wary in her shoes."

"I think she might ... maybe for his wife's sake. But she is pretty scared."

"How will she know where we are?"

"I slipped one of your business cards under my mug for her to find when the police took me away. It's got all your details on it, so she can get in touch at the office or on your mobile."

"My *business card!*"

"What's the matter?" said Anne. "I thought you wouldn't mind. It's the only thing I could think to do and – "

"Of course! That's how they knew my mobile number for the trick message about the parking space. I gave my card to that Fran woman."

"It's a good job they got out of the house before the police came," said Anne. "Otherwise they'd have found it on Fran."

"God, yes," said Marnie. "Bruere would've had a field day. And Bartlett ..." She rolled her eyes and looked at her watch. "We've got to get a move on. I can't leave the car there much longer. I'll be glad to get home. I've had enough of London."

"So we'll just have to wait for Marlene to get in touch, then," said Anne.

"Don't count on it. And frankly, after what we've been through, I for one ..."

"But we've got to help her if she does, Marnie," Anne said urgently. "Maybe it means more to me ... I've met her. We've got to get her away from there ... get her life back. We can't let her down. Not now we've found her ... almost."

"Where've I heard that before?"

# Part 28

Amazingly, the normal world was still waiting for them when they returned to Knightly St John. Marnie looked out at the builders moving round the farmhouse, one of them singing as he climbed a ladder. She saw the men turn and smile at Anne as she took out the tea tray. Anne knew all their preferences: who took milk, how many sugars. They knew her as the girl from the office with the friendly face. They had no idea that on the day before she had been picked up by the police at a house suspected of being used by drug dealers and vice rings, and driven through London in a squad car.

Marnie had collapsed bone-weary into bed the previous night after a supper that consisted of hot chocolate and two biscuits.

In the office early, they hit the ground running from the sheer pleasure of leading a normal life, even if they knew it could not last. When the phone rang, Marnie picked it up with a feeling of apprehension.

"Walker and Co, good morning."

"Hallo, my dear." A warm and homely voice.

Relief. "Hallo, Mrs Jolly. How are you?"

"Oh fine, and I won't keep you long. I know how busy you are. I just wanted to ask if you'd heard the news on the radio this morning ... the *Today* programme."

"'Fraid not. We leapt straight in at the deep end of the in-tray. What did we miss?"

"It was about that MP chap ... you know ... Well, it was about his wife actually. The inquest verdict was suicide committed while the balance of her mind was ... something or other ..."

"*Disturbed*, perhaps? Did they say anything about Anthony himself?"

"Only that he hadn't been seen since those photos appeared in the paper. Paul Pinder hinted that a lot of the blame rested on the MP because he'd left his wife to face the music."

"Paul Pinder seems to have forgotten that he himself orchestrated some of that music on his own programme."

"I'd forgotten that. I suppose he's what you'd call an *investigative* reporter. He's usually very good."

"You seem to be a fan, Mrs Jolly."

The old lady laughed. "I always thought he performed a public service, exposing things people wouldn't otherwise know about, especially the secret lives of politicians. But listen to me rambling on. You must have lots to do in the *deep end* of your in-tray, so I'll leave you to get on. Bye, my dear. Give my love to Ralph and Anne."

Anne walked in as Marnie was putting the phone down.

"That was Mrs Jolly. She heard the inquest verdict on Anthony's wife. Suicide. Not much of a surprise."

"Talking of surprises ..." Anne nodded towards the window.

Marnie looked out and frowned. "I thought you said *surprises*."

A grey Vauxhall Cavalier was coming down the field track.

"I think that's Sergeant Marriner's car," said Anne.

"Perfect."

The detective sergeant was alone. He parked in his usual place, and Marnie opened the office door as he approached.

She called out, "The 'reserved' sign with your car's number on it is nearly ready."

Marriner smiled faintly as Marnie offered him a seat, and Anne waved a mug at him.

"Thank you, Anne. Milk and one sugar, please."

"Now you have got me worried," said Marnie. "Accepting a cup of coffee for the second time in a matter of days."

"After the morning I'm having, Mrs Walker, I'd be glad of anything."

"And it's only just nine o'clock," Marnie pointed out. "When did you start?"

"Just after six."

"Have you eaten?"

A wry smile. "Tough question. My memory's not that good."

Marnie turned towards the kitchen, but Anne was already rummaging in the fridge. She held up two packets.

"The choice is ... in the blue corner, crumpets ... in the red corner, croissants."

"Don't know when I last had crumpet," he said, without a trace of innuendo.

• • • • •

Ralph was at first puzzled as to why his scanner was not functioning. The message on the computer's screen told him it was unplugged, and he knelt down to follow the cable back to the socket. Its place had been taken by the lead for Marnie's mobile phone charger. Before pulling the plug, Ralph pressed the button on the phone to check if it was fully charged.

In the mobile's window, words came into view: *1 message*. Ralph tried another button to check the charge, and a longer text appeared. He tried to return to the main screen, and the text changed to: *Calling*. He put the phone to his ear, and a woman's voice came on, brisk, efficient.

"Becky Thornton."

"Er ... sorry, I think I've pressed the wrong button."

"Who d'you want?" She sounded busy, anxious to get on with whatever she was doing.

"No idea. I accidentally pressed a button on a friend's phone and there you were."

"Who's the friend?"

"Marnie Walker."

"Ah ..."

"She's not here just now, but I'll be seeing her very soon – "

"Perhaps you can get her to ring me."

"Yes, of course I'll – "

"Let me give you my number in case you've *accidentally* wiped it."

Feeling hugely inadequate, Ralph took down the number and disconnected. He had no sooner pressed the red button to end the call than it began ringing and vibrating in his hand. Muttering that it seemed to have a life of its own, he pressed the green button and hoped he was now mastering the technology.

"Hallo?"

"Ah … I seem to have mis-dialled … unless you've had the operation." A man's voice, educated, confident.

"Who did you want to speak to?"

"I was hoping to speak to Marnie Walker."

"This is her phone. Who is that, please?"

"Randall Hughes. Is that … Ralph?"

"The very same. Hallo, Randall."

"So you're working the switchboard now …"

"Yes … promotion at last."

"Marnie all right?" An edge of concern in his voice.

"Fine. She left her phone in my study. Can I ask her to ring you back?"

"Actually, it involves all of you. I wondered if you might be free to pop over this afternoon. I want to talk to you about Tony."

"Everything okay?"

"Yes, but I'd rather talk to you in person … and in private."

• • • • •

Marriner picked it up carefully so that the butter did not drip over the edge. Anne certainly knew how to do crumpets. Hidden talents, that girl. He winked at her, and she smiled in return.

"So … no Inspector Bartlett to hold your hand?" said Marnie.

"No. It doesn't work like that. Don't believe what you see on television. It's the sergeants who do the real detective work. And the DCs."

"Is this visit *real detective work*? I thought it was a social call."

"Partly. We don't really do social calls in the CID."

"You surprise me. Tell me something, then. Why was Chief Inspector Bartlett involved when Toni was murdered? Do inspectors handle the murder cases? Is that how it works?"

"Not in the field, not normally. They're usually back at base, masterminding things from behind a computer."

"Then why was he here?"

"Good question. Bit of an exception … the church and all that … words in ears in high places. He got involved at the start as normal and then it all started happening around us."

"And Bruere, in London? He's a DCI. He was very much involved when Tim Edmonds was murdered at Christmas."

"That case was special, too. One MP as victim … another as a suspect. Anyway, I think Bruere likes to get stuck in … hates being desk-bound. Course, I've never met him in person. But I gather you've been paying him a visit, Anne. Social call was it?"

"Is that what this visit is all about?" Marnie asked.

Marriner said to Anne, "DCI Bartlett was curious to know why you were found in a house known to be frequented by some of our friends."

Anne had stopped smiling some time before. She had guessed where the conversation would be leading.

"I was visiting someone," Anne said simply. "It's the truth."

Marriner stared at her. "Well, it's not a crime … just an odd coincidence. They turn up expecting to find some villains, and there you are."

"They had nothing on Anne's friend," Marnie said. "She was just renting a bedsit in a house. Not her fault if the house was used for other things."

"We were wondering what she was doing in London, Anne, this *friend* of yours. She wasn't a student, had no job, no family in the area."

"Probably looking for work," Marnie suggested. "You'll have to ask her that, or rather your friends in the Met will."

"Difficult," said Marriner. "She's disappeared."

• • • • •

They were on the road again, this time heading for Brackley, with Ralph at the wheel, Marnie beside him, Anne in the back. They looked like a family out for a drive, except that Anne was checking through her 'Jobs to do' list and sending text messages on the mobile. For much of the journey Marnie had her eyes closed.

"You okay?" Ralph said.

"Still a bit weary. How about you?"

"I'm all right. But then I haven't been running around masterminding the escape of you-know-whom."

Laughter came from the back seat. Ralph looked in the rear-view mirror and saw Anne grinning at him.

"What's the matter with you?" he asked in mock indignation.

"*You-know-whom*," she repeated, laughing again. "No one would ever guess you were a professor, Ralph!"

"Huh!" he exclaimed, smiling. "So, Marnie, tell me about Becky Thornton. What did she have to say?"

"Not a lot. She was under pressure ... deadlines."

"Is she a journalist?"

"No, a researcher. She's with that *Lifelines* programme on television."

"Can't say I've ever heard of it," said Ralph.

"It's quite famous," Anne chimed in. "Do you know *This is Your Life?*"

Ralph looked at her in the rear-view mirror again. "Of course."

"Well, it's its rival on another channel."

Ralph said, "They must be running out of lives by now. That programme's been going for centuries. I wouldn't have thought they needed another one ... doesn't seem much point."

"Ah, but it's different," said Marnie. "*Lifelines* goes out live, just like *This is Your Life* did years ago. Makes it more spontaneous."

"Does that make it better? Have you seen it?"

"Not a whole programme. I saw a bit once when I was tuning the video. And I read an article. Apparently it's all arranged in utmost secrecy. Even the audience don't know what they're going to see. They get tickets, thinking it's a variety show with famous stars. Millions watch it."

"So the person whose life story they're telling thinks they're doing something else."

"That's the idea, and suddenly ... surprise, surprise! *It's your Lifeline!* Then they have the usual ego-trip orgy with famous people queuing up to say wonderful things about them. It's all hugs, tears, *dorling-dorlings* ... you know the thing."

"Sounds ghastly."

"Sure," said Anne. "That's why millions switch on to watch it."

Ralph glanced up at the mirror. "Millions?"

"Prime time TV," said Marnie . "No editing, no script."

"Is this somehow relevant to us?" said Ralph doubtfully.

"Not as such. It's just that Becky Thornton knows so many people through working on the show, she's got loads of contacts."

"Good. It must be the most interesting sort of research, delving into people's private lives."

"And all top secret," said Marnie. "If the word got out, all the spontaneity would be lost. This is our turning up here, Ralph. This road leads straight to Randall's place."

Anne said, "I saw it once ... it was a star from *Coronation Street* ... they were all practically in tears. Not your sort of thing, Ralph. I bet you haven't even heard of *Coronation Street*."

"Yes, I have."

"Ralph," said Marnie. "This is our ... er, that *was* our turning. Didn't you hear me? It's all this talk of television. It's true what they say. Too much television warps your brain. What are you doing now?"

"Turning the car to go back."

"No need. We can take the next on the right. It's just as quick."

Ralph pulled over and stopped, waiting for traffic to go by before turning the car.

"I think I've become invisible," said Marnie. "That's why you can't hear me."

Anne snorted in the back of the car. "What are you doing, Ralph?"

"Apart from doing a U-turn, I'm wondering if the blue Ford Sierra that's just gone past has been following us since we left Knightly."

• • • • •

Randall had wasted no time. He had been in the rectory for less than a year and it looked as if he had lived there all his life. As they stood in the hall shaking hands, kissing cheeks, Marnie quickly took in the decor that was unmistakably Randall: primrose yellow walls and dense matt white paintwork, set off by a carpet of deep blue Wilton. None of these came cheap.

Randall ushered his guests ahead of him into the living room, turning to Marnie, who was last in line, to mutter, "In case you're wondering, the diocese pays for the materials and I do the work myself. Not the normal arrangement, but I got them to do a deal so I could get what I wanted."

"You're very perceptive, Randall. You know you're destined for promotion as soon as they bring back the Holy Inquisition."

"Great," he said instantly. "It's starting up again next week. I've ordered the instruments of persuasion from a catalogue. *And* I'm taking Spanish lessons."

Marnie gave him A Look. He put an arm round her shoulder and squeezed affectionately. He really did not seem like a normal churchman at all. She wondered why he was so frisky. As he moved aside to let her enter the room, she saw Angela Hemingway sitting in an armchair, smiling. Of course.

Randall insisted on serving the tea himself. Angela looked as if she enjoyed being served. She also looked as if she was part of the furniture. When they were settled, Randall came straight to the point.

"When you first asked me if Anthony – *Tony* – could come and stay at the hostel, I must say I had some misgivings. I wondered how he'd cope. He was used to enjoying status and privilege. Coming here could cause severe depression. I was sure he'd see himself reduced to living in a community of *tramps*."

"You're right," said Marnie. "He thought he was coming to a *doss house*. Sorry to put it like that, Randall, but that's what he said."

"Understandably. But that feeling didn't last. Very quickly I realised he was coming to terms with his situation. And I think I understand why."

Marnie said, "It's obvious, Randall. You took him in and offered him – "

"No. Well, perhaps partly yes. But I believe his time on the canals had a big impact on him. And so did all your efforts to help him survive, especially after the death of his wife."

Ralph said, "Did you hear the verdict of the inquest on the radio this morning?"

"Yes," said Angela. "That's what made us think of asking you to come round."

*Us*, Marnie thought. Out loud she said, "How did Anthony take it? Did he hear it himself or did you tell him?"

"I went to tell him straight after breakfast," said Randall. "But he already knew. I found him in the chapel."

"In the *chapel*?"

"Yes. It's not so unusual, Marnie. People do turn to God in times of trouble."

"Of course. But it's just ... well, Anthony ..."

"I found him in tears. He seemed to be praying. I asked if he wanted to be left alone. He said he'd heard about the inquest and it had brought it all back. He asked if I could stay and hear his confession."

"*Confession?*"

"Yes. I sat with him and we talked for a while."

"What did he ..." Marnie began, but checked herself. "Ah, *confession* ... that would be confidential, of course."

Randall seemed to ignore Marnie's interjection. "He told me that he'd caused her death, that he was responsible for killing her."

The three visitors all but gaped at him. Marnie broke the silence. "He said *what?*"

"Yes," Randall said quietly. "And I'm quite sure he meant it."

"But he was at Knightly," Ralph protested. "Anyway, why should he want to do such a thing?"

"There's more than one way to kill someone," said Randall.

"You think," Marnie said, "he meant he'd driven her to take her own life?"

"More than a possibility, don't you think?"

"Did he say anything else?"

"Well, I told him that he should think very carefully about what he'd done and what he'd told me. I asked him what he wanted to do, and he said he was almost ready to face the world, but not quite yet."

"That's what he always says," Ralph muttered.

"In my job I've had quite a bit of experience of people who've hit rock bottom. I believe he was genuinely sorry for what happened, contrite and ready to repent. I'm sure you all helped him to get that far."

"How did you leave things?" said Marnie.

"I took his confession and gave him absolution. It was all I could do ... what I had to do."

"I suppose so," said Marnie. "Thank you for telling us the details."

"Of course, if he'd actually confessed to murder, I would've kept the details, as you call them, strictly confidential."

"And would you still have granted him absolution?" said Ralph.

"Yes. A priest isn't a judge. That's out of our hands."

Marnie said, "It must've been a great comfort to be able to speak about his sense of guilt for Melissa's death ... get it off his chest."

"No doubt. I also think I may have found a possible solution to his problem."

Randall glanced at Angela. They had been discussing this. She smiled.

"A solution?" Marnie said. "What is it?"

"You'll probably think it strange, but we've been wondering if the Church might offer him a way out ... a future."

$$\bullet \quad \bullet \quad \bullet \quad \bullet \quad \bullet$$

They were in the galley on *Thyrsis*, Marnie and Ralph making supper together, a simple pasta with tomato and basil, garlic bread in the oven already adding a spicy note to the air. Marnie washed grapes and peaches, dried them on kitchen paper and put them in a bowl. Anne had gone over to *Sally Ann* to fetch a bottle of bardolino from the 'cellar'. She seemed to have been gone a long time.

Marnie heard her mobile warbling in the sleeping cabin and skipped along to find it.

"Hallo, Marnie Walker."

"Did you say Marnie Walker? Sorry, you're rather faint." A man's voice. Not one she recognised. Crackly.

Marnie moved quickly out of the cabin and down to the boat's side entrance. "Just a sec." She put her head through the hatch. "That better?"

"That's fine. A friend gave me your number."

"Oh, yes."

Marnie had the feeling this was not about a redecorating job on a barn conversion or a loft in Docklands.

He continued. "You were asking about ... Jeremy Hawksby. Is that right?"

"You know him?"

"I used to ... quite a long time ago. A very long time ago, actually."

*Gently does it*, she thought. "Can you tell me anything about him?"

"Possibly."

"But not on the phone?"

Marnie wanted to ask a hundred questions, but reined herself in, worrying that she might frighten him away if she pushed too hard.

"No."

Quietly she said, "Would you like us to meet?" There was a long silence. Marnie decided to ride it, but after a while she wondered if he had gone. She tried again. "We could find somewhere neutral. I'm in the country about fifty miles north of London."

"I'll ring you back."

Marnie immediately pressed a button on the phone. The message in the mobile's tiny window read: *Number withheld*.

• • • • •

Anne had found the wine as soon as she opened the cupboard door. Putting the bottle on the workbench in the galley, she went along to the key rack, bursting with impatience. When they had returned from Brackley, Marnie and Ralph had headed straight for *Thyrsis* to make supper, still talking about Anthony's apparent change of character, his *repentance*. They had stopped at a supermarket on the way and each of them was carrying bags of groceries, so Anne had been obliged to walk through the spinney to the docking area. Now she was desperate to find out if Marlene had kept her promise and phoned her.

She grabbed the key and ran out of the boat, taking the shortest track through the trees to the office barn. When she saw the number 4 in the answerphone window, she had a foreboding that Marlene would not be one of them. She pressed the button and reached for the pad. One: Beth. Two: the builders' merchants wanting instructions about slates. Three: Willards wanting to discuss completion dates. Anne knew the last message would not be Marlene. She was right.

• • • • •

"You don't think it might have been one of the rat pack?" Ralph said. "The man who's been watching Anthony?"

"He seemed different," said Marnie, looking out of the window. "I wonder what's happened to Anne."

"What do you mean? She's here on board, isn't she?" Ralph put the garlic bread into a dish and rinsed his hands.

"No. I sent her to get a bottle of wine on *Sally* some time ago. Where *can* she be? "

"Don't get paranoid," said Ralph. "She's not going to get abducted again. Not here. Anyway, I think she's coming. I can see movement in the spinney."

Marnie peered out. "The *spinney*? You're sure it's her?"

"It's her."

They saw Anne step aboard *Sally Ann* and re-appear moments later holding a bottle. She looked pre-occupied, and Marnie had her usual feelings of guilt at exposing her young friend to so many problems. She wandered along the corridor and pushed the side doors open as Anne approached.

"What's up? You look glum."

Anne turned to come in backwards down the steps, sighing. "No message from Marlene. I don't suppose she's tried on the mobile?"

Marnie took the bottle of wine. "No. But I had a call from a man. I think it was the contact from Judith."

"Did he give his name?"

"No, hardly said anything."

Anne pondered for a few moments. "You don't think it could've been someone from the press?"

"Don't think so. Come on, let's eat." She turned and led the way towards the galley. Over her shoulder she said, "Anything interesting on the answerphone?"

"Nothing earth-shattering. I've made a list."

· · · · ·

Marnie poured the last of the wine into their glasses. She and Ralph helped themselves to fruit while Anne put the dishes in the sink. In the cleared space on the table Marnie put a notebook.

"I've been drafting a press release and writing a sort of plan of campaign."

Ralph quickly read the details: girl made pregnant by Hawksby, boy sexually assaulted at school, Anthony set up with girl in garden, hounding in the paper, girl's disappearance, hounding all over the country, wife's suicide. Marnie turned the page.

"I've put all that in the press release. I'm going to send it as soon as I get names of contacts in the media world."

"From this Becky Thornton?" said Ralph.

"Or whoever."

"You're still hoping Marlene will contact you?"

"Perhaps she's been delayed," Anne said, sounding unconvinced. "Do you think she could be in any danger?"

"Who from?" said Ralph. "Hawksby? I doubt it. He got what he wanted from her. My suspicion is she might just decide to lie low."

"That's what worries me," said Marnie. "I have this feeling that after everything we've done, it's going to lead nowhere."

# Part 29

"So things aren't going too well," Beth said sympathetically. "Must be disappointing."

Marnie was determined not to sigh. "Yes. I mean no. Both. In reverse order."

As she spoke, she put a line through Beth's name on Anne's list of phone messages. It was almost eight-thirty, Wednesday morning.

"And this Anthony is over at Randall's place. Is that right?"

"Yeah. Randall thinks he might want to take up Holy Orders. Can you believe that?"

"He must've been reading books about monks and nuns in the Middle Ages," Beth suggested. "We all know what they got up to."

"Something tells me you don't have a high opinion of Anthony."

"Well, Marnie, after what I've read in the papers, what do you expect? Sorry if he's become a mate of yours, and all that, but you know what they say about leopards and spots. Oh dear, was that a sigh?"

"No," Marnie said firmly. "I've given them up for Lent."

"Lent finished at Easter."

"I'm in training for next year. It's all this talk about religion."

"Do you think he's changed his character?" said Beth.

"Well ... he's certainly changed quite a bit since he first came here. Anyway, I'm past caring. All I want is to get things resolved. And nothing's happening. It's all gone ominously quiet."

"And you take that as a bad sign ... that it's all gone quiet?"

"Sure. I'm trying to make things happen. That's the whole idea."

"Oh well," said Beth. "You never know. Look on the bright side. This might just be the lull before the storm."

"Thanks, Beth. That's very comforting."

"We aim to please."

"Gotta go. Calls to make. Plans to lay. Decisions, decisions. I'll ring you."

"Okay. Keep smiling."

Marnie checked her list and was about to ring the builders' merchants when the phone rang first.

"Hi Marnie."

"Simon, hi."

"Progress?"

"What's the opposite of progress?"

"Ah ... Look, I'm going to a meeting in Birmingham on Friday. Any chance of calling in on my way back? You around?"

She checked her filofax. "We'll be here. What time?"

"Late afternoon ... ish."

"Come for supper?"

"Great. But I can't stay late, early start on Saturday morning, business trip."

"We can have an early supper. No problem."

"Fine. And you can fill me in on whatever's the opposite of progress. Oh, er ... and I'd like us to have a chat."

Marnie made the rest of her phone calls, pleased that the real world seemed to be going forward. The only name on her list not to be crossed through was Marriner, yesterday's fourth message. He was out of the office till after lunch. She turned to her drawing board and began finalising a scheme for one of the Willards' jobs.

Anne took the next call. "Walker and Co, good morning."

"Has anyone told you, Anne, you've got a very good telephone voice?"

"Is that … Mr Leyton-Brown?"

"Yes. Anthony. You sound very professional … make a good impression."

"Good. I'll pass you over to Marnie."

With Marnie on the phone, Anne made drinks for the builders and took them out on the tray, enjoying her few moments of friendly banter with the men on the site. By the time she returned to the office, Marnie was back at her drawing board, but there was a stillness about her, even seen from behind, that made it clear to Anne that her mind was not on colour schemes. Anne asked if she was ready for a drink and, when Marnie made no reply, Anne walked over.

"Anything bothering you? Anything I should know?"

"Anthony wants a talk. I said we'd go over this afternoon."

"I've got my driving lesson today."

"I know. I'll go with Ralph. We'll drop you off in Towcester on the way."

"Did he say what he wanted to talk about?"

"He was on the payphone in the hostel, so he just said … planning the next step."

"Sounds like progress. Is your mobile charged up, Marnie?"

"I think so. Why?"

"I don't want to miss Marlene when she … *if* … she rings."

· · · · ·

Anthony's room was plain and simple, with two beds, only one of which was in use. There was one window, a chair, a wardrobe and a bedside cabinet. A landscape print on the wall. No crucifixes or biblical quotations.

Randall had told Anthony that numbers were down, so he could have a room to himself, but they both knew this was special treatment, minimising the risk of recognition and giving him solitude to clarify his thoughts.

Anthony offered Marnie the chair, while he sat on one bed and Ralph took the other. They both noticed a calm about his manner.

"I'm afraid I can't offer you refreshment up here. Funny, the things you take for granted. Still, it's private and we won't be disturbed. Thank you for coming."

Marnie began, "You wanted to talk about plans for the future."

"I'm genuinely touched by what you've done for me … you two and your friends. I know I don't deserve so much help, and I know it's not been easy."

Ralph smiled faintly. "There hasn't always been a great deal of choice about it."

"No. But there is now."

"What kind of choice do you have in mind?" said Marnie.

"I think the way ahead has become clear. This is your last chance to pull out before it gets too late. So far you've been in control – to some extent – of what's happened. All that is about to change."

He spoke quietly, but it added a sinister edge to his words.

"Why do you think things are going to change?" said Marnie. "Why now?"

"It's simple. Because the only way to clear my name involves bringing Marlene out of the shadows, which means it's going to get tough from here on."

"*If* she comes out of the shadows," Ralph said. "We don't even know where she is just now."

"All the more reason to be clear about what we're doing. Things could happen quickly, and we may not have time to sit around talking about plans by then."

"Good point," said Marnie. "You always said you wanted to clear your name. You still think you can?"

"After coming this far, it's got to be my aim. I may not be vindicated, but I want to be understood or at least heard."

Ralph said, "I suppose that's fair enough ... wanting to put your side of the story."

"You could've done that from the start," Marnie said. "I don't want to seem callous, but it would've saved a lot of trouble if you'd given your explanation when the story blew up."

"You're absolutely right, Marnie." His voice was still calm. "But when something like that blows up, you can't tell how you're going to react. In my case I was so shaken, I just fled. You can't imagine what it's like to be vilified in the national press ... not what it's *really* like ... not when it actually happens to *you*. It's horrifying."

"But now you're ready to face the world," said Ralph. "You want to issue a statement?"

"Not yet."

"When?" said Marnie.

"As soon as Marlene is ready to speak. Without her I can't clear my name."

"But you could achieve that by yourself," Marnie said. "A public statement would do it."

"But it would only be my word against theirs. And they'd print their side of the story in bigger print than mine. Banner headlines."

"But better than nothing," Ralph said. "The other media will give you a fairer hearing when they report it."

"You always were more of an optimist than I am, Ralph. No. I need the girl to back me up. And without her testimony I can't get even with the paper for what it did to me."

"*Get even?*" said Marnie. "You want to do that as well?"

"Of course. That's why I've been waiting for you to find Marlene and bring her out of hiding."

"Getting even doesn't sound very Christian," said Marnie.

Anthony looked at her as if she had spoken in a foreign language. "*Christian?*"

Marnie was going to say what Randall had told her, but changed her mind. "Just a turn of phrase."

"Getting even may not be very Christian," Anthony said. "But I've come to learn that revenge is a very pure motive."

• • • • •

"*Get even!*" Marnie said in exasperation as Ralph drove out of Brackley. "*Bloody hell!* It's as much as we can do to keep going and try to make a statement, let alone *get even.* Who does he think we are ... the *Mafia* ... the SAS? There's no way we're going to be able to get even with a national newspaper and all the power of the press. He's living on another planet."

"I wish he was," said Ralph. "And please don't remind me it's because of me that we're in this position."

A gloom settled on them for the rest of the journey, though they comforted themselves with the thought that things could not get much worse. That thought was dispelled when they bumped down the field track and saw Sergeant Marriner's Cavalier waiting in the yard in its usual space.

They walked into the office and found him sitting with a cup of tea. Anne was at her desk looking anxious. When she saw Marnie and Ralph, she headed straight for the kitchen area.

"Sergeant Marriner, good afternoon. I tried to return your – no, please don't get up – your call, but they said you were out."

"In the circumstances I thought a personal visit was preferable after all, Mrs Walker." He looked tired and drawn.

"Do we have *circumstances*?"

"I'm afraid so."

Marnie glanced over to Anne at the sink. Anne shrugged. Whatever it was, Marriner had not told her. Marnie and Ralph pulled up chairs and sat down.

"You're here on a serious matter, then," said Ralph.

Marnie thought this was not as intelligent a comment as she usually expected from Ralph, until she realised what he was suggesting. Marriner understood immediately.

"Yes, sir. Of course normally I would've come with a woman colleague, but as Mrs Walker is always here ..."

"So what you've come to say concerns Anne?"

"That's right. That's why I waited until your return before asking her any questions."

Marnie looked at the cup of tea in his hand. "She's the fastest draw in the West, Sergeant."

A faint smile. "So I've noticed."

Ralph stood up. "Anne, I'll do that. You come and hear what Sergeant Marriner has to say."

Anne walked back to her chair. As she passed Ralph, he squeezed her arm. She sat facing the detective, looking very young and vulnerable, and Marnie wished she was anywhere but there.

Sergeant Marriner said, "Anne, there isn't an easy way to put this. I understand that when you were questioned in London you said you'd been looking for your friend in Limehouse. Is that correct?"

"Yes. It was true."

"Okay. But DCI Bruere found you and your friend at a house in Stoke Newington."

"Yes. Those are her digs."

"So why were you looking for her in the Limehouse area? It isn't a trick question, Anne."

Anne immediately got his drift and frowned. "I am telling you the truth, Mr Marriner."

He gave an encouraging nod. She decided to give as full an answer as she could and knew that Marnie regretted that she had not always been frank with the police. Anne was about to reply when Ralph came over.

"Sergeant Marriner," he said. "I'm sure Anne has nothing to hide, and I'm sure your questions aren't hostile, but don't you think you ought to tell us why you're pursuing this line? If Anne is likely to find herself in any kind of – "

"She isn't, sir. Otherwise I'd be spelling out her rights. I just need to get something clear."

Anne said, "I was looking for Marlene around Limehouse because I'd heard from someone that she might've been there. When I asked about her, someone else told me where she was, and that's how I came to see her in Stoke ... Thingammy."

"Thank you. Anne, how well do you know Marlene?"

"Not *very* well."

"Can't you just come to the point?" Marnie said.

"This *is* the point. Do you know her well enough to recognise her?"

Anne looked puzzled. Marnie felt a shiver down her spine. She saw the point of the question and dreaded its implication. She could tell by Ralph's expression that he also understood where Marriner's question was leading.

"Recognise her? Of course I recognise ... why?"

As she asked her question, Anne's eyes widened. She knew the answer before Marriner spoke, and put a hand to her mouth.

"I'm afraid the Met have found the body of a girl answering Marlene's description in the canal by Limehouse Basin."

"Are you absolutely sure of this?" Marnie said.

"That's why I'm here."

"They once told me about a tramp's body being found, and it turned out to have nothing to do with their enquiry. I think they knew that at the time but were just trying to make me react."

"I can't comment on that, Mrs Walker. But I can assure you that is not the case now. In fact, the reason I've come here is to ask ..." He turned towards Anne. "It's to ask if you will go to London to identify the body."

• • • • •

Later, sitting together on the bed in Anne's attic room after supper, with the dread of the next day hanging over them like storm clouds, Marnie asked Anne if they should contact her parents. Anne simply shook her head.

"Don't you think they ought to know?" Marnie said softly. "Wouldn't you like your mum to be with you tomorrow?"

Anne looked alarmed.

"God no! But you'll come, won't you, Marnie?"

"Of course I will. But I thought you at least ought to tell them what's happening."

"I can't. If I did ..."

"They'd worry about you and want you to go back home?"

"I don't know what they'd do. That's the point. I don't want to risk what I've got here. It's my whole life ... everything I've wanted since I first met you."

"I can understand that, Anne. But I do feel a responsibility to your parents – "

Anne interrupted her. "Let me look after them. I talk to my mum a few times a week on the phone, like you've always said I could. She was worried about these muggings, but she was all right when I promised not to go out alone. It's not my fault this poor girl's dead … but she's nowhere near here. I know it must seem callous, Marnie, but I don't want her death to stop me having my life."

# Part 30

An unmarked car had been waiting for them at Euston station, indistinguishable from thousands of other Vauxhalls. Anne had thought it was just like her father's, but this was unlike any other journey she had ever made. She sat quietly with Marnie in the back, not noticing where they were going. The streets were a blur. In front, two women police officers sat in silence. They had threaded their way through heavy traffic past King's Cross and down towards the City of London. This time they did not see Tower Bridge or Docklands. This time there was no pleasure in modern architecture, only a hollow feeling in the pit of the stomach.

The building in which they were sitting was like a small plain office block. They were shown into a waiting room and offered tea or coffee. They refused both, but Anne asked if she could have a glass of water. When it arrived, it was icy cold. They had expected a drab depressing mortuary, but this was a bright, well-lit place with pale blue walls and white paintwork. The floor was covered in dense grey carpet tiles that deadened the sound.

The WDC left them and returned a minute later, asking Anne if she was ready. Marnie admired Anne's calm manner as she stood up, nodded once and took a deep breath. She touched Marnie's sleeve, and the WDC led them both along the passage. The police officer stopped at a door.

"The chapel of rest is just here," she said quietly, her hand on the door knob. "Inside, you'll see a window on your left. When you're ready, I want you to look in through the window. Take your time. There's no rush."

Anne's eyes moistened and she chewed her lip. She blinked a few times and whispered, "Okay."

Marnie fought back an urge to grab Anne by the arm and run with her down the corridor and out of the building into the fresh air. Instead she touched her hand lightly. Anne did not look at her but kept her face towards the door.

She said softly, "I'm ready now."

The police officer swung the door open and went in first. They entered a space the size of a domestic living room with a picture window. Anne swallowed and turned towards the window, stepping forward slowly. The chapel was a simple space with a small altar table on which stood a brass cross and two unlit church candles. In the middle stood a coffin of light wood, with a cream lining. Anne glanced briefly down and quickly raised her eyes towards the opposite wall. Marnie heard her breathing. Anne looked down again at the face, all that was visible of the girl in the coffin. She stared for several seconds and turned towards the WDC.

"All right?" said the police officer.

"Yes."

The WDC led them back out into the corridor. "Thank you, Anne. I'm afraid it's never easy. They've tried to make it as painless as possible for you. Were you able to identify her?"

Anne said simply, "That wasn't Marlene. I've never seen that girl before."

• • • • •

The police Vauxhall came out of the car park at the back of the mortuary and eased into the late morning traffic. Marnie thought Anne was looking better. With her habitually pale skin, it was inappropriate to think of colour returning to her cheeks, but there was a light in her eyes again, her expression no longer dulled with anxiety. She even managed a weak smile in reply to Marnie's unspoken question of whether she was okay.

The WDC turned in her seat to look round at them. "We can take you back to Euston. Is that all right?"

"Do you need a statement or anything?" Marnie asked.

"Not in the circumstances, no. So Euston, then?"

"Please."

"If you'd like to give me your address and the receipt for your train tickets, I'll arrange for your travel expenses to be sent to you."

"Thanks."

Marnie opened her wallet and took out a business card and the receipt for the train fare. A thought flashed through her mind, so fast that she could not bring it into focus. It flashed past again. She studied the wording on the card. There was her name, the Glebe Farm address, the phone numbers, the e-mail. Cream with dark blue lettering, *Sally Ann*'s colours. So?

"Is that your card?" It was the WDC looking back again.

Marnie passed both items forward. At that moment, the thought became clear and formed itself into a question.

"How did you know to contact us?"

"Sorry?" said the policewoman.

"You – or rather your colleagues – got in touch with us about the girl found in the river."

"Yes."

"Why? How did you know it might have something to do with us? Inspector Bruere found Anne in Stoke Newington. That's miles north of here, up Hackney way. What connected him to Anne?"

The WDC looked puzzled. "I see what you mean ... but I don't have an answer. My orders were just – "

"Your card," Anne broke in.

"My card? What about it?"

"Someone must've got the address from one of your cards."

"Of course!" said Marnie. "That's it. But how ... and who?"

"It must've been me," said Anne. "I gave them to the shop people to get in touch with us if Marlene came back ... that day I was in Limehouse with Ralph."

Marnie sat back, deep in thought. Quickly she said to the policewoman, "Could we have a change of plan? Would you mind dropping us near the old Limehouse Town Hall?"

• • • • •

They stood on the corner where Marlene had first picked up Anthony and started the chain of events that had led them back to this spot. The gloom of the mortuary hung over them, the memory of that other girl, that quiet shape in her box. The efforts made to reduce the pain of the identification process for Anne, had brought Marnie close to tears. Now they stood on the windy pavement with the noise of the city traffic and the dust swirling round them, both wondering who she had been, that poor lonely girl, dead and unclaimed. Marnie wondered if it was only a matter of time before they were back again, looking at the real Marlene in a box in that chapel.

"What a morning!" Marnie said wearily. She put her arm round Anne's shoulders. "You've been brilliant, you know that? What an ordeal!"

"Marnie, what are we doing here? I don't understand. Why have we come to this place?"

"Elementary, my dear Watson."

It was one of their old jokes, but Marnie often asked herself which of them was Holmes and which his faithful friend.

Anne said, "Put your deerstalker on, then, and tell me the answer."

"It's not a clever deduction," said Marnie. "I just thought that perhaps the shopkeepers might've seen Marlene again ... that she might be around here for some reason. It's just a forlorn hope that we might find her, the only thing we've got."

"Is it that long a shot, you think, finding her again? Are we really back to square one?"

Marnie fought back a sigh. "I think we may be, yes."

"Right," said Anne. "Newsagent's or chippy? Which one first?"

Marnie looked across the road. The choice was obvious.

They emerged from the fish-and-chip shop with the knowledge that the owner, who was clearly more at home in Cantonese, had no recollection of ever having had the card from Anne. But they did each have a portion of haddock and chips to console them. The frying smell had made them realise how little they had eaten that morning. Barely a slice of toast had sent them on their way. Marnie managed to bring out the first real smile of the day.

"I'm not really surprised he didn't remember you, Anne."

"No?"

"I expect to the Chinese we all look alike."

They loitered on the pavement across the street, eating their lunch out of newspaper – inevitably pages from the *Globe* – before going into the other shop.

The newsagent remembered at once. He was a tall stately Indian, very dark and handsome, with clear unaccented English. They both thought he should have been in films instead of running a shop in the East End.

"Yes, of course, I remember you coming in and giving me the card. I stuck it up on the board behind the counter. That's why I thought of you when the police came in asking about a missing girl. I thought it might have been you. I'm glad it wasn't. But did I do the wrong thing?"

"Not at all," said Marnie.

"Good. I didn't want to cause you trouble. I wanted to help find you."

"Very kind of you." Marnie reached into her shoulder bag and pulled out a folder. She slid out a cutting from the *Globe* and held it up. "This is the girl we're looking for. Her name's Marlene ... or sometimes she was called Avril."

The man studied the paper with dark intense eyes. "I'm not sure. It's hard to tell."

"When she was here," Marnie said, "she sometimes wore a yellow cagoule ... like a light jacket ... with a hood."

"Mm ... maybe. I think I did see her, but that was weeks ago. Is that the girl the police were asking about?"

"No. The girl they found had darker hair, like mine but more auburn ... reddish."

"Oh, yes ... yes," he said thoughtfully.

"You've seen her?"

"I think so. I may have seen them hanging around together once or twice."

# Part 31

Friday morning's major achievement was to persuade the council's planning officer of the logic of fitting Welsh blue slates to the farmhouse, matching the existing cottage roofs. Marnie tried not to gloat when confirming the order to the man at the builders' merchants. He tried not to smirk when informing her that the price of victory would be a four week's wait for delivery and a twenty per cent increase in cost.

Anne had recovered well from her ordeal in London. Marnie had asked if she wanted to sleep on *Sally Ann* and offered to stay on board with her, but Anne was adamant. She reminded Marnie that a young woman had hanged herself in that very barn, directly beneath Anne's loft, back in the time of the Civil War, and she did not believe in ghosts. The only anxiety for Anne was discovering on their return that there was no message from Marlene.

When Randall rang just before ten, Marnie suspected they would be having a visitor at break-time, but she was wrong. That evening he was coming to Knightly to take Angela to a concert. Anthony had asked if he could travel with him to do things on his boat. He had not sorted it out since the journey with Andrew and Kate and he wanted to *clear the decks for action*, as he put it, in case he found himself needing to make a discreet getaway in the near future. Marnie thought this made sense, though she did not want Anthony arriving while she was talking with Simon. They agreed that Anthony would go straight to his boat and stay on board overnight. That would leave Randall flexible for the rest of the evening, and Marnie or Ralph would deliver Anthony back to Brackley some time the next day.

Ralph set off at the end of the morning for a meeting and dinner with his publishers in London. He would be back late. With Simon due to arrive after work, Marnie left Anne running the office while she went to prepare supper for three on *Sally Ann*. As she chopped vegetables she turned over in her mind the problem of Marlene. Although she was thankful they had not found her body in the mortuary, she despaired that they would ever bring her out of hiding.

By six-thirty Marnie was beginning to be concerned about the ratatouille, fearing it might turn into a glutinous mass. She was bending towards the oven, trying to find the lowest possible setting, when her mobile rang.

"Hi, it's me. Am I eating in the doghouse? I'm sorry about this, Marnie, but the meeting over-ran and I should've been okay, but I've hit roadworks."

"Where are you exactly, Simon?"

"Coming off the M6, picking up the M1. Traffic's crawling."

"You're facing south?"

"South? I suppose so."

"Can you see a big black cloud in the distance?"

"A big black ... All right, I'll buy it."

"That's our oven going up in flames ... with your supper in it."

Simon laughed, an open full-blooded laugh. "You haven't changed! You and your one-liners! I do love you, Marnie. See you in a bit. I'll be as quick as I can."

Marnie lifted the casserole dish from the oven and set it down on top of the cooker. It was like old times. Too much like old times. She knew he had probably not given any thought to what he had said, reacting to her joke, but the words were still echoing in her head. Looking at the mobile lying on the workbench, she had an overwhelming urge to ring him back and ask him not to come. Later, she had reason to wish she had picked up the phone.

• • • • •

Simon came through the spinney at a rapid pace, clutching a bunch of flowers. They had the look of the bouquets on sale at motorway filling stations – usually for husbands with a guilty conscience – but the thought was there.

When he came aboard *Sally Ann*, he kissed Marnie on the cheek and shook hands with Anne. Marnie was wondering about drinks, with the ratatouille heating up again in the oven. Simon opted for water; he had more driving to do that evening and he could not stay late as he had to get ready for his early start the next morning. Anne produced three tumblers filled with chunks of ice, sparkling water and a slice of lemon. They took their seats for supper as Marnie cut up a French stick and Anne tossed a green salad in vinaigrette.

"This looks great," said Simon. "No sign of fire damage. Nice of you not to hang the guilt thing on me for coming late."

Marnie shrugged. "Ratatouille doesn't suffer from being re-heated, as long as it doesn't dry out."

Simon smiled. "I know."

Over supper they talked over the Anthony campaign and their lack of progress. Marnie briefly outlined the visit to London the day before, and Simon listened without comment. As soon as they finished eating, Anne looked at her watch, announced that she needed an early night and excused herself. She walked back through the spinney as dusk was falling, and Simon volunteered to clear things away while Marnie made coffee. She lit the two oil-lamps, and they settled back in their safari chairs in the soft glow.

"That was a wonderful meal, Marnie. Thank you."

"Just something simple. Thank you for the flowers."

He laughed. "Think nothing of it! I mean that."

"I ought to say something about the thought counting ..."

"Yeah. I'm glad you've ... got your life worked out, Marnie. I know you've got this Anthony thing hanging over you, but that won't last. It's got to be resolved sooner or later, and you'll get back to normal."

"*Normal*. I live in hope."

"I think you do ... literally. And I'm glad you're happy. You are, aren't you?"

"Yes."

"Good. You know, I'm sorry about us ... our marriage ... failing the way it did. I really regret that."

"I know. Me too ... but it is in the past now ... it's history." Marnie hoped she did not sound harsh.

"Yes. Still ... I hope I haven't only been a negative experience in your life."

"Of course not, Simon. We had some great times, lots of them. Things just didn't work out."

"More's the pity. Marnie, this is difficult, but... I don't think it's a good idea ... seeing you the way I have been."

"Oh ..."

"I wanted to know you were okay and I'm glad about that, but I think on balance it was probably a mistake. I've been finding it tough, and I can't think it's easy for you, having me barging into your life like this."

"It has been good seeing you again, Simon."

"Yeah. But I know I keep seeming to forget how much things have changed and I start saying things that are over-familiar and ... well, you know ... I don't want to disrupt things for you."

"No." She felt this was a less than adequate response and added, "I understand."

He stared into his cup and without looking up said, "Do you know the idea they had in the Middle Ages about wounds bleeding?"

"About what?"

"When someone was killed, to find the person who'd done it, they'd get people to stand one after another next to the victim. If the wounds opened up and started bleeding again, that person was the murderer."

"I'll have to tell Bartlett and Bruere," Marnie said quietly. "They could find that useful."

"That's how it is for me, Marnie ... seeing you again ... like opening up old wounds."

●　●　●　●　●

Arriving back at the office barn, Anne went straight to the answerphone. No light glowing, no messages. It was her usual habit to switch the machine to immediate reply and turn the volume control to zero when she went to bed, but that evening she left the machine in daytime mode in case Marlene rang.

Climbing the wall ladder to the loft, she slipped into bed and settled down with the latest edition of *Interiors* magazine. Finding concentration difficult, she let her gaze wander round the room. It was her Aladdin's cave, softly lit by three table lamps, with colourful fabrics setting off the pastel-washed stonework and dark oak beams, Oriental rugs scattered over oatmeal carpet and a Moroccan throw as bed-cover. How gorgeous it all was, she thought, compared with the squalid house in Stoke Newington where Marlene had to live. Marlene ...

A soft scuffing sound reached her, and she began smiling seconds before she saw movement over by the wall. At the top of the loft ladder a head appeared by the open trap door. Dolly had mastered the art of climbing the ladder and now leapt expertly onto the platform. The big black cat trotted straight to the bed and jumped up beside Anne with a warble, turning in circles to make a nest for herself.

Anne reached down to stroke her. The steady sound of a motor on tick-over.

"You're right, Dolly. For us, it's *purrfect*. Aren't we the lucky ones?"

●　●　●　●　●

Simon looked at his watch and shifted in his seat. Marnie was surprised how apprehensive she felt. After their divorce, she had never expected to see Simon again, and now she was feeling the same old jumble of emotions as when they were splitting up. Half of her wanted him to leave quickly; half of her wanted to find the right words to draw a line under that part of their lives, before he went away.

Suddenly his head snapped up from contemplating the dial. "I meant to tell you … Did you know Leyton-Brown had been sighted?"

"*What?*"

"Yes. It was on the car radio. I seem to have been listening to news bulletins for hours on the way here."

"Where was he seen?"

"Edinburgh." Simon chuckled.

"*Edinburgh?*"

"Yep. That's what they said. Apparently the *Globe* has offered a reward of £1,000 for a confirmed sighting. They're going to run a competition in the paper starting tomorrow."

"You've got to hand it to them," said Marnie. "They sure know how to keep a story running and sell papers. You see what we're up against?"

"You'd better tell your guy what's happening and warn him to be extra-vigilant in his hiding place, wherever it is."

"You could tell him yourself. His hiding place is here."

"What do you mean?"

"He's on his boat. Randall was bringing him over for this evening. He's there now, moored just along from *Thyrsis*."

"Are you serious?"

"Sure. You really could tell him, if you wanted."

Simon inclined his head on one side. "Yeah. That might be quite interesting. Do you want to come with me? I can't imagine he'd open up for a casual visitor."

Marnie shook her head. "Knock on the hatch twice, pause and knock twice again. He'll open up."

Simon smiled. "Cloak-and-dagger stuff, eh? I'm intrigued. Okay, I'll hop along and see him before I go. I shouldn't be long."

Simon grabbed his jacket, blew a kiss to Marnie and went out, still smiling. While he was gone, Marnie washed up without noticing the dishes.

• • • • •

After a while Marnie got absorbed in an article on new architecture in Catalunya and lost track of time. She was surprised how dark it was when she looked up as the boat rocked gently and she heard a footfall on the stern deck. Simon and Anthony must have had a heart-to-heart talk rather than a quick chat.

But it was not Simon's voice that called through. "Hallo. Anybody home?" It was Ralph.

Marnie quickly examined her watch. "Hi!" she called out. "You're early."

Ralph walked through to the saloon. "I got away as soon as I could. You seem surprised to see me."

"Actually, I was expecting to see Simon. He went over to have a word with

Anthony. He's been gone a long time."

"I'd better hide in the cupboard if your husband's due back at any minute." He smiled, put down his briefcase and kissed her.

"Would you like coffee or something stronger?"

Ralph opened a cupboard and extracted a bottle of brandy. "Do I put out one glass or two?"

Marnie shook her head. "Not for me." She checked the time on the wall clock.

"Are you worried about Simon?" said Ralph, sitting down opposite her, where Simon had sat.

"No. It's just that I was sure he'd be coming back before he went home."

"He drove here, presumably?"

"Of course."

"Then he's gone. His car's not at the farm."

"Oh well," said Marnie, "I expect he stayed longer than he planned with Anthony and had to get off. He said he was in a hurry."

· · · · ·

Marnie was restless that evening and eventually allowed Ralph to pour her a brandy, while she struggled to maintain concentration on the magazine. Simon's rapid departure had left a feeling of unfinished business, even if it was only to say good-bye. Had he planned it that way, deliberately leaving so that there was no farewell scene between them? At around ten she suggested a stroll before she and Ralph retired to *Thyrsis* for the night, and they walked hand-in-hand through the spinney towards the office barn. Marnie saw that Anne's light was on and she quietly opened the office door and crossed to her desk.

"That you, Marnie?" Anne called down from her room.

"Sorry if I disturbed you."

"No probs. You didn't. Don't bother with the answerphone. No message from Marlene."

Marnie smiled up towards the hatch at the top of the wall ladder. "Thank you, radar." She walked back to the doorway where Ralph was standing. "Anne?"

"Yes?"

"Did your antennae notice when Simon's car left?"

A pause. "Quite a while ago ... couldn't tell you what time ... it was dark outside, I think ... not long before Ralph arrived."

"Thanks. Goodnight, then."

On the way back to *Thyrsis*, they could see lights still showing round the curtains on Anthony's boat.

"Marnie," Ralph said quietly. "It's none of my business, but did you and Simon possibly have an argument? You seem a little anxious about something."

"Oh no, not at all." She squeezed his hand. "No. It's just not like him to go off like that ... somehow out of character."

"You did say he was in a hurry."

"Yes. That's what it was."

"But it's still bothering you," Ralph said as he reached in his pocket for the boat key. "You could call in on Anthony and check how Simon was when he left. The light's still on."

Marnie frowned. "I don't want to involve Anthony, really."

"Couldn't you give Simon a ring?" said Ralph. "He'll have easily got home by now."

"Mm ..."

"Why not? Then you can put it down. I'll leave you to it. I'm going to have a shower."

Marnie leaned forward and kissed Ralph, and they went on board *Thyrsis*, going in opposite directions at the foot of the steps. In the saloon Marnie rang Simon's flat. The answerphone immediately cut in. She disconnected. Same result with his mobile. From her wallet she took out Simon's card and checked the number for the Porter's Lodge.

"No, madam. Mr Walker hasn't been in this evening."

"You're sure about that?"

"Quite sure. I've been on duty since seven o'clock ... here all the time. His mail hasn't been collected, and there are two messages marked urgent waiting for him."

"Perhaps he's been held up somewhere," Marnie muttered.

"I'm just checking the car park cameras, madam. One moment ... No. His space is empty. He hasn't returned yet. If you'd like to leave a message I'll ask him to phone you as soon as he gets back."

Marnie gave the porter her mobile number asking Simon to ring at any time, however late it was. An idea was growing in her mind. What if Simon had not been going back to his place after all? Perhaps he was staying with someone. Perhaps that was why he wanted to stop coming to see her in future. *Someone.* She got up to draw the curtains and noticed the lights again on Anthony's boat. On an impulse she rang his number.

"Simon?" said Anthony. He sounded surprised. "That was ages ago. He was only here a couple of minutes ... said he had to be away ... some meeting or other."

• • • • •

Marnie jumped. She had not noticed Ralph enter the saloon. He was in his dressing gown, rubbing his hair with a towel, when he sat down beside her.

"Sorry. Did I startle you? Didn't mean to. You were lost in thought there."

"Yes."

"Am I disturbing you?"

"No, of course not. I was only thinking. Actually, I was wondering if Simon had a girlfriend."

"A *girlfriend*?"

"He didn't go back to his flat and ... well, he said he probably wouldn't be coming here any more."

"I see," said Ralph. "Did he give any reason?"

"Only that he'd originally contacted me to check that I was all right, and now he wanted me to be able to get on with my own life without intruding."

"Seems fair enough." He stood up, rubbing his hair again. "But something's still bothering you, isn't it?"

"I know it shouldn't, but he said he'd be gone a minute and would then come back to say goodbye. Anthony confirmed that he did only stay for a minute – I just rang him to check – but then he went off without another word. It's just odd."

"Unless he was rushing off to see a hypothetical girlfriend, you think," said Ralph.

"Then why didn't he just say so? No need to keep it a secret. Though perhaps he thought it was none of my business."

Ralph shook his head and stood up, heading back to the bathroom. After two paces he turned. "Sorry I can't solve your mystery, Marnie. It is curious. I can only think he realised it was later than he thought and went off in a hurry. You've tried his phone numbers?"

Marnie nodded. "All of them, and he's not got back to the flat. That's what made me think he might be going somewhere else."

Ralph pondered. "Logical." He smiled. "If he doesn't return your call by tomorrow, I'll get one of my contacts at the MoD to track him down with a spy satellite."

Marnie smiled back. "Good idea."

As Ralph padded back to the bathroom, Marnie felt her cheeks tingle. She reached over to the bookshelf and grabbed a thick volume with a silver cover decorated with the emblem of a three-pointed star. She quickly thumbed through to the helpline section and began scanning the pages. After a minute or two she turned to the inside back flap and looked at Simon's handwritten notes. Her mind was racing. She picked up the mobile and hit the buttons.

"Good evening. Mercedes helpline." A man's voice, calm, efficient. "Can I first take you though security, starting with your registration number and your postcode." Marnie supplied the details. "Thank you. And may I have the third letter from your password."

Marnie looked at the word in block capitals printed inside the flap. "S, sierra."

"And the fourth letter?"

"T, tango."

"And finally your mother's maiden name."

"Oakham."

"Thank you, madam. Actually I see the car is registered to a gentleman."

"Yes, In fact, that's the point. It's my husband, Simon Walker."

"And you are?"

"Marnie Walker."

"That's no problem. What difficulty are you experiencing, Mrs Walker?"

"It's … well … my husband has been taken ill. He's been admitted to hospital in Northampton. I want to fetch the car, but I don't know exactly where it is. It's not the sort of vehicle you'd want to leave lying around, obviously, and for all I know it might be unlocked. You see the problem."

"Yes, of course."

"A friend's offered to drive me to collect it, but I can't talk to Simon at the moment. Can you tell me where it is using your satnav system?"

"One moment, please." Marnie looked at the password as she held on. OYSTER. Strange choice, she thought. Simon had never liked them. In seconds the voice returned. "It's on the A508 in Northamptonshire. Do you have a pencil ready, Mrs Walker?"

Marnie took down a six-figure OS grid reference. "Just one other thing. Did Simon report any fault with the car by any chance?"

"No, madam."

She thanked the helpline operator, disconnected and walked through to Ralph's study to search the bookshelves.

"Did you manage to get hold of him?" Ralph was standing in the entrance, his hair now combed. "I heard you talking on the phone. Everything okay?"

"I took your advice and got him traced by satellite."

"You did what?"

"Seriously. Mercedes have a satnav tracking system, for security. They gave me a grid reference. I'm trying to find it."

Ralph stepped forward and pulled a local map from the shelf. Marnie checked the numbers.

"That's odd. It's hardly any distance at all." She ran her finger along the co-ordinates and stopped. "On the main road between Hanford and Stoke Bruerne."

Ralph craned forward. "That's where it crosses the canal between the locks. He must've stopped in the car park. Perhaps he wasn't feeling well and had to pull over."

Marnie suddenly felt guilty about telling the helpline operator that Simon had been taken ill. "Hang on, Ralph. That doesn't make sense. It's north of here. Simon said he was going back to London. He wouldn't pick up the M1 at junction 15. That's miles out of his way. He was heading south."

"Unless your supposition about visiting someone was correct."

"Whether it was or not, he's hardly gone any distance at all. The car didn't break down. And I can't imagine Simon arranging an assignation in a canalside car park." Marnie raced over the options. *Simon wanted a breath of air and a stroll by the canal to clear his head.* In the dark? *He was feeling unwell and stopped for a rest.* All very sudden, but not impossible. *He realised he'd gone the wrong way, stopped to turn round and for some reason decided to wait a while.* What for? "No," she said out loud. "Something's wrong. It doesn't add up."

Ralph turned to leave. "I'll be ready in two minutes," he said over his shoulder.

• • • • •

There was scarcely any traffic as the Volvo sped north. The road wound its way though darkness, passing Yore and Hanford. Five minutes after leaving Knightly St John they crested a hill and looking ahead saw light in the distance a mile or so away.

"What's that up ahead?" Ralph muttered.

"Working late on one of the locks?" Marnie replied, peering into the distance. "They're always doing something up there."

Ralph eased back at the end of a long straight, slowing as the road approached the bridge over the canal, ready to take the tight right turn into the car park. Through the trees on their right they could see lights flickering. It took Marnie a moment to realise that they were not flickering but flashing. They were blue lights: emergency vehicles. Her heart froze, and her stomach tightened.

Ralph stopped the car in the parking area. They could see two patrol cars, with dayglow stripes on the side, an ambulance, people in uniforms, purposeful movement. They climbed out of the Volvo and rushed forward. Before they had gone six paces a uniformed policeman stepped towards them, hands raised in an unmistakable gesture.

"Sorry. You'll have to go back. There's nothing to see." He stood solid and immovable, blocking their way.

Marnie strained to look round him.

"I told you there's nothing to see, madam. Now I'm asking you to leave."

"Who's in charge here?"

"Please." The policeman stepped closer.

"Is that Sergeant Marriner over there?"

A hesitation. "And if it is?"

"I need to speak to him."

"He's busy at the moment. Now I'm asking you again to move away and – "

Marnie suddenly called out, "Cathy!" The policeman stared at her. "Cathy!" Marnie shouted, this time much louder. At the sound of footsteps behind him, the officer looked over his shoulder. WDC Cathy Lamb appeared at his side, her face puzzled.

"Mrs Walker? Marnie?"

"What's going on, Cathy?"

"There's been an accident. What are you doing here?"

The policeman began, "I was telling them – "

Ralph interrupted. "It's a long story. Who's been involved in the accident?"

"We don't know. It's too early to tell."

With a gasp, Marnie grabbed Ralph's arm and pointed across to the lockside. To Cathy Lamb she said, "That car ... is it involved?"

All four turned to look at the car illuminated by arc lights, its metallic silver bodywork shining like the centrepiece at a motor show or a photo-shoot for a magazine. The light glinted from the three-pointed star on the bonnet.

"Can you identify it?" said Cathy Lamb.

Marnie nodded. In the background cameras were flashing intermittently around the lock chamber like fireworks on Guy Fawkes night. There were voices, among which she recognised Sergeant Marriner's, giving orders.

To the policeman Cathy Lamb said, "It's okay, Rob. I'll take them through."

The Mercedes was parked neatly in the bay nearest to the lock. Marnie went to try the door handle, but Lamb reached out to restrain her hand.

"You know this car, Marnie? You're sure?"

Marnie walked to the rear to look at the number plate. "Yes, I know it. And you could easily work out who it belongs to by checking the national computer."

"We would, once we'd sorted out ..." She inclined her head towards the lock.

Marnie followed her gaze, her eyes seeming hollow in the harsh floodlighting. "My former husband, Simon, owns this car."

Ralph moved closer and put an arm round her. "Perhaps he's here somewhere," he said softly, scanning the groups of men and women moving round the lock.

Two men began pushing the balance beam to open the lock gates. Marriner and a few others descended the steps down to the lower level at the canalside.

"When did you last see Simon?" asked Lamb.

"Earlier this evening."

"So you can describe what he was wearing?"

"Yes." Marnie's voice was flat.

"Will you both wait here, please. And don't touch anything."

She walked quickly away towards the steps. Marnie leaned against Ralph, drained of all feeling. They knew what was coming next.

• • • • •

Marnie squatted on the canalbank in the glare of the white lights, with Simon's body lying beside her where they had dragged him out. He lay on his back, eyes closed, his head turned towards her as if he was telling her something in confidence. His lips were parted, and a piece of weed was stuck to his forehead like an errant curl of hair. His fine clothes were smeared with mud and slime. Ralph had offered to do the identification, but Marnie had insisted she was all right, and everyone had withdrawn to give her space. Closest to her now was Cathy Lamb, hovering attentively.

After a few minutes, Marriner walked slowly forward with Lamb at his side. Marnie raised her head.

"This is Simon."

To her ears it sounded absurd, as if she was making introductions. She reached out to touch Simon's hand. It was unpleasantly cold, all life gone. For always and ever. She did not want this to be her memory. There was a pricking sensation in her eyes, and her vision blurred. Someone spoke, but she did not make out the words, aware only of the water cascading over the further lock gates and a rushing sound in her ears. It was time to go. She lifted the hand and stretched towards it, bringing it to her lips. As she kissed the pale flesh, she saw that Simon's wrist was grazed, dark blue and red blemishes marked the skin where it had been scraped against hard surfaces, the stone, iron and timber of the canal lock. A hand was on her arm, easing her up. Marnie lowered Simon's hand gently onto the stone edging as she stood.

"Are you all right, Marnie?" said Lamb.

"I suppose so."

Ralph was beside her again, holding her as she walked away. The group came to a halt beside the Mercedes. It seemed to Marnie like a monument to the man Simon had become, the new Simon with all the trappings of success, the Merc, the designer clothes, the luxury watch.

"I'm very sorry, Mrs Walker." It was Marriner. "There are some questions I'll need to ask you, but they can wait until tomorrow."

Marnie was looking at the car, dazzled by the reflected light glinting off every surface. She turned to Marriner.

"Why are you here?"

"Why?" Marriner looked puzzled. He had seen the effects of shock on many victims of catastrophe, but even so the question seemed odd. Perhaps Marnie Walker was not as strong and composed as she always seemed to be. Perhaps she was after all just like any other woman.

"Why did you come here? Why you? You're a detective."

Cathy Lamb touched her arm. "We were still on duty when a call came in from people on a boat. It's routine for us to be involved when there's a fatal accident that's in any way unusual."

Marnie turned her head towards the bank where Simon lay. She ran her tongue over her lips.

Marriner began, "I think it would be best now if you – "

"Oyster," Marnie said clearly, to no one but herself. "Of course."

Three faces looked blank.

"It's not an accident."

"What do you mean?" said Marriner.

"Simon's Rolex is missing. He's been robbed ... of everything."

# Part 32

It was one minute past nine when the phone rang in the office barn the next day. Sergeant Marriner apologised for phoning on a Saturday morning, but wanted to make an urgent appointment to see Marnie without delay. She told him he could come as soon as he wanted. Barely twenty minutes later the familiar grey car arrived bringing Marriner with DCI Bartlett and WDC Cathy Lamb. They walked in to the office barn to find Marnie, Ralph and Anne waiting for them, all three looking tired and subdued.

Anne had been waiting for the Volvo to return the night before and had intercepted Marnie and Ralph by the garage barn. They had no choice but to tell her what had happened, and she had heard the news in silence, her eyes widening, tears making tracks down her cheeks. None of them had slept that night.

They sat in a loose circle between the desks, and Anne did not ask if anyone wanted a drink. She simply busied herself in the kitchen area with kettle and pot to occupy her hands while the others talked.

"You'll appreciate I've got to ask you about last evening, Mrs Walker," said Bartlett.

"Of course. I'll tell you everything I know, but I don't think it'll help you very much. I've no idea why Simon went to the car park by the locks."

Cathy Lamb opened a notepad.

"Let's begin with *how* you knew he'd gone there rather than *why*," said Bartlett. "Presumably you must've had some idea he'd be where he was. You didn't arrive on the scene by chance."

"It's quite simple. Simon had been here for supper on his way back to London after a meeting. After he left I needed to have a word with him, but I got no replies from his phone numbers. Later in the evening I tried again, and the porter at his block in Docklands said he hadn't returned."

"What was his state of mind when he left here?" Bartlett interrupted.

"He was fine."

"You and your former husband often had supper together?"

"No. He just called in for a chat as we were on his way home from Birmingham."

"We?"

"Anne was here too. The three of us ate together."

"And the atmosphere was friendly?"

"Certainly."

Anne set down the tray, and Bartlett looked up at her. "We had a nice supper together," she said, her voice trembling slightly.

Bartlett turned back to Marnie. "So you needed to talk to Mr Walker again later that evening?"

"That's when I became concerned."

"What was worrying you? Was he agitated about something when he left?"

"No, nothing like that." Marnie sounded weary. "I told you, he was fine. It's just that he said he was in a hurry and … when I found he hadn't got home much later … well, it made me wonder if he was all right."

"You didn't wonder if your husband had gone somewhere other than home?"

"My *ex*-husband, Inspector. Simon and I ..." Marnie's voice faltered. "We split up years ago."

"And your relationship now?"

"I've seen him a few times lately. He got in touch after hearing about what happened to me last year. It's all been very friendly."

"And you, Professor Lombard, how would you describe your relationship with Mr Walker?"

"Amicable, though I must admit I hardly knew him."

"You didn't regard him as a threat to your relationship with Mrs Walker?"

"Not at all. As far as I was concerned, he was welcome here any time. And he knew that."

"You weren't here during the meal, sir?"

"No. I arrived later ... some time after Simon had left."

"Would you mind telling us where you were last evening?"

"At a meeting in London. I left at about nine and came up on the train."

"Would you be able to give us the names of people at your meeting, sir?"

"Certainly. Roland Miles and Max Womark of Kensington House Publishing. We ate at Max's club off Pall Mall."

"Very well. Mrs Walker, you were telling me how it came about that you knew your ex-husband was at the car park where we found him last evening. Presumably you hadn't just guessed that?"

"No. I knew exactly where to go. At least, I knew where his car was." Marnie explained about the Mercedes tracking system, and the police officers looked suitably impressed. Bartlett asked her to describe the enquiry process in detail, step by step.

"You knew Mr Walker's password," he said. "Also his postcode and the car's registration number. Is that right?"

"And his mother's maiden name," Marnie confirmed.

"You'd know that anyway, surely, as she was your mother-in-law. What I'm interested in is how you knew the other private details."

"Simon lent me the car manual. He knows I like that kind of thing ... he *knew* ..."

"And he told you his password? Why would he do that?"

"He didn't, not directly. I spotted it in his notes at the back of the manual. I guessed what it was."

"How did you guess? The chances must've been very slight of guessing something like that."

"It was OYSTER. It was obvious."

"His favourite food?"

"He had a Rolex watch. Oyster is a famous type of Rolex movement. When I saw it written there, I realised it was his password."

"He wasn't wearing a watch when we found him, Mrs Walker."

"But you will have seen the marks on his wrist where he would've been wearing it," said Marnie. "Either it was dragged off his wrist when he fell into the canal, or somebody removed it in a hurry. I saw the grazing clearly. Did you find his wallet? It was two-tone leather, made by Bugatti."

"You're exceptionally observant, Mrs Walker."

"I gave him the wallet years ago as a birthday present. He'd always wanted a Bugatti – they were great classic cars, you know. This was the nearest I could get."

Bartlett shook his head. "No wallet, Bugatti or otherwise."

"A mugging that went too far?" said Ralph.

"That's the big question," said Bartlett.

"No it isn't," said Marnie. The police stared at her. "The big question is why Simon was there at all."

• • • • •

Marriner drove more carefully then ever as the police car climbed the sloping, rutted track up to the village from Glebe Farm. He did not want to put his DCI in a bad mood by bouncing him roughly against the roof of the car, and he knew that Bartlett could be on a short fuse when faced with a possible murder investigation. Past experience taught him that it was better to drive in silence leaving the DCI to his private thoughts.

"Do you think it was a murder, sir?" said Cathy Lamb from the back seat. Marriner grimaced inwardly. "Or perhaps manslaughter if he was mugged and it went too far?"

"Let's not jump the gun," said the DCI.

"But the watch and the wallet ..." Lamb continued.

"The watch could've been dragged off his wrist when he went into the lock. And the wallet ... perhaps he wasn't carrying it for some reason. Or maybe it's in a special compartment in the car. That thing seems to be full of secrets. Pity we can't just dial up the Mercedes helpline and get them to solve the bloody thing for us."

Marriner pulled out onto the village street at the top of the track. "I expect they log the calls they get at the helpline," he said.

"Yeah," said Bartlett. "You'd better get onto them and check out Walker's story. You've got the manual?"

"Yes, sir."

"You think Marnie – Mrs Walker – was telling the truth, sir?" Lamb asked from the back seat.

"What I *think* is irrelevant, Cathy. It's of no importance. We've got to build up the picture with facts. I want you to check with forensic when they'll be able to let me have the report on the car. And dig out the file on the muggings while you're at it." He looked at his watch. "I'll want it on my desk when I get back from the autopsy."

• • • • •

Anne cleared the cups and saucers and began washing up. It gave her something to do to occupy her mind. Ralph returned the chairs to their normal places and put a hand on Marnie's shoulder; she was sitting staring in front of her.

"You okay?" he said quietly.

"Yeah." She reached up and put her hand on his. "I wonder what happens next. Bartlett will probably want a statement, I expect."

"He seemed more courteous than usual," said Ralph. "At least he won't be suspecting you of anything this time."

"I wouldn't bet on it, if I were you." She stood up. "It's all so awful and somehow … unsatisfactory … Simon just popping out like that, saying he'll be back in a minute, and then … that's it … for ever."

Marnie walked back through the spinney with Ralph. She felt hollow inside and needed some fresh air. Reaching across to take his hand, she said, "I wonder what happens about Simon. What needs to be done … and by whom? Who handles his affairs? I keep thinking I ought to be doing something, but strictly speaking it has nothing to do with me these days."

"Who's his next of kin?" said Ralph.

"I don't know. He was an only child. His parents married late and both of them died years ago. Perhaps there was a note in his wallet to say who should be contacted in the event of …"

They came to a halt at the edge of the spinney, facing the water. Marnie looked over to Anthony's boat moored snug against the bank beyond *Thyrsis*.

"What do we do about him?"

"I think he'd better lie low," said Ralph. "If we try and move him, we risk running into the police or journalists."

"Yeah, we can do without that complication. We'll stock him up with supplies and pretend he isn't there. As if …"

In the trees above them rooks were crowing. To Marnie the eerie sound seemed appropriate to the desolate feeling inside her.

"I think it must've been a mugging … can't think what else it could be. But why was Simon there in the first place? What reason could he possibly have for going in that direction and stopping in that car park?"

"Could he have been meeting someone, do you think? Did he have any connections round here apart from you, Marnie?"

"None that I know of. In fact, now that he's gone, I realise how little I know of his life these days."

"I'm sure the police will be able to go through his papers and find out who was his next of kin, who'd be his executor … that sort of thing."

Marnie put a hand to her mouth.

What is it?" said Ralph.

"Executor," she muttered. "It sounds like 'executioner' …"

• • • • •

Anne was putting crockery in the cupboard when the phone rang. She dashed to her desk to pick up.

"Walker and Co, good morning." She tried to sound positive and businesslike. There was no answering voice at the other end of the line. "Hallo, Walker and Co. Anne Price speaking." Still nothing. "I'm sorry but I can't hear you at all." She waited a few moments. "Hallo? There must be a problem with the phone, I'm afraid. I'm going to hang up, but please try again. Good-bye."

She sat at the desk waiting. Ten seconds, thirty seconds, a minute. Marnie came into the office and looked at her. Anne picked up the phone and dialled one-four-seven-one.

"You were phoned this morning at ten forty-three. The caller withheld their number."

The automatic message was given by the usual calm, impersonal voice, but it made Anne want to scream in frustration. She wanted to throw the phone through the window and smash it to pieces in the yard outside. Looking up at Marnie with her sad eyes, Anne got her cares in perspective and felt herself calm down.

"What was that, Anne?"

"Nobody there when I answered the phone. I thought it might've been Marlene."

"Oh yes," said Marnie. It was like an afterthought, as if the whole business with Anthony was a million miles away and a hundred years ago. "And?"

"Nothing." The statement seemed to sum up how they both felt that day. "I'll get drinks ready for the builders. There are only three on site this morning. Things are slowing down till we get the roof slates."

Two minutes later, while Anne was loading the tray, a car was heard pulling up outside. Neither of them went to see who had arrived, and it was a surprise to both when the door opened and Angela Hemingway looked in. She went straight to Marnie, who stood up, and put her arms around her.

"I'm so sorry, Marnie. I've just heard about your loss."

"You've heard? How?"

"Molly Appleton. I was in the shop when she had a call from her brother. His wife's cousin is a paramedic and was on duty last night. He was there by the canal. I came at once."

"That's very nice of you, Angela. The old bush telegraph … Have a seat. Will you stay for coffee?"

Marnie explained what happened the previous evening and asked Angela if she could think of any reason why Simon – or anyone – might go in that direction when they were heading for London: roadworks, an accident, a diversion, anything. Angela had no ideas and apologised that she was unable to help.

"All I can do, Marnie, is offer my support and my prayers. I know you're an agnostic, but I really do believe in the value and the power of prayer. I shall pray for Simon's immortal soul, for his sake, that he should be at peace."

"Bless you, Angela," said Marnie. "That's really kind of you. Though I suppose I shouldn't say 'bless you', given that I'm not religious, but you know what I mean."

"Of course I do, Marnie. And there's no reason why you shouldn't wish someone God's blessing, if it's sincerely meant. No blessing is ever wasted."

Marnie smiled. "I'll try to remember that, Angela."

"And if you don't mind, Marnie, I shall pray for you, too. I think you could use some peace right now."

$$\bullet \quad \bullet \quad \bullet \quad \bullet \quad \bullet$$

There were no more phantom phone calls, and Marnie and Anne occupied their time with work, immersing themselves in practical everyday business to take their minds away from the unhappiness that hung in the air like a grey cloud.

At bedtime Marnie kicked off her slippers and slid under the duvet beside Ralph. She cuddled up to him, realising that her thoughts had been on Simon all day.

"I'd ask how you're feeling, Marnie, but that would be a silly question. I can remember what it was like when Laura died."

Marnie raised her head from the pillow. "But it's not the same at all. Laura was your wife, the centre of everything. With Simon it was ... different. Our closeness was in the past. It was over long ago."

"Even so ..."

"Of course. Loads of memories ... and the strange feeling he left behind ... just going off. And being found at the lock like that ... So many unanswered questions."

"I suppose we'll never know the answers," said Ralph.

"Well at least I see how to sort things out now, thanks to Angela."

"*Angela*? You think praying will help?"

"No, but seeing the organised way she approached the problems, it made me get my own thinking organised, too. And it's quite straightforward, really. I'll get in touch with our solicitor, the one who handled our affairs when we were married. He dealt with the divorce for Simon when we split up. He'll know what to do."

# Part 33

Unusually for her, on Sunday morning Marnie wrote a letter by hand to explain the situation to Colin Parfitt, who was both Simon's solicitor and his squash partner. In the past he had been *their* solicitor and had handled the conveyancing on their house. When Marnie and Simon split up, it seemed logical that Colin would act for Simon, so Marnie had used her father's solicitor. It had all been managed as amicably as possible in the circumstances, but Marnie could not face the prospect of phoning Colin, and the idea of sending an e-mail seemed crass.

Anne offered to take the letter up to the post-box, but Marnie wanted to post it herself, and Ralph thought it best to let her have a solitary walk. Marnie was a bundle of emotions, too numb for tears, she knew they would come later. Tramping up the field track, she recalled the words of her old yoga teacher: *listen to yourself, follow your instincts.*

By the time she got back to Glebe Farm, Marnie seemed composed, the colour was in her cheeks and her self-possession had returned. They agreed to have a quiet hour or two catching up with paperwork and other chores, leaving till later the decision on how to spend the rest of the day. Anne already had an idea of what would be decided, but said nothing, contenting herself with tidying up the filing and making the office ready for the coming week. She did not stray far from the phone all morning and was growing increasingly disappointed and concerned that there was no word from Marlene.

Shortly after noon Ralph walked into the office. Marnie gathered her files together and looked up from the drawing board.

"Finished?" she said.

"As much as I need to do for today. How about you?"

"Sure. Anne?"

"Me too."

"So, what's it to be?" said Marnie.

• • • • •

*Sally Ann* chugged steadily in mid-channel with Anne at the tiller. There were furrows on the canal surface, and flashes of light on the water from the sun half-hidden among high wisps of cloud. It was the kind of day to restore the human spirit, and Marnie needed such a day more than at any time she could remember.

Shortly after setting off, she noticed a puff of grey smoke from the engine and spent some minutes hanging over the stern rail watching the exhaust pipe and listening to the beat of the engine. She realised that with all her other preoccupations she was probably neglecting *Sally Ann*, and her mind was busy with the thought of the routine checks she should be making at regular intervals. She told herself not to take for granted the things that were in her care. But *Sally Ann* had a stout heart, and the old two-cylinder engine thumped steadily once it had warmed up and seemed happy enough.

"Are you all right, Marnie?" said Anne. "I thought you were being sea-sick over the back of the boat."

A pale smile. "I'm fine. Just listening to the engine."

"I think it's okay. I did the usual checks the other day – engine and gearbox oil, grease in the stern gland, drop filter, bilge pump – the things you showed me."

Marnie hugged her friend. "Where would I be without you?" At that time of asking it was meant only as a rhetorical question.

"I'd better make us a drink and earn some brownie points too," said Ralph, stepping down into the cabin.

Marnie perched on the lid of the gas bottle holder, leaned back against the bulkhead and closed her eyes in the intermittent sunshine. The familiar sounds and movement of the boat brought some comfort, but she had a weight in the pit of her stomach that she thought would be with her for the rest of her life. Without opening her eyes, she heard the engine note diminish as Anne slowed for a moored boat, heard a called greeting and Anne's cheerful reply. She felt *Sally Ann* take a bend and straighten up, listened as the engine boomed louder in a bridge hole, noting the solid banging of a healthy machine, followed by Anne's cry of thanks to a boat that must have given way to them. The everyday sounds and experiences of the canals that she had come to know and love, the restorative power of the waterways. Life would never be quite the same again.

Marnie wanted the journey to go on like that forever, Anne's steady hand guiding them along, Ralph caring for her needs. She felt a slight sway as the boat responded to the tiller and knew they were swinging round the bend with trees on both sides, one of them overhanging at the mid-point of the curve, obscuring the way ahead. It was the sudden deceleration and the clanking of the gear lever, coupled with a muttered "Uh-oh!" from Anne, that told her something was amiss. Marnie opened her eyes and stood up quickly. It took a second or two for her to focus, and she felt momentarily dizzy. As the feeling passed, she was aware that the canal was partially blocked by a boat adrift across their path. By now, Anne had the engine running fast in reverse, and *Sally Ann* lost all momentum. The obstruction was a forty-five footer, green and red, with yellow lining and a faded black hull, and as she looked at it Marnie had a sense of *déjà vu*. She could not see the bows, but knew the name of this boat before it came in sight. Sure enough, within seconds she could read it on the side: *High Jinx*.

"This is becoming a habit," she muttered.

"It's the boat that was adrift the other week," said Anne.

Ralph came up from below. "D'you see who it is? What on earth's going on?"

Marnie pointed. "I think it must be another of your Oxford chums. Look ... he's punting."

On the stern deck a stocky man in jeans and sweater could be seen trying to push the boat towards the bank with a pole. Anne eased *Sally Ann* as close to *High Jinx* as she could without ramming, and Ralph went forward to speak to the 'punter' from the cratch. He would offer to tow the other boat to the side.

It was an easy task, and soon the stranger was waving his thanks, at the same time reaching in his pocket for a mobile phone. Ralph walked back along the gunwale to the stern deck.

"What was the matter this time?" said Marnie.

"Transmission packed up, apparently. He reversed away from the bank because of the muddy bottom, and when he put it in forward, nothing happened ... couldn't get it to go in either direction. Said he'd been there for about ten minutes when we showed up."

"Did you tell him we'd already rescued him once before?"

"Yes. He said he had no idea ... probably the afternoon he'd taken a siesta after a long journey the previous day and he probably failed to tie her up correctly."

"Yeah," Marnie agreed. "So what's he doing now?"

"I gave him Pinkerton's emergency number. They'll come out and sort it for him."

"On a Sunday? He'll be lucky."

• • • • •

They were both proved to be right. On the return leg of their trip, with Marnie at the tiller, they came upon *High Jinx* where they had left her. Coming closer, they could see that the panels of the stern deck had been removed and in the open engine compartment two men were bending over, examining the machinery. One of them was in dark blue overalls with the name *Pinkerton* written across the back. Neither looked up as *Sally Ann* slid past at half speed.

As Marnie nosed *Sally Ann* into the docking area, she resolved not to go near the answerphone. Anne had made no such resolution and as soon as the boat was tied up securely, she ran through the spinney to the office barn. All three messages – from Beth, Mrs Jolly and Philip Everett – were personal to Marnie, and she saved them. There was nothing else, no faxes, no e-mails, and even though Anne had been assailed by other anxieties, she was becoming increasingly worried about the fate of Marlene.

# Part 34

The report on the autopsy carried out on Simon reached DCI Bartlett on Monday morning. It confirmed the views expressed orally by Dr Rod Gregory, the forensic pathologist, when conducting the examination. The results were inconclusive. Bartlett called for Sergeant Marriner and pushed the report across the desk for him to read.

"Don't bother going through the whole thing now," said Bartlett. "The point is, we haven't got clear evidence one way or the other."

"Some water in the lungs, but not enough to make drowning the cause of death," said Marriner, reading the summary. "The fatal injury was the skull fracture."

Bartlett grunted. "Blow to the head or contact with a hard object while falling. You see the impact was at the back of the head."

"So he slipped and fell badly?" said Marriner. "It's not impossible. His feet could've shot out from under him, he went down hard and caught the stone edge of the lock. Very nasty. That way, he would've ingested some water, and he'd have died in a few seconds."

"Reading between the lines," said Bartlett, "That's what Doc Gregory seems to think happened."

"But you don't, sir?"

"I dunno. What else've we got that's suspicious?"

"What Walker said, you mean?"

Bartlett shrugged. "There was a time when I couldn't believe anything she said, but now ..."

"You don't think she knows more than she's telling us, sir? It wouldn't be the first time."

"Two questions, Ted. Why did she turn up at the lock just like that? What did you get from Mercedes?"

"Just as she said. They had a call from someone calling herself Mrs Walker, describing herself as Simon Walker's wife, at about the right time. She gave all the right ID information, including the password; they gave her the location of the car. They record their calls for monitoring the service, and they can let us have the tape."

"It must've been her, Ted. No doubt about that."

"No, sir. I've arranged for the tape to be collected from their call centre near London. You said you had two questions."

"The watch. Walker seemed to think he was wearing a Rolex when she saw him that evening. The autopsy report mentions grazing of the left wrist, consistent with a metal bracelet being dragged off. The Rolex would've had a steel wristband."

"You're wondering if it got pulled off when he went in the lock?"

"Either that or someone pulled it off in a hurry."

"There's one way to find out, sir."

"Get on with it, Ted. Tell British Waterways we want that lock drained. If the watch is in the mud at the bottom, there's a fair chance the whole thing was an accident. If not, it looks as if our mugger might've gone too far this time."

• • • • •

First thing that morning Marnie had returned the calls left for her on the answerphone, and then buckled down to finalising designs for the projects in her programme. Anne fielded all the incoming calls and spent the morning typing invoices and checking delivery dates. Hardly a word was spoken between them until a call came in shortly before noon.

"Sorry to disturb you, Marnie, but I've got Guy Pinkerton on the line. He says he wants to speak to you in person."

Marnie picked up. "Good morning, Mr Pinkerton. What can I do for you?"

"Call me Guy, for a start." It was his usual gruff way of speaking. "First of all, I want to say I'm very sorry about what happened. I heard about it from the local BW officer. You know they've closed the canal at the Stoke Bruerne locks?"

"The second lock from the bottom, yes. That's where it happened."

"No, this is different. They're draining the lock, as well as the pounds on either side. The whole section's closed. That's one of the reasons I'm phoning. I want to ask you a favour, Marnie."

"Go ahead."

"You know the boat that broke down on Sunday? Needs a new gearbox. I've got one coming tomorrow, and we were going to tow the boat up to the yard. The closure's put the kybosh on that ... God knows for how long. The customer's putting pressure on me ... you know how it is."

"So how can I help?"

"If I can get the boat somewhere where a van can reach it, I can get the gearbox sent directly there. One of my mechanics can get on with the work at that point. It should only take half a day. Could I get the box delivered to your place?"

"No problem. But what about the boat itself?"

"We could take it along the towpath in a barrow or bow-haul the boat. It's not far, I gather. The two of them should be able to manage."

"It's best part of a mile," Marnie protested. "Look, I'll go up after work today and tow it here with *Sally*. We can pop it in our docking area to work on."

"Oh no ... I wouldn't dream of it – "

"It's fine, Guy. I owe you, remember, for the loan of your wharf. You make your arrangements, and we'll fit in."

•  •  •  •  •

The search began that afternoon inside the lock. It was surprisingly clear of mud and debris as it had been drained in the spring for the fitting of a new pair of gates. Yellow tapes were stretched across the towpath to cordon off the area. Three police officers looking like cosmonauts in protective clothing picked their way slowly and systematically along the floor of the chamber. The air was filled with the throbbing of heavy diesel pump engines. On both sides of the canal, uniformed police were conducting a thorough search of the hedges and grass borders.

•  •  •  •  •

For the third time that month *Sally Ann* made her way along the canal to rescue the narrowboat, *High Jinx*, only this time the mission was planned in advance. Marnie was glad to help a fellow boater in trouble, but there was one aspect that caused her concern. Ralph noticed her serious expression as they motored north up the canal and he leaned over the tiller to speak to her.

"I think I know what's bothering you, Marnie."

She looked at him in surprise. "Is it that obvious?"

"We don't have to offer him hospitality ... not in our present circumstances. If it would make you feel any better, I can invite him on to *Thyrsis* for a drink or something later this evening."

The stranded boat came into view, and Marnie turned *Sally Ann* while Ralph went along the towpath to alert the owner of *High Jinx* who immediately set about releasing his mooring ropes with profuse thanks. Anne helped push *Sally Ann* away from the bank while Ralph held the towrope clear of the water, and they set off at a slow but steady pace, meeting no other traffic on the short journey.

They were hardly moving when Marnie brought *Sally Ann* alongside *Thyrsis*, where Ralph untied the towrope. The owner of *High Jinx* had turned the stern into the bank, and it was a simple if heavy task to manhandle the boat backwards into *Sally Ann*'s dock. Marnie manoeuvred *Sally Ann* across the entrance to the dock and made her secure.

Ralph coiled the end of the stern mooring rope neatly on the deck below the T-stud. "You needn't have worried, Marnie. Our *guest* has promised himself an early night."

"Did you explain ... about Simon, I mean?"

"I did mention it, yes. He'd heard the news on the radio and when he realised who we were, he straight away said he already had plans for tonight and didn't want to trouble us further. He seems quite a shy man ... rather embarrassed ... so I just left it at that."

• • • • •

After darkness fell the search continued under arc lights powered by a mobile generator. Bartlett turned up as the evening wore on, and Sergeant Marriner reported progress. The two detectives stood together at the edge of the empty lock chamber like mourners staring into a giant's grave.

"Do you get the feeling all this might be a waste of time, sir?" said Marriner softly.

"Wish I knew, Ted."

Down below them the cosmonauts conferred in a huddle. They looked up at Bartlett and Marriner and shook their heads wearily.

# Part 35

There were no builders on site the next day. The delay with the roof slates had held up the farmhouse project, and Marnie had agreed they could work on another job for the rest of the week. From force of habit Anne went out to look at the site and returned to the office with the news that a van was bumping down the field track towards them. The gearbox for *High Jinx* had arrived.

The driver parked almost outside the office, opened the rear doors of the van and cheerfully invited Marnie to help herself. Anne suggested that Marnie leave everything to her and offered the driver a choice of wheelbarrow or sack barrow. But he produced his own trolley, onto which he carefully slid the gearbox, and Anne led him off through the spinney. Meanwhile, Marnie rang Guy Pinkerton to report the arrival, and he confirmed that a mechanic would be sent along in the early afternoon. Deciding that she could not hide away indefinitely, Marnie took herself out to let her guest know what was planned. She passed the van driver and Anne coming back from the dock, signed the delivery note and left Anne to see him on his way.

It seemed strange to have another boat occupying *Sally Ann*'s dock, recalling the first sight of the grey boat that brought Anthony Leyton-Brown several weeks earlier. This would be her year of unexpected visitors, a year she would never forget. At the edge of the spinney she stopped, took two deep breaths and walked towards the boat. It had its curtains drawn, and for a moment after knocking on the stern door Marnie had the feeling that there was no one aboard. She was on the brink of turning away when she heard a bolt being drawn, and a face appeared round the door.

"Sorry to disturb you, but I've just had a word with Guy Pinkerton. Someone's coming down this afternoon to fit the new gearbox. I thought you'd like to know."

"Thank you. That'll be fine. It's, er … very kind of you to let me stay here."

"You're welcome. Do you have everything you need? I'm afraid I've not been a very good hostess."

"I do understand. Your … the man … told me what happened. I'm very sorry." He shook his head.

"Thank you. That's why I've been … you know …"

"Of course … I'm sorry, I don't think I know your name."

"Forgive me. I'm Marnie Walker." Automatically she held out her hand.

"And I'm John Hewitt," he said reaching forward.

There was a pause, and it seemed for a second as if Marnie was going to draw back. They shook hands.

"Are you all right, Mrs Walker?"

"Oh yes," said Marnie, adding, "You're left-handed."

"How did you know that?"

"Like my father. You wear your watch on your right hand."

"That's true, but lots of left-handed people wear them on the left wrist, you know."

"And you have the watch on the inside of your wrist. My father always does that … it's what I noticed. He says you can see it better when you're driving."

Hewitt raised his hand, palm towards his face. "That's why I wear it that way round."

"Okay, well if you need anything our office is in the barn facing the cottages just through the spinney." She pointed over her shoulder. "And here's my card with our phone numbers." She pulled one from her back pocket. Hewitt took it with his left hand.

On her way back to the office barn Marnie was frowning again. She was still frowning when she sat at her desk.

Anne was at the back, pouring milk into a saucer for Dolly. "D'you want coffee, Marnie?" She stroked the cat's head. "Marnie?"

"What?" Marnie seemed to be reading something.

"I thought I'd make some ... Marnie, are you all right? You're shaking." Anne quickly crossed the room. "What's the matter?"

Marnie held up her hands and stared at them. There was a distinct tremor, as if she was freezing. She spoke slowly and quietly. "I'm not sure ... but I think I may have come face-to-face with Simon's killer."

Anne gasped, her eyes like dinner plates. "What did you say?" she whispered.

"I've got to think what to do. I'm sure he'll be suspicious ... I think I blew it ..."

"Phone the police," said Anne. "Straight away."

Marnie already had one hand on the phone, the other flipping open the address book to find the number. "Anne, lock the door, will you."

Anne flew across the office, flicked the snib on the lock and forced home the bolts, top and bottom. She looked quickly through the window. Marnie was pressing buttons on the phone.

"Who is it?" said Anne. "How do you know? Are you sure?"

"Hallo? I need to speak to DCI Bartlett. ... Marnie Walker, Knightly St John. ... What? Oh, then try Sergeant Marriner. ... Please interrupt their meeting. This is *very* urgent. ... Look, I don't care if he's having tea with the Queen, I've got to speak to him. ... Thank you. Yes, I'll hold." She put her hand over the mouthpiece. "Does he think I'm going somewhere? *Come on, come* – Oh Mr Bartlett. It's Marnie Walker. Listen ..."

• • • • •

Chief Superintendent Scutt listened patiently while Bartlett reported on progress with the search of the canal. Nothing had been found at the bottom of the chamber but a windlass used for operating the lock paddles. It was the modern design made of solid aluminium and was capable of delivering a blow that could cause serious injury. Forensic were examining it, but it was more than likely that someone had simply dropped it into the lock by accident.

Sergeant Marriner confirmed that statements had been obtained from the boaters who had found the body, plus everyone on boats within a mile of the lock in both directions, and the residents in the lock cottages nearby. So far no one had seen or heard anything suspicious that evening. No one had heard a car drive into the car park. There had been no sound of a fight or any kind of commotion.

"There must've been a splash when he went in," said Scutt.

"Not so's you'd notice," said Marriner. "There's a constant sound of rushing water at the lock. It's either pouring in through the gates if the lock's empty, or pouring out over the top if it's full. We had to have pumps going all the time when our men were searching in there."

"Why didn't anyone hear the car?"

"It's very quiet sir, a brand new Merc."

"You've checked for footprints, of course."

"Nothing there. Dozens of people will've been there that day, working the lock. The ground was firm and grassy. There are no indications of a scuffle."

Scutt turned to Bartlett. "So what are your conclusions, Jack?"

"Well, sir, on the evidence so far, it looks like it could've been an accident. He stopped there for some reason unknown to us – "

"Such as?"

Bartlett shrugged. "Could be to do with Marnie Walker, but that's only a guess. He'd come back to see her for the first time in a couple of years. Perhaps he wanted to show her what success he'd achieved in business and maybe try to start over again. Wouldn't blame him. She's an attractive woman. But she's got her professor now, and they're all nice and cosy together ..."

"You're thinking suicide?" Scutt sounded sceptical.

"No, sir. I'm just saying, perhaps he wanted to have a walk by the canal for a quiet think ... got lost in his thoughts, went too near the edge in the dark, slipped ..."

"What about what Walker said ... he was going home to get ready for an early start?"

"It could just've been an excuse. We'll check his diary when we get hold of it."

"What about the watch ... the missing Rolex?"

"We're assuming Walker was right when she said he was wearing it that evening," said Bartlett. "We don't know that for a fact."

"Something caused the grazing on his wrist," said Scutt.

"If it had come off in the canal we'd have found it, sir," Marriner joined in. "I'm sure of that."

"That seems to be the one sticking point," said Scutt.

The intercom buzzed on his desk. Scutt pressed a button. "What is it, Sandra?"

"There's a Marnie Walker on the phone, sir, wanting to speak to DCI Bartlett. She says it's very urgent."

"Okay, you'd better put her on the line." Scutt pressed the button marked 'conference' and pointed at Bartlett.

"Hallo?" Marnie sounded strained.

"Bartlett here, Mrs Walker. What's happened?"

"I know this is going to sound crazy, but I think I know who killed Simon."

All three police officers straightened in their seats. "Go on," said Bartlett.

"To keep it brief ... there's a boat being repaired here. The man on board seems to be wearing Simon's watch ... his Rolex. I may be wrong, but it's a very distinctive wristband in steel and gold. I've never seen another one like it. The man's a stranger round here, calls himself John Hewitt. There's something odd about him. His boat seems to turn up every now and again looking as if it's deserted. I think he's hiding out on it."

"Could it be our mugger?" said Marriner.

"Mrs Walker, can you give us any details of the boat?" said Bartlett.

"Yes. It's called *High Jinx*, and the licence number is 1704426, registered at Watford."

Bartlett nodded towards Marriner who was scribbling rapidly on a pad. "Good. Tell me, where is this Hewitt at the moment?"

Marriner took out his mobile and left the room.

"I saw him not five minutes ago," said Marnie. "He's on the boat here."

"Is he aware of your suspicions?"

"I don't think so ... at least I ... actually I'm not sure. He might be."

"Are you somewhere safe?"

"Yes. We're in the office with the door locked."

"That's good. Stay where you are and don't go out for any reason at all. Got that?"

"Yes. Do you think it could be him?"

"We're checking him out now, but it's best not to take any – just a minute."

Marriner came in at the double. "I spoke to my contact at BW. There's no such boat with that number and no record of anyone called John Hewitt owning a boat at all."

"*Jesus!*" said Bartlett. "Did you hear that, Marnie?"

"Yes."

"Sit tight, do nothing. No curiosity, no heroics. You can ring me on the mobile if anything develops. I've gotta go now."

"We'll wait here."

They disconnected. Marnie immediately rang Ralph on *Thyrsis* to put him in the picture and warn him to batten down the hatches, literally.

Bartlett said, "Sir, I want authorisation to call in the armed support unit. It's not definite, I know, but this man could be a killer. We've got to move fast."

"Get going, Jack." Scutt was pressing buttons on the phone before Bartlett was out of his chair.

• • • • •

Ronny Cope was looking forward to seeing Anne for the first time in a couple of weeks. He cycled round to the high street from the executive housing development where he lived and turned into the field entrance, moving onto the grass to avoid the rutted surface of the track. He had promised himself a break from exam revision, just an hour before lunch to clear his head, and he liked nowhere better in the village than Glebe Farm. Marnie and Anne were different from other people. They made everything seem magic.

Where the track sloped more steeply, he could see the rooftops of the farmhouse and cottages, and he dismounted so as not to be riding the last section on his brakes. He had intended ringing Anne with his mobile to ask if it was all right to come down, but he worried that she might put him off till later and he knew that if he arrived they would make him welcome.

The sound of a car made him look back, and he hoped it might be Marnie in her old MG, but the engine sounded modern, and it was no surprise when a Cavalier came into view. He thought it was going faster than was wise on the bumpy track, and he pulled over to give it plenty of space to pass. It was being followed by a dark blue van, like a Transit, and as he watched, the van peeled off and headed down the slope towards the canal. Behind it was another, and then another. What the hell was going on?

Moving into cover behind a tree, Ronny grabbed his mobile, scrolled to Anne's name on the dialling menu and hit the green button.

• • • • •

"What's going to happen now?" said Anne.

They were both standing at the back of the office, leaning against the kitchen workbench, arms folded. Dolly was sitting on the floor beside them, washing.

"I suppose the police'll come and question our visitor. Oh god, Anne ... I think I've probably made myself look a *complete* fool. They'll probably scramble helicopters, the commandos and a tank division, only to find this is a man who needs peace and quiet because he suffers with migraine."

"Well I think you did the right thing," said Anne. "After everything that's happened round here lately, you can't take any chances. Do you really think they'll send a helicopter?"

"Dunno. But I can't imagine them asking Cathy Lamb to pop round for a quiet chat with him, not after I've virtually accused him of being a murderer. And I heard Sergeant Marriner say perhaps it was the mugger."

Anne's mobile began ringing across the room, and they both stared at it for some seconds as if mesmerised before Anne went to pick it up. Dolly followed her and jumped up to sit on the desk. Anne looked at the tiny screen.

"It's okay, Marnie. Nothing to worry about. It's only Ronny." She pressed the button. "Hiya!"

Marnie saw Anne's smile vanish as she listened. "What's up?" she mouthed.

Anne held the phone away from her face, looking even paler than usual.

"They're here," she said.

• • • • •

Ronny put the mobile in his pocket and tried to think things through. He had never been in this kind of situation before. Suddenly his thoughts about the interesting lives led by Anne and Marnie seemed to be slapping him in the face. Marnie had taken over the conversation from Anne. *Get away as quickly as you can,* she had said. *Don't stick around. It could be dangerous. No time for explanations, just go. Now!*

He reached for the handlebars of his bike, but straightened up again, leaving it propped against the tree. Marnie had been very firm, but how could he just go off and leave them if they were in danger? He had seen those police vans and was sure the people inside were carrying guns, the butts resting on their knees, barrels pointing upwards. They were wearing helmets with raised visors like the riot police he had seen on television. But what could he do? The realistic answer was ... nothing. His only weapon was a bicycle pump. And if the police were arriving in force, armed with assault rifles, what did the opposition have? He was looking at a potential battlefield. And in the middle of the action were Anne and Marnie and presumably Ralph.

He agonised for several more seconds before reaching his decision. Leaving the bike, he slowly made his way down the slope until he reached a clump of bushes, where he could see the whole of the Glebe Farm complex laid out before him. The place looked deserted and peaceful. Nothing stirred. Fleetingly, he wondered where the Cavalier had gone.

An urge came over him. He wanted to rush headlong to the office barn and drag Anne and Marnie away to safety before the storm broke. But perhaps he would only make it worse and put their lives in danger. He felt desperate and suddenly had to relieve himself in the bushes. This brought comfort, but a feeling of shame, and he realised that all he could do was watch and wait.

• • • • •

Bartlett and Marriner drove off the field track before reaching the farm buildings. They had glimpsed a cyclist on their way down, but had no time to stop and turn him away. With any luck he would be clear before any action started.

Marriner brought the car to a halt at one side of the spinney, annoyed that new foliage made it impossible to see through to the canalside about fifty metres away. They got out of the car, and Bartlett called up the leader of the armed support unit by walkie-talkie, his voice barely a murmur. There was a faint burst of static, and the ASU officer announced in a whisper that they were approaching the boat.

Bartlett told him to move in as soon as he was ready and use minimum force. His heart was pounding as all manner of emotions conflicted inside him. There could be a gun battle and casualties. Lives could be lost because of a decision he had taken. The man on the boat might be innocent of any crime. This could be a fiasco, and a deadly one at that.

Peering ahead, Bartlett saw movement between the trees, dark shapes blurring in the background. He heard a banging that was not gunfire, and a splintering, crunching sound, a door being smashed. He waited an eternity. Was it all over? A voice on the walkie-talkie. Boat empty. Damn, damn, damn!

The armed men began to comb through the spinney, fanning out to cover the whole area. They were working their way steadily towards Glebe Farm.

• • • • •

"What was that?" Anne tilted her head on one side. "Did you hear that, Marnie?"

"It's started," said Marnie. Anne was going to speak again, but Marnie raised a hand to stop her. "Listen."

They could hear only silence and their own breathing. Even the cat stopped washing. No birdsong, no movement, nothing. Marnie walked to the window.

"Perhaps it's all over."

• • • • •

The leader of the ASU joined Bartlett and Marriner by their car and raised his visor, holding his weapon down by his side.

"Looks like he's done a runner. Everything neat and tidy."

"You don't think he might just've gone out ... to the shop, perhaps?" said Bartlett.

"It all looks too clean for that. No clothes on board. He's legged it."

That brought some relief to Bartlett, but the problem still remained. Somewhere not far away a suspicious and potentially dangerous character was at large. He could be their mugger and may well be a murderer, too.

"Let's hope we can pick him up before he vanishes," said Marriner.

The ASU leader scanned the spinney where his men were advancing in a line. If the fugitive was here, he would be found. The question on everyone's mind was whether he was armed. He would certainly be desperate.

Suddenly, one of the ASU men raised a hand. All the others stopped and squatted down, watching him as he indicated twice with a finger pointing ahead and over to the right. Someone had been spotted moving towards the edge of the spinney in the direction of the cluster of outlying barns.

"Can we head him off?" said Bartlett. "If we can catch him before he gets in among the barns, it'll be easier. We don't know if he's armed."

The ASU leader nodded and signalled to his unit to move forward, keeping low. One of the men halted, raised himself to a stooping position and stared ahead. He looked back to his commander, shaking his head slightly, before moving forward with the others.

"What's all that about?" said Bartlett.

"He's seen something," said the leader. "Something's bothering him. I don't want to use radio at this stage. We'll just have to be on our guard."

He moved off swiftly and silently, catching up with his men, veering towards the barns. Bartlett and Marriner turned out from the spinney and began to walk quickly along its perimeter on a course that would converge with the unit when they cleared the trees.

"Sir!" Marriner grabbed Bartlett by the arm and pointed ahead.

There was no doubt about it. Someone – not in uniform – was making a break for it between the barns. They only caught a glimpse of a shape but whoever it was, he knew he was being pursued. There it was again, this time much further ahead. He was moving at speed like a frightened hare. It was almost as if he was in two places at once, he was so fast. Bartlett and Marriner were jogging forward, and they lost sight of their quarry behind the barns. They wanted to shout to the armed unit, but were worried it would give their position away. One false move at this stage and they could lose him up the slope in among the bushes. And if he had a car – or could get hold of one in the village – that really would be a disaster.

• • • • •

Ronny heard the sound of the boat's door being smashed in. Otherwise, everything was eerily quiet, as if the world was holding its breath. Ronny was certainly holding *his* breath. At the edge of his field of vision something caught his eye, and he turned his head to see a narrow boat threading its way along a silver strip of water about half a mile off. He wondered if it was going to blunder into a disaster area. Just then, more movement made him snap back to the farm and the spinney. He was sure he had seen something, though unsure about what it was.

His eyes became dry with staring, and he thought he might have been hallucinating. He blinked and rubbed his eyes and had the frustrating impression that he had missed the sight of someone leaping out of the spinney and who was now concealed behind the barns. There was no doubt in his mind, and he was in an agony of indecision. If anyone came his way what would he – could he – do about it? How would he know if they were the hunted or the hunter? Half wishing he had followed Marnie's orders, he took a few deep breaths and watched for developments.

He did not have to wait long. A head came round the corner of the nearest barn, about twenty-five metres downhill from where he stood. Simultaneously he spotted two men running up the side of the spinney and beyond them, in a gap between the farm buildings, he saw dark uniforms creeping forward where the trees began. Without waiting to think, he stood out from his clump of trees and yelled.

"Down here! Quick! This way!"

He screamed so loud he was almost hoarse with the effort, and he swallowed hard, resisting the urge to cough. For a second he nearly choked, but he saw that his cry had been heeded. The two men were sprinting towards the barns, and the ones who looked like commandos were moving stealthily forward, guns at the ready. He just caught a glimpse of the man being pursued as he charged from one barn to another and dived over a pile of paving slabs beside the farmhouse. But something was not right. Was that the man he had seen? Somehow he looked smaller. Could there be two of them? No, he was getting confused in his excitement. He could almost feel the adrenaline pumping in his veins. Here he was, playing his part, practically directing the operation. When this was all over, he would be able to feel he had pulled his weight, helped Anne and Marnie and the police, even though he had no idea what was happening in front of his eyes or why.

One group of armed men was now gathering in the shelter of the end cottage. Ronny worried that they might break cover and come under fire. Again he stepped out from behind his tree, cupped his hands and yelled.

"Over there – that way! In the farmhouse!"

He leapt back, his heart thumping. Risking a glance, he saw more armed men rounding the office barn, where they were joined by the two men in plain clothes. These two were in urgent discussion with one of the 'commandos', and Ronny was gratified to see them looking in his direction. He was part of the action.

• • • • •

"Someone's shouting," said Anne. "Not far away. What do you think's happening?"

Marnie went to the further end of the window to look out. "Someone's out there. I can see something over there by the cottages. Oh my God!"

"What is it?" said Anne.

"Men with guns. Loads of them in uniform ... must be police ..."

Anne rushed across to where Marnie stood, the two of them keeping as far back from the window as they could. The shouting voice rang out again.

"Did you hear that, Marnie? He said the farmhouse, I'm sure he did. Funny ... sounded like Ronny."

"Can't be," said Marnie. "Surely not. Must be one of their men, spotting."

Suddenly, another voice could be heard outside, amplified by a megaphone, speaking slowly and clearly. "Armed police. The building is surrounded. Throw out any weapons and come out slowly with your hands on your head."

Marnie strained to see if there was any movement visible across the yard. The site was deserted for once, and she stared at the open doorway of the house, but saw nothing. As they watched, there was a soft bump behind them, and Anne turned her head to see Dolly, who had jumped down from the desk. Anne gasped. To her horror, the cat trotted across the room towards the door.

"Dolly no!" Anne screamed.

But it was too late. Before Anne could reach her, Dolly dived through the catflap and out into the yard. Marnie pressed her face against the window, trying to see which way the cat went. Dolly was surprised by the unexpected sight of all the men with their dark uniforms and guns. She sprinted across the yard, ran straight through the open door of the farmhouse and disappeared inside. In her consternation Marnie failed to hear Anne run to the door. The bolts were already drawn before she realised what was happening.

"Anne!" she shouted, rushing to restrain her.

Again it was too late. Anne leapt out, pulling the door behind her, spraying stones from her shoes as she accelerated away. From that moment, Marnie later recalled what happened in the next few minutes only as a blur. She had a dim recollection of a man visible at a downstairs window, carrying a rifle or shotgun. There was shouting. Men yelling at each other, others calling to Anne to get back. But the girl took no notice and kept running with her head down. In seconds she reached the doorway and dived in without hesitation. Marnie wrenched open the office door and through all the sounds, clearly heard an exclamation from Anne. It was part shock, part surprise.

For Marnie everything happened in slow motion, lasting an eternity. She set herself to run towards the farmhouse, but her arms were grabbed from behind. Sergeant Marriner held her in a firm grip.

"Don't struggle, Marnie!" he yelled. "There's nothing you can do."

"But Anne – "

"Looks like he's got a gun. Listen to me. Did you have a shotgun in the farmhouse?"

"A shot–? No, of course not."

"Then it's his, and he's armed. Get back inside the office."

Marriner tried to turn her back, but she resisted. There was more shouting. A sound of breaking glass. Anne screamed. The sound was suddenly cut short. The fugitive with the gun flashed into view inside the house, partly concealed in shadows.

"There!" shouted Bartlett.

A rifle shot rang out from beside the office barn. More shots. An order from the leader to cease fire. One man sprinted in a crouch towards the house followed by three others. They formed up either side of the doorway, and one dived inside while the others covered him, slipping inside, one after another. The leader spoke curtly into his radio. Marnie did not catch what he said, but she heard the reply. It would stay with her for the rest of her life.

A faint burst of static and then, "Girl's down."

"Say again."

"Girl's down, sir."

"Wounded?"

"Dead, sir. No chance."

Marnie closed her eyes as a wave of dizziness and nausea swept over her. Marriner released his grip on her arms. Bartlett stared at the ASU leader.

"What the – " he began.

Before he could finish, a shape became visible at the rear of the house, a man clutching a rucksack. He dived into the overgrown patch of garden to make his escape. Marnie broke clear of the group by the office barn and sprinted across the yard. She leaped the low pile of paving slabs in a volley of shots, heard bullets slap the foliage, ricochet off the wall beside her. She was still running, gaining on the man, when he fell headlong. More shots echoed, stone dust sprayed her, and she was struck from behind by a giant hand smacking the back of her head. She tripped and scrambled in the earth to regain her footing, tasting dirt, the blood pounding in her brain. Her efforts only pitched her forward on hands and knees, and weakening she grabbed at the legs of the man she had chased, now lying on his side in amongst the weeds. His breath was coming in short sobbing gasps, staccato and uneven.

Marnie pulled herself to her knees, shook her head, winced in pain and seized him by the shoulder. She wanted to beat him with her fists for killing Simon and being the cause of Anne's death, but he was close to death himself, and she was weighed down with anguish. Blood was forming a puddle under the man's chest, and his mouth was hanging half-open. He turned his eyes, already beginning to glaze over, to look up at her. All her rage, all her desire to harm this man, to kill him, drained from her body in exhaustion, and she hung her head.

"Why did you kill Simon?" she muttered breathlessly. "And Anne."

"Never ..." he murmured. "Never ... killed ... anybody."

"At the lock," said Marnie. Her voice was weak and weary. "Simon."

"No ... no ... never killed ... no ..."

"I know you did. You killed him for his watch."

"Never ..."

"Liar!" she screamed and reached forward along his arm to take hold of his wrist, pulling at the watch.

The man's head went limp, and a trickle of blood rolled from the corner of his mouth. Marnie knew he was dead, knew she had found Simon's murderer, and a great wave broke over her. A thousand images flooded into her mind. Simon and his precious watch, Simon standing with her in a hotel bedroom in moonlight all those years ago. Her last sight of Anne alive, racing to the house to rescue Dolly. Anne at her side, collapsing in laughter at a sign in a shop window that read 'Ear-piercing while you wait'. Anne pretending her name was Anne Withaney. All the images were overflowing in her head as despair overwhelmed her. Marnie felt herself slipping away like a leaf carried by water over-spilling the lock gates. She knew she was fading and wondered if, like the man beside her on the ground, she too had been hit by the bullets, that she too might be dying.

When she lost consciousness seconds later, she was not even aware that Marriner caught her as she collapsed. He noticed with surprise that she was clutching the dead man's watch.

· · · · ·

Ronny knew he ought to keep his head down, but he was mesmerised by the action unfolding before his eyes. He saw Anne race into the house, heard her exclamation followed by the gunfire. He left his shelter and began running down the slope, not knowing where he was going or what he could do. He vaguely registered the sound of vehicles coming down the track, but had no thought for them.

Sliding over the grass, he was nearing the farmhouse when a man jumped out of a ground floor window and began running up towards the bushes. Seeing Ronny, he hesitated and veered off into the garden where the weeds were high and dense. At the moment the man changed direction, Ronny saw Marnie hurl herself across the yard, and simultaneously more shots were fired. The fugitive arched his back and pitched forward into the planting as Marnie herself tumbled under the hail of bullets. He saw her crawl towards the fugitive, but before he could get nearer two armed men ran at him, each with a hand outstretched, yelling at him to get away.

Reluctantly he stopped and began walking backwards up the slope, seeing two ambulances rolling into the farmyard under guidance from the armed men. Paramedics immediately jumped out and began a rapid dialogue with the ASU men, who were pointing towards the farmhouse and its scrappy garden.

Ronny stopped to watch, but one of the men shouted at him and he turned away to find his bike in amongst the bushes and go back to the village. His head was spinning with all that he had seen, and plodding up the track he felt overburdened by the weight of terrible events that he was carrying alone.

· · · · ·

On *Thyrsis* Ralph was beside himself with anxiety. After Marnie's phone call telling him to bolt all doors and stay inside the boat, he had strained every nerve and sinew trying to assess what was happening around him.

Pressing his face against the windows, he caught sight of movement in the spinney, but he was unable to judge who was on the move. All he could make out was dark shapes crouching low, hidden by undergrowth and tree-trunks. The silence was eerie. No twigs cracked, no branches rustled. The scene looked peaceful and still, except that there was no sound of birds singing. The whole place was waiting.

He was on his way to open the centre doors to gain a better view, when he heard a voice, magnified and echoing, coming from the far side of the spinney. It reminded him of the commentary amplified by loudspeakers at a sports event, and he stopped with his ears pricked to listen. In the middle of the boat, he was badly situated to hear what was said, but he caught one or two words.

*... police ... building ... weapons ... head ...*

Ralph raced to the doors and tugged at the bolts, mounting the steps to throw back the hatch and lean out. All was silence again. He was scanning the area when new sounds reached him, muted cries, men's voices, urgent, alarmed. The frustration was unbearable, and Ralph began easing himself onto the gunwale when a loud crack rang out, flat and hard. It was unmistakeably gunfire. More shots followed and more cries, one of the voices definitely a woman's. Marnie? *Marnie!*

He leapt onto the bank, heading for the farm when a voice called from the opposite direction.

"Ralph! What the hell's going on?" Anthony at the side doors on his boat.

Ralph wanted to wave him back, but a sudden thought flashed into his mind. If the police came checking the boats, they would find Anthony and their whole plan would be blown. He turned towards Anthony.

"Get away from here!" he shouted.

"What are you talking about?"

"The police could be swarming over us at any minute. Just take the boat and go ... anywhere. Don't come back till this evening and then be careful."

"What's all that noise about?"

"Gotta go, Anthony. Just do as I say."

Without another word, Ralph turned and ran into the spinney. Anthony watched him go and for several seconds stood undecided in the doorway. The unfamiliar sound of assault weapons firing broke out again. He hesitated no longer, started the engine and pushed off from the bank.

· · · · ·

The news that Anne had been killed reached the village minutes later when the incident almost claimed another victim.

George Stubbs was driving down the high street in his Range Rover when Ronny cycled round the corner from the field track in the middle of the road. For a second, George was sure the boy would move over, but when he kept coming, he hit the brakes and brought the big car shuddering to a stop as the cycle veered across his bows. At that point Ronny seemed to wake up and he stopped suddenly, hopping on one foot to keep his balance, leaning on the handlebars.

George switched on the emergency lights and leapt out of the car at great speed for a man of his bulk. He ran up to Ronny and put his hands on his shoulders.

Angela Hemingway was crossing the road by the shop, when the flashing lights caught her attention. Her first inclination was not to interfere. If Ronny Cope had done something to upset George Stubbs, that was a private matter. But there was something about the body language, the Range Rover stationary in the road just before a bend, George holding on to Ronny whose face was turned down. She ran towards them.

Molly Appleton notice Angela's sudden change of direction, and she came out onto the pavement to look down the street. Thus it was that in a few minutes Ronny found himself at the centre of a small crowd, being led into the shop for a glass of water. George propped the bicycle against the field hedge before parking his car outside the pub. He was crossing the road when two ambulances drove through the field gate and sped past him up the high street, blue lights flashing. Before he could reach the shop, the vicar rushed out. She grabbed him by the arm and begged him to take her at once down to Glebe Farm.

On their way down, a grey Cavalier came up towards them, and as it passed, a hand reached out on the passenger side and planted a blue light on its roof. George found the way to Glebe Farm blocked by a blue police personnel carrier. A man in full combat gear with a stubby assault rifle at his side raised a hand, and George pulled up beside him. Angela at once got out.

"What's happened here?" she cried.

The man shook his head. "There's nothing to see. You must go back."

"I've not come to see anything," Angela barked at him. "I'm the vicar in this village. What's going on? Is anyone injured or dying?"

The policeman eyed her dog collar and glanced across at George, who was now out of the car. "I can't tell you anything," he said. "You'll have to go back. I'm sorry."

"Look." Angela brought her face close to his. "I know the people who live here. I've not come out of idle curiosity. If there's someone injured or even dying, I can help them. It's my parish."

He glanced over his shoulder. "They've gone. There's nobody here now."

"Is it true that someone was killed?"

The man hesitated.

"Was it a girl called Anne?"

"I don't know her name. Look, I'm not supposed to be talking about this. You shouldn't be here."

"She was killed?" Angela persisted, staring him in the face.

He nodded. "The girl, yes."

The colour drained from Angela's face. She took a step back and swayed. George put his arm round her shoulders.

"What about the others?" he said.

"They've gone, all of them."

"So others were wounded," said George.

The policeman said nothing, lowered his eyes.

"I see."

George looked at Angela, worried that she might faint. He himself felt numb. Slowly, Angela turned towards him. He felt her shaking as her head hit his shoulder and she was racked with convulsions, shuddering. Standing with an attractive young woman in his arms, George Stubbs felt as cold as a block of marble.

•  •  •  •  •

In the late afternoon Alex and Jill Burton arrived home from work and were surprised to see the blue and white tape surrounding the farmhouse. Their first thought was that this was a safety measure, perhaps there were holes in the ground. But they saw the inscription on the tape: *Police – do not enter*, and exchanged anxious looks.

Jill was the first to see the flowers, bunches stacked against the door of the office barn, as if Interflora had made deliveries and found no one at home. Still puzzling, the couple walked across and examined them, obviously posies cut from gardens, a cheerful mixture of wallflowers, tulips, anemones and sweet William. Every bunch bore a label, and Jill stooped to read them. When she turned to look up at her husband, tears were filling her eyes.

The messages on the labels were simple: *In loving memory of Anne; We will miss you forever; God bless you and keep you in his love.* More than one of them asked the question: *Why?*

In the still afternoon, Jill and Alex clung to each other in the abandoned farmyard.

# Part 36

The taste of dirt had gone. With eyes closed, Marnie ran her tongue over her lips. Slowly she became aware of the smell of fresh cotton, a soft pillow, the sounds of footsteps nearby. She moved her head, and pain struck her at the same time as memory returned. Her heartbeat quickened, and she knew she had no desire to wake up, no wish to know where she was. Lapsing back into sleep, she had the faintest impression that a hand touched her forehead.

When next she drifted up to the surface, Marnie could hear Ralph's voice not far away, and a woman's, answering him in the same measured tone. They were talking without emotion, as if the world had not fallen apart. Marnie was thirsty and knew exactly where she was. The smell of clean sheets was mixed with the antiseptic of hospital. She could feel now that her head was bandaged, and knowing better than to move quickly, she opted not to move at all.

She opened her eyes and waited as they struggled to focus, gradually fixing on a plain cream wall, with a picture above a trolley. It was indistinct, no more than a tangled abstract of colours. The thirst needed to be tackled, and Marnie knew that if she could look in the other direction she would find a bedside unit and, with any luck, a jug of water. She closed her eyes and very slowly and gently began to turn her head. No stab of pain this time, she continued steadily one centimetre at a time until her left ear was touching the pillow. She paused, opened her eyes and jumped with shock. Wincing, she shut her eyes tight and let the spasm of pain rage through her head. It was all so unfair. This would be her waking nightmare forever. She felt a cool hand touch her hand, another smooth her forehead and warm tears formed under her eyelids. A tissue touched her face, a voice murmuring softly. She tried again to see, and this time it was the tears that blurred her vision. She reached up and took the tissue, wiping it across her eyes. She blinked, the room swirled in and out of focus like a mirage in a sandstorm, and a face took shape.

Anne!

Marnie choked, closing her eyes again, and felt herself supported under the shoulders as she wriggled to sit up. She ignored the pain in her head, held a tissue to her mouth and coughed dryly. A glass of water was pressed to her lips, and she felt cold splashes on her bare arms. She turned to stare at the girl standing at the bedside, reaching for more tissues, taking the glass from her.

"Anne," she said in a croaky voice.

"With an 'e'," said Anne, smiling. "How are you feeling?"

"How am I – " Marnie burst into tears, dabbing her face with a sodden tissue, having it replaced by Anne who was simultaneously pulling the pillows up behind her for support.

The door flew open and Ralph crashed into the room, rushing across to hold her.

"I think I'm going to ..." Her head fell back as she passed out.

• • • • •

Marnie awoke to find Anne wiping her face with a cold flannel. Ralph was holding her hand, while a nurse popped a thermometer attached to a blue curly wire under her tongue.

"Are you hurting anywhere, my love?" said the nurse.

Marnie seemed to consider the question for a long time. Her body was aching in every department, with head and left knee singled out for special attention.

"I'm fine," she mumbled round the thermometer.

She looked from Ralph to Anne as the nurse removed the instrument and read the dial.

"I can't believe this," said Marnie. "Is it all a dream?"

"No," said Ralph. "It's been a nightmare, but it's over now. And Anthony's back on his boat."

"I didn't dream about what happened to Simon?"

"No."

The nurse rearranged the pillows and tucked the sheets around her. "You need more rest, Marnie. Your family can stay with you, but I want no more talking for a while. You must try to sleep."

"My family," Marnie repeated quietly. "Yes ..."

•   •   •   •   •

"Tell me about it."

Marnie had surprised herself by going back to sleep, and when she woke for the third time she was feeling more refreshed. While she had slept, Ralph handled the press and had a long conversation with Bartlett and Marriner. The nurse told her they had given her a sedative the previous day to help her rest, and they insisted on keeping her in hospital for at least one more night.

Now she was able to sit up in bed and sip tea. "Tell me what happened. I still can't believe this ... that you're here ... that Anne's alive ... any of it."

Ralph nodded at Anne.

"Well," she said. "You can remember the policemen with guns?"

"In the yard, yes."

"That's right. And Dolly jumped through her catflap – "

"Dolly! Is she – "

"She's fine."

"Truth?" said Marnie, looking at Ralph.

"Yes. Trust me ... I'm an economist."

Marnie pulled a mock grimace. "Go on, Anne. You ran out and chased her into the farmhouse. Then you made a strange sound. What was that?"

"It was shock. I ran straight into them."

"Them?"

"Yes. There were two of them. That's what surprised me."

"And Hewitt had a gun," said Marnie. "I saw that when I came out of the office."

"Gun? No. He had a piece of scaffold tube. He was trying to break open the back door to get out. Is that why the police opened fire? They thought he had a gun?"

"Yes," said Ralph. "They were convinced he had a shotgun, so when they got sight of him they opened fire. Only it wasn't him they hit."

"But it wasn't you either," Marnie said to Anne. "They told their leader that they'd killed you."

Anne looked down. "It was horrible," she murmured.

"But it was untrue," said Marnie.

"No. They killed his partner ... a woman."

"Oh ... That's what they meant ... *the girl's down* ..."

"She was about your age Marnie. The bullets hit her and ... she flew back against the wall ... and there was blood and ..." Anne's face was a picture of misery.

"What about you?"

"I dived for the floor as soon as I heard the first shot. She was too slow. I saw these red lights on her chest – like little dots – as I went down, and next thing they all started shooting ... it was *terrible* ..."

"A woman," said Marnie in a dreamy voice. "What Frank was talking about ..."

"Yes, perfume," said Ralph. "He said he'd smelt perfume when he was attacked."

"Of course."

They fell silent. The wall clock ticked. Marnie spoke first.

"They must've attacked Simon that evening. Perhaps they followed him, drawn by the expensive car. How dreadful ... to lose his life for a wristwatch." She closed her eyes.

"You had it in your hand when they brought you in," Anne said in a subdued voice. "I couldn't get it free until they gave you that injection."

"You came in with me?"

"I was with you all the time. I rang Ralph to tell him what was happening. You were out like a light. The paramedics gave you oxygen ... I sat beside you in the ambulance."

"And Bartlett took the watch as evidence?"

"No. I er ... hid it. I thought you'd ... want to keep it."

Marnie stared in front of her. "I wanted to kill that man ... beat him to death with my own fists, but when it came to it ... it was just so *awful* ... to see it happen like that."

"What did happen?" said Ralph. "Bartlett seems to think you're a hero."

"I saw John Hewitt – if that was his name – climb out of the kitchen window in the farmhouse. I thought you were dead, Anne, and I blamed him for everything. I wanted ... well, you know. He was going to make a break for it up the slope, but suddenly swerved left into the old garden. That slowed him, and I almost caught up with him just as the men opened fire. Something knocked me flying, and we both went down."

"A ricochet," said Ralph. "It caught you as you stumbled, apparently."

"You're not going to tell me I was lucky."

"Not quite. But you had a lucky escape."

Marnie touched the dressing on the back of her head. "More shaved off?"

"Not much. Your favourite hairdresser will be able to work her usual magic, I expect."

"What did you do with Simon's watch?" she said to Anne.

"It's at the back of the drawer." Anne glanced at the bedside unit.

"I'll have to give it to the police," said Marnie.

Anne reached in and pulled it out from the furthest corner, where it lay hidden behind a box of paper tissues. She gave it to Marnie, who gazed at the bracelet, rubbing the back of it with her thumb. She turned it inside out, revealing the name – *fixoflex* – on each link. Marnie could not help herself; a single tear ran down each cheek. In sorrow for Marnie's pain and at the thought of Simon, Anne's eyes also filled with tears and she reached forward to hug Marnie. Ralph enveloped them both in his arms.

At that moment there was a knock, and the door opened to admit DCI Bartlett and WDC Lamb.

"I'm sorry to intrude," said Bartlett, hesitating in the doorway. "Would you prefer it if we came back another time?"

"It's all right," said Marnie as they separated, each mopping their eyes from the box of tissues that Anne passed round. "There's never going to be a good time."

"I just thought," Bartlett began. He sighed. "You'll be having me at it next …"

"Blimey!" Lamb exclaimed, quickly adding, " … sir."

"You'll be wanting this," Marnie said, holding up the watch. "I suppose it's evidence, but if it's at all possible, I'd like it back some time."

"I quite understand," said Bartlett. "Though strictly speaking, that is a valuable article, and it may be that Mr Walker's solicitor might have a view on what becomes of it."

"Of course," said Marnie. "I hadn't thought of that. I'm not Simon's next of kin. This will have to go to them."

"Do you know who they might be?" said Bartlett.

Marnie shook her head and regretted it. "No idea, I'm afraid."

She reversed the bracelet back to the right position and turned the watch over, looking down at its face for perhaps the last time. Her eyes seemed to be out of focus again. There was no distinctive five-pointed crown on the dial surmounting the name *Rolex*. Instead she saw the last letter of the Greek alphabet above the name *Omega*. Where she expected the words *Oyster Perpetual*, she saw *Seamaster*.

She looked up at Bartlett. "This is not Simon's watch."

• • • • •

It was late morning when the Volvo arrived back at Glebe Farm. They had been at the hospital with Marnie since noon the previous day, and neither had had any real sleep in that time. They were stopped at the entrance to the field track by two policemen in a car before being allowed to drive down to the farm. Anne yawned as Ralph parked outside the garage barn. They walked in silence to the courtyard and stopped on the corner by the office to stare across at the farmhouse. It was cordoned off with blue and white tape. The builders were still away, and the site was quiet and deserted. It was difficult to imagine the horrific scenes that had been played out there yesterday. Anne moved closer to Ralph and held his arm.

Without speaking, they turned the corner and headed towards the office. They promised themselves a few hours of rest, but first Anne wanted to check for messages on the answerphone. Rounding the corner of the office barn, they stopped in their tracks. The entrance was stacked with flowers. They knelt down to read the cards.

"They think I'm dead," Anne said quietly. "All these nice words about me."

"I'm sure they're sincere, Anne. You're a very popular person you know."

"But I can't have them thinking I'm dead. I'd better phone Molly and all the others. Some of the cards haven't got names on."

They picked up the flowers and pushed open the office door. It was unlocked. From nowhere Dolly bounded in behind them, warbling a greeting, rubbing herself against Ralph's trouser legs before taking up position by the fridge. Anne laughed and hugged Ralph. He kissed the top of her head. She broke free and pirouetted in the middle of the room. Dolly blinked but held her ground, and Anne stroked her ears before filling the food bowl and milk saucer with generous measures.

"You appear to be recovering from your ordeal," said Ralph.

"Yes, oh yes! We're alive, and Marnie's alive, and it must be the first time ever that the person commemorated by flowers after being killed can put them in vases to decorate her room."

Ralph smiled. "You've probably got a point there."

"I'm not being cruel, really I'm not. It was terrible about Simon and the couple who were shot. It was all horrible, and I wish none of it had happened. But seeing the flowers, and thinking what might've been, and knowing I'm alive after all ... I just wanted to jump in the air. Is that wicked, Ralph?"

"Not at all. I think it's probably a very healthy reaction."

"Good. And for the moment I feel awake again. I know it won't last. I must ring Mum and Dad. Then I'll make a few local calls before I collapse."

Ralph made for the door as Anne sat at her desk pressing buttons on the phone. Turning, he said, "Be sure to break it gently to our neighbours. People are going to have a tremendous shock, receiving a phone call from someone they believe to be dead."

Anne looked up, the receiver pressed to her ear. "I will, don't worry. I'm just checking the messages first and then I'll ..." Her voice faded.

"What is it?" said Ralph.

Anne looked as if she had seen the proverbial ghost. "It's Marlene!"

• • • • •

The knock was so soft that Marnie scarcely heard it. Angela Hemingway looked drawn, as if she had not slept for a week. She stepped in and closed the door quietly behind her.

"Oh Marnie, I'm so sorry."

She looked as if she was going to cry, and if she did, it would obviously not be the first time that day.

"About?"

"About Anne."

"You haven't heard. Come over here and sit down. I have a pleasant surprise for you and I don't want you fainting on the floor. Anne is alive and well and on her way back to Glebe Farm with Ralph. In fact, they're probably home by now."

"Oh my goodness." Angela crossed the room unsteadily and took the visitor's chair. "I prayed for this. Wow ... I don't know what to say. You must feel *absolutely* ... Actually, Marnie, you don't look absolutely ... you know."

"Maybe it's because I've caused two people to be killed for murdering Simon, only to find that they may not have done it."

"Oh, no! Can you bear to talk about it?"

Marnie outlined the situation, the chance meeting with the broken-down boat, recognising Simon's watch, the pursuit by the armed police. Angela knew the rest.

"The trouble is ... when I got a proper look at the watch, I saw that it wasn't Simon's at all. It was just a similar bracelet. It could've been Hewitt's own watch ... or one he'd stolen from somebody else."

"That's dreadful, Marnie. And you really think they were innocent of – "

Before she could finish the sentence, another knock announced the arrival of DS Marriner, accompanied as always by WDC Lamb.

"Bad timing?" said Marriner.

"Come in," said Marnie. "The more the merrier."

"Truer than you think."

Marnie made introductions.

"I'd better be going," said Angela.

"You've only just come."

"I know, but I don't want to be in the way."

"Don't go unless you have to," said Marnie. "Is that all right with you, Mr Marriner?"

"Of course. I only wanted to let you know that the couple who were ..."

"Shot dead, is the correct way to put it," said Marnie.

"They were our muggers."

Marnie sat up. "You're certain of this?"

"We found several items in their bags and on their boat that had been reported as stolen, and a substantial amount of cash. One of the items has been identified as Gary Rawlings's camera."

"Whose?" Marnie looked blank.

"The photographer?" said Marriner. "The one who was attacked near the towpath in Blisworth."

"Ah ... the one you thought I'd beaten up and robbed."

Marriner looked uncomfortable. "Yes, well, we got that wrong. That was the time you were telling the truth. You took us by surprise."

"Did you find Simon's Rolex?"

Marriner shook his head. "No watches."

"You searched the boat really thoroughly?"

"Practically dismantled it. It's a miracle it floats."

Marnie lay back against the pillows. "Can I ask you something? When someone knows they're going to die, would they lie about something they'd done?"

"Depends," said Marriner. "If they thought it might cause trouble for one of their family, for example, they might tell a lie."

"But this isn't like that," said Marnie. "There was nothing to stop John Hewitt admitting he'd killed Simon. He just said he didn't do it ... and then he died."

"That's strange," Angela chimed in. "In their last moments most people experience a strong urge to confess, get something off their conscience, before they die."

"You can't be sure, though," said Marriner. "When someone's fading, their brain can do strange things. It's not like in films where they manage to say something sensible and then they go. All sorts of things can happen."

"So you do think they killed Simon."

"Personally, yes, I do."

"What about his watch?"

Marriner shrugged. "It's valuable and conspicuous. They would've wanted to off-load it as soon as they could."

• • • • •

Chief Superintendent Scutt listened to Bartlett's report without interrupting. The third man in the room was Sergeant Pat Robson, who had led the armed support unit at Glebe Farm. When Bartlett finished, Scutt asked Robson if he had anything to add.

"No, sir. I think the DCI's covered everything."

"Including your back," said Scutt tersely. "There'll be an inquiry, of course. The Chief Constable is under siege from the press."

"I believe we acted appropriately in the circumstances, sir," said Robson.

"And two people were killed. Do you know what today's headline is in the Milton Keynes Echo? GUNFIGHT AT THE MK CORRAL."

Bartlett and Robson winced.

"Sir, I wasn't trying to cover their backs. Sergeant Robson and his men did what they had to in a dangerous situation. They thought Hewitt had a shotgun. We all did. Everything happened very quickly. It could've been worse. Hewitt could've killed Anne or Marnie Walker or taken them hostage ... all sorts of possibilities."

"I know," said Scutt. "But the fact remains, both of them were unarmed."

"They had already killed one person, sir, and injured others. It's not as if they were being picked up for a minor offence. They were violent criminals."

"And that's what makes the difference," said Scutt. "I'm sure it'll all come out right in the end. In the meantime, no comment to the press or media pending the inquiry. We'll play it by the book."

"That won't stop the papers running the story, sir."

"No, Jack. it won't. But they'll be concentrating on the human angle. After the first report that the girl had been killed – Anne Price – they'll be able to tell the world that she's alive after all. That'll keep 'em happy."

• • • • •

By early evening, Ralph and Anne were back with Marnie, who had recovered so well that she was asking to be sent home. Anne had rung her parents to warn them not to be alarmed at the news that would be broadcast and published, and they arranged to come up to see her in a few days, 'once normal life had been resumed'. Anne felt that was being over-optimistic, but she thought it best not to disagree.

Ralph sided with the medics and insisted that Marnie should have another night of nursing care. The three sat eating grapes reviewing their situation. It had been a busier afternoon than they had anticipated. The phone in the office barn had been ringing constantly as journalists tried to arrange an interview or at least obtain a statement. Ralph decided to take action.

After agreeing it with Bartlett, he fixed a brief press conference at the police station – determined not to have Glebe Farm featuring in any newspaper photos – and drove Anne there on the way to the hospital. Bartlett chaired the proceedings, stressing that the police investigation was still in progress. Anne was allowed to say that she had been present when the police engaged the criminals and that there had been a misunderstanding about her being shot. The session came to an end when Bartlett made it clear that no further details of the action would be revealed as the matter was the subject of a formal inquiry, like any incident involving the fatal use of firearms.

"Did Bartlett say anything to you about their investigation in general?" Marnie asked.

"I gather it depends on how his report is received by the top brass," said Ralph. "But he told me his conclusion. These were the muggers who injured Frank Day and one or two others. He believes they also killed Simon, though that was probably an accident, he thinks."

"It's so obvious," said Marnie. "They were hiding out in a boat, able to travel about at night, rob their victims and just vanish afterwards."

"It's easy to see it all with hindsight."

"So the case is closed?"

"That's Bartlett's recommendation."

"He'll be glad to be able to put it down," said Marnie. "All neat and tidy. Another case solved." She took a grape from the bag on the bed. "I've been thinking about *our* case ... the Anthony affair. I've come to a conclusion, too."

"Marlene phoned," Anne said quickly.

Marnie sat up. "When?"

"This morning. She'd heard on the news about me being ... well, killed ... and she tried to get in touch with you. I rang her back. She was in a terrible state, and when I told her it was me and I was all right, I thought she'd blow a fuse."

"Where's she staying?"

"She's camping out for a few days in a flat with two other girls, till she finds somewhere permanent."

Marnie frowned.

"What was your conclusion ... about the Anthony business?" Anne asked.

"Not as conclusive as I thought, perhaps."

"You were going to say we should drop it, weren't you? Let Anthony make a public statement. Put it all behind him ... make a fresh start."

"Something like that."

"And now?" said Ralph.

"I'd overlooked Marlene. Not forgotten. I just didn't think we'd ever hear from her again. How was she ... apart from hysterical?"

"More hysterical," said Anne.

"Figures."

"At least she got in touch, and we know where she is."

"What's the good news?" said Marnie. "Seriously, I don't know whether to be glad or sad. I just wanted to draw a line and get on with life, encourage Anthony to do the same. But Marlene ..."

"Not easy to abandon her," said Anne. "And she said she wanted to help sort out Anthony."

"Oh well ..." Marnie sounded weary. "Can you ring her again and say we'll contact her tomorrow with a plan."

"You've got a plan?" said Ralph.

"I'll think of something."

# Part 37

"Is it really Saturday?" Anne said, clearing the breakfast table on *Thyrsis*.

The days since Marnie left hospital had passed in a surreal atmosphere of heightened emotion, as people learned that Anne had not perished. Several had made the trek down to Glebe Farm where, with varied outpourings of feeling – tearful, embarrassed, exultant – they grasped her to their bosom, so that by Friday evening she had complained that if she had to endure any more displays of affection, she would need a neck support collar.

The only one not to give her the bear-hug treatment was Ronny who, struggling with self-control, recounted his part in the action while they walked together by the canal. It had been his testimony that had spread the news of Anne's death, and the combination of confusion and heartache he had brought about, added to his own turmoil at confronting her loss, had overwhelmed him. All this was balanced by a return to normality as Marnie applied herself to working up designs for her clients, supported by Anne between scenes straight out of *Lassie Come Home*.

Marnie looked up from writing a list of phone calls. "I know how you feel. Do you realise there are people out there looking forward to going shopping, walking the dog, enjoying a spring weekend?"

Anne smiled ruefully. "Sounds good to me, compared with my journey to the morgue in London and visiting you in hospital after we'd both nearly been shot."

"Shouldn't be too hard to improve on that," said Ralph. "How would you like to spend the day, Anne?"

"Well … Best of all, I'd just like a tootle on *Sally* … and perhaps Ronny could come with us?"

• • • • •

Anne fed Dolly who purred her way through a generous bowl of salmon and shrimp in jelly, with no apparent after-effects from coming under fire. Next, Anne jogged through the spinney to check for faxes and e-mails in the office. As usual, she carried Marnie's mobile to use as an intercom, and before she reached the office barn it began to ring in her pocket.

"Hallo? Marnie Walker's phone." There was a strange sound on the line. It could have been static, but it might have been a sob. "Hallo?" she repeated gently. "This is Anne. Who's that, please?"

"I knew her, Anne." Definitely a sob. "That girl they found. It said in the paper the police thought it was me."

"I know. Where are you, Marlene?"

"She didn't have anything …"

"Marlene, tell me where you are."

"I'm really scared, Anne. Perhaps next time it *will* be me."

"You can come to us. We'll look after you." Nothing. "You'll be safe here. No one'll find you, honest."

"You told me they'd followed you home … they knew where you lived."

*Damn!* Anne thought. But Marlene was right. There was no point promising her safety at Glebe Farm. For all she knew there might be a photographer behind every tree in the spinney.

"You're right, Marlene. Let me talk to Marnie and Ralph. Have you got a phone where we can reach you?"

"No."

"Will you phone me back in half an hour?"

"I can't."

"Where are you?"

"King's Cross."

"When can you phone?" Silence. "*Please*, Marlene."

"Later."

The line went dead.

• • • • •

When Anne ran back to the boats she found Marnie and Ralph in high spirits, carrying boxes of provisions from *Thyrsis* to *Sally Ann*, chatting as they went. Marnie called out to her as she approached.

"Guess what? We're going to have a big crew today. You know who's coming to join us?"

Anne was panting. "No."

"Angela and Randall. They're obviously an item, those two. I thought I'd see if they fancied an outing, and they said yes. You okay, Anne? You look less than delighted."

"Oh, no ..." She gasped for breath. "It's nice ..."

"But?"

Anne outlined her conversation with Marlene, and the atmosphere became sombre.

"Did you try recall?" said Marnie.

"It didn't work. I think she was in a phonebox."

"She's slipping away," said Marnie. "We're gonna lose her."

• • • • •

They travelled just a few miles along the canal in fine breezy weather, Angela taking the tiller with a natural talent for steering. Randall kept a hand on hers, and it had nothing to do with guiding the boat. Ronny and Anne sat on the cushioned benches in the cratch, watching the scenery float by.

They pulled over for a buffet lunch of hot quiches filled with salmon and broccoli, baked jacket potatoes and coleslaw, with Beaujolais and an Aussie white that Randall had brought.

When Marnie's mobile sounded, everyone fell silent as she took the call. She quickly came to the point. "Marlene, we want to get you away from London, somewhere safe. Will you trust us?"

"I don't think I've got much choice." Her voice was sullen.

"So you'll you come?"

"I've got my bag ready." There was no enthusiasm.

"Good. Do you have enough money to buy a train ticket to Milton Keynes?"

"I suppose so."

"Can you find Euston station?"

"Just up the road."

"Right. Get the first train up here and we'll meet you. I'll give you the money for your ticket. Okay?"

"Okay."

"My car will be recognised," said Ralph quietly.

Marnie said, "Hang on, Marlene." To Ralph, "Taxi?"

"If she comes here, she could still be seen by anyone watching us. Everything depends on secrecy."

Suddenly another voice joined in. It was Angela. "She can come to me. I've got loads of room in the vicarage."

"But a taxi arriving in Knightly could be conspicuous," said Marnie.

"Then I'll fetch her," said Angela brightly. "Nobody would suspect a vicar of anything, especially a woman vicar."

"Except the Rural Dean," Randall muttered under his breath.

• • • • •

When Marnie's phone rang, she was checking the boat's mooring ropes in the docking area with Anne. She feared it would be Marlene calling the whole thing off, but it was a man's voice, and she recognised it at once.

Anne watched Marnie as she spoke, admired the patient coaxing, heard her call him 'Nigel', and knew she was making progress. They talked for several minutes until Marnie eventually slipped out a biro, wrote a number on the palm of her hand and the conversation ended.

"I think," she began slowly. "I think it's falling into place. I'm not sure how it'll turn out, but at least the people are coming together."

"Nigel?" said Anne.

Marnie nodded. "Hawksby's other victim. He said he's willing to come and meet the others ... join in with the statement."

"You asked him why he was willing to help now. What did he say?"

"He thought we might stand a chance of getting somewhere. He'd never thought that before. He said it wouldn't do *him* any good, but it could be his only chance of getting back at Hawksby. He wants to try and settle the score."

"So that's it ... another one wanting revenge?"

"Hard to blame them," said Marnie. "I always thought that was a totally sterile emotion. But the other day Anthony said more or less the same thing ... revenge was a very pure motive."

# Part 38

Marnie felt almost guilty about what she was doing, how ruthless she had become. Heads turned as the trio entered the church that Sunday morning and took their seats towards the rear of the congregation. Now Marnie knew how the Royals felt when they travelled on duty. There were smiles and greetings, hands raised, even one or two blown kisses, as the whole village strained to see their neighbours who had been in the middle of a gun battle.

They looked like any other family in Sunday clothes: Ralph in a charcoal grey suit, Marnie in a dark blue dress with a tiny flower design, Anne in black trousers and a cream shirt. They had never been seen attending a service before, not surprising as they were all agnostics. Some of those present made a shrewd deduction; Marnie and Ralph were planning a church wedding. It was obvious, they were making token appearances for the calling of the banns.

Even those who were dozing off perked up and paid attention when the Reverend Angela Hemingway gave out the announcements. But no banns were called, and muted comments were made around the church. At the end of the service no one noticed that the trio were the last to file out, and only a few living near the church observed that they waited and accompanied the vicar across the road to the vicarage. Any outsider would have found nothing unusual in the small group of parishioners walking along with the vicar, chatting in the morning sunshine.

Once the front door was closed, Angela said, "You're looking even better than you did yesterday, Marnie, much more like your old self. You, too, Anne. I didn't realise you were actually going to come to church. Did you think it would be a better disguise than just turning up at the vicarage after the service?"

"I'm afraid I did," said Marnie. "I feel rather badly about that."

"Well don't. You're always welcome in church ... for whatever reason, or should I say 'motive'. It might even do you some good." She smiled and turned to call up the stairs. "Marlene, we're back."

Immediately there was the sound of footsteps and the girl came down to join them.

"Right," said Angela. "Coffee while we talk? It won't be up to your standard, Marnie ... only instant, I'm afraid."

Anne stepped forward and from her shoulder bag took out a box of biscuits. "These are from us. We got them at Marks and Sparks, Belgian chocolate."

"Wicked," said Angela.

They settled round the dining room table, and Angela passed a plate crammed with biscuits to her guests.

"I expect you have a plan."

"Only a very simple one," said Marnie. "I think the simpler we keep it, the better. I've no confidence I can organise anything complicated that will actually work."

"That's no bad thing," said Angela. "Keeping it simple gives a better chance of success."

Marlene said, "What will I have to do?"

"There are four of you. Apart from you, there's Anthony, a man called Nigel that Hawksby abused as a schoolboy, and Jenny Poulter who was left holding the baby when she was sixteen. You're all his victims, and now's the time for you all to speak out."

"How are they going to speak out exactly?" said Angela.

"I'm going to fetch them by car and bring them together here at Glebe Farm," said Ralph. "We're going to take a group photograph and send copies to the media with a statement signed by all four of what Hawksby has done."

"They've all agreed to this?" said Angela.

Marnie said, "I spoke to Jenny on the phone this morning. She said she'd co-operate as long as everybody else did. She completes the picture ... literally."

"When does it all happen?" said Marlene.

"Some time in the coming week."

Marlene turned to Angela. "Is it all right for me to stay here till then?"

"Of course."

"You don't have any problem with this, do you?" Marnie asked Angela. "From a moral point of view?"

"As far as I can judge, you're just telling the truth. That can't be wrong."

"And the truth shall make you free," Anne quoted.

"Saint John eight, thirty-two," said Angela. "Well done! One visit to church and you're a bible-basher."

"We did it at school ... RE ... I got a B for the course work."

• • • • •

Marnie left Ralph and Anne preparing lunch in the galley on Thyrsis, on the pretext of having something to do in the office. For the second time that day she felt guilty at being less than honest, a feeling compounded by their easy acceptance of what she had told them, and she had slipped away while they worked amicably together. Marnie felt a pressing need to be alone.

She pulled the barn door partly open and sat at her desk in the cool office, a hazy half-light filtering in from outside. Alone with her thoughts, she felt the strain of events bearing down on her shoulders and longed for expert hands to massage the ache away. Was it really only a few short weeks since the boat without a name had arrived in Sally Ann's docking area, and everything had turned upside down?

Now here she was, poised on the brink. She wondered if you could teeter on more than one brink at a time. In front of her was the last stage of her crazy plan to expose the media as completely hypocritical. The further she had gone down that road, the more she suspected that Anthony was right; everyone in public life had something to hide; everyone exposed to temptation would probably succumb. Was this the beginning of cynicism? She hoped not.

Another brink was her own private life. She had promised herself after the failed marriage with Simon that she would never become dependent on someone else for happiness. Yet here she was, cheerfully planning a joint future. She had come this far, giving up a secure job in London to run her own show, taking her own decisions, making her own mistakes. Was she really going to gamble everything on another relationship? She stood up and walked round the room. What's the matter with you, Marnie?

She dropped down onto her chair, emitting a sigh. It was immediately followed by its echo as Dolly jumped up onto the desk. The big black cat blinked slowly at her and began purring, settling herself down in front of Marnie, who reached out to stroke her head. Dolly closed her eyes and the two of them communed without words, Dolly turning her head to push against Marnie's hand movements. Marnie felt her face muscles relax and a smile ease its way into her features. The cat made a barely audible sound of undisguised pleasure.

"Oh, Dolly ..." Marnie breathed.

She reached across for the phone and dialled a familiar number.

"I was just thinking about you! Do you believe that stuff about sisters being able to communicate without speaking?"

"Not in your case, Beth."

"Thank you. So what's new?"

"I'm about to do the most stupid thing of my entire life, that's all."

"What particular stupid thing do you have in mind, Marnie? You have such a wide repertoire."

"I've got everybody lined up to expose the newspaper editor in public. All four of them. We're sending out a group photograph and a press release this week."

"And that's it? All over? Or does he sue you all for slander or libel or get you thrown in the Tower?"

"I phoned you because I wanted cheering up, Beth."

Beth laughed. "There's gotta be a first time. Seriously, though ..."

"I don't know what he'll do. But I do know we'll only send out hard facts. Ralph thinks we should get sworn statements, affidavits drawn up by a solicitor."

"Well, if that's what Ralph says, you should do it. He's reliable, that one. For once you've made a good choice. I approve."

"What do you mean, for once? I thought you always liked Simon."

"He was great ... in the beginning ..."

"You had doubts about him? You never said."

"And I don't want to now, Marnie. I wouldn't want to speak ill ... you know. I really thought you were ideal for each other ... for a long time."

"So did I."

"I thought you were lucky, both of you. Do you believe in Big Love ... capital B, capital L?"

"You think there is such a thing?"

"I don't want to cause pain, but I thought Simon was yours, if I'm honest. And you were the same for him."

"That's funny. I've sometimes wondered if Laura was that for Ralph. They must've been so suited to each other."

"Does that mean you think you're both settling for second best, you and Ralph?"

"What a thought!" said Marnie, taken aback. "That's not how it should be. All your life you see yourself centre-stage, and one day you wake up and find you're somebody's compromise?"

"Hey, this is getting too heavy, Marnie. You said you wanted cheering up."

"Yes. But how can everything go so wrong when it started out so well?"

"Things change – that includes relationships – then you move on. You can't look back ... can't afford to ... it's just too painful."

"That's what Simon said."

"There you are, then. Wait a minute ... Simon? You've been talking about that sort of thing with Simon? Was that a good idea?"

"Beth, do you know the things they believed in the Middle Ages ... about wounds bleeding? Ever heard of that?"

"Wounds ... You're losing me. What wounds bleeding?"

"Simon told me about this idea they had. You stood a suspect next to the body of someone who'd been killed, and if that person was the killer, the wounds started bleeding again. They believed it in mediaeval times."

"Sounds weird. Anyway, what's that got to do with anything?"

"Nothing, I suppose."

• • • • •

A Sunday afternoon outing. It was becoming a traditional English Sabbath: morning church, Sunday lunch, a ride in the car. Only that was where the comparison ended. This ride was transporting a Member of Parliament secretly back to a hostel for down-and-outs, with the aim of finalising a plan to expose hypocrisy in the establishment. Not quite the traditional English Sunday.

As a precaution, after dropping Anthony at the back of the hostel, Ralph parked the Volvo a little way down the street. He and Marnie walked hand-in-hand towards the blue front door. They had left Anne at Glebe Farm, going for another walk along the towpath with Ronny.

Randall loaned them the room that he and the housekeeper shared as an office during the week, with cream walls and white paint, desk and chairs in lightwood, a pale grey filing cabinet in the corner. An honest room. It looked an unlikely place for conspirators.

They went over the plan one last time. Four people standing against a wall, one group photograph, one individual close-up of each person, a statement outlining how Hawksby had touched – and contaminated – their lives. Plain facts, all verifiable, cut and dried.

"You're sure they've all agreed to this?" said Anthony. "And you can somehow reach Marlene?"

"All of them have agreed," said Marnie. "And we've brought Marlene up from London."

"You've brought her up?" Anthony looked astonished. "Where is she?"

"You drove past her half an hour ago. She's safely tucked away in the village."

"Good god," said Anthony, suddenly pale. "I can hardly believe it."

"Well, you'd better believe it because she's here, but she's very shaky. When you see her again – "

"No, it's all right. I won't say anything. No reproaches. I don't blame her any more."

"Good."

"When do we do this?"

"We've yet to organise getting everybody together," said Ralph. "We're not sure exactly which day that will be."

"But this week?"

"Yes. The timing's very important. We have to spring the whole thing as a surprise. Hawksby mustn't suspect what we're up to. That's how Marnie's planned it. We've gone to great lengths to cover our tracks."

"That's brilliant, Marnie." Anthony smiled. "Elegant simplicity. The essence of good design, I believe. How appropriate."

"I don't know about brilliant," said Marnie. "It's the best I can think of, that's all. I'm way out of my league."

Anthony walked with them to the front door.

"You'll be glad to see the back of me, Marnie. I know I've been an imposition in your life. I'm sorry for that ... and for other things that have happened, of course. And I'll always be grateful for what you've done for me."

"Let's wait till things are sorted out before congratulating ourselves. We've still got a long way to go. Anything can happen."

Ralph put a hand on her shoulder. "Marnie's right. I won't be able to rest until we've completed our part and sent off the photos and statements."

"Oh well," said Anthony, "Not long now. It'll be a big relief to me, I can tell you."

"Are you ready to face the press?"

"Yes, Ralph. I'm ready."

He turned the handle and pulled the heavy Georgian door open. Late afternoon sunshine poured in, inviting them onto the doorstep. They shook hands, Anthony smiling, Marnie and Ralph turning to walk back to the car. From the corner of her eye, Marnie caught sight of something across the street. She reached out to touch Ralph's arm, but he had seen it too.

"What is it?" Anthony said, recognising their concern.

Marnie pointed. "Over there by that tree."

As she spoke, a face looked out, below it the end of a long camera lens. The man raised the camera quickly, bracing himself against the tree trunk. Marnie dived to one side. Ralph pushed Anthony in the chest.

"Get back inside! Quick!" He began to race across the road, but Marnie pulled his sleeve, half spinning him as a car scorched past, inches away from running him down. A horn blared. When they looked up, they saw a man sprinting off. He leapt into a car, hit the starter and pulled out with tyres squealing. It was a blue Ford Sierra.

Marnie held on to Ralph, who looked shocked after his near miss with the passing car. Anthony was still frozen in place on the doorstep, mouth half open.

"Damn!" Marnie said hoarsely. "Are you all right, Ralph?"

"Thanks to you, yes."

Anthony said, "Was that – "

"Yes," said Marnie. "It was."

Anthony thumped the wall with his fist. "They're onto us. Jesus!"

"They're onto us," she repeated. "And it's all coming apart."

It was a common enough sight. The jogger trotted up over the field towards the village from the direction of the canal. At that time on Monday morning, around seven, the only stirrings in Knightly St John involved commuters heading towards the station ten miles away to begin their trek to the capital.

The jogger pounded steadily up the slope, lightly-built, in green tracksuit, dark glasses, bobble hat and *Walkman*, turning right at the gate at the end of the track, keeping a regular pace past the primary school, past the church and on towards the shop. At the last moment, the jogger changed course abruptly just as one of the newspaper boys pushed the door open to heave a bundle of papers into the pannier on his bike, and darted into the shop before the door closed.

Once inside, the jogger pulled off the hat and glasses, gasping for breath, to reveal a head of very short pale blond hair.

"Ouf! The things I do for Marnie! I must be mad."

Molly Appleton, checking newspapers at the counter, smiled broadly. "I didn't know you were a jogger, Anne. Is this a new hobby?"

"I'm in training for the Knightly St John Marathon."

Molly looked bewildered. "There isn't one."

"Great! I can announce my retirement."

She crossed to the counter and examined the papers.

"Tim's taken your *Guardian*, Anne. He's just gone out. You might still catch him if you hurry."

"No, it's all right, Mrs Appleton. I only wanted to see what was in the other papers. Can I look through them?"

"Help yourself. Looking for anything in particular?"

Anne sifted through the pile and found the *Globe*. There on the front page, under an *Exclusive* banner and the headline *Bingo!* was the photo of a man in a doorway. He was bearded, with dark thinning hair, and staring straight at the camera. On either side of him, mostly out of shot, were two blurred shapes, probably a man and a woman. Below the photo was a question: *Is this the missing MP?* Another photo – Anthony without the beard – invited readers to compare the likeness and judge for themselves.

As casually as she could, Anne said, "I'll take this one, Mrs Appleton."

• • • • •

They bent over the table in the galley on *Thyrsis* and studied the article. Anne was pulling off the tracksuit, still panting in the background.

"*Damn, damn, damn, damn, damn!*" Marnie muttered, turning the front page. "Wait a minute ... is that all it is? Where's the rest?"

She turned the next few pages before flicking back to the cover story. Ralph pointed to the foot of the page.

"Look there. It says there'll be more revelations over the next few days."

"They're going to spin the story out like they did when they first printed the photos of Anthony with Marlene."

"That's how you sell papers."

Marnie banged the table lightly with her fist. "What a *drag!*"

"Mm ..." Ralph began. "Could be worse."

"I'd love to know how. They've completely blown our cover. Any minute now the place'll be swarming with paparazzi."

"No, it won't. The *Globe* isn't going to reveal where Anthony is. It wants the story to remain exclusive for as long as possible."

"Ye-e-s." Marnie turned and looked out of the window across the canal. "Actually, I think you're right, Ralph. And we could use that to our advantage ... if we move quickly enough."

. . . . .

It was a common enough sight. Mid-morning and the vicar was going off on her rounds. In grey blouse with dog collar and grey skirt, she climbed into the Ford Escort and set off out of the village towards the Towcester road. At the Shell station she stopped for petrol and Polo mints. Two miles up the dual carriageway, she turned left into a narrow country road that led to Brackley through a series of byways.

Arriving in the town centre, she turned off the high street and threaded her way round to park at the back of the hostel. From there it was just a short walk to the rectory where the Rural Dean invited her to stay for a chat. Half an hour later, she emerged and walked up to the shops.

At about the time Angela was taking her leave of Randall at the rectory, a Volvo drove down the high street and parked outside the hostel. Ralph got out, rang the doorbell and was admitted by the housekeeper. A few minutes later, Randall let himself in with his own key. The two men came out of the building after a short while and drove off. They only went as far as the rectory before Randall got out, leaving Ralph to continue on his way back to Knightly St John.

It was a quiet Monday morning.

. . . . .

It was almost noon when the vicar's car crossed the ancient Roman highway of Watling Street and launched itself across the modern city of Milton Keynes from one roundabout to the next. In ten minutes she reached the eastern edge of town and pulled into the grounds of a canalside pub. She left the car at the far end of the parking area, almost under a willow tree within two steps of the water.

The sky, which had been overcast all morning, was clearing and it was warm enough to sit outside. Angela took her sandwich and glass of cider out to one of the tables in the garden to enjoy her snack lunch overlooking the canal boats that lined the bank. As she took her seat, one of the boats a short distance away down the car park started its engine, burbling gently as the person in charge walked to the front end to push the nose out. It was painted in dark blue and cream. When the boat eased away from the bank, Angela and some of the other customers glanced up. The steerer was a girl with fine blond hair, cut very short. The name on the bow was *Sally Ann*.

. . . . .

Half an hour later, the same boat pulled in to the bank opposite another pub. This one was in a rural setting, far from any visible habitation, at a point where the canal was crossed by a minor road. This pub had been built two centuries earlier as a hostel for the men digging the Grand Junction Canal and was very popular with walkers. Barely five minutes had elapsed before a couple wearing jeans and sweatshirts came marching along the towpath. They stopped beside *Sally Ann* to confer about their plans, exchanged a few words with the steerer, quickly stepped on board and went below.

Some of the pub's customers looked across at the boat when its engine started again, and they waved at the girl holding the tiller as she guided the boat out into mid-channel and headed north. The girl smiled and raised her hand to them. A pleasant day for a boat trip.

Within fifteen minutes they found themselves in a remote spot with woods on one side of the canal and fields of cows and sheep on the other. Anne eased *Sally Ann* carefully in shallow water to tie her up fore and aft to trees on the opposite side to the towpath. She turned off the engine and went below.

There was an appetising smell in the cabin of hot soup and rolls warming in the oven. Ralph and Anthony were sitting at the table that was set for four, Anthony checking the newspaper for any other references to the cover story.

Anne took steaming soup bowls from Marnie and put them on the table. "Do you think anyone spotted you, Anthony?"

"No. The only tricky part was coming out of the back door of the hostel, but Angela signalled all clear and I dived onto the back seat. I assume you were the decoy, Ralph."

"Yes. If that photographer was around, he knows my car well enough."

Anne cleared the paper away, tucking it down beside her chair.

Marnie said, "I don't think Angela has any doubts now about our policy of covering our tracks. We've shown her that if anything we weren't careful enough."

Ralph shook his head. "We've all had a rude awakening."

"At least I'm out of their clutches for the time being," said Anthony.

"Don't count on it. They've got enough to run the story again. They'll have photos of you on the front page every day this week, and they'll drag the whole thing up for a second time. The PM will be furious. The last thing your government wants is another sleaze row."

"I know. I realise I've got to make a move ... and quickly. I just didn't want to be seen to be on the defensive. If your plan had gone smoothly, Marnie, we would've had the advantage."

"Too late for that now," she said. "We're into damage limitation. We've got to have a whole new plan."

"You don't think we can go ahead as we intended ... the four of us in a photograph with a press statement?"

"You really would have your backs to the wall," said Ralph. "Hawksby would dismiss it as a stunt."

Marnie agreed. "Definitely. And there's another worry. The new campaign in the *Globe* could well frighten the others off."

"At least Marlene's here. She'll be better than nothing."

"Even that may be optimistic, Anthony. For her it'll be the nightmare starting all over again."

"So what do you suggest?"

*Why is it always me?* Marnie thought. "I don't know. It was the best I could do to come up with the first plan. God knows what we do now."

Anne had finished her soup while the others were talking. Absentmindedly she picked up the paper and, as she thumbed through it, a name jumped out at her.

Anthony began, "I don't want to – "

"Look at this," Anne said suddenly. "There's more about Anthony."

She held up the editorial page. It appeared under the heading, *Time for the Truth.*

"Read it out," said Ralph.

*The Globe has been tireless in its exposure of sleaze at all levels of politics and government ... bla-bla-bla ... never cease to reveal the truth behind the scandal of those in the public eye who exploit their position ... those who hold themselves up as models of how we should all behave ... bla-bla-bla ... once again we bring to light the man the whole country has been looking for ... in hiding for weeks ... abandoned his wife ... bla-bla-bla ... at last we have tracked him down ... will soon reveal his whereabouts unless he does the decent thing ... This newspaper challenges Anthony Leyton-Brown MP to come out of the shadows and give a full explanation of his conduct ... only a public appearance will satisfy the British people ... Now is the time for the truth to be told.*

"Wonderful," said Ralph. "Go public now, and it'll seem like Hawksby's dragged you all out."

Marnie nodded. "We've lost the initiative. We're on the back foot. Again."

Anthony slumped in his chair. "So ... rock bottom. I thought I'd been there before, but this time ..."

"We've got to find some way of hitting back," Marnie said. "And in the meantime we have to have somewhere to conceal you. We're running out of hiding places."

"Yes, and every journalist in the country will be hunting me."

Ralph said, "It's a pity there isn't somewhere at Glebe Farm."

"The builders have started up again," Anne muttered. "They're working all over it."

"I know."

Marnie looked up. "What did you say?"

"I said," Ralph began, "You've got all those buildings at Glebe Farm but – "

"No. Not you, Ralph. Anthony. What did you say just then?"

He shrugged. "Nothing much. Only the obvious. The investigative journalists will be trying to track me down. It's going to make hiding all the more difficult."

Marnie narrowed her eyes. "Then maybe it's time they found you."

• • • • •

Marnie, Ralph and Anne sat in the office barn that afternoon, leaving Anthony on his boat. They had work to do. Anne took notes and wrote a list of the phone calls they had to make. Marnie made the easy ones first.

"Jenny? Hi, this is Marnie."

"I was wondering when we'd be starting."

"Look, Jenny ... the fact is ... we're not."

"What's happened?"

"You haven't seen the Globe this morning?"

"That rag? No. Why?"

"They've found Anthony ... at least, they know where he's staying. We've had to change the plan. We're not going to ask you to come here. No photo. No statement."

"Oh ... okay. Funny ... I'd kind of resigned myself to doing it."

"Thanks, but you can stand down."

"Good luck."

Next, Nigel. It was almost the same conversation.

"Well, Marnie, I can't say I'm not relieved, but I was ready to have a go. Do you think you'll get Hawksby?"

"I think that's gone by the board now. We're just trying to sort out Anthony ... and of course, Marlene."

"I wish you luck, Marnie."

Marnie put the phone down. Good luck! she thought. She ran a hand down her face, feeling the tense muscles.

"You okay, Marnie?" said Ralph.

"Sure. One more call and we can move on to the next step."

Suddenly Anne said, "Can I make the call to Marlene?"

"Are you sure?" Marnie said.

Anne nodded, picked up the phone and rang Angela's number. The vicar answered. Seconds later Marlene came on the line.

"Listen, Marlene, we've had to make a new plan, and we've got to move fast."

"What have I got to do?" Marlene sounded wary.

"Just sit tight for the moment. Anthony's going to give a statement to the press. You'll have to be prepared to back up what he says. And we might need a photo of you."

"Is that it?"

"No. You might have to appear in public. We'll organise that when the time comes."

"Well ... if you think it's really necessary ..."

"There's more," said Anne. "You might have to appear in court if the paper takes legal action."

"In court?"

"Maybe. We can't tell. It all depends on what happens in the next few days."

There was a long pause. "Anne, what would you do if you were me? Try and imagine how I feel."

Anne said softly, "I'd go for it."

"Yeah ... I suppose so. Since I got involved in this business, my life's been a nightmare. What've I got to lose?"

Marnie took the receiver from Anne after the call and replaced it.

"Well," she said. "This is it."

• • • • •

Back on *Sally Ann* for tea, Anne rang the driving school to cancel her

Wednesday lesson. When she finished, Anthony took the phone, keyed in the code to stop the number being traced and rang the Radio 4 newsdesk. Marnie, Ralph and Anne watched him as he pressed the buttons on the phone, taking deep breaths. When the call was answered, he spoke slowly and calmly.

"Hallo, newsdesk? This is Anthony Leyton-Brown ... yes, the MP." He was put through to the producer and replied to a number of personal questions to satisfy him of his identity, before being allowed to continue. "In response to the article that appeared in the Globe this morning, I'd be willing to be interviewed on your breakfast news programme ... Tomorrow? Yes. Who'll be doing the interview? ... I see ... Very well. Thank you."

# Part 40

"It really is very good of you to put us up like this, Mrs Jolly."

Marnie settled herself in the kitchen facing a mound of scrambled eggs on toast. Anne beamed at her from across the table. It was the first time since the shootings that Anne looked relaxed and cheerful. In the background, the radio was adding a quiet murmur to breakfast.

"I'm only sorry I couldn't have you to stay last time you were here. Have you both got everything you need?"

"More than enough, thank you. You're spoiling us."

They had arrived the previous evening after the old lady had offered them a base for a few days. Marnie had thought of staying with Beth and Paul, but that left the problem of where Anthony could go. In the end they found the solution to all their needs in Little Venice, when Roger Broadbent agreed to them borrowing Rumpole. The boat was almost opposite Mrs Jolly's house that faced the canal across the road, and they smuggled Anthony on board after dark.

"What time will he be on?" asked Mrs Jolly, joining them at the table.

"About ten to eight. He's got a slot for three to four minutes."

"A slot," Mrs Jolly repeated. "That's not very long."

"It's the usual time they give for an interview ... unless it's with a government minister. Anyway, I expect it'll be more than enough for anyone to bear. I'm dreading it."

"Oh, yes," said Mrs Jolly. "It'll seem like an eternity up against someone like Paul Pinder. He's very sharp. Nobody gets away with anything when he's around."

Anne nearly choked on a piece of toast and had to take a hurried gulp of orange juice.

"That's very reassuring," said Marnie, patting Anne on the back.

As they ate, Marnie was assailed by conflicting feelings: relief that they had almost reached the end of the line; resignation that they had no more shots in the locker. It was up to Anthony now, and Ralph had reminded her of his reputation in parliamentary debates for thinking quickly on his feet. Now that the time had come to prove what he could do, Marnie felt uneasy. She liked to be running the show herself, and once Anthony was out in the open, they were at the mercy of other forces.

Her final stroke had been the press release. Late the previous night they had gone to Paddington station and used public fax-phones to send a statement, including a contact phone number, to all the national newspapers ... with one exception. It was a simple message: Anthony Leyton-Brown MP would be interviewed that morning on the breakfast news. The Exclusive banner on the front page of the Globe did not look so impressive that day, when it was the only paper not carrying the story. To keep other reporters off the scent, it had been arranged that he would be interviewed at a local radio station, and he had set off alone by taxi at an early hour.

The time came round for Anthony's 'slot' while they were finishing breakfast. Mrs Jolly turned up the volume as Paul Pinder was making the introduction.

*... and has now agreed to be interviewed on this programme. Good morning, Mr Leyton-Brown.*

*Good morning.*

*Why have you decided to come out of hiding at this particular time?*

*I was ... I think I've had a kind of ... a kind of breakdown, and it's taken me this long to get myself together.*

Anthony did not sound impressive. Marnie had the awful feeling he was going to make a mess of this one chance to reclaim his life.

*Can we go back to that time when you were exposed in the press? Is it fair to assume that your disappearance was an admission of guilt, that you were in fact caught with your ... well, this is a family news programme ... let's say – in a compromising position?*

*It was a compromising position, yes.*

*So you fully admit that you were betraying the standards that you – and let it be said, your party and your government – have gone on record as saying are the values the country should follow?*

*So it appeared.*

*Appeared? Come on ... the evidence seemed all too plain ... don't you think?*

*If you can believe what was shown in the paper.*

*You don't think that evidence was clear enough?*

*I came here this morning to clear up one or two points.*

*But presumably not to try to clear your name, Mr Leyton-Brown? Some might think it's rather too late for that.*

*I came fully prepared to talk about what you would call 'scandal'.*

*What would you call it?*

*Look ... any man put in my position would have done the same thing.*

*Are you trying to justify your actions? You surely can't deny the evidence of the photos.*

There was a pause in which Paul Pinder asked repeatedly if Anthony was still there, explaining they were not in the same studio. When Anthony came back on the air, his voice seemed even more strained, as if on the point of collapse.

*What I'm saying is ... I was set up.*

*You're claiming you were the victim of entrapment?*

*Yes.*

*And what about the girl? You're saying she was part of that? Or was she in reality your victim? I notice she has not come forward to give evidence.*

*She was part of the plot to trap me. I never so much as laid a finger on her until –*

*But whatever the circumstances, Mr Leyton-Brown, the fact of the matter remains that you were caught with the girl in a situation that was absolutely plain to see. Surely there can be no explanation or excuse for that?*

*At the very least you must see it was an invasion of my privacy.*

*Privacy? You're a public figure, in the party that insists on high moral standards.*

*But you're a public figure too, Mr Pinder. You must know how sometimes the media distort the truth.*

*I think this is one public figure having no way of concealing the truth. Or don't you agree?*

*Do you think entrapment can ever be justified, Mr Pinder?*

*I think we have to focus on the situation as it now stands. Sadly, our situation is that we're running out of time –*

*So you think exposing someone's shortcomings is okay, whatever means are used to do it?*

*It's the duty of the press to expose hypocrisy. That can sometimes involve unorthodox methods.*

In his earpiece, Pinder could hear the producer telling him to wind up and move on to the next item. He made a signal that he was coming to the end.

*Well, we're going to have to leave it there for now, but I think this story is far from concluded.*

*I agree. Can I just say one thing?*

*Briefly, very briefly, please.*

*It's awful when public figures who want to be respected are revealed to be not quite what they seem –*

*Yes, well that's all too clear. Thank you Mr –*

*I used to relax with my colleagues in the Pugin room in parliament over a drink, or Annie's bar where journalists are allowed –*

*I know it well, but now we have to end it there –*

*But some people prefer the Pink Flamingo Club in Soho, don't they? Don't they, Mr Pinder?*

*The ...?*

*You know where I mean. It's famous, the Pink Flamingo Club. Its members are ... liberated spirits with – what do they call it – alternative lifestyles? Is that right? Mr Pinder?*

Pinder turned to the window where the producer was sitting with a baffled expression. Why was Leyton-Brown rambling on about a gay club? Could it be that they were about to have a further revelation? He told Pinder to keep it going.

*I don't think that really concerns us here and now.*

*Oh, I think it does. You see, I came here to talk about scandal, hypocrisy. What if I said that I knew someone was a member of the Pink Flamingo Club ... meaning they were gay in their private life, and I came here deliberately to state that in public? Would that be entrapment? Would it be okay? I ought to say I have nothing against the gay community myself. Some of my closest colleagues ... well, that's perhaps another story ... or two. What do you think, Mr Pinder?*

*I ... I ... I fail to see the relevance of what you're –*

*Oh, you do. I'm quite sure you do. And so do your listeners, Mr Pinder ... I'm sure they do now.*

There was a squawk on the air, but no reply. Anthony continued.

*I'm not sure if I'm still on the air, but I would just say this in case anyone can hear me. Okay, I was in the wrong. I'm a politician ... and a hypocrite. But I was set up and only reacted like any normal man exposed to that kind of temptation. It was entrapment by the media. And they don't like having a taste of their own medicine. I'd like to thank this programme for giving me the chance to make my point.*

Mrs Jolly looked stunned as the radio went dead. Seconds passed, and there was a sound of shuffling papers. Paul Pinder's running mate in the studio that morning was Fiona McLaren, an experienced regular on the programme. She stumbled back into earshot.

Well, we ... er ... yes ... I think we've slightly overrun and it's time to go over to the BBC weather centre where Steve Young has the latest forecast. Steve, good morning.

Mrs Jolly stood up and turned off the radio. "Well … That was a turn-up. I've never heard anything like it."

"No." Marnie looked equally surprised.

"Did you know he was going to do that, Marnie?"

"Not exactly. The idea was that he was going to make a veiled hint that media people might have secrets, too … something rather more general. I didn't realise he was actually going to out him like that."

"And is it really true, my dear?"

"We've only got someone's word for it, of course. But I don't think they'd lie."

"What does that mean for us?" Anne said. "Could it be trouble?"

"I'm not sure. As long as it is the truth …"

"Oh, I think Paul Pinder's reaction meant it was the truth," said Mrs Jolly. "Don't you think?"

· · · · ·

Marnie was upstairs making her bed when the mobile rang. She checked the number on the tiny screen. Another mobile.

"Marnie Walker."

"This is Becky Thornton. I heard the programme. *Christ!* You play hard ball."

"Yes. Actually it wasn't quite – "

"Listen. I've got to talk to you. You're not going to believe this."

"What's happened?"

"Not now. We have to meet. Can you do lunch?"

"Sure. Where?"

"Make it that pub, the boater's pub, round the corner from Little Venice. Can you be there before it gets busy, say, twelve o'clock?"

"I'll be there."

· · · · ·

Anthony was out of the studio before the weather forecaster had finished the general synopsis. He hailed a cab and was quickly on his way to King's Cross station. There, he went straight to the taxi rank and queued for two minutes, concealed behind an open newspaper, and asked the driver for a turning off the Edgware Road. Anne was loitering near the towpath gate and swung it open as he paid the cabbie and crossed the pavement. She fastened it with the padlock behind him. Seconds later, Anthony boarded *Rumpole* and had vanished before anyone had become aware of his presence.

Anne went to the far end of the towpath, exited via the public gate and walked up to the newsstand by the tube station. She bought a copy of the *Guardian* and the *Globe* and returned to Mrs Jolly's house, letting herself in with a key. She met Marnie coming down the stairs.

"I got the papers."

"Good. I saw you let Anthony in. Did he say anything?"

"He just muttered something under his breath."

"Anything significant?"

"Vaguely blasphemous, I think."

Marnie smiled. "Right. Listen, Becky Thornton rang. I'm meeting her in the pub round the corner at twelve. It's all very mysterious."

"Black cloak or beret and shoulder-holster?"

"Both. *And* … We've had a request for another radio interview. The Beeb wants Anthony on the lunchtime news programme tomorrow. You know who the producer is … *Tim Rodgers!*"

"Bingo!" said Anne.

Mrs Jolly was standing in the kitchen doorway. "Won't they be able to trace your number and know how to find you, my dear?"

"Not without great difficulty," Marnie said. "We've given out an ex-directory number that we use for faxing and hooked the answerphone up to it. I check messages using the mobile."

The old lady shook her head. "I don't know where you get these ideas, Marnie. It's all very cloak-and-dagger."

Marnie laughed. "I know. I don't mind the cloak … but I can do without the dagger."

• • • • •

Marnie and Becky Thornton converged on the boater's pub from opposite ends of the street. Marnie reached the door first but went in without waiting for Becky. They found a table in the corner and sat with sandwiches and spritzers trying not to look like plotters. Becky did most of the talking while Marnie listened in silence. At the end of the narrative, they both took a drink.

Marnie put down her glass. "I can hardly believe it."

"It's true, Marnie. You'd almost think it was fate, wouldn't you?"

"It's certainly bizarre."

"So?" said Becky. "What are you going to do about it?"

"I've got to take it in … think things over … work something out."

"Well, don't hang about."

Marnie sipped her drink. "Are you sure about this? I mean, about going through with it?"

Becky shrugged. "I wouldn't be here if I wasn't."

"Why are you doing this? You're taking one hell of a risk, putting your whole career on the line."

"I heard that interview this morning, Marnie. It made me think. Frankly, I'm no fan of Leyton-Brown, but he was definitely set up, and the point is, he's no worse than anyone else."

"That's what he says."

"He's right. I see it all the time. There are so many hypocrites in public life. The cameras go on … they're all smiles. The cameras turn off … they're shits. You wouldn't believe it. I figured … well, he's going down anyway. He might as well take a few with him."

"Mind you don't get dragged down too, Becky."

"Don't remind me. But I can cover my tracks … with a bit of luck." She drained her glass. "Gotta go. I'll keep you posted."

Pulling open the pub door, Becky glanced back at the corner table. Marnie was already on the phone, talking quietly and urgently.

# Part 41

There was nothing unusual about Marnie Walker being seen on the towpath in Little Venice that Wednesday morning. She was a familiar sight, well-known and well-liked by the canal community whose colourful narrowboats lined the banks on both arms leading in and out of the pool itself. No one would have been surprised to see her board *Rumpole*. It belonged to her friend Roger Broadbent, and everyone knew he often let her use it.

The surprise would have been to know that Anthony was living on board, a fugitive from the press, whose notoriety had rocketed since his radio interview of the day before. There was no outward sign of his presence, and the curtains stayed closed all day. Marnie pulled them apart now and opened the windows to air the boat. Only the saloon porthole covers remained in place.

Marnie sat in one armchair and Anthony in the other. "They want you there by half twelve at the latest," she said, looking at her watch. "That gives us an hour before we need to leave."

"*We?*" said Anthony.

"Yes. You can't rely on taxis today. We need mobility. We have to assume the word will be out that you're on the programme. You can bet your life the press will cover all the exits you're likely to use."

"I can't go to another studio like I did yesterday?"

"No. We're upping the anti now. This time you come out with all guns blazing."

"Go on."

"We've got two aims today. You hammer home the point about entrapment and the corrupt practices of the *Globe*."

"But there's nothing new there."

"No. But that's just the first message, and we need to keep plugging it. The second is, we carry the battle to the enemy. You spring the surprise on Tim Rodgers."

"He's the producer?"

"Yes, and he'll be there in the control room. You'll be able to see him through the window that looks into the studio. That's the point. You'll expose his past life right in front of him. If we're going to put the frighteners on the media, we have to make a good job of it."

"This is about the woman who had his baby and he left her in the lurch?"

"Judith. Her name's Judith, and the baby – she's a little girl now, a sweetie – she's called Rosie."

Anthony wrote the names on a pad. "Judith ... Rosie. Okay. And she's agreed to this?"

"She agrees. I've been to see her."

"What about transport? Ralph's car?"

"No. He's getting a hire car. It'll be something unremarkable. People might recognise the Volvo."

"Fine. How long's the interview?"

"The PA said three to four minutes. And they won't over-run like yesterday. This is just a thirty-minute programme, and the main news will be the interest rate rise to be announced by the Chancellor at noon."

Anthony looked amazed. "How the hell did you know that? That'd be top secret."

"Ralph told me last night."

"Huh!" Anthony laughed. "That smart-arse! Could you get him to forecast horseracing results in his spare time? We could make a fortune."

Marnie smiled. "Let's just concentrate on your campaign, shall we?"

"Sure. Do we know who's fronting the programme?"

"Olivia Munnings."

"That makes sense. Everyone knows she's Miss Squeaky-Clean."

• • • • •

In the meeting room down the corridor from the studio, the lunchtime news team completed their pre-programme briefing, and Olivia Munnings collected her papers together. As usual she was meticulous and had marked each item in order with a number in a circle in the top right-hand corner of the page. The lead story was an interview with the Chief Financial Secretary to the Treasury, and she would enjoy probing below the surface of the government's boast that the economy was on the mend.

Across the table, Tim Rodgers took a cigarette from a packet and twisted it between his fingers, a reflex born of long habit. This was a strictly no-smoking building.

"You okay about the Leyton-Brown story, Olivia?"

"Why shouldn't I be?"

"No guilty secrets, skeletons in the cupboard?" He teased her with the boyish smile he thought women found appealing.

"I'm not likely to be outed, if that's what you mean," she retorted. "I thought that was why they invited him when I was doing the programme … to be on the safe side."

"Just coincidence, Ol. But I know you don't really like doing this sort of thing. Not heavyweight enough for you, is it?"

"It's fine … quite straightforward. I'll press him on moral values and hypocrisy; he'll protest he was framed. I don't know why we're so keen to give him a platform."

Rodgers smiled and shrugged. "Because it's news, that's why."

"Yesterday's news," she countered. "And tomorrow it'll be forgotten. Dumbing down, I call it."

Rodgers winced. "*Horrible* Americanism. I hope it doesn't catch on over here. *Ghastly*. I'm going for a smoke. Coming?"

"No. Ladies' room for me. Got to freshen up."

They walked down the corridor together and parted company outside the ladies' loo. Rodgers waved a cigarette as he went on his way.

"Change your mind?"

She began pushing the door. "You go ahead. See you in fifteen minutes."

"Okay. I know you've got your standards to keep up."

• • • • •

It was a dark grey Ford Mondeo estate of the kind used by reps all over the country. No one glanced at it as it turned in from the street at the back of the BBC building in the area of west London known as the White City.

The car pulled up at an unmarked door and a man climbed out from the rear seats. He was slim and tanned, as if he worked out of doors, with close-cropped brown hair, tending to thin, and a short beard. He wore a faded denim shirt, stone-coloured chinos and brown deck shoes. Beside him was a slender woman of almost the same height, with short dark hair, in black trousers and a silk top in charcoal grey. They pushed the door open and went in. The car moved across the yard and stopped in a reserved parking bay.

• • • • •

Olivia Munnings, immaculately groomed as always, with every hair in place, applied a fresh layer of lipstick and worked her lips together to even out the colour. Some colleagues used to joke with her that she was wasted on radio. But hers was the most famous and easily recognised voice in Britain, her best feature. Some said she *was* the voice of Britain and represented everything the BBC stood for in the world: honesty, truthfulness, accuracy. She had upheld these standards for more than twenty years and had built her professional reputation on personal integrity, becoming a national institution. Then why was her hand shaking?

She looked into her eyes in the mirror. Why had Tim Rodgers asked if she had any guilty secrets? Silly thing to say! He knew nothing of her life. She closed her eyes to compose herself, but she could not keep the thoughts out.

The child would have been twenty-one that autumn. As a student she had felt too ashamed to let her parents – or even the baby's father – know of her indiscretion and had rejected the idea of adoption. It would have caused havoc to her university course, having a child and repeating the year. At the end of the Lent term she had quietly gone to a private clinic and used all the money left to her by her grandmother to have a termination.

Could anyone have discovered her secret? Was it remotely possible?

The door opened and in came two secretaries from News and Current Affairs. Olivia Munnings greeted them confidently and strode out to start the programme.

• • • • •

Halfway down the passageway, Marnie and Anthony were met by a brisk young woman in a black trouser-suit. She guided them towards a lift and took them up three floors to a waiting room, offering them coffee, tea or 'perhaps something a little stronger'. There was a trolley on which stood a variety of bottles. They both declined. The woman asked them to take a seat and left the room, promising to return in five minutes.

Marnie took out her mobile to check the answerphone at Glebe Farm. Messages had been coming in at frequent intervals on the number given out in the press statement. Before she could hit the buttons, the phone began vibrating in her hand and she took an incoming call.

"Marnie?"

"Yes. Is that Judith? Hi. We're in the studio, waiting to go in. I can't really talk at the moment. Can I ring you back?"

"I can't go through with it, Marnie." Her voice sounded flat.

"Say again?"

"I can't … I can't let you do it."

Marnie's expression changed. Anthony saw the cloud pass over her face and he mouthed, *What is it?* Marnie turned the phone so that he could listen. He moved his head close to hers.

"Judith," she said. "We're in the studio. Maybe you didn't hear me. We're actually there now. In two minutes Anthony's going through to be interviewed. This is going out live. You said you agreed."

"I'm sorry … so sorry, Marnie." Judith was close to tears. "But I still … you know … I can't let him bring it all out in public. I couldn't bear it. Not Tim."

"God almighty, Judith! This is *great* timing."

"Please, Marnie. You said I could count on you."

Marnie closed her eyes. "Leave it with me. I'll have to think of something." She ended the call and stared at Anthony. "*Bloody hell!*"

"Too bad," he said.

Marnie bit her lip. "It's worse than too bad … it's a total disaster."

Anthony shook his head. "Too bad for *her*, I mean. We can't turn back now. It's too late."

"But – "

"What does she expect me to do … go on the air and just trot out the entrapment thing I said yesterday? Does she want me to commit hara kiri in public? *For Chrissake!*"

"Anthony, I gave her my word. I don't see how you can – "

Before she could finish the sentence, the young woman in black entered the room and extended a hand towards Anthony. She had been about to smile, but the atmosphere made it clear that something was amiss. She noticed the mobile that Marnie was holding.

"Sorry, but you can't use that in here. I should've asked you to turn it off. Mobiles aren't allowed. They can cause big problems." She gestured to Anthony and led him out.

"You can say that again," Marnie muttered to herself.

· · · · ·

Outside in the car park, Ralph was fiddling with the radio trying to find Radio 4. "This is all very complicated," he was muttering. "It's quite different from the Volvo."

"Yes," said Anne. "Nowhere to shovel the coal in." She reached forward from the back seat. "Shall I have a go?"

"It'll do untold damage to my ego if you get it working. You do realise that, don't you?"

The mobile began ringing.

"You take the call, I'll twiddle the knobs," Anne suggested.

"Hallo, Ralph Lombard."

"It's Marnie. Listen. We're in deep trouble."

"Tell me."

"Judith rang just as Anthony was going in. She's cried off."

"What?"

"She won't let us expose Tim Rodgers. And of course, I promised to respect her wishes."

"Oh, my God! The whole thing'll fall flat on its face. He'll be a sitting duck."

"Worse than that, Ralph ... much worse. Anthony doesn't feel bound by my promise. He thinks she's let him down."

"You mean he's going ahead with the plan? Oh boy ... So we'll end up alienating one of our allies."

"Exactly. What a mess!"

"How did she contact you?"

"On the mobile."

"They don't allow mobiles to be used in there."

"I wish I'd thought of that. Could've saved a load of trouble."

"How are you phoning now, as a matter of interest?"

"I'm using the mobile. I don't care any more. I'm secretly hoping it'll jam their transmission ... or better still, blow up the studio ... with Anthony in it."

Suddenly and noisily, Anne succeeded in finding the right wavelength, and Radio 4 burst into life on the car radio. They heard Olivia Munnings putting a complex financial question to the minister.

"Your jamming attempt seems to have failed," Ralph said. "Can you hear the programme up there?"

Marnie sighed. "Yes. It's piped into the room. I'd better listen. See you later."

• • • • •

Marnie turned off the mobile and settled back to listen to the programme. It seemed that Ralph had been right about the interest rate. Clever clogs! She tried hard to be impressed, but had no enthusiasm. Her plans were already hitting snags, and they had hardly begun.

She had only half an ear listening to the minister, but she caught a reference to him, sending a clear message to the rest of the world that Britain was in control of its economy. She was determined not to sigh again, but suddenly heard an echo in her brain: sending a clear message. Yes. How could she get a message to Tim Rodgers? She could tell him that Anthony knew all about Judith and Rosie and would broadcast it here and now if Olivia Munnings even hinted at a hostile line in her questioning. Could a producer control an interview like that from the background? She could not wait to find out and quickly scribbled a note. She folded it in two, wrote 'Tim Rodgers – Confidential' on the back and rushed out into the corridor.

It was deserted. She did not even know which way to turn.

• • • • •

Tim Rodgers fiddled with the cigarette packet on the deck in front of him in the control room. Through the triple-glazed picture window that separated his area from the studio, he could see Munnings and the minister locked in deep discussion. Both protagonists rocked gently as they spoke, leaning in towards the bulbous microphones suspended before them from the ceiling to emphasise the points they were making.

On his computer screen, Rodgers saw a newsflash appear. As the minister tackled the last question, Rodgers pressed a button and spoke into a microphone.

"Olivia. Incoming story. Big car bomb – West Bank in Israel. Patching it through. Announce it as breaking news at the end of the programme. We'll cue you."

Olivia quickly glanced at the screen on her left and raised a finger to acknowledge. She checked her notes for closing remarks to the minister while an assistant ushered Anthony into the studio. Seamlessly and smoothly, Olivia introduced Anthony's story as the assistant led the minister silently to the door. He did not look twice at the bearded man who was taking a seat.

• • • • •

Ralph and Anne listened to the interview in the car, leaning back in their seats one behind the other. They concentrated on every word.

The interview began with factual questions.

*Do you accept that the newspaper photographs were genuine?*

*Do you admit you were involved in a sexual act with a girl in your garden?*

*Was the girl a member of your staff?*

*How long had she worked for you?*

*Had you been having an affair with her prior to that event?*

*Why did you go into hiding?*

Anthony's replies were brief and to the point. He accepted that the photographs showed him in a compromising position, but denied having an affair. He maintained the girl had been planted on him by the Globe, and had lured him into position for the camera. He had gone into hiding to gain time to think things out.

It was the mixture as before, and it sounded feeble. It was his word against the newspaper's and it was leading nowhere. After this, there would be no more interest in his story. All the efforts made by Marnie, Ralph and the others – all the plotting, all the running, all the scheming – would have been wasted. There would be no redress, no retribution. Anthony would appear weak and foolish; Marlene would feel cheapened and used for the rest of her life; Melissa would have died for a sordid and soon-to-be-forgotten scandal dreamt up to sell newspapers.

• • • • •

Marnie sat alone in the waiting room. She had thrown her message into the waste bin after giving up the attempt to find Tim Rodgers. Restless, frustrated and unable to settle, she had spotted the collection of bottles on the trolley and poured herself a generous measure of cognac. She flopped into an armchair waiting to hear Anthony bringing misery and unhappiness to a woman he had never met, who had done him no harm and whose only fault was that she still loved the father of her child, a man who was about to have his shortcomings broadcast to the nation with untold consequences for his life. And it was all Marnie's idea, her plan to hit back at the faceless media that could ruin lives and reputations. Now she would become part of it herself. She took a drink of the brandy and felt it burn a path down her throat.

She could hear Anthony telling Olivia Munnings that he had gone to stay with friends who had helped him put his life back together. Priceless! she thought. One slip of the tongue and he'll 'out' us as well. She sipped more cognac, put her head back and closed her eyes.

*But if you felt you were a victim of a conspiracy, why did you run away? Could you not simply have issued a statement denying that you were in a relationship with the girl?*

*You make it sound so easy. Try to imagine the whole of the media hounding you.*

*Some people might say that you had set yourself up as the custodian of national morals and that you were only running away because you'd been found out.*

*How would you feel if your private life was being held up for attack as mine was?*

*We're not really here to judge my private life, Mr Leyton-Brown.*

*Oh, but we are, you see. We are. You in the news media also have a great responsibility. I wonder how you can judge others when your own life may be no better.*

*I think you're evading the issue here –*

*No, with respect, I'm not. Tell us about your guilty secret. I challenge you ... here and now. Are you going to make it public ... or shall I?*

Marnie sat bolt upright. What was he going to say this time? Did he have something on Olivia Munnings? Before she could reply, Anthony continued.

*That's the point, you see. You think I'm here to talk about me and my shortcomings. You're all happy to judge and attack me. Why? Because it's newsworthy. Am I right? Of course I am. And you all think you're safe on your side of the microphone. But what if I turned the tables and revealed your secret? Would that be entrapment ... or a new kind of investigative politics?*

*I'm not sure what you're getting at, Mr Leyton-Brown, I –*

*I'm getting at you actually ... or to be fair, I'm getting at the media through you. And really, it's not personal. Isn't that what gangsters are supposed to say? I'm only using you as an example. Mind you, judging by your expression, you've got me wondering whether you might have ... never mind. No. My real target is someone else ... part of the same machine.*

Marnie thought, Oh no ... he's going to do it. He's going to go for Tim Rodgers. She braced herself mentally as Anthony went on.

*Listen carefully to what I say. Don't just think I can be brought here to be pilloried in public. I was trapped, I was set up, I was used. Think about it. I'd like all your listeners to think about it, too. And what I would say is this. You can't be complacent. You can't live your life through ... rosie-tinted spectacles.*

Marnie strained forward. Did she hear that right? Olivia Munnings was talking again.

*... though I'm not sure I fully understood what you were saying there.*

*It was a warning. Now it's my turn to declare open season on hypocrites, on anyone who pretends their standards are better than mine and tries to judge me after setting me up. That's all I have to say ... for the moment. Just watch this space.*

• • • • •

In her kitchen in Little Venice, Mrs Jolly sat by the radio pondering the interview she had just heard. It was all very curious. Did Anthony Leyton-Brown mean to suggest that Olivia Munnings had some sort of guilty secret? Surely not. Or did he? She wondered if he had a point, not about Olivia Munnings, of course. *She* was beyond *any* kind of suspicion. Wasn't she?

Mrs Jolly wondered what she really knew about Olivia Munnings, the *real person*. Or about any of the people who were household names. Was corruption – or this new word everybody was using these days – *sleaze* ... was it rampant in public life? It would be very sad to think that the people who came into her living room every day by television or radio or the newspapers were not what they seemed to be.

• • • • •

In her living room in St Albans, Judith sat back in the armchair. All the toys were neatly tidied away on shelves or in the toy box under the window. Rosie was at nursery school. Judith's mind was a jangle of twisted emotions. She had listened to the interview with dread gradually creeping over her as she waited for Leyton-Brown to talk about Tim and her ... and Rosie. She had been shaking with nerves and had almost cried out when he had said 'rosie-tinted spectacles'. And then it was all over.

She had heard nothing after that. Her brain had shut out the world, and she had come back to reality with Olivia Munnings introducing a foreign correspondent at a meeting of oil-producing countries in the Middle East. Of one thing she was sure: Marnie Walker was a person who could be trusted.

• • • • •

In the control room of the lunchtime news programme at the BBC, Tim Rodgers was telling the production assistant to cut to the live report from the OPEC meeting in Riyadh. It was business as usual, split-second timing bringing world-class reporting into millions of homes. *Rosie-tinted spectacles* ... he had really said that. What did he know? It could not have been a slip of the tongue. Tim had seen that slight turn of the head towards the control room window as Leyton-Brown had said it. He knew, all right. But *how*? And what use would he be prepared to make of it?

At that moment a breaking news item came up on the computer screen. A man armed with a shotgun had barricaded himself into a house in Leeds with two children. Rodgers quickly looked down the list of remaining items to assess how and where to slot in the story. Decisively, he adjusted the order while an assistant phoned the local radio station in readiness for live commentary. Across the country the listeners had no idea what went on behind the scenes.

• • • • •

The door to the car park opened and Marnie stepped out alone. The hire car was now standing two paces away, the engine running. Marnie was followed almost at once by Anthony. Ralph was standing by the rear passenger's door, and Anne was sitting in the front. Ralph pointed to the driver's seat.

"You drive, Anthony."

He climbed into the back, where Marnie joined him. As the car exited through the gates, Ralph was reading a newspaper that all but concealed his face.

"Go left and take the first right at the lights."

Marnie looked at him curiously. "What's all this about?"

"Just a precaution. I'm getting as paranoid as you are. I thought that anyone spotting the car would look at me with the newspaper rather than Anthony."

Anne laughed out loud. "It's Professor Bond ... Professor James Bond." Her voice was three octaves lower than usual, with a slight lisp.

Marnie joined in. "My God, Ralph, you've turned yourself into a diversionary tactic. Must be an all-time first for Oxford."

"Mock not. Look, I'm doing my best here – "

Before he could finish, Marnie reached across and kissed him full on the lips. Seismologists in Stockholm registered earth tremors in the London area far up the Richter scale.

When he was allowed to breathe again, Ralph said, "I like this Bond lark ... think I'll change career."

"Sounds okay to me," Anthony said, looking in the rear-view mirror. "Did you manage to hear the piece, Ralph?"

"Thanks to the techno-wizard on your left, yes. That was very enigmatic at the end ... the rosie-tinted spectacles. I thought I'd mis-heard you."

Marnie leaned forward. "Thanks for that, Anthony. Quick thinking."

"You're welcome. I think it got the message across to the person concerned."

Ralph said, "And you gave Olivia Munnings quite a fright, I thought. Interesting."

"Yes," Anthony said. "That made me wonder, too."

"You may have done enough to scare every journalist in the country ... apart from those with blameless lives. I suppose there must be some ..."

Marnie said, "Anthony, I want to ask you something."

"What do I do at these traffic lights?"

"Go straight on. I want to know if you would really have used the information about Judith and Tim Rodgers on the air."

The car rolled to a halt at the red lights. Anthony pulled on the parking brake and turned in the seat.

"Some things it's better not to ask, Marnie. Sometimes it's better not to think the unthinkable."

"Good lord!" Mrs Jolly exclaimed. The three of them were scanning the newspapers at breakfast. She had picked up the *Sun*.

"I think Mrs Jolly's reached page three," Anne muttered, grinning.

Marnie and Anne were sharing the Globe, heads close together across the table. Anne had gone out early and bought one of every paper on sale at the news-stand by the tube. They were reading intently, like students on the morning of an important exam.

"Good lord!" the old lady said again.

Marnie looked up and smiled. "Good lord *what*, Mrs Jolly?"

"Well ... I mean ..." She shook her head. " They're *all* at it. Everybody's ... what's that strange term ... *coming out of the closet*. Or is it *cupboard*? No, that's *skeletons*. Actually, it amounts to the same thing."

Anne laughed. Mrs Jolly continued.

"You're going to tell me I'm rambling, I know, but it really is quite amazing. Everybody's confessing to just about everything imaginable. It's a kind of national outpouring of the soul. Your Mr Leyton-Brown seems to have lanced a boil and ..." She pulled a face and shuddered. "Well, I don't want to continue that, but you know what I mean."

"Not exactly *my* Mr Leyton-Brown," Marnie said gently. "But yes, I do know what you mean. All the papers are full of it."

She held up the *Globe* to reveal a whole page of photographs of the Great and the Good. Each caption seemed to be a confession. Here, a television chat show host revealed that he had been abused as a child – Marnie thought that explained why he now spent his life abusing the guests on his show. There, a heartthrob pop singer confessed he was gay – Marnie wondered if he was the only one in the country who thought that was news. Public figures were confessing to having mistresses and lovers. Activists were outing bishops; bishops were admitting to doubts about God. An unprecedented, unnatural wave of honesty was pouring over the country.

"I've never known anything like it," said Mrs Jolly. "What's he up to today?"

"Ah ..." Marnie began. "Today we probably get arrested."

"My goodness! What are you going to do? Or is it best not to ask? Though perhaps I ought to ask, in case I have to come and bail you out."

"Don't even joke about it," Marnie said ruefully.

"Was I joking? I didn't think I was."

Marnie said, "Today we have to split forces for a while. Ralph has commitments in Oxford, then in London. We may see him later, or we may not. Anthony's doing an interview on the early evening news on Radio 4."

"Who's he outing this time?" said Mrs Jolly, proud of her command of the jargon.

"It's just a straight interview ... no pun intended. He thinks people are willing to listen now to what he has to say, and he wants to make a simple statement."

"I don't see how any of that could get you arrested, my dear. So what will *you* be doing?"

"Nothing till later this evening probably, though my plans aren't clear just yet. May we hang out here for the morning while I make phone calls and plan things?"

"Of course. I'll get lunch for whenever you want it. Will Anne be going out with you?"

"Probably. I'll know the details when I've made my calls."

• • • • •

At lunchtime Anne went out first, alone, carrying Mrs Jolly's old-fashioned shopping basket. The sandwiches and fruit that were Anthony's lunch were covered with a striped tea towel. On the doorstep she scanned the street for suspicious characters, but everything seemed normal and she crossed the road in the direction of the towpath gate. She felt like Little Red Riding Hood on her way through the woods to visit Grandma. The hatch on *Rumpole* was already unlocked in readiness, and Anne stepped aboard and went below unnoticed by passers-by. Marnie followed minutes later, carrying a shopping bag.

"Everything sorted?" Anthony asked.

"I think so ... as much as it can be. We'll see. Meantime, I've brought you some papers." She unloaded the contents of the shopping bag onto the galley table. "They should keep you amused for a while."

"Any more interviews lined up?"

"No, but an interesting cancellation."

"Cancellation?"

"I had a call from the *Newsnight* programme on television. They'd seemed quite keen the other day. This morning I phoned them to check timings, only to be told the idea'd been dropped."

"One high place too many. The TV people don't seem too keen to have me, do they? What a surprise." Anthony opened the papers. "Look at this lot! *Wow!* It's confessions time. *Jeez.*"

He pointed at a photograph. "I knew her. She used to be in old Rodney's private office when he was a junior minister at Defence. Here she is saying that ... well, it's sexual harassment, isn't it?"

"Certainly is," Marnie said, unsmiling. "Does it surprise you?"

"Not that that particular minister tried to put his hand up her ... not that actually, no. What surprises me is that she's gone public about it."

"Don't you think she was justified?"

"Sure, but it's still a surprise. Most women don't have the guts to do such a thing."

Two heads snapped up. Marnie and Anne traded glances.

"It takes a lot of courage to do that," Anthony said.

They decided to give him the benefit of the doubt.

"So what's the schedule for today?" he asked.

"Just the one radio slot. They want you there by about five."

"Who's interviewing me?"

"They didn't say. One of their regulars, I suppose. It varies from day to day."

"Same travel arrangements as yesterday?"

"No. Ralph's got appointments. Me, too. I don't know how long I'll be ... may be some time. You take the hire car."

"All right. Anne going with you?"

Marnie shook her head. "Not this time ... could be tricky. Anne can hold the fort."

Anthony said, "What about her coming with me ... in case I need a gofer?"

Marnie stared at him. "Why might you need a gofer?"

"I don't know. I've kinda got used to having a minder these days. Forget it. I'll be all right."

"I don't mind," Anne said. "Better than staying indoors all afternoon by myself."

"Er ..." Marnie began.

Anthony shrugged. "It's okay. I quite understand if you'd rather I went alone."

"Unless you think I might be in the way," Anne muttered.

"No," said Marnie, torn between conflicting thoughts. "An extra pair of eyes could be useful, I suppose. You never know ..."

•　•　•　•　•

The late afternoon was clouding over as Mrs Jolly and her guests made their way to the front door.

"I don't know what time I'll be back exactly," the old lady said. She fished in her purse. "Look ... take my spare door key. Then you can come and go as you please. Help yourselves to anything you want. You know where to find tea and such."

Marnie slipped the key in her pocket. "Thank you."

Outside, Marnie and Mrs Jolly walked together towards the tube station, while Anne watched for the grey Mondeo to approach. She felt the first drops of rain falling on her head when she opened the front gate and crossed the pavement to climb in beside Anthony.

•　•　•　•　•

Ralph was sitting in an office in Whitehall when he noticed the first raindrops streaking the window. It was a vast office with heavy dark furniture, harking back to the days when Britain ruled a huge empire. Opposite him over the mahogany desk sat a *Mandarin*, a senior civil servant, in fact a *very* senior official of Her Majesty's Treasury. They had been discussing Ralph's appointment to a new committee on economic policy, and there was a pause while a young woman came in with tea and biscuits.

On the corner of the desk lay a copy of that morning's Times. The mandarin nodded towards it.

"Did you see the Times this morning, Ralph? Every bloody paper's become a scandal sheet these days. It's *appalling!*"

"So I'd noticed." Ralph remained enigmatic.

"It's ever since Leyton-Brown started exposing everybody. Did you hear that radio interview with Paul Pinder the other day? *Ye gods!*"

"I did, yes. Quite a surprise. Hung him out to dry in public." Inscrutable.

"Certainly did. I was at the Press Complaints Commission yesterday, having a row with the vice-chairman about regulation and standards of reporting. He didn't know what to make of it. The whole media world's shaking in its boots. *I tell you ... that's what I call self-regulation!*"

The mandarin guffawed. Ralph stirred his tea.

• • • • •

Anthony was becoming visibly agitated at the wheel, wiping condensation from inside the windscreen with irritated hand movements. He grabbed the control stalk for the wipers, trying to make them go faster to cope with the downpour. Anne heard him muttering under his breath, but thought it better not to ask him to repeat.

"It's all right," she said. "We've got plenty of time, and it's not far now."

"We should've come by taxi," Anthony grumbled. "God knows where we'll be able to park."

"But Marnie thought we needed to be independent with our own transport. She didn't want you to be stranded somewhere trying to get a cab and exposed to reporters."

"Marnie's a control freak," he growled, adding, "And she's absolutely right, as usual."

"Are you missing your minder?"

He stopped at traffic lights. "Probably. It's just nerves." He looked down at the street atlas on Anne's lap. "Not far, you say?"

"Two more blocks and we turn left. Then it's almost a straight run for half a mile and we're there."

"What about parking?"

"There isn't a car park. We'll have to find somewhere."

"Oh well ... that should solve everything. I probably won't even make it to the interview. I'll be driving round Broadcasting House."

In an attempt at levity Anne said, "With any luck we might get a crack at the lap record. Marnie says the thing to do is think positive and deal with the situation when you get there."

Anthony spoke but Anne could not hear what he said as the engine revved and he pulled away from the lights. She suspected it was not complimentary.

"What did you say, Anthony? I missed that."

He cleared his throat. "I was just ... er, trying to look on the bright side and think positive ... or something like that."

They pressed on through the steady rain, Anne leaning forward to keep the screen clear of mist with the palm of her hand, Anthony silently concentrating on the traffic. Soon afterwards, Anne pointed ahead.

"That's it. Now we've just got to find a slot."

"A slot," Anthony repeated through gritted teeth. "Let's think positive then ... like Marnie says."

Anne could understand Anthony's display of nerves. She was glad that her part in the operation was limited to finding a parking space. The idea of facing a hostile interview on national radio at peak time would have filled her with dread. She wanted to remind Anthony that parking the car was the least of his worries, but she thought better of it. Soon his prediction of lapping Broadcasting House was becoming a reality. They reached the front of the building for the second time.

Anthony growled. "Oh God ... this is hopeless. We're going to be doing this till nightfall. How much longer have I got, Anne?"

"They're expecting you in about ten minutes."

More muttering from Anthony.

"Look," Anne said suddenly. "Stop here."

Anthony braked outside the main doors. "I can't stay. It's a double yellow line. It'll get towed away."

"I know. You go in, and I'll find somewhere to park. Easy."

"You?"

"Sure. I know how to drive. I'm having lessons. I can do parking. No probs." Her voice was full of youthful optimism.

"I think it's only insured for me to drive," Anthony said, frowning.

"No, it's not. I know all about the hiring conditions. I was there."

"Oh .. okay ... that's fine, then," Anthony said, opening the door as Anne slid across to the driving seat.

"Yes," Anne called out gaily. "It's actually only insured for Ralph to drive."

As Anthony's jaw dropped, Anne pulled the door shut, leaving him no choice but to dive into the building to escape the rain. She gave a brief good-luck wave as she put the car in gear, indicated and edged cautiously away from the kerb.

Thinking positively all the while, she had gone barely a hundred metres when she saw a car up ahead signalling that it was pulling out of a parking space. She swung over and put on the hazard lights. No one would be in any doubt that she was having that slot, as she eased forward and reversed gingerly into the space. It was a perfect manoeuvre. She put a pound in the meter and jogged back to the building through the rain. A uniformed commissionaire raised an eyebrow as she pushed open the heavy door and entered the reception hall. Breathless and dripping, and holding up the car keys, she gasped that she was collecting someone who was being interviewed on the news. The man indicated a row of seats where she could wait.

•  •  •  •  •

A young woman dressed in black and clasping a clipboard led Anthony down a long corridor, explaining that there was not enough time to offer him a drink before he went on air.

"That's okay. Who's on tonight? Who's doing the interview?"

"Granville Boyce."

"Who? Never heard of him."

"He's new. This is only his second time on."

"What's his background?"

The young woman pushed open a door and ushered him into an anteroom. "Local radio. He's joined us from Liverpool ... very bright."

Anthony wondered if this was good or bad news. Could it be that they did not want to run the risk of him exposing something in the past of the well-known presenters? Was it coincidence? Or was it a chance for a young Turk to make his mark? "Liverpool," he muttered.

"Yes. I think he was the local reporter for somewhere called Skelmersdale." She pronounced it hesitantly, as if it was a new planet, only recently discovered.

"Skelmersdale? That's a new town, isn't it? I've barely heard of it."

"Nor has anybody else." She smiled. "Are you ready to go through? They're waiting for you."

I bet they are, he thought. "Yes, of course," he said brightly. "Let's go." He sounded completely confident.

The interview began with no surprises. Granville Boyce looked too young to be in gainful employment and had greased-up hair. Anthony expounded his familiar line. He was beginning to wonder if the campaign was fizzling out when the interviewer threw in a casual question.

*So, do you think you're going to get away with it, then? Is it all going to blow over? Back to normal?*

Anthony saw a glint in Boyce's eye. He was trying to trip him up, trying to be clever. This would be the start of his reputation as a big-hitter.

*Nothing will get back to normal again, I think,* Anthony said cautiously.

*But you don't seriously think you can go round exposing people's shortcomings, do you? Surely these indiscretions aren't as widespread as you seem to make out? Is this just the pot calling the kettle black?*

*Playing hardball,* Anthony thought. He said, *Well, it's a funny thing, but whenever I delve around in someone's past, I never fail to dig up something. Isn't that strange?*

*You delve around ... that's how you'd describe it?*

*Yes. But that isn't what I want to do this evening. I've just come to explain how I was tricked by devious means.*

*And you want people to believe that?*

*Yes. It's the truth. Despite what your listeners may feel, I honestly haven't come here this evening with the intention of exposing ... shall we say, your little – or perhaps not so little – indiscretion, perhaps more than a peccadillo, in* (pause) *Skelmersdale, for example. That is not my purpose.*

Silence. Boyce made a croaking sound. Anthony pushed a glass of water towards him. All over the country smiles were spreading across faces that a few moments earlier were beginning to register boredom. Motorists turned up the volume of car radios; mothers stopped pushing spoons of baby food into the mouths of their infants. Anthony grinned at Boyce across the studio deck. The young man struggled to regain his composure.

*Well, at the rate you're going, it'll soon only be safe to report stories about the Pope and Mother Theresa.*

Anthony smiled.

*I think you should be careful whose names you link together these days ... could be controversial.*

• • • • •

Downstairs in the hall, Anne was making a small puddle on the woodblock floor. It was frustrating not being able to hear the interview. She did not even know if Anthony would be leaving the building via the main entrance. Outside, it was still raining steadily. She shivered and wondered if she could find the ladies' loo and stand under an electric hand-drier for a few minutes. Not a good idea, she thought; she might miss Anthony. There was nothing for it but to wait patiently and make a damp patch on the chair. She sneezed.

• • • • •

The interview was drawing to a close. Boyce knew there were some risks not worth taking at this stage in a career. He let Anthony have a clear run, and Anthony soldiered on.

*I challenge any public figure to state categorically that they do not have a guilty secret or two. Nothing could make up for the fact that my dear wife committed suicide. But if I can expose the hypocrisy that is rife in Britain, at least I will have achieved something.*

*Mr Leyton-Brown, is it fair to say that you are out for vengeance?*

*I want to redress the balance. Hypocrisy is the British malaise. Politicians stand for election promising to cut taxes and at the same time increase spending. We all know it's absolute nonsense. Any fool can see that. But it's the game we play. We vote people into office as if they were saints and then cry foul if they stray from some imaginary path of virtue.*

*And you want revenge on the system?*

*Why not ... after all I've suffered? Revenge is a very pure motive. It's always sincere. Don't forget that.*

Anthony had given the newspapers their headline for the next day.

• • • • •

When the lift doors opened, Anthony burst into the entrance hall like a rocket. He caught sight of movement and saw Anne leaping to her feet. She rushed to join him at the door and was surprised to find him smiling.

"It went well, obviously."

"You could say that. Where's the car?"

"Round the corner."

"Positive thinking, eh?" He looked at her. "Goodness, you're drenched. You look like a drowned rat!"

She sneezed on cue. "And it's still raining. Look, there's no point in us both getting soaked. You wait here, I'll fetch the car."

She was gone before he could protest. A minute later, the Mondeo appeared outside, and he raced to get in while Anne slid across to the passenger seat.

"Sorry if I've made it damp for you."

"That's all right. What's our direction?"

"It's the TV studio, but we're not due there for nearly two hours. I'd really like to have a hot bath and get out of these wet things."

Anthony pulled into the traffic. "Where to, then?"

"Mrs Jolly's, please, if you don't mind. We've got plenty of time." Anthony was changing gear when Anne raised a hand to her mouth. "Oh, no ... that's no good."

"Why not?"

"Can't get in. Mrs Jolly's out ... Marnie's got the spare key."

"There's a shower on Rumpole," Anthony ventured. "Better than nothing, perhaps."

"I'm still stuck with these wet clothes." Anne's next sneeze was seconds away. "I'm soaked through to my underwear."

They moved slowly forward in silence. Anthony quickly switched lanes and made a right turn, gaining ground by threading his way deftly through side streets, joining the main road network further on. Anne checked the atlas.

"Where are we going? This is the opposite way from Little Venice."

"Trust me," said Anthony. "I've got an idea."

· · · · ·

A few miles to the west, Marnie finally put her mobile down, having ticked the last name off her list. She had been so absorbed in the task in hand that she had not given a moment's thought to Anthony's interview. What she had planned was probably not illegal, but Ralph had warned her that if she was ever found out, she could face the risk of being sued by at least two of the biggest companies in the land. She shuddered.

· · · · ·

Anthony needed no navigator for this journey, pressing on over roads he knew well. When they encountered traffic, he took short cuts, staying ahead of the game. Anne realised they were going down towards the river, but a long way west of Docklands. They surged past the buses on Putney Bridge and charged up the High Street, squeezing through gaps and jumping the lights when Anthony judged he could do so without being caught. Their route and destination were a mystery to Anne.

Three or four more turnings and they found themselves in a residential area, large houses set back with gravel drives and spacious grounds. Something about the place seemed familiar, though Anne had never been there in her life. Anthony slowed at each junction and eventually slipped round a corner and stopped, staring forward into the distance through the rain that was falling more lightly now. He eased the car away, cruising slowly down the road. Anne noticed that he pushed his neck back into the headrest so that his face was half-concealed by the door pillar. He reached the end of the road and turned back. This time, he travelled at normal speed and pulled sharply into the drive of a house on the corner, bringing the car to a standstill under the branches of a weeping birch tree. He scanned the house and grounds while the engine was running. No one stirred. He switched off. Anne knew he had come home.

"Let me go first to open the door," he said. "I'll need a moment or two to switch off the alarm." He turned in the seat. "This is the best I could think of, Anne. I hope it's all right."

"Yes," she said simply.

At once he leapt out, walked briskly to the door and went in. Anne followed and waited to be told she could enter the hall. It was a Victorian house of generous proportions, with a tiled floor and heavy doors of dark wood. There was an unlived-in smell, but at least it was dry and solid. Anthony emerged from a walk-in cupboard.

"Right. We haven't got long. Let me show you the bathroom." He led the way upstairs, Anne trying not to think she was alone in a strange house with a man notorious for dubious morals and unsavoury relations with young girls. He continued talking as they climbed the stairs that were covered in thick, deep red carpet. "The bathroom has a heating system that works separately, like the Paloma on the boat. You can have as much hot water as you like."

"But what about clothes?"

"That's why I've brought us here. I can find you something from Melissa's wardrobe. She was about your size, more or less." He saw Anne's expression. "No, it's okay. There are plenty of clothes she never wore. I'll find new things. She was always shopping."

He turned on the taps, and the bath, a huge white enamelled structure that was probably original, began to fill with steaming gushes of water. It looked so good to Anne.

"There are loads of oils and things," said Anthony. "Just help yourself. Let me get my razor and I'll leave you to it. It's time this beard came off … time I came out of hiding. I'll fetch you some towels."

"Do you want to shave in here?"

"No, I'll use the downstairs cloakroom."

He returned in a minute to find Anne perched on the side of the bath, running her fingers in the rising water.

"There's some Chanel bath oil on the side there. Do use it. You'll need a couple of capfuls for a deep bath. And here are some things to put on. I've … er … taken the liberty of including some underclothes. I hope that's all right." He seemed embarrassed, saddened.

"Thank you."

"Not at all. I think your shoe size is a little larger than Melissa's. Put some toilet tissue in them, and they'll dry out a bit. Okay, it's all yours. You can soak for about twenty minutes. I'll be downstairs." He paused in the doorway. "Oh, and … er … there's a bolt on the door. Do use it."

"I'm sure that won't be necessary."

"Please, Anne. I'd like you to bolt the door."

"All right."

She shut the door and pushed the bolt home. The bath oil smelled luxurious. Slowly she peeled off her wet things and laid them in a pile on a shelf at the foot of the bath. Standing naked while the water level climbed, she examined the clothes that Anthony had brought for her. They were new, as he had promised, good labels with price tags still attached. He had made an apt choice: two skirts in summer prints, a few cotton blouses in pastel shades and white cotton underwear. There were even some pairs of tights and a box of earrings. She tried not to think of the woman who had bought them that spring, and who now lay quietly in her grave.

Anne stepped into the bath, swirling the water round. She lowered herself carefully into the hot scented foam. It caressed her skin and took away the discomfort of the drenching rain. She rested her head against the bath edge and closed her eyes. It was blissful.

The twenty minutes passed too quickly, and Anne had to leave time for a shampoo. When she went downstairs, she found Anthony sorting through mail at a glass-topped occasional table in the drawing room. He seemed in better spirits than she had ever known. The beard had gone, and he had changed into a jacket and slacks, with an open-neck shirt.

"You look great," he said. "Feeling better?"

"Much. That was a brilliant idea. Thank you."

"Good. Okay, let's get going."

"Are you coming too?" There was an edge of doubt in her voice.

"You bet I'm coming. I wouldn't miss this for the world."

• • • • •

Marnie was pacing conspicuously up and down in the entrance to the theatre and saw Anne and Anthony as they spotted her. She stared at Anne's clothes.

"What are you wearing?"

"These … er … belonged to Melissa, but she'd never worn them. I got soaked in the rain, had to have a bath and change. I'll tell you about it later. Everything was okay."

"Nothing to worry about, Marnie," said Anthony. "I took Anne back to my house. There was no one there to see us."

"Okay. We'd better go in before they shut the doors. We'll be right at the back."

They presented their tickets and were shown to seats in the back row near the exit. The floor manager was already explaining that this was a live show and the audience was allowed to show its appreciation. For the sake of continuity, as he put it, they would at times indicate when they wanted applause. He held his hands above his head and clapped. If he did that, everyone should applaud. They could cheer and even whistle, but not stamp their feet.

Anne was gazing at the elaborate stage set, with its sweeping staircase, chairs laid out for guests and a rostrum for the presenter. There was a film screen over the stairs and, to one side, a five-piece band was sorting out its instruments, occasional notes being practised as a humorous accompaniment to the floor manager's instructions. Dotted about were television cameras, each one served by an operator and a minion holding cables. On each camera a tiny monitor glowed, and a red light appeared on top of them at intervals.

Above the whole set, glowing in fluorescent blue splendour, hung the programme's title: *Lifelines*.

With one last wish that everyone should enjoy themselves and make the audience at home know they were having a great time on the show, the floor manager introduced the presenter, Lance Gallagher.

He was a household name, a television personality, and he glided down the staircase as if it had been built for him to descend from Mount Olympus. He explained that they expected a national audience for the show of around six million viewers. The 'victim' that evening was someone who had enormous influence over how the country was run. He was not a politician or an actor, or even a football player. That elicited a burst of laughter.

Gallagher droned on, revealing that their guest's story was an enthralling tale of risk-taking, boardroom intrigue and the pursuit of ambition. He had claimed credit for ensuring the elections of Mrs Thatcher and Mr Major to number ten Downing Street. He was the maker and breaker of reputations. But despite his awesome authority, he remained a human being of discerning taste, who had made donations to art galleries and endowments to universities. And yet he was rarely seen in public, preferring to stay in the shadows. This would be a rare glimpse behind the scenes in the real corridors of power.

As the lights went down, and the scripted applause went up, Marnie leaned over to Anne.

"You smell nice," she whispered. "Expensive."

"Chanel, my dear. Nothing but the best."

Marnie moved her hand up to Anne's face and touched an earring. Anne stuck out her chin and smiled impishly. The sound from the band became louder as a disembodied voice announced Lance Gallagher to even more rapturous applause. Marnie moved her hand away and crossed her fingers. Anne's smile changed abruptly to a grimace. Anthony sat impervious beside them.

The applause rang out again when Gallagher introduced Jeremy Hawksby, to whom the whole event seemed a complete surprise. Perhaps it was, Marnie thought, but she had lately begun to wonder if anything in the media was quite what it appeared to be.

So there he was before them, *The Monster*. Marnie glanced at Anthony, but his face revealed nothing. Hawksby was tall and smartly dressed in a dark suit, with a grey silk shirt and matching tie, both shimmering under the studio lights that also picked out the grey handkerchief in his top pocket. He exuded confidence and seemed to be enjoying this rare sortie into the public gaze.

For the first fifteen minutes the audience was treated to a parade of film and television stars, sports celebrities and government ministers, all apparently queuing up to heap praise on the guest of honour. Marnie was impressed with the sheer efficiency of the operation. They must have had a line of the Great and the Good waiting behind the scenes to make their way down the gilded staircase. Each new arrival was heralded by their image on the film screen as they spoke lines that may or may not have been rehearsed, but always sounded sincere.

She had never quite understood how television people got their jobs and kept them over the years, but she could see why Gallagher was likely to be in secure employment forever. He combined smoothness with an unerring talent for finding just the right turn of phrase to suit every occasion. He was unflappable and totally professional, making his whole presentation seem utterly effortless. If anyone was going to survive the evening, he would.

A member of the England football team was just taking his seat among the guests, having warmly embraced the editor who had demanded his recall to the national squad after a period in the doldrums, when Gallagher announced that life had not always been caviar and champagne for Jeremy Hawksby. He had grown up in London and gone to school there. He was still remembered for his lively membership of the Debating Society at his old school and for a recent generous donation to build a new library and media centre. Gallagher turned to look up at the screen. But it was not the former headmaster, or even the current one whose face appeared. It was a child.

Hawksby was looking towards the audience, waiting for a familiar voice to ring out, and the first intimation he had that things were not quite right was when the theatre went completely silent. He looked quickly up at the screen, but it was now blank. There, at the top of the glowing staircase, stood a woman in jeans and sweater, holding up a large photograph of an infant.

"Something else to be remembered for, Jeremy," she said in a voice that was wavering with nervousness.

Gallagher swiftly turned towards the floor manager, who shook his head in puzzlement.

"My name used to be Jenny Poulter. This is our baby, Jeremy. Of course, she's grown up now, but you've never helped her, so I thought you might like to see what she was like when you dumped me."

Hawksby was riveted to the chair, struggling but failing to switch his smile back on. His mouth gaped open. The audience was buzzing. Some wondered if it was a stunt and if they should applaud. A few laughed momentarily. The cameras tracked the woman as she walked down towards where Hawksby was sitting. Marnie tried to imagine the pandemonium in the producer's gallery.

There was a gasp from the audience as another new person appeared on the stairs, and one camera swung up like a curious animal to film the girl in the yellow cagoule. It was Marlene, and she looked terrified, but she walked down without flinching.

"My name's Marlene. I was the girl in the newspaper photographs with Anthony Leyton-Brown, the MP who's been causing all the fuss this week. I want to tell you it was all a set-up. I was hired by this man, Mr Hawksby, to trick the MP so the pictures could go in the papers. I never had a real relationship with Mr Leyton-Brown. It was all a sham, and I'm sorry for my part in it, very sorry. Please believe me. You mustn't let that man get away with it."

She pointed at Jeremy Hawksby, sitting in the chair of honour, his face the colour of an aubergine.

Lance Gallagher had all but given up trying to keep control and was frantically talking into a tiny microphone on his lapel. Marnie longed to know what form the conversation took between the presenter and his producer.

*An even louder gasp went up from the audience when a man came out onto the staircase and walked elegantly and steadily down towards the stage. He was handsome and beautifully dressed in a lightweight cream suit and a shirt of pale blue. Hawksby was dabbing his face with the grey silk handkerchief.*

"Hallo, Jeremy," the man intoned in a smooth voice. "I'm Nigel. You won't remember me. And I guarantee you won't want to. I was only a child when you abused me at school. I suppose I'm here to show what a wonderfully rounded character you are … at least in terms of sexual preference. *AC / DC*, I think is the term for what you are. That's why I could never understand why you were so beastly to everybody else."

Hawksby was on his feet, pulling at his collar. Marnie wondered if he was going to have a seizure and worried that it might spoil the show. The newspaper editor staggered off towards the wings as the man in the cream suit continued, speaking direct to the front camera. A red light glowed on top. It was transmitting.

"We have all signed affidavits in front of lawyers this afternoon, all three of us. We are all willing to testify in court if Mr Hawksby seeks legal redress. If he doesn't, you'll know why. Well, Mr Gallagher, I think that's the end of your show. Goodnight."

With that, he put an arm round the shoulders of both women and walked them off in the opposite direction to the one taken by Hawksby.

Marnie leaned over to Anne. "I think I've stopped breathing."

"I think Hawksby probably has, too," Anne said.

"What did you think, Anthony?"

"Words fail me, frankly. I've never seen anything like it."

Marnie said, "When they started coming onto the set, I thought you might be tempted to join in."

He shook his head. "No need to, Marnie. It was perfect. You should've been a general in the army. It was a total rout."

The members of the audience were talking heatedly among themselves. The guests and celebrities on the set were in huddles. Even the camera crews, who thought they had seen everything in their time, were arguing about what had happened. There had been little instruction from the gallery, and they were now feeling exposed for keeping the show running.

Anthony stood up. "Come on. Let's get out of here."

It had stopped raining, and the streets were glistening. In the car, swishing its way through traffic, Marnie put her face in her hands.

"Are you all right?" Anne said from the back seat. "You're not going to be ill are you?"

"No, I'm fine, just a little shell-shocked. I can't get over what happened in there tonight. Up till now I'd never thought *Lifelines* was any more dangerous than *Blue Peter*."

Anne and Anthony laughed, and they made steady progress back to Little Venice. They left the car in a long-term parking slot, and Anthony quietly disappeared on board *Rumpole*. Lights were on in the house, and Marnie rang the bell as she used Mrs Jolly's key to open the door.

"We're back, Mrs Jolly."

"Wonderful timing, my dears. Have you eaten?"

"Not really. I can go and get pizzas, if you like. There's a place round the corner."

"That sounds like fun," said the old lady. "I think I've got one of those bottles of Italian wine wrapped in raffia. We can have that with it. What a pretty skirt that is, Anne. Have you been shopping?"

"Not exactly." Everything felt surreal.

"Oh. Well, you can tell me all about it when we have our pizza."

"Okay. Shall I lay the table?"

"Thank you, dear."

Marnie turned back to the front door with a sense of detachment from reality.

"Where did you go this evening?" Mrs Jolly asked. "I can't remember if you told me."

"We went to see the TV programme, *Lifelines*."

"Really. I must say I don't watch that as a rule. All rather predictable, don't you think? All that *gushing* ... strikes me as rather insincere. Still, if you liked it, I wouldn't want to spoil your fun."

Marnie and Anne exploded with laughter.

Mrs Jolly looked bewildered. "I've said something silly, haven't I?"

# Part 43

Marnie drove the hire car that morning while Anthony dozed on the back seat. Anne sat in the front, but there was no need for her skills at map reading. They were going home.

Knowing that Mrs Jolly was an early riser – *Always have been, my dear, since I was a girl growing up in the country, and now, at my age, I get by with very little sleep* – Marnie had asked if they could leave early on Friday morning to miss the traffic. She had waved them off – after insisting on providing coffee and toast – with wishes for a safe journey and a happy outcome to their plans.

Marnie had wanted to let Anthony return to his house in Putney, but his borrowed boat needed to be brought back to London from Glebe farm to await decisions about its future. So it was that the three of them headed north up the motorway as the sun was rising on a hazy late spring morning. Anne lay back against the headrest and closed her eyes, contented. Marnie admired her friend's resilience after all that had happened in the past week. She reached across to squeeze Anne's arm gently and could almost imagine her purring beside her. Marnie's thoughts turned to Dolly, wondering how the cat was coping with the stress of living through a gun battle. Stability and a normal life were her greatest wish now that the Anthony campaign was over.

They had a clear run in light traffic, and soon Marnie was turning off the main road towards Knightly St John. It was wonderful to be coming home without fear of harassment. There was no need to hide or cover their tracks. They were normal people again. Marnie turned into the high street and drove past the village shop. Leaning against the wall was a bicycle, and she caught a glimpse of Molly Appleton inside, bundling the newspapers for delivery. By an automatic reflex she found her foot moving towards the brake pedal, but thought better of it and motored past without stopping. She made a vow not to buy any papers that day; a symbolic gesture that their lives would not be dominated by the press for the first time in weeks.

Past the church and the pub, Marnie turned down the field track to Glebe Farm and parked beside the office barn. Ralph's Volvo was back in its usual place. As she got out and stretched her legs in the pale sunshine, a hand waved in the kitchen window of cottage number one. Marnie waved back to Jill Burton. Two bottles of milk stood guard by the office door. It was a perfect morning.

Walking through the spinney towards the boats and a second breakfast, Marnie realised that Anthony had not spoken on the entire journey.

"You're very quiet this morning," she said to him.

"Mm ... feeling rather tired ... bit of a headache ... probably the strain of events. It sometimes gets me like this."

"Same here. But for once I'm feeling fine. Do you think you'll feel better after something to eat?"

"Actually, if you don't mind, I think I'll go and have a lie down."

"Can I get you anything?"

"No. It's okay. I'll be all right."

They split up by *Sally Ann*, and Anthony turned towards his boat, moored beyond *Thyrsis*.

Unlocking the door of *Sally Ann*, Marnie said quietly, "I'll look in later and see how he is. He might be going down with a migraine."

"He's looking very pale," Anne agreed.

Marnie was pushing the hatch open when a movement in the spinney made her look up. For a second her instinct was to be suspicious, but it was Ralph on his morning walk. She jumped ashore and hugged him.

"Oh Ralph, it is *so* good to be back!"

"*Absolutely.*" He held her tight. "I heard about the *Lifelines* programme. *My God!*"

"Do you think there'll be repercussions?"

"Definitely. I thought that was the idea."

"Will I be in trouble?"

He smiled and shook his head. "Let's talk over breakfast."

• • • • •

For several seconds after Anne had cleared the table, the only sound to be heard in the cabin on *Sally Ann* was Dolly purring as she ate. Marnie leaned over and was stroking her back when the mobile warbled. Anne picked it up.

"Hallo. Is that Anne?"

"*Marlene!*" Anne exclaimed. Marnie and Ralph looked up. "I was going to ring you. Are you all right?"

"More than all right." It was the first time Anne had ever heard her sound like a normal girl. "I'm so relieved it's all over."

"Where are you? Do you want to come and stay with us ... have a break?"

"I'd love to, but ... well ... after the programme I phoned Mum and Dad ..."

"And?"

"They want me to go home. They saw the programme. They were so shocked, Mum said Dad was in tears. He wanted to phone the TV studio ..."

"But they had no idea how to contact you."

"I know. Anyway, I rang them and Mum was crying on the phone. Then Dad came on and he was crying. I thought they'd put Jenny on next – that's their Jack Russell – but she'd probably cry as well."

Anne laughed. "That's brilliant! So when are you going?"

"I'm at Euston station now. They said I had to come home straight away – first class! Dad's treat."

"Great," said Anne. "But I'm sorry I'll not be seeing you. Would you like to come here some time?"

"You bet! When things have settled down a bit. I've got some serious thinking to do ... about my future. I never thought I'd have one. I'm not going to mess things up this time."

They agreed to keep in touch, and Anne hung up after giving Marlene good wishes from Marnie and Ralph.

"I'm *really* really pleased for Marlene," said Anne. "I can hardly believe everything worked out in the end. Phew!"

"You can say that again," said Marnie. "I think we were amazingly lucky to get away with it."

"We're lucky to be *alive!*" said Anne with feeling.

"Of course, but then everything we've done since Anthony arrived has been crazy when you think about it."

"Totally," said Ralph. "And yes, you were lucky ... we've all been lucky. It's been a very close run thing."

"And there really will be no repercussions after what happened on Lifelines?"

"According to the radio, it was 'sabotage by persons unknown.' There'll be an inquiry, of course, but the view is that they'd been following Hawksby and trailed him to the TV theatre by chance. They somehow infiltrated the studio – a window in the toilets was mysteriously found to be open – and hid until they could get to the stage. Because there are always various guests and hangers-on milling around the back, no one thought they were suspicious characters ... until it was too late."

"And they won't get into trouble?"

"What for ... telling the truth? It hasn't yet been made a crime. And Hawksby won't dare take action against them. He doesn't want a rerun of the whole thing in a court of law. It would be like printing newspapers for the *Globe's* rivals."

"What about Becky Thornton? Will they find out she leaked the news of his appearance to me?"

"She only has to keep quiet, and no one can prove anything. She's just one member of a big team, and there are no links between her and the three infiltrators. No one saw her fit them up with lapel microphones."

"Good." Marnie was relieved. "No harm done, then ... except to Hawksby."

"No. I suspect *Lifelines* won't be broadcast live any more, but that's no great hardship. Oh ... there is one other result ... in many ways the most serious of all."

Marnie and Anne frowned in unison. "What is it?"

"Well ... it's an open secret – put about by Hawksby himself, of course – that he was about to be awarded a knighthood. It's always been his burning ambition."

"O God," said Marnie.

Anne's mouth opened in disbelief.

"Wait for it," said Ralph. "I've heard ... *very* confidentially ... that the offer is being withdrawn. We can never talk about it, but my source is entirely reliable, as they say."

"That's great," said Marnie. "The main thing is that Hawksby knows it. It's only a pity it can't be made public."

"I wouldn't count on that."

"An unattributed leak?"

Ralph nodded. "From an entirely reliable source, I wouldn't wonder."

"Good. That means we can start to put it all behind us ... at last."

•　•　•　•　•

They revelled in the idea of being ordinary again. Marnie and Anne went to fetch bags from the boot of the Mondeo and took everything back to *Sally Ann* for sorting while Ralph showered and changed. There would follow an orgy of washing, hoovering and tidying up. Anne wondered what to do with Melissa's clothes and decided to wash and iron them and give them back to Anthony. Marnie had declared that after checking the post and the messages, they would have a three-day weekend and go for trips on *Sally Ann*. This was unanimously agreed.

"What do we do about Anthony?" Anne asked. "Do we invite him along?"

"That depends on his plans," said Marnie. "He should be able to sort out his life from now on. But I think at least for today we should leave him to recover. My guess is he'll want to set off for London without delay. In his place, I'd be away tomorrow. A journey on the canal will help restore his spirits. It never fails."

"What do you think he'll do now ... with his life, I mean?"

Marnie shrugged. "Dunno. I have a suspicion he'll try to hang on as an MP. What do you think?"

"Not sure," said Anne. "Ralph says Mr Major thinks he's a liability." As an afterthought she added, "I wonder how he is."

"Perhaps I should look in on him," Marnie offered.

"No, I'll go. If he's awake and sees you, he'll want to talk about plans and we'll never get our tootle on *Sally*. If he's got a headache I'll see if he's got any tablets. Okay?"

"All right," Marnie agreed. "Don't be long."

On the way to Anthony's boat, Anne thought of the care he had taken of her when she was drenched. That wonderful soak in the bath, and Anthony lending her the fresh clothes had revived her. She resolved that if he was still sleeping, she would look in the medicine cabinet in the shower room and find him something for his headache. She would simply leave it near at hand for when he woke up. Passing *Thyrsis*, she heard Ralph singing in his shower, a rousing version of the Beatles' *Yellow Submarine*, and she smiled broadly. It was great to be back.

Anne stepped silently down through the side hatch of Anthony's boat. Inside, she paused, listening for any sounds, and moved noiselessly towards the sleeping cabin. When she peeped in, Anthony was lying on his side on the bed fully clothed, facing away from her, breathing steadily. She tiptoed along to the shower room and opened the cabinet.

• • • • •

Marnie rummaged in a cupboard under the galley workbench and found a black plastic rubbish sack. She poured the entire contents of her overnight bag into it, apart from her sponge bag. Anne's things followed, including the clothes she had worn the previous evening, Melissa's last purchases. They made Melissa seem all the more real, not just a story in a newspaper, and all the more tragic. *Rest in peace*, Marnie thought.

The last bag was Anthony's. She pulled open the zip fastener and took out a small document case. It was of fine quality leather with his initials embossed in the corner, and she laid it on the table. There was also a sponge bag, a pair of leather slippers and a camera case. The remaining contents were clothes, and she tipped them all into the sack.

Dolly rubbed her side against Marnie's leg. "Have you forgiven us for leaving you behind and for everything else, Dolly? Come for a cuddle." She picked her up, and the purring increased in volume as Marnie rubbed her face into fur that felt like thick-pile carpet. "Look how untidy I'm making it in here, Dolly. This will never do."

Marnie set the cat down on her favourite chair and, while Dolly washed herself, began gathering the things together. One by one she put them in her own overnight bag to take them up to the office barn. She noticed that the camera was a Polaroid like the one she used for work. Perhaps Anthony had kept a record of his time on the boat. Perhaps he was already thinking of producing his memoirs, illustrated with photos and some of Kate's sketches. Some newspapers would probably pay a fortune for his story, especially if it would discredit Jeremy Hawksby and the *Globe* empire. How ironic that he might now earn pots of money from the very sector that he had been trying to escape. Marnie shook her head. Funny old world.

She liked the document case. It was very smart, probably Italian, beautifully stitched. She went to pick it up, not realising that it was open, and a collection of papers slipped out onto the table. Reaching over to gather them up, she saw that they were photographs, Polaroids. Without curiosity, she patted them together to put back in the case. As she did so, something caught her attention and she paused. She did not mean to look, but there was something that drew her eyes more closely. Barely visible near the top edge of one photo was a head. More precisely, it was a hairstyle that was unmistakable: very short, very pale blond, very familiar.

Marnie moved the photo out of the folder to reveal the rest of the head. She had been right. Why did Anthony have a picture of Anne? Perhaps he had photos of all of them. The last thing she wanted was to feature in newspaper stories of Anthony's time in hiding. She picked up the folder to examine the photographs. But they were not a collection of all of them. Every one was of Anne, and as she studied them, Marnie felt her cheeks glowing. Here was Anne pulling off a sweatshirt. Here she was standing looking at clothes, holding up a skirt and a blouse. Next, she was bending over, swirling water in a bath with her hand. There must have been a dozen or more. And in all of them Anne was naked.

For a second she saw how Anne had changed in the two years that she had known her. She was no longer just a skinny girl, but developing a charming slim figure, the kind that could appeal to someone who liked young girls with boyish lines. Marnie pushed the photos back into the folder, overcome with sadness and anger to think that her friend had been defiled, but unsure what to do. Her instinct was to confront Anthony and demand an explanation. How could he have taken the photos? Anne was obviously completely unaware that she was being watched. What should she do?

Of one thing she was certain. She would never let Anne see them. As for the rest, she needed time to think.

• • • • •

Anne tried to explore the contents of the cabinet without making a sound. It was surprisingly full, and she thought most of the things must have belonged to the boat's real owner. Moving a bottle of herbal remedy, she dislodged some sachets of cold relief powders and they fell to the floor. She left them while she studied the labels on the bottles. The prescription remedies carried the patient's name and a date, and several were for a Mr P. Catesby or a Mrs S. Catesby. There were some homeopathic medicines, including a bottle of echinacea on the top shelf, which might help his immune system if there was nothing stronger to be found. She reached up and took it down. There were other bottles behind it, and she studied the labels to see if there was anything she recognised.

• • • • •

Marnie desperately needed someone to consult about the photos, the one person in the world who conformed to her needs. She was on the point of hanging up when Ralph answered his mobile.

"You caught me in the shower," he confessed.

"Are you able to talk?"

"*And* stand dripping on the carpet? Of course. I'm a very talented – "

"Ralph, listen." A serious edge to her voice stopped him in full flow. "I need your advice." She explained about the photos. "I don't know what to do for the best."

"You want to protect Anne," he said.

"Yes, but part of me doesn't want him to get away with this."

"No. Tricky. Would you like me to talk to him?"

"What would you say?"

"First, I'd warn him about ever doing anything like that again. Then I'd find out if he had any more and demand that he hand them over for us to destroy."

"It makes me so *angry*," Marnie said. "After all we've done for him, especially Anne, risking her neck for him in London. God knows what might've happened to her."

"Where is she now?"

"That's just it. She's on his boat trying to find something to help him feel better. How *ironic* when he's betrayed her. You know, I could really – "

"Marnie, listen. All this revenge business can get out of hand. The best thing is simply to try to sort out the problem. He'll be out of our lives by tomorrow. I'll talk to him."

"Yes. You're right. I knew you'd be sensible about it."

"Sensible sounds dull."

"It sounds dependable," said Marnie. "And that's what I need right now. Your approach is best. Above all, I don't want Anne to suffer any more distress." Marnie said goodbye and disconnected.

"Marnie there's something I – " said Anne, entering the cabin. She stopped in mid-flight. "Distress about what?

Marnie turned so sharply that she cricked her neck and dropped the folder of photographs on the table. Anne rushed forward.

"Sorry, Marnie. I didn't mean to startle you like that. Are you okay?"

Marnie rubbed her neck, turning her head slowly from side to side, a pained expression on her face. "Apart from a broken neck, I'm wonderful."

"What were you talking about then? And who to?"

Marnie sat down. "Ralph. Look, I need time to think about something that's come up. It's complicated. We can talk about it later."

"Was it about you and Ralph ... something that would upset me?"

"No. Nothing to do with Ralph and me. Don't worry about it."

Anne's eyes strayed to the folder on the table. She picked it up and glanced inside. Marnie looked up quickly and had another spasm in her neck. "Ow!"

"What's this?" Anne said.

"You mustn't look. They're private."

Anne was bewildered. "Why not? Don't you trust me?"

"It's not like that, Anne."

"What is it, then? I'm your very best friend. You can trust me with anything, Marnie. There's nothing I can't handle."

• • • • •

Anthony rolled onto his back. The headache was getting worse. Much worse. He tried sitting up and felt dizzy. If he could take some codeine, he might just get it under control. Then he realised that something had disturbed him. There had been a sound in the distance, a long way away in his dreams, but close at hand in reality. Something had fallen. There had been movement on the boat, barely audible, but enough to stir him.

He stood up awkwardly and plodded towards the galley. Passing the shower room, he noticed some sachets of Lemsip on the floor. Someone *had* been on board. Someone had been in the medicine cabinet.

He staggered to the galley and found the box of codeine in a drawer, quickly taking two tablets with water. Unsteadily, he went back to the shower room and opened the cabinet door.

• • • • •

Anne sat in the galley, staring at the photos. She had spread them all out on the table to examine them clearly. Tears were running down her cheeks. Marnie took her hand.

"That's why I didn't want you to see them, Anne," she said gently. "I didn't want you to be hurt."

Anne's voice was surprisingly firm and calm. "I'm not hurt. I'm not upset by the photos ... not just upset. These are tears of anger."

"I'm so sorry, darling."

"So am I. I'm sorry that we ever helped him. I'm glad we did something for Marlene and the others. And for Melissa. I'm glad your plan worked out. But I'm sorry he benefited from it."

Marnie passed her a tissue. Anne wiped her eyes and blew her nose.

"What do we do now?" she asked.

"Ralph's coming over. He's going to talk to Anthony when he gets up. The best thing is for him to go away and never come back. He must leave as soon as he's well enough to drive the boat."

"I don't want to see him again, Marnie."

"No. Nor do I."

"What will we say to Randall and Angela and everyone else who joined in with us?"

"I'm not sure. My mind's still confused."

"The truth is best," said Anne. "Even when it hurts."

Marnie got up, filled with emotion for her friend. "There's only one thing for it."

Anne nodded and smiled grimly. "Yes. I'll have a spoon of sugar in mine ... to help with the shock."

Marnie put the kettle on the stove and lit the gas. When she put the teacups and saucers on the table, Anne left the photographs where they were. They had barely taken a sip of the hot tea when they heard a footfall on the stern deck and knew that Ralph had arrived.

"Hallo." The voice, though weary and subdued, made them both start, wide-eyed. It was Anthony. "Anybody home?"

He came into the galley looking far from well. His face was pale and drawn, his skin greying and damp. He looked at them sitting at the table and attempted a smile, seeming not to notice their reaction.

"This looks cosy," he said faintly. "Kept the British Empire going, tea did. Made us what we are."

He took two steps forward and for a long moment stared down as if his eyes were not focusing. Then, realisation struck him in the face. He saw the pictures, saw Anne's innocent bath time turned into a sordid peepshow. He swayed where he stood and steadied himself against the empty chair.

"I know this must look bad ..."

Anne drew breath audibly but said nothing. Marnie was struggling to keep control of herself. She wanted to strangle him. Slowly. Anthony pulled the chair out and sat down.

"I'm sorry. It was a moment of weakness. I shouldn't have done it, I know. But she looked so ... I mean, in those wet clothes ... women don't realise ..."

"Anthony, she was shivering with cold and discomfort trying to help you." Marnie's voice was even colder. "And you abused her. She wasn't taking part in some wet T-shirt competition to titivate boys at the seaside. She was soaked to the skin on account of protecting you."

"There was no real harm done, Marnie," he pleaded.

"You don't think Anne feels cheapened by this?"

"She was never meant to see them. Nor were you. Nobody was. If you hadn't gone through my things – "

"I was going to do your washing for you. I wasn't prying."

He lowered his face, even paler than when he had come in. "What are you going to do?"

"I feel like telling the whole world about you," Marnie said very quietly, not trusting herself to use her normal voice. "What kind of person you really are. I feel like phoning the police. I'm sure this is illegal."

"But you won't do that, will you? That would only hurt Anne."

*Most women don't have the guts ...* Marnie heard the words, his words, at the back of her mind. Yesterday she had let it pass, but now she realised that men like him counted on it. And most often, they were right.

*Most women don't have the guts ...* Anne heard Anthony's words echoing in her brain.

"Tell me something," Marnie said. "How did you get these photos? Where did you take them?"

Anthony spoke without looking up. "In the airing cupboard ... a sort of hiding place."

"Is there a hole in the wall or something?"

"Nothing so complicated. There's a built wall mirror ... Victorian ... some of the silver backing has worn away from the glass. With the door closed and the cupboard in darkness, no one in the bathroom would ever know it's there. I found it by chance one day. I didn't make it on purpose."

"What did you use it for?"

Anthony shrugged. "Haven't you heard of sex games?"

Marnie looked puzzled. "I don't get it. You took clandestine pictures of your *wife* in the bathroom?"

There was no reply.

"Au pairs," Anne said quietly. "It was in the papers."

"Au pairs," Marnie repeated. "You used your hiding place to take nude photos of young women ... guests in your house. Did your wife find out? Is that why she killed herself? Was it just one step too far – getting up to your sordid little games and then leaving her to face the music, so she took her own life?"

"No!" he protested. "It wasn't like that. Not at all. You've got it all wrong."

"Oh no, I haven't," Marnie was raising her voice.

"Yes you have, Marnie," said Anne in a whisper. "You've got it all wrong."

Marnie stared at her. "What do you mean? Are you defending him? I ... I don't understand."

"I'm not defending him, Marnie. But I am agreeing with him."

Anthony looked up. He was gaunt and hollow-cheeked. "You understand?" he murmured. "It isn't easy. It's like a sickness."

Marnie said, "I'm totally bewildered here. What are you saying, Anne? That Anthony has some kind of psychological illness that makes him take nude photos of girls?"

"I don't know about that," Anne said. "You asked if that was why Melissa killed herself. I'm saying that she didn't take her own life."

"*What?*"

"She was murdered."

"*Murdered?* I don't think I heard you right."

"Ask Anthony if he denies it."

Anthony looked bemused and wary at this new direction, as if he had little idea what was happening around him.

Marnie said, "Anthony, what's going on?"

He rubbed a hand across his forehead. "You tell me. It's Anne who's making the wild accusations. I think she must be in a state of shock."

"She's not alone," said Marnie. "But she's also not a fool."

"Maybe not, but she has no proof to back up what she says. She can't have. There is none."

Marnie said, "When people say that, it makes me think they've lost the argument. What do you know, Anne?"

"He's got to tell you himself. I'm sick of playing games."

Anthony put his head in his hands. "All right. I'll tell you what happened. I'll tell you everything." He pointed at the photos. "Do we have to have these here?"

Anne gathered them together and put them back in the folder.

Anthony began. "It was after she was on the radio. I had to speak to her."

"And Ralph lent you his mobile," Marnie said.

"Yes. I used it to fix a time to go down."

"Go down? How did you go down? We thought you were here all the time."

"We didn't see him every day, Marnie."

"Marnie, Anne … can I just tell the story without interruptions and questions the whole time? It's bad enough talking about – "

"Okay … okay. Go ahead. No interruptions."

"I got the early bus into town and caught the train to London. I wore a baseball cap that I found on the boat and dark glasses. No one recognised me. When I got home, Melissa was very strange. I put it down to the stress of it all and the effect of taking sleeping pills. She often did. Suddenly, when I went to put my arms round her, she pushed me away and started screaming. I told her I'd had a kind of breakdown and I was sorry I'd run away. But this was something different."

Anthony touched the teapot. "Is there any chance of …" Marnie poured him a cup, and he began again as he stirred the tea.

"Melissa ran upstairs, still yelling at me … calling me all sorts of names. I followed her up and saw the airing cupboard door standing open. It's a walk-in cupboard like a small room. Melissa said she'd gone in one evening to fetch a clean towel when the light was on in the bathroom. She'd discovered the place where you could see through. She'd found the camera and a box of photos hidden behind towels and sheets. She went ballistic."

He sipped the tea, reliving the scene in his mind.

"She said she would've stood by me over Marlene. She was convinced that was entrapment, and there was nothing in it. But after seeing the other photos, she could never forgive me for leaving her to face everything alone. I asked her what she was going to do, begged her to stick by me until the story had blown over. Then we could make a fresh start, put it all behind us." He shook his head. "She laughed at me … except it wasn't real laughter. It was hysterics. She wouldn't stop. She screamed that she was going to tell everyone the truth, go to the press, make statements to the media, get a divorce. I told her it would ruin me, my whole career. She said she was glad … I deserved it."

He closed his eyes and sat quietly. Marnie glanced at Anne who was looking down at her cup. Eventually, Anthony took a sip of tea.

"I simply wanted to quieten her … for her own good. If she could just calm down, she'd feel better and get things in proportion again. I wanted her to see that there was no sense in throwing everything away for the sake of a few pictures. It was crazy. After a time she seemed to have exhausted herself, and I got her to sit down. She was in quite a state, rambling and muttering to herself. I urged her to take one of her pills. I found one left in the bottle in the bathroom cabinet. And I got her a drink … just a small whisky. I made her promise to think it over before doing anything else, told her we'd talk about it again when she felt calmer. She said she would. That was my one comfort … the thought that we could have sorted things out together, as we always had in the past."

He put his head in his hands and sobbed quietly. Marnie wished Anne could have been spared all this, but was surprised to see that Anne seemed lost in her own private thoughts. And where was Ralph?

Anne broke the silence. "Just one pill? That wouldn't do any harm."

Anthony rubbed his eyes with the palms of his hands. "After I left, Melissa must've found another bottle of pills. I didn't know she had any more. I thought things were going to be all right. That's why it was such a shock."

"What happened to the photos that Melissa had found?" Marnie said.

"I destroyed them. If the police had ever got hold of them, they'd have become public. I'd have been ruined."

"And after she died, you didn't think of telling the police what had happened ... the truth?"

Anthony sighed. "No. It was all too much. What could I have said? It seemed easier just to ... end it all and have done with it. A bottle of whisky and a bottle of sleeping pills seemed to be the best way out. If you hadn't stepped in when you did, Marnie ... you and Simon."

Marnie frowned. Something was going round in her mind. Doctor Siddiqui in the ITU ... what had she said? The tablets ... they were for ... depression. Not sleeping pills. *He may not have drunk enough alcohol and may not have taken enough tablets to kill himself.* It could have been a cry for help ... or an accident ... or made to look like suicide ...

"They weren't sleeping pills," Marnie said. "They were treatment for depression."

"I was there, Marnie. They were my pills. I know what I took."

"No. The doctor told us they were anti-depressants. And she said you didn't drink enough to do real damage to yourself. It only looked like a suicide attempt."

"Look," he said. "It doesn't matter. When you're in the state I was in, you don't care about minor details. You grab what you think will do the job. Believe me, Marnie, one bottle of pills is very like another."

Suddenly, Anne stood up and leaned against the workbench. "No they're not."

"It doesn't matter," Anthony said. "I took what I thought would do it. I was in shock. I tried to kill myself. You all saw me. There was no faking involved."

"I didn't mean those pills," Anne said. "I don't know anything about that. I meant the ones Melissa took."

Marnie touched her arm. "How could you know about those, Anne?"

"I do."

"Why do you think that?" said Marnie. "Did you see something in London ... in the bathroom, perhaps?"

"No. I wouldn't look in someone else's cupboards ... not without a proper reason."

Anthony said, "Anne, you're not making sense. The police took away all Melissa's medicine bottles. They know what she took and how many. You couldn't have seen anything. You're making a mistake."

"You must've bought sleeping tablets that day in London," Anne said quietly.

"That's nonsense. The police had all the evidence they needed to prove Melissa took her own life. They were in no doubt about it. Nothing can change that fact. Nothing can prove anything different."

"I can."

Marnie said, "How can you be so sure of this, Anne?"

Anne looked Anthony in the eye. "I've got the bottle in my pocket."

Marnie stared. Anthony's mouth opened. He put his hand to his head as if in pain.

"That's ridiculous," he said. "You don't know what you're talking about."

"I can prove you bought the sleeping pills in London that day."

"That means nothing."

"If Anne's right, it means whatever happened was premeditated," said Marnie.

Anthony groaned. "Even if it were true – which it isn't – it doesn't make any kind of case against me. No one can prove anything different."

"Do you really believe you can prove it, Anne?" Marnie asked, incredulously.

Anne reached in her pocket, pulled out a small bottle of tablets wrapped in a paper tissue and gave it to Marnie.

"I don't think you should open it. The police might want to check it for fingerprints. It came from a chemist's in London, near Limehouse. It's got Anthony's name on it."

"I get them regularly," he said. "Repeat prescriptions. I've been taking them for years."

Anne said, "It's got the date on ... the day Melissa died. It proves he bought them that day in London."

"It would never stand up as evidence," Anthony said firmly. "Someone must've put the wrong date on the label. That isn't proof."

"Surely it would raise enough doubts to make the police investigate further," Marnie said.

"It would be entirely circumstantial. My word against ... who's? There's no one who could testify against me. You've just cleared my name in public, both of you. You've personally vindicated me. And I'd deny everything. The police wouldn't even bring charges. They'd have to give me the benefit of the doubt."

"Not when they see the photos you took of me in the bathroom," Anne said.

"*Anne!*" Marnie exclaimed. "You couldn't do that!"

"Marnie's right, Anne. Think about it. You couldn't ... you won't do that."

Anne looked at him steadily. She could tell he was still in much pain, but his expression was confident. He was not in the slightest doubt that he was right. She could hear his voice again – *Most women don't have the guts.* He was on safe ground. How often had he exploited that knowledge?

"We've come all this way," Anne said. "I'm not giving in now."

Marnie began, "But Anne – "

"No. I don't care. He mustn't be allowed to get away with it. I don't know if the police can make a case against him, but someone has to start. Otherwise it's all been a waste of time ... everything you've done, Marnie. All our efforts for nothing."

"My God," Marnie said. "Do you realise ... nothing has been what it seemed? Everything's been an illusion. We've been trying to protect Anthony, and all this time we've been sheltering a murderer."

Anne picked up the mobile phone. "Let's do it here and now ... phone Sergeant Marriner."

The boat rocked gently, and footsteps were heard on the stern deck. Ralph came down into the cabin.

"Sorry to take so long. The Master rang just as I was leaving ... wants me to ..." He looked at the three faces turned towards him. "What's up?"

Anne said, "Everything's fine, Ralph. Couldn't be better, really. Who was it who said – *revenge is such a pure motive?*"

• • • • •

The red boat looked strange with the blue and white police tape attached all round it, like bunting for a waterways festival. But there was nothing festive about the officers who clambered on board to examine the boat. They were wearing white overalls that covered every inch of their bodies, with hats, gloves and goggles to complete the ensemble.

Anne's bottle of pills had been taken away for examination in the same car as Anthony, and she perched on the stern rail on *Sally Ann*, watching the proceedings with grim fascination. She had asked to be allowed a few minutes to herself, a space in time to be alone until she had to face more questioning. Marriner and Cathy Lamb were on their way from the station to interview her and were expected at any minute. Dolly had crept under the bed in the cabin, unwilling to leave while all the police officers were swarming around the boats. Marnie and Ralph were with Bartlett in the office barn. They had a lot of explaining to do about Anthony.

The arrival of Marriner and Lamb coincided with a commotion on the red boat, and the two detectives veered off when hailed by one of the scene-of-crime officers. After a brief huddle, Cathy looked across at Anne and waved to her to join them.

As she approached, Anne saw they were holding a transparent envelope. Cathy passed it to her.

"Do you recognise this, Anne?"

Inside the envelope was a watch, and Anne knew it at first glance. She had seen it before, heard all about it from Marnie, knew the gold and steel case and the five-pointed crown on the dial. She did not even need to read the name *Rolex*.

"Yes," she said softly.

"Is it …?" Cathy began.

Anne nodded. "It's Simon's."

"It seems to match the description that Marnie gave us," said Marriner.

Anne handed it to him. "Marnie will tell you for sure, but I'm pretty certain about it. If you want to check, look on the back of the bracelet. It should be a different make from the watch … a *fixoflex*."

Marriner brought the envelope close to his face and peered in at the watchband. "*Fixoflex*, yes."

"Does this mean that Anthony killed Simon?" Anne said quietly.

"It means we have some questions to ask."

"I'd better come with you."

"That won't be necessary, Anne," said Cathy Lamb gently.

"I want to be there when you show the watch to Marnie."

• • • • •

After the police had left, Anne made a phone call to let her parents know what had happened. Marnie and Ralph and Anne sat in silence on deckchairs beside *Sally Ann*.

Eventually Marnie said, "How are you feeling, Anne?"

"All right. But I've felt better. How about you?"

"So-so."

"It must've been a shock for you, seeing Simon's watch like that."

"Yes ... and no."

"How come?"

"That day ... when the muggers were shot ... the man – John Hewitt – said he never killed Simon. I couldn't see why he'd lie when he knew he was dying."

"So what did you think had happened?" said Ralph. "Did you think it might've been an accident?"

"I always had my doubts. There was no reason I could see why Simon would've chosen to head in that direction."

"Why did he?" said Anne.

"He didn't ... not alive, anyway. Bartlett thinks he must've spotted something that made him realise what had happened to Melissa. I expect it'll all come out at the trial. Simon was always very perceptive ... had a quick brain. But he was obviously taken unawares by Anthony, who probably grabbed the nearest weapon to hand. The only way to get rid of ..." Marnie's voice faded. "He needed Simon's car to get up to the locks ... no doubt had the idea of making it look like a robbery that had gone too far. That's why he kept the watch."

"And why he couldn't throw it away," said Ralph. "Too much risk of it being found and identified. I wonder if they'll find his wallet."

Marnie shrugged. "Who knows?"

"How did he get back?" said Anne.

Marnie pointed across the canal. "Along the towpath and over the bridge. It's only a couple of miles. It'd be deserted at night, and even if he'd been seen, he'd have been just another jogger."

"Do you think they'll have enough to make out two cases of murder?"

"Marriner seemed to think so. What do you think, Ralph?"

"That was my impression," he said. "And whatever they decide, I don't think the photographs of Anne will ever see the light of day. My guess is, Anthony will confess and plead guilty. There's nowhere for him to hide any more ... no Marnie to rescue him this time."

Marnie said, "You were pretty perceptive, Anne. You did well to spot that medicine bottle in the cabinet when you were looking for tablets for Anthony. Pure Sherlock Holmes, that was."

"Not really," Anne replied. "It was easy ... *elementary*, you might say."

"How did you make the connection?"

"The same way that Simon did, maybe. It was the date on the bottle. The twelfth of May. The day Melissa died was the day of my first driving lesson. And Simon knew that, too. It was my Red Letter Day ... a day I'll never forget."

# Part 44

Towards the end of that afternoon, Marnie began to feel restless and thought she too might go down with a headache if she did not stir herself. Leaving Ralph and Anne dozing at the water's edge, she wandered through the spinney and met Dolly stalking dragonflies. They walked together to the office barn.

It seemed an age had passed since Marnie had last checked the post, and she unlocked the door, bending to retrieve the letters lying on the mat, while Dolly remained outside, washing behind her ears on the doorstep.

Not wanting to stay long, Marnie left the barn door covering the windows unopened, and switched on the main office lights. She quickly sorted through the collection. One envelope bore the franking stamp of Ridger, Parfitt and Anderson, Simon's solicitors. She picked up the paperknife and tipped out a letter and another, smaller envelope. The letter from Colin Parfitt began with condolences that were brief but sincere, and went on to explain that Colin was Simon's sole executor. He would make all the necessary formal arrangements, but wished Marnie to know that, with the exception of a few small donations, she had been named as the only beneficiary in Simon's will. Marnie felt her stomach tighten, and tears filled her eyes.

She reached for a tissue from the box on her desk and read on. There was one matter on which Colin needed to consult her: he had been notified by the police that the Mercedes could be released to his custody, and he asked for Marnie's instructions. She made a pencilled note in the margin – *Sell*.

He had been to Simon's flat to check that it was secure and had obtained keys that he would pass on to Marnie when they met. Colin ended with the promise to phone her in the next few days to arrange a meeting. In a PS he added that he had found the enclosed envelope on Simon's desk and thought she would wish to have it without delay.

She looked at it with curiosity. It was a plain white envelope with the single word Marnie handwritten on the front. She flipped it open with her thumb and discovered no letter but a solitary piece of paper with a few lines of writing.

### Old Wounds
*Time heals*
*It takes away the pain*
*Time washes over scar tissue*

*But were they right who said*
*That wounds open*
*That blood flows again*

*In the presence*
*Of the malefactor*

Marnie stood quietly for a few seconds and read the poem again. Somewhere in the back of her mind she could hear Angela Hemingway's voice ... *no blessing is ever wasted.*

*God bless, Simon,* she said in a whisper, *and keep you safe ... wherever you are.* She raised the paper to her lips and held it there for a few seconds before slipping the poem into the top drawer of her desk. She walked to the door and put out the lights.

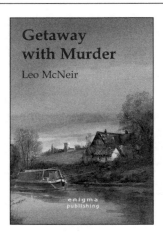

# Getaway with Murder

## Leo McNeir

Marnie Walker is an interior designer with a passion for boats, in particular her sister's boat Sally Ann, that she borrowed a year ago for an extended trip on the Grand Union Canal during the summer. While on her travels, Marnie had discovered a derelict farmhouse in a Northamptonshire village.

A year later, wishing to set up her own company, she finds herself buying the farm to restore it as an investment and a base, aided and abetted by her sister Beth and her friend, Anne with an 'e'. But she does not reckon with the tensions underlying the peace and tranquillity of her new home. All is going well until Marnie finds herself embroiled in not one unsolved murder but two, separated by almost 350 years.

The old feuds of the Civil War period seem to be fermenting again in a village becoming torn apart by factions. It is only a matter of time before something sinister emerges to shatter the calm of the countryside, and Marnie herself is dragged into the ancient conflict with terrifying results.

"... is destined to become a classic of crime fiction."
*Canal and Riverboat*

" ... the story has many fascinating twists – great holiday reading."
*Inland Waterways Association*

Available from enigma publishing: ISBN 0 9524052 6 1

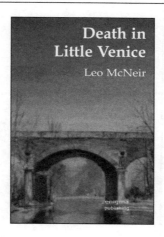

# Death in Little Venice

## Leo McNeir

A winter's afternoon on a deserted stretch of canal in Regent's park, and the discovery of a body under the 'blow-up' bridge, the body of a famous MP. A nasty shock for Marnie Walker, but more surprises lie in wait for her. Why do the police try to link her with the murder victim? Who is going to great lengths to try to eliminate her? Why should anyone want to destroy her if she really knows nothing?

Marnie finds herself pursued by unseen predators, who seem to know her every move, read her every thought. Out of her depth in a world of political intrigue and treachery, she is thrown together with the dead man's best friend, ally and fellow MP in an attempt to get to the bottom of the mystery. But the police appear to regard them both as suspects, despite every effort they make to clear their names. Neither Marnie's guile, nor the MP's connections can shake off their pursuers on both sides of the law.

In the heart of London's Little Venice, in the idyllic setting of her canalside Northamptonshire home and in the corridors of power at Westminster, there seems to be no escape. Sooner or later someone else could become a second victim, and the pursuers have Marnie firmly in their sights.

"Political intrigue in the corridors of power at Westminster and alongside the canals add spice to the story and flashes of humour combine to make this a most enjoyable whodunit."          *Waterways World*

"His are the only books our reviewer read twice, just for the fun of it."
*Canal and Riverboat*

Available from enigma publishing: ISBN 0 9524052 7 X